PRAISE FOR CATHERINE ASARO

"With a mixture of technology, physics, action, romance, and characters you can't forget, Catherine Asaro's *The Radiant Seas* offers an insightful look at human nature, a roller-coaster of emotions, and a most engrossing read—far better than the vast majority of books sold as 'great' hard science fiction."

—L. E. Modesitt, Jr.

"Catherine Asaro is one of those rare authors who can write accurately and lovingly both about science and about the minds and hearts of her characters. *Primary Inversion* is vivid, thoughtful, and exciting, the kind of story you want to read at one sitting. It sweeps you along with the force of its action. Throughout it are sprinkled jewels of scientific speculation that enhance the story with their clarity and cleverness. The changes in the main character are evoked so carefully and with such understanding that only at the end do you realize how far she, and so you as the reader along with her, have come."

—Kate Elliott

"What a great read! In her newest book, *The Radiant Seas,* Catherine Asaro shows herself to be a writer with depth and sensitivity. Her signature strengths—dynamic characters, real human emotions, and cutting-edge scientific background—here flower into a story that reaches past the individual lives of her characters to engulf entire interstellar empires. Unlike writers who focus on technology as an end in itself, she uses her stunningly original vision to weave a story of loyalty, love, courage, and sacrifice. I'm looking forward to reading more!"

—Deborah Wheeler

"Rising star Catherine Asaro exploded onto the science fiction scene with all the blazing glory of a supernova with her first book called *Primary In*

"Ms. Asaro reveals fasci

with each new book, and r

thing fresh, different, and a

Tor Books by Catherine Asaro

THE SAGA OF THE SKOLIAN EMPIRE

Primary Inversion

Catch the Lightning

The Last Hawk

The Radiant Seas

Ascendant Sun

The Quantum Rose

Moon's Shadow

The Radiant Seas

Catherine Asaro

A TOM DOHERTY ASSOCIATES BOOK
NEW YORK

THE RADIANT SEAS

Edited by David G. Hartwell

A Tor Book
Published by Tom Doherty Associates, LLC
175 Fifth Avenue
New York, NY 10010

www.tor.com

ISBN: 0-812-58036-2
Library of Congress Catalog Card Number: 98-7979

First edition: January 1999
First mass market edition: November 1999

Printed in the United States of America

0 9 8 7 6 5 4 3 2

In Memory of Jo Clayton
1939–98

A friend, mentor, and admired colleague
who graced the world with her talent
and her spirit

See what a scourge is laid upon your hate,
That heaven find means to kill your joys with love.
And I, for winking at your discords too,
Have lost a brace of kinsmen:—all are punish'd.

—*Romeo and Juliet,* by William Shakespeare

Contents

Acknowledgments

I would like to thank the following readers for their much appreciated input. Their comments have made this a better book, and any mistakes that remain are my own.

To Major James Cannizzo, USAF, for advice on the military; to Professor Todd Jackson and his Goucher geniuses, the students in his class at Goucher College: Abby Callard, Margaret Slack, Claire Willey, Mei-Ling Johnson, and Pat Lenehan, for their insightful analyses and an absolutely delicious dinner; to my sister, Nina Smith, for her excellent suggestions; to NASA scientist Marc Millis at Lewis Research Center, for his much appreciated insights; to Professor Davide Cervone in the Math Department at Union College in Schenectady, New York, for making me the diagram of the Klein bottle; to Jan Howard Finder, for his coinage of the word *bytelock;* to my editors Jim Minz and David Hartwell, to my publisher Tom Doherty, and to the many people at Tor who made this book possible; and to my agent Eleanor Wood for her excellent work on my behalf. A special thanks to the shining lights in my life, my husband John Cannizzo and my daughter Cathy, for their love and support.

Important Characters, in Order of Appearance

KURJ SKOLIA — Imperator of Skolian Imperialate. Military commander in chief of forces within Imperial Space Command (ISC): the Imperial Fleet, Pharaoh's Army, Advance Services Corps (ASC) and J-Force. Firstborn son of Roca Skolia. Stepson of Eldrinson Valdoria. Military Key of Triad. Member of Ruby Dynasty. Rhon.

STARJACK TAHOTA — admiral and eventually commander of the Imperial Fleet.

SAUSCONY LAHAYLIA VALDORIA (SOZ) — Kurj's heir and half sister. Sixth child of Roca Skolia and Eldrinson Valdoria. Married to Jaibriol Qox II. Narrator of *Primary Inversion.* Also called Primary Valdoria. Member of Ruby Dynasty. Rhon.

JAIBRIOL QOX II — firstborn son and heir of Emperor Ur Qox, grandson of Emperor Jaibriol I, and great-grandson of Eube Qox, the founder and first emperor of Eube. Married to Sauscony Valdoria. Member of Ruby Dynasty by marriage. Rhon.

DYHIANNA SELEI (DEHYA) — the Ruby Pharaoh. Highest ranked and oldest member of Ruby Dynasty. Sister of Roca Skolia. Assembly Key of Triad. Married to Eldrin Valdoria. Rhon.

ALTHOR VALDORIA — Kurj's second heir and half brother. Second child of Roca Skolia and Eldrinson Valdoria. Uncle and namesake of Althor Selei in *Catch the Lightning* (which takes place sixty-nine years after *The Radiant Seas* begins). Member of Ruby Dynasty. Rhon.

ELDRINSON VALDORIA (ELDRI) — Web Key of Triad. Husband of Roca Skolia and sire of the ten Valdoria children. Member of Ruby Dynasty by marriage. Rhon.

ROCA SKOLIA — Foreign Affairs Councilor in the Imperial Assembly and heir to Assembly Key. Wife of Eldrinson Valdoria, sister of Dyhianna Selei, mother of Kurj, and mother of the ten Valdoria children. Member of Ruby Dynasty. Rhon.

ELDRIN VALDORIA (DRYNI) — oldest child of Eldrinson Valdoria and Roca Skolia. Consort to Pharaoh Dyhianna Selei. Member of Ruby Dynasty. Rhon.

BARCALA TIKAL — First Councilor of the Skolian Assembly. Civilian leader of the Imperialate.

U'JJR QOX (UR) — emperor of the Eubian Concord, also known as Trader Empire. Son of Jaibriol I and father of Jaibriol II. Assumed to be a Highton Aristo.

VIQUARA IQUAR — empress of Eubian Concord. Wife of Ur Qox. Highton Aristo.

JESSIE TARRINGTON — son of Senator Jack Tarrington. Captured by Trader pirates.

AMI — mistress of Kurj Skolia. Originally a War Room page.

JAIBRIOL QOX SKOLIA (JAI) — firstborn of Soz and Jaibriol II. Also known as Jaibriol III. Member of both Ruby and Qox Dynasties. Rhon.

ROCALISA QOX SKOLIA (LISI) — second child of Soz and Jaibriol II. Named for Soz's mother Roca. Member of both Ruby and Qox Dynasties. Rhon.

ERISTIA LEIROL VALDORIA — illegitimate daughter of Althor Valdoria and Syreen Leirol.

SYREEN LEIROL — friend and former companion of Althor Valdoria. Former actress turned linguist.

COOP — an artist. Companion to Althor Valdoria.

KRYX QUAELEN — Trade Minister of Eube. Highton Aristo.

CIRRUS — pleasure girl and provider owned by Emperor Ur Qox. Mother of Kai, her son by Ur Qox, making Kai Jaibriol II's half brother.

VITAR QOX SKOLIA — third child of Soz and Jaibriol. Member of both Ruby and Qox Dynasties. Rhon.

DEL-KELRIC QOX SKOLIA (KELLI) — fourth child of Soz and Jaibriol. Named in honor of Soz's brother Kelric (the main character in *The Last Hawk*). Member of both Ruby and Qox Dynasties. Rhon.

IZAR VITREX — Eubian Minister of Intelligence. Highton Aristo.

CORBAL XIR — patriarch of Xir bloodline, which controls Sphinx Sector in Eube. Related to the Qox Dynasty, as the son of Eube Qox's sister Ilina. Highton Aristo.

CAYSON — pleasure youth and provider owned by Empress Viquara.

CALOPE MUZE — High Judge of Highton Aristo. Related to Qox Dynasty, as the daughter of Eube Qox's sister Tarquine. Wife of Admiral Lassar Ajaks. Highton Aristo.

WILLIAM SETH ROCKWORTH III — retired naval admiral and ex-husband to Dyhianna Selei. Their arranged marriage established the Iceland Treaty between Earth and Skolia.

TAQUINIL SELEI — firstborn son of Pharaoh Dyhianna and her consort Eldrin. Heir to Ruby Throne. Member of Ruby Dynasty. Rhon.

DAYAMAR STONE — general and commandant of the ASC.

NAAJ MAJDA — General of the Pharaoh's Army.

BRANT TAPPERHAVEN — Jagernaut Primary and commandant of the Jagernaut Forces, or J-Forces.

Prologue

I swear I meant well. I sought only to benefit humanity, to increase the human tolerance for pain. But none of that matters now. These creations of mine that call themselves Aristos—they feel no empathy for the pain of others. No, it is worse than that. They are anti-empaths, like vampires that feed on human suffering. You know I have dedicated my life to healing. Would I beg you to destroy them if I saw any other choice? Open your eyes! We must stop them before they spread beyond our ability to contain. For if we don't destroy them, they will surely destroy us.

—*From the testimony of the geneticist Hezahr Rhon*
to the Parthonia Ethics Committee,
four days before his murder by the Aristos

Kurj Skolia strode down the corridor, past walls lit with a muted radiance. Admiral Starjack Tahota kept pace at his side, speaking into the comm on the flexible gauntlet she wore around her wrist. They stalked through the skyneedle toward his office, two towering figures, he seven feet tall, she six-foot-six, he a metal giant more machine than human, she long-legged and muscular, with a bronzed face and gray-streaked dark hair.

"Imperator Skolia." A man's voice snapped out of the comm on Kurj's wrist gauntlet. "This is Colonel Casestar. We've intercepted a signal between the two ships on the roof of your palace, the flier and the racer. Jaibriol Qox is piloting the flier. Primary Valdoria has control of the racer, and she is threatening to destroy Qox's flier if he doesn't surrender."

"Understood." Kurj glanced at Tahota. "What's the status on the planetary cordon?"

"It's complete," Tahota said. "No ship can get out unless we let it."

Kurj spoke into his comm. "Casestar, have you established communication with my sister yet?"

"Negative, sir. Primary Valdoria doesn't respond on any channel we've opened to the racer."

"Get me through to her," Kurj said. "I don't want her shooting down Qox's ship." He still didn't know how Jaibriol Qox had escaped his prison cell, but Kurj wanted him alive, this heir of the Aristo emperor. He couldn't interrogate a dead man.

Casestar spoke again. "Sir, Qox's flier is taking off."

"He must be desperate," Tahota said. "He has to know we have a cordon set up."

"Maybe he doesn't care," Kurj said. "In his place, wouldn't you prefer death to recapture?"

"What the hell?" Casestar said. "Sir, Qox has engaged the stardrive on his ship. Primary Valdoria is bringing her inversion drives on-line as well—saints almighty, they're trying to invert from standing still."

Kurj scowled. "Casestar, get me that line to my sister *now.* I don't want her pursuing Qox. If you can't reach her, cripple her racer." Bad enough he might lose his prize prisoner if Qox engaged the stardrive of his ship while it was at rest on the surface of the planet. Kurj had no intention of letting his sister and heir risk her life to stop him.

"Sir." Casestar's voice sounded odd. "Both ships just melted out of real space."

Kurj stopped, with Tahota at his side. "Repeat that last."

"Both ships tried to invert," Casestar said. "They disappeared. Dissipated into nothing."

Kurj stared at Tahota. Speaking into his comm, he said, "Find them." But even as he spoke, he saw his thoughts mirrored in Tahota's broad face. To activate its stardrive, a ship had to be traveling at near light speed, far from the gravity well of a planet. As far as Kurj knew, no ship that had tried otherwise had survived.

I

Exile

356 ASC on the Imperial Calendar
379 EG on the Eubian Calendar
A.D. 2259 on the Gregorian Calendar
Ie 5262 on the Ruby Calendar
About 6275 on the Iotic Calendar

1

They spent their first evening of exile staring at the sky of their new world, watching the sea of stars. While the long sunset died, the two of them sat on the edge of a cliff, a laser carbine across their knees, the mountains rolling away at their feet.

In the initial flush of their escape, Soz Valdoria had felt a rush of optimism. As a Primary, one of Imperial Space Command's highest ranking officers, she well knew the odds against evading a planetwide cordon set up by ISC. That she and Jaibriol had succeeded exhilarated her. But as daylight waned, her adrenaline-provoked rush of euphoria faded. She glanced at Jaibriol Qox, suddenly unsure what to say to this man who, as of one hour ago, was her husband.

Jaibriol turned to her. "Perhaps we should go back to the cave. Take shelter for the night."

"All right." She stood up with him, holding the carbine.

A warning entered her mind. Alert.

What's the problem? Soz asked. Bio-electrodes in her neurons converted the thought into pulses that it sent to the computer node in her spine, using fiberoptic threads that networked her body.

Something is coming, her node thought. As Soz turned to the forest behind them, a map "appeared" in her mind. Her node accessed her optic nerve and the map jumped out in front of her, a translucent image superimposed on the landscape. It had few details, given their scant data on this primitive wilderness, but a red triangle blinked in one corner.

Estimated distance: 12–15 meters; weight: 200–300 kilograms, her node thought. Predicted trajectory shown. A blue line appeared on the map.

Unaware of her silent communication, Jaibriol stepped toward the trees. When Soz laid her hand on his arm, he froze, and she glimpsed an image in his mind: herself, sitting naked on a bed, smiling as she held out her hand to him. Then he flushed and raised his mental barriers. His mind became a fortress, unreadable and closed.

Disconcerted, yet also flattered, Soz pulled back her hand. "Something is coming toward us."

He indicated the carbine. "Can that deal with it?"

"Possibly. But I'd prefer to conserve the charge."

On her map, the red triangle stopped, then moved again, this time away from them. Path cleared, her node thought.

Soz glanced at Jaibriol, trying to relax. "We can go now."

They entered the forest together. Although it was dark under the canopy of foliage, her enhanced optics let her see in both the infrared and the ultraviolet. When she toggled her IR, the landscape smoldered in dim reds and Jaibriol glowed in the colors of flame. The trees resembled giant palms a hundred meters tall. They whispered, crackling and shushing, their crowns forming an intertwined roof, with huge stiff fronds that clattered together or floated to the ground. Fragrances drifted in the air, the delicate, bittersweet smells of unknown foliage and loamy soil.

Jaibriol stumbled on an exposed root. "Sauscony," he said. "Can you see where we're going?"

She stopped, surprised to hear her full first name, and he plowed into her. Her node toggled the hydraulics that augmented her skeleton and muscles, and she caught her balance with enhanced speed.

Jaibriol pulled away from her, a flush of heat showing on his face. "My apology."

"Soz," she answered.

"What did you say?"

She started to repeat *Soz*, then surprised herself and said, "Soshoni."

He was looking lower than her head, unable to judge the exact location of her face in the dark. "I don't understand."

"Only my parents call me Sauscony," she said. "Everyone else calls me Soz."

"Who is Soshoni?"

"It's a nickname my family used when I was young." She hesitated. "You can use it too. If you'd like."

A charming smile lit his face. "I would like that."

His boyish expression startled her. Faced with his prodigious intellect and highborn manner, she tended to forget he was only twenty-three, less than half her age. She kept her hale, hearty youth courtesy of biotech and good genes.

As they started to walk again, a high-pitched cry undulated in the night. Another followed, then others, fading with distance. Leaves rustled like chattering spirits.

When they reached the cave, Soz turned off the quasis screen that protected the entrance, but as soon as they were inside she reset it. In this unknown wilderness, they had no idea what might come to visit.

The action-sensor lamp turned itself on, lighting the small cave that defined their new life. It contained everything they owned: crates of supplies, computers, excavation bomblets, tools. An axe stood in one corner, its alloyed blade gleaming.

As Soz leaned the carbine against the wall, Jaibriol sat on a pile of crates, then swayed, his face paling.

"Are you all right?" she asked.

He sat up straighter. "Yes. Fine."

Quietly she said, "We have a medkit. I can help."

Jaibriol exhaled, then nodded. As she unpacked the kit, he took off his shirt. She felt ill when she saw his bruises, welts, and scabs. Had his interrogators forgotten the Halstaad Code of War? All three interstellar powers had signed the Code: her people of the Skolian Imperialate, the Eubian Traders ruled by Jaibriol's father, and the Allied Worlds of Earth. That Skolian ISC questioners had gone so far beyond the humane forms of interrogation mandated by the Code gave harsh reality to their fear and hatred of the Trader Aristos he represented.

She cleaned his injuries, using a salve and a nanomed spray. Then she bandaged his back. As she worked, an odd sensation touched her mind, as if a clumsy hand had brushed against it.

Kylatine inhibitors released, her node thought, reacting to what it interpreted as an invasive mental probe. The kylatine molecules attached to neural sites in her brain, blocking her reception of Jaibriol's brain waves.

Cease block, she thought. But it was too late. He had already felt her cut him off.

"I didn't mean to intrude," he said.

"You didn't." She tried to relax. "I just need time, to readjust."

"We've time." Uneasily he added, "Unless someone finds us."

"I doubt they will." Only three people knew she and Jaibriol had gone into exile: the president of the Allied Worlds of Earth, the pilot who had brought them here, and Soz's father.

It was hard to believe less than a year had passed since she had met Jaibriol and shared with him the miraculous joining of minds that showed they were alike, both Rhon psions. The word *Rhon* came from the geneticist who had done pioneering work on the DNA mutations that produced empaths and telepaths. Rhon psions exhibited the traits in their strongest form. She had never expected to find a Rhon mate; healthy psions were rare, the Rhon almost extinct. The only other known Rhon psions were her family, the Ruby Dynasty.

Jaibriol was watching her face. "We should name this planet."

She thought about it. "New World."

His laugh gentled the night. "Well, it's literal."

"You have a better idea?"

"How about Prism?" He hesitated. "Splitting ordinary light into a rainbow—that seems right somehow. For us."

"All right. Prism." She wasn't sure she understood his reasoning, but she liked it. *Prism* was aesthetic. Like Jaibriol. Broad-shouldered and tall, with a handsome face, he was a pleasure to look at.

But his appearance also made her uneasy, his red eyes, his shimmering black hair, his classic aristocratic features. He looked Aristo, pure Highton Aristo, of the highest caste. Seeing him, she remembered the Aristos she had fought in battle. How could he resemble a people so saturated in their own cruelty and yet be so gentle himself?

"It's not real," he said.

"Real?"

"My face. I wasn't born like this." An edge grated in his voice. "My father had me 'fine-tuned' to the Aristo ideal of perfection. Never mind what you inflict on the rest of humanity. It's how you look that matters." Bitterly he added, "The only reason I exist is because he felt no price was too great to make a Rhon psion, even 'polluting' his genes with those of a psion."

"Jaibriol—"

He just shook his head. "I can't."

Soz understood his reluctance to talk about it. Had knowledge of his true heredity ever become public, it would have destroyed both him and his father. Aristo DNA included none of the mutated genes that produced psions, and Aristo law forbade legitimizing children who weren't Aristo. So no true Aristo could ever be a psion. Jaibriol's father had created him anyway, in secret. His purpose was to destroy the Ruby Dynasty. Her family.

"We should unpack these supplies," Jaibriol said.

"All right."

Setting up home didn't take long. They had no amenities, just survival gear. After a while Soz paused, watching Jaibriol spread out a blanket. She hesitated to join him. On the one hand, it was natural they desired each other; the Rhon were driven to each other like salmon driven upstream to mate. In the months since they had met, she and Jaibriol had spent no more than a total of six hours together, yet they had forged a Rhon-driven bond so strong it survived the hatreds of two empires. But would they also come to *like* each other, the affection that grew only with time and compatibility? She had no idea.

For once she actually appreciated her appearance. She had a heart-shaped face with large green eyes. Wild black curls spilled to her shoulders, shading into burgundy and then metallic gold at the tips. She stood a bit taller than average, her body lean but well shaped, or so she had been told. As far as she was concerned, her decorative looks served no purpose for a military officer. A craggy, hardened aspect would have been more functional. Her new husband seemed taken with her appearance, though, so apparently it had some use after all.

He sat back on his heels, his mouth quirking in a smile. "Apparently so."

Soz reddened. "Stop eavesdropping," she grumbled, to cover her embarrassment.

"Come sit with me." As she knelt next to him on the blanket, his face gentled. "Greetings, my wife."

Her face relaxed into a smile. "Greetings, Husband." She slid her hand behind his neck and drew him into a kiss, her fingers tangling in his hair. At first, when he stiffened, she feared she had misread his signals. Then he put his arms around her and returned the kiss. So they sat, surrounded by crates in a cave, the heirs of two interstellar empires necking in the night.

Eventually he pulled back to look at her. "Ai, Soshoni. I've spent my life isolated from people. This is better."

"You had no one at all?" Most of the memories she picked up from his mind showed him alone, in a huge palace run by robots.

He shrugged, trying for a nonchalance she knew he didn't feel. "My father visited sometimes. Afterward I would go on about it for days to the robots." Dryly he added, "It is good they were robots; otherwise I would have bored them catatonic."

Soz smiled. "I've never seen a catatonic robot."

"I had human tutors every now and then, when I was

small." He paused. "When I was a baby, there was a Camyllia. My wet nurse."

She caught his mental image, a beloved woman who resembled him, except for her brown hair and eyes. "Your mother."

He stiffened as if she had slapped him. "My *mother* is the Empress Viquara. My father's wife. Not a slave."

Soz said nothing. They both knew Viquara couldn't be his mother, not if he was Rhon. The genes manifested only if a person inherited them from both parents. She didn't doubt the emperor was his father; not only did Jaibriol resemble him, but Soz had no doubt the emperor would never let an heir with no Qox blood inherit his throne—which meant his father also carried the genes of a psion, another unspeakable secret for the Qox Dynasty. But Jaibriol bore no resemblance to Empress Viquara.

He spoke in a low voice. "Camyllia died when I was four."

She touched his cheek. "I'm sorry."

"My father told me that I must be stronger; I must never become close to anyone." He sounded subdued. "He kept me isolated my entire life. I had nothing to do but study. I've the equivalent of advanced degrees in math, physics, and philosophy. No idea what to do with them, but I have them. I can sing operas, speak more languages than I have fingers, play sports at an elite level, recite the history of empires." Softly he said, "But I have no idea how to love another human being."

"Ai, Jaibriol." In his mind, she saw the Aristos as he saw them, parasites who preyed on empaths to fill the void where their capacity for compassion should have existed. In his own harsh way, his father *had* protected him. The emperor taught his son to barricade his mind until Jaibriol became an emotional fortress unassailable by the Aristos he was destined to rule.

He leaned against the wall, drawing her with him. She laid her head on his shoulder and rested her palm on his chest. Outside, an animal howled, its voice rising in a wavering scale of notes.

Exhaustion soon claimed them. While they dozed, Jaibriol's defenses eased and one of his memories drifted into her mind, vivid and complete. He was fourteen. Standing by a window, he stared out at gardens slumbering in the night. Silvery starlight gleamed on statues and arbors, on the ball courts where he worked out, and on the hills beyond, with their groves of trees.

He turned to look around his room, with its elegant furnishings more appropriate for an elderly statesman than a boy. The gold upholstery was emblazoned with the Trader insignia, a black puma extending its arm, claws bared. Paintings hung on the walls, originals by long-dead artists, a fortune in art. Although he understood their significance, he had no concept of their worth. To him that beautiful room, with its chandeliers and priceless vases, was a prison.

He went over and lay on his bed, rubbing his hand on the velvet spread, comforted by the feel of it. Loneliness pressed on him with an unrelieved pressure he took for granted, simply assuming he was meant to live with that weight, unaware companionship could alleviate it. He didn't believe love existed; he considered it a literary metaphor used in books.

He touched a panel on his nightstand, and a voice drifted into the air. "Attending."

"Cryo?" Jaibriol asked. "Is that you?"

"Yes, Your Highness."

"Come to my bedroom."

A robot soon entered, a household appliance rolling on a gilded tread. About two meters tall, made with antiqued platinum metal, it consisted of a fluted tube varying in diameter from half a meter to only a few centimeters. It was lovely to look at, though odd, having six pairs of arms, each over a meter long. Their joints allowed them far more flexibility than human arms, and the hand on each arm supported eleven multijointed fingers.

"Do you want me to clean the room?" Cryo asked.

"No." Jaibriol rolled onto his side. "Attend me."

Cryo came to the bed and bent its body with the eerie

grace of flexi-metal, lowering itself next to him. With the careful touch of a machine that calculated it needed more care with its frangible human owner than with the rooms it tended, Cryo readied Jaibriol for sleep.

After Cryo had folded his clothes on the nightstand, Jaibriol tugged down the covers. "Here. Come under with me."

"My temperature is already balanced," Cryo said.

"I know. But come anyway." He arranged the covers so he and Cryo lay under them, then laid his head against the robot. With an almost convincing display of tenderness, Cryo folded him in its six pairs of arms, cradling him in a cage of metal limbs. Jaibriol said, "Lights off," and the room dimmed as he slid his arms around the robot and pulled it close.

Later Jaibriol had murmured, "Tell me, Cryo."

"I love you, Your Highness."

"Of course . . ." Jaibriol had finally drifted to sleep.

Soz opened her eyes into blackness. The motion-sensitive lamp had turned off and she had deactivated her IR. She hid in the dark, feeling guilty for trespassing on Jaibriol's privacy.

He spoke in a low voice. "You're soft."

She jerked, surprised he was awake. "Soft?"

Still holding her, he pressed his lips against the top of her head. "We've all a place inside that needs to be soft. Even warriors. Even you." His fingers trailed over the socket on her wrist that could link her internal web to external computers. "Aristo propagandists claim you Jagernauts are inhuman killing machines. But then, propagandists would say that, wouldn't they?"

"Jaibriol—"

"Of course, they say slaves aren't human either." The edge on his voice could have cut casecrete. "But that's all right. Slaves have benevolent Aristos to care for them."

"You aren't a slave. And I'm not inhuman."

It was a moment before he answered. "Kryx Quaelen made me his provider."

Soz went rigid. As Trade Minister of Eube, Kryx Quaelen

held a position high in the hierarchy of Aristo power. "You're the emperor's *son.* The Highton Heir. How could he make you a slave?"

He gave a harsh laugh. "Slave? Of course he never used such a word for me. He has been my esteemed 'mentor' these past few months. After all, I needed to learn a great deal." His voice cracked. "What a shame I required such severe training. I never realized before what screaming can do to your vocal cords."

"Saints almighty," Soz said. "Couldn't you tell your father?"

"Quaelen guessed I was Rhon. He never said it outright, but he left no doubt. He threatened to reveal my father and me as false Aristos if I said anything." His hair brushed her cheek, its distinctive shimmer hidden in the dark. "Everyone believes my father hid me all those years because assassins from your people were trying to kill me. Why bother with assassins? A few months with Kryx as my mentor and I was ready to do the job for them."

Softly she said, "You're safe now. No one can hurt you here."

His voice took on an odd quality. "Do you know, when I was young I read everything I could find. Eubian literature, Skolian, Allied. Humans write so much about love. As far as I can tell, none of it is true." He stroked her hair. "I took what I liked from stories and made up better parts for the rest."

"What did you like?"

"*Oklahoma.*"

"Oak Lahome? What is that?"

"A place. On Earth. The people there fall in love a great deal, dance at odd times for no reason, and sing about their problems, which are hardly problems at all. It is quite absurd. They don't even have computers. In the end, love wins and all are happy except for the villain."

She had never heard of the story. "It sounds, uh, pleasant."

"It's nothing like Eubian literature. In our great works, Highton Aristos are like deities. They all have beautiful naked suffering slaves who worship their owners, gods know why. Or your Skolian literature, where everyone is so nauseatingly grateful to be dominated by your brother's thugs—excuse me, by his benighted military police." He made an incredulous sound. "Why are the tales of my and your peoples so hellaciously *dark?*"

Literature had never been one of her strong points. She tended to be too literal for allegory. "Maybe because we've been at war so long."

For a long time he didn't respond. When he spoke, he caught her off guard again. "I wonder if you and I can have children."

The thought of bearing the Highton Heir's children was a concept she had yet to grapple with. "I don't know."

"If we do, I want them to know laughter."

Her voice softened. "I too."

His hand searched for her in the dark and brushed through her curls. Lifting her chin, he kissed her, less self-conscious than before, already adapting to her unspoken responses.

As they lay down together, she thought, **Activate IR.** The cave became visible, radiating heat it had absorbed during the day. Jaibriol was lying on his side with his eyes closed, one arm around her as he unfastened the front of her uniform vest. As he slid his hand over her breast, he opened his eyes and looked straight at her, though for him it was pitch-black.

"You have the advantage over me," he said.

"Advantage?"

"I see you seeing me. In your mind."

"You can pick up that vivid an image?"

"Why does it surprise you?"

"Even the Rhon can't usually do that with each other."

"Turn off your eyes." His fingers brushed her face. "We can see each other this way."

Deactivate IR, she thought. The cave became black again.

The scent of his Rhon pheromones saturated her senses, invoking her Rhon instincts, the inescapable drive to seek her own kind, just as he sought her. On this, their wedding night, they touched each other with hands, bodies, and minds, speaking a language far more eloquent than the stumbling words they had used earlier.

Afterward they fell into a deep sleep, the first either had known for days.

2

Is it true what they claim, those scholars who read the artifacts of our past? Are we the Lost Children? They say our ancestors were taken from Earth four thousand years before the birth of Christ and stranded on this bitter world. Then I ask this: Why would an unknown race move our progenitors to this land of dying seas and parched deserts, leaving no help, no rationale, nothing but the wreckage of ancient starships? *Why?*

We speak with pride of our ancestors who conquered space flight while Earth languished in her Stone Age. We glorify the Ruby Empire, which rose in antediluvian splendor five millennia ago. We have no more than whispers for its fall only a scant three centuries later. That it took us another four thousand years to regain the stars; we have no boasts on this either. Yet for all that our empires rose and fell, we the Lost Children of Earth never found our legendary home.

Until that day, in Earth's twenty-first century, when her other children ventured to the stars—and found us already here.

—From The Lost Empire, *by Tajjil Bloodstone*

Kurj Skolia, Imperator of Imperial Skolia, was a large man. At seven feet tall, broad-shouldered and massive, he claimed a physique too heavy for Earth. He was descended from Ruby Empire colonists who modified their DNA to survive on a low-gravity world with a bright sun. His gold metallic skin and hair reflected light. His gold irises shimmered. When lowered, his inner eyelids became one-way mirrors that let him see the world but remained opaque to the outside. His was an implacable face, the visage of a metal dictator with shields for eyes.

He had, himself, ordered other modifications to his body. Fiberoptics networked it, webbing together the nodes in his spine with his brain. High-pressure hydraulics augmented his muscles and skeleton, and a microfusion reactor powered him. But blood still flowed in his veins, the blood of his ancestors, the Ruby Dynasty that had once, long ago, ruled an empire.

At ninety-one years of age, Kurj looked a hale forty. He had commanded Imperial Space Command for fifty-six years. The loyalty of his officers was legendary, his brilliance as a war leader undisputed.

He had assumed his title at his grandfather's death. The Imperial Assembly ruled the death an accident, an unintended tragedy. But legend whispered that Kurj Skolia murdered his grandfather in his unquenchable ambition to achieve a title none dared deny him. The Assembly governed modern Skolia now, rather than the Ruby Dynasty, but its councilors trod with care in the presence of this man known as the Fist of Skolia.

He had no wife. No legitimate children. His legacy was further constrained in that his heir had to be Rhon. Only the Rhon were strong enough to power the psiberweb, which was created by machines from the Ruby Empire. Knowledge of how to build those ancient machines had been lost, but a few still operated. They created a psiberweb outside of spacetime, unfettered by light speed. It made possible instant communication across any distance.

The psiberweb gave Imperial Space Command, the Skolian military, an unmatched speed in communications. It was why they survived against the Traders. So Kurj needed Rhon heirs to ensure the web's survival. He chose three of his half siblings: Althor, a Jagernaut Secondary; Kelric, a Tertiary who later died in battle; and Soz, a Primary, equivalent to an admiral.

Soz.

Kurj stood at the wall of dichromesh glass in his office and looked at HeadQuarters City far below. Laid out in squares and angles, the city formed a precise metropolis. Chrome, metal, ceramoplex: it gleamed under the red sky and splintering hot sun of Diesha.

Soz will someday stand here. For three months he had maintained that hope. For three months he had waited for her to reappear with Jaibriol Qox as her prisoner. But now his operatives had found the ships. As wreckage. That inescapable fact registered in his files.

Soz was dead.

Kurj stared at his city, his hands clasped behind his back. She had been his first choice among his heirs. He had only one living candidate now, his half brother Althor, his second rather than first choice, but still a fine candidate. Soon Kurj would make the announcement. Althor would follow him as Imperator.

A, he thought, summoning the primary node in his spine.

Attending, **A** answered.

Explain, Kurj thought. **Why am I unable to stop dwelling on the death of Sauscony Valdoria when such serves no useful purpose?**

Analysis complete, **A** answered.

Already?

Yes. You are grieving.

Kurj looked at the pale wash of sky above HeadQuarters City. **It achieves no useful result. End process.**

It is a necessary process. It will stop when you have made peace with her death.

Peace is not in my nature.

I can delete your memories of her. However, she is embedded in your processors, files, and neural patterns. Removing her will delete data crucial to your optimal function.

No deletions. Kurj didn't want to forget his sister.

Suggestion, node **C** thought.

Yes?

Work, **C** thought. Occupying your mind with tasks will decrease the amount of time it spends in attempts to calculate models that would have led to your sister's continued existence.

Very well. Kurj turned from the window. His office took up the top floor of the skyneedle known as Spire A. His desk extended the length of the room, a slab of dichromesh glass studded by web units and supported by glass columns embedded with more equipment, a mechanically beautiful array designed from precious metals and ceramoplex. He settled into one of the control chairs and sat back while its exoskeleton folded around his body, clicking prongs into sockets in his spine.

Activate Kyle gate, he thought.

His office web responded. Activated.

A psicon appeared in his mind, the symbol Ψ from an old language. Greek. As a descendant of Earth's Lost Children, Kurj found himself fascinated by those ancients from Earth and their legends. Antigone. Agamemnon. Oedipus.

The psicon vanished, replaced by his mindscape, an ordered mesh that extended in all directions. Just as a Fourier transform took a time-dependent function into frequency space, so the Ψ gate transformed his mind from spacetime into psiberspace.

Kurj interacted with machine intelligences using the synthetic nodes and fiberoptics implanted in his body; he interacted with other telepaths using organic bodies in his brain. As he entered the web, his Kyle Afferent Body picked up signals sent by other telepaths and routed them to the *para* neural structures in his cortex, which translated them into the thoughts of the other users. The *paras* also translated and conveyed his thoughts to his Kyle Efferent Body, which sent them into the web. Without psiberweb amplification, he could still pick up and send thoughts to a limited extent, but it depended on fields produced by the brain, in particular Coulomb effects, which meant he had to be near the people he interacted with. In the web, spatial location became irrelevant.

Clearance verified. That came from the Evolving Intelligence in the computer that monitored security in his office.

Dusk icon, Kurj thought. He became a dark figure cloaked in shadows.

So he strode across the grid, passing through psiware that waved like filaments in the glimmering atmosphere. One flicked his leg, as often happened near a node where his telops were working on ISC business.

Kurj stopped. He distrusted subtle events like psiware fronds flicking his leg. The Rhon powerlink that created the web was a Triad: himself, his stepfather Eldrinson, and his mother's sister Dehya. When it came to Dehya, he took nothing for granted. Where he was force, she was subtlety; where he radiated power, she created nuances. And he didn't trust nuances.

Kurj knelt to study the filament. It waved innocuously, like seaweed.

Access location. He sank down, into a bare room with gray walls. **Torpedo,** he thought, calling one of his search-and-destroy routines.

Attending, Torpedo rumbled.

Apply key codes.

Done. Large keys appeared, hanging from a rack on the wall, each representing a different security routine. No hidden locks found at this location.

Go deeper into the web, Kurj thought.

The walls peeled away as Torpedo searched. Each time it stripped down a wall, the debris disappeared, swept away by macros Kurj had created to keep the web well-ordered.

No locks detected, Torpedo thought.

Upload the filament under analysis, Kurj thought.

The ceiling above him misted and the filament fell

through, dangling in the air. The disruption of the room's symmetry aggravated Kurj. He resisted the urge to eject the filament; if Dehya had created it, she might intend for it to evoke exactly that reaction. She knew him too well.

Isolate filament code from its environment, he thought.

The filament dropped to the floor. When Kurj crouched down to take it, the code came alive and whisked out of his hands. It sped up the wall, but the ceiling had solidified, controlled by his security routines. The filament whipped across it, slid down the other wall, and disappeared into a seam where the wall met the floor.

Go get it, Torpedo, Kurj thought.

Code captured. It is corrupting itself.

Bring back what's left.

A glass box appeared on the floor. The filament inside dissolved in erratic sparkles until only glitter winked on the bottom of the box.

Analysis of code, Kurj thought.

It is a monitor to track your web activity.

Kurj snorted. **Mail Server attend.**

Server 36 answered. Attending.

Send the following to Assembly Key Selei: "I ate your spy, Dehya." End.

Mail sent. Reply received.

That was fast.

The response came from an automated routine in Selei's mail server. It says: "My spies proliferate. I call them hydra. If you cut down one, two more grow in its place."

So. Dehya was playing on his penchant for Earth mythology, using the battle of Hercules and the hydra. Every time Hercules cut off one head, two more appeared. He defeated the hydra by having the stumps cauterized before they grew new heads.

Send reply, Kurj thought. **"Hydras are easy to scorch." End.**

Message sent.

Any reply?

None.

Kurj grinned. **Close memory location.**

He rose out of the room, and its ceiling re-formed under his feet. Filaments of web code waved around its edges.

Torpedo, he thought. **Search out and destroy any psiware produced by the corrupted code.**

Procedure implemented.

Good. Kurj continued across the web, surrounded by its glittering atmosphere. Each speck of "glitter" specified the process of a user. His Watchers ran continual security checks without need of his attention, but from time to time he examined a speck at random, to gain a sense of web activities. Today he turned up little worth his time: three telops in a quarrel, a private group meditating together via psiberspace, and someone checking flight times at a starport.

One nodule resolved into a petition written by a colonist on a fringe world. He was protesting an ISC order to disband the colony's Union of Web Analysts. Kurj deleted the petition even as the man was writing it and ordered a monitor to remove any rewrites. The UWA created disorder by agitating for privileges reserved to ISC. And Kurj disliked disorder.

A sparkle danced in front of him. Attention.

Expand, Kurj thought.

It grew into a shimmer that engulfed the web. When it cleared, Kurj was standing in Selei City on the planet Parthonia, capital of the Imperialate. A boulevard stretched in front of him, bordered by wrywillows, with stately houses set far back from the street and a lavender sky overhead.

What is the purpose of this representation? Kurj asked.

The sparkle reappeared. An advertisement for the Imperial Ballet triggered security monitor 484.

Show me the advertisement.

The street moved past him as if he were traveling in one of the open teardrop cars popular in Selei City. He came into view of Ascendance Hall, home to the Imperial Ballet. A mural on its facade glistened in a holographic display of dancers, along with performance dates and times.

The mural's most striking aspect was a dancer in a diaphanous blue dress. Her skin, eyes, and hair gleamed gold. Hip-length curls streamed out when she whirled and leapt, then swirled around her when she paused. A sweet smile curved in her angel's face. She had the body of an erotic holomovie actress rather than the more angular form of most dancers.

Kurj clenched his teeth. He raised his hand and red lasers shot out of his fingers, searing the mural. In a node owned by Ascendance Hall on the planet Parthonia, a marauding section of computer code cut a swath of destruction through the directory of advertising files for the Imperial Ballet. In Kurj's mindscape the mural exploded, shards of color flying everywhere.

Offense nullified, the sparkle thought.

If they show her image again, Kurj thought, **shut them down.**

Monitoring of Imperial Ballet updated, the routine answered.

Kurj had no objection to the Imperial Ballet—provided they used no displays of this woman. Let the tales of her spectacular beauty become legends no one could verify. He had no intention of letting audiences drool over his mother.

He waved his hand and the city disappeared, replaced by the web grid. **Transfer to Comtrace,** he thought.

Transferred. That came from a new source, cold and rumbling. Any other user accessing Comtrace, the heart of ISC intelligence, would have faced extensive security protocols. Unauthorized attempts could result in execution. Kurj's Dusk psicon simply re-formed in a region of splintering whiteness.

Attending, Comtrace thought.

Download Admiral Tahota's reports to node 5, Kurj thought.

Download commenced.

Kurj went to work. First he read the reports from Starjack Tahota, his second in command at ISC. Then he studied ISC maneuvers against Trader battle cruisers, analyzing them for weaknesses in strategy. Next he moved on to intelligence reports on military officers in ESComm, the Trader equivalent of ISC.

When Kurj finally left Comtrace, he felt more settled. Thoughts of Soz still weighed on him, but the pressure had eased, at least for now.

Incoming message from Assembly Key Selei, Mail Server 19 thought.

What does she say? Kurj asked.

"Hercules is the wrong icon."

That's it?

Yes.

He frowned. Dehya was the one who had invoked the hydra myth. And what did she mean, *icon?* It could refer either to a computer icon or to an icon as a figure of note. Knowing Dehya, it might be both, in a riddle that made sense only to her enigmatic, albeit towering, intellect. What was she up to, on this eve of his announcement that he had chosen his heir?

Seeker, respond, Kurj thought.

A rotating sphere the size of his fist appeared, with colors swirling on it like rainbows on oil. Attending, his Search-and-Summon monitor thought.

Is Secondary Althor Valdoria in the web? Kurj asked.

Seeker paused. No.

Summon him.

The sphere darted off, vanishing into the glimmering mist. If Althor was near any form of console with IR capability, he would receive the summons through IR signals sent to receivers in his body. Given the ubiquitous presence of computers, from full-sized consoles down to picowebs embedded in buildings, almost nowhere in the Imperialate existed where one could avoid a summons from the Imperator.

Kurj focused on the grid under his feet. **Access memory location.**

The ground descended, taking him into another gray room. **Office,** he thought, and a macro created a massive office for him, all dichromesh glass and gleaming components. As he sat behind the huge desk that spanned the room, Seeker reappeared, hovering in the air.

Secondary Valdoria requests permission to access your location, Seeker thought.

Let him in.

The door opened and a man entered. A psicon, actually, but this man's symbol of choice was simple; it looked like him. Althor Valdoria stood nearly two meters high, six-foot-six. He was built like Kurj, with a massive physique. He too had inherited their mother's gold coloring, but his violet eyes came from his father, Eldrinson Valdoria, the man Kurj refused to acknowledge as his stepfather.

Althor wore a Jagernaut's black uniform with black knee boots. Two gold armbands on each arm indicated his rank as a Secondary, about equivalent to a naval commodore. Picochips packed the conduits embedded in his leather-and-metal gauntlets, and were linked through his wrist sockets to the biomech web in his body. He saluted Kurj, extending his arms straight out, his fists clenched and his wrists crossed.

At ease. Kurj motioned to a chair. After Althor sat down, Kurj said, **Tomorrow I will announce you are to assume the title of Imperial Heir. The ceremony will be at 16:45, Dieshan time, from my office.**

I am honored by your confidence, Althor thought.

You've given me good reason for it. Kurj paused. **Has Dehya discussed this with you?**

No, sir.

Have you had contact with her recently?

A tenday ago, Althor answered. **She and my brother Eldrin invited me to dinner at their home on the Orbiter.**

What did you talk about?

Althor rubbed his chin. **A ballad Eldrin is writing. The remodeling on their house. Mother's birthday.**

Anything about your position as the Imperial Heir?

Nothing.

Very well. Kurj doubted he would discover anything even if Dehya had intended more than a quiet family dinner. Her methods were too subtle. He needed a different approach to unmask them.

Watching Althor, Kurj was concerned for other reasons. His brother's psicon reflected moods, at least those that Althor's spinal nodes considered safe for him to express. Right now he looked tired. Dark circles showed under his eyes.

How are you? Kurj asked.

Althor swallowed. **I will be fine.**

Quietly Kurj thought, **Nothing makes up for Soz's loss.**

I had kept hoping.

I also, Kurj thought. **I miss our sister.**

Grief flicked across Althor's face, and also surprise. Kurj supposed it wasn't often he revealed emotions even to his family.

I too, Althor thought.

Kurj nodded. **Report to my office tomorrow at sixteen hundred hours.**

Yes, sir.

Kurj raised his hand. **You may go.**

Althor stood and saluted, then left as he had come, through the door.

Seeker, Kurj thought.

The sphere appeared. Attending.

Where is the Web Key?

On the Orbiter space station, repairing a damaged section of the web.

So. His stepfather also combated grief with work.

Kurj had never come to terms with his mother's marriage to Eldrinson. But Eldrinson Valdoria—a simple farmer from a backward world—was Rhon. The difficulty in creating Rhon psions in the lab made sexual reproduction the most reliable source. In the past, that had prompted the Assembly to overlook the ethics, or lack thereof, in coercing the Ruby Dynasty to interbreed. It all became moot when Eldrinson and Kurj's mother began having Rhon children, which they had done at a frequency Kurj found altogether inappropriate. Even more annoying, they bequeathed some form of Eldrinson's name to numerous of their sons. However, they named their third son Del-Kurj, which meant "In honor of Kurj." In any case, their ten offspring ensured a hefty reserve of Rhon psions for the web, enough so the less important children even enjoyed a degree of freedom rather than having their every move monitored by the Assembly.

The web grew larger every year, a voracious ocean as deep as the stars, requiring ever more Rhon strength to power it. But the powerlink could support at most only three minds; more would overload the link and short-circuit the web. Nor could just any Rhon psion join the Triad. Just as no two fermion particles could have the same quantum numbers, so no two minds could occupy the same region in psiberspace—a condition difficult to satisfy when the Rhon were all related, which made their minds more similar.

The original powerlink had been a Dyad, formed by Kurj's maternal grandparents. Kurj had tried to make it a Triad, but he and his grandfather were too much alike. The strained link shattered—and killed his grandfather. His grandmother died soon after of old age, and Dehya, her eldest daughter, assumed both the Ruby Throne and the title of Assembly Key. So Dehya and Kurj had formed a new

Dyad, shaken by grief, afraid to add a third Key because their close genetic ties made them too much alike. It could kill.

Except Eldrinson had no Ruby Dynasty genes. Fate played the ultimate joke on Kurj; the stepfather he so wished would vanish turned out to be the only person who could complete the Triad. Having Eldrinson to maintain the web freed Kurj and Dehya to focus on using it. Which they did in service to the Imperial Assembly, but also in pursuit of their own purposes, such as maneuvering control of the Imperialate away from the Assembly. So they formed a volatile Triad: Dehya, Kurj, and Eldrinson; Assembly Key, Military Key, and Web Key; the Mind, the Fist, and the Heart of Skolia.

Summon Web Key, Kurj thought.

Seeker darted off again.

A moment later a thought came out of the air, its lustrous resonance a reminder of its owner's extraordinary singing voice. ***Yes?*** Eldrinson asked.

Where are you? Kurj thought.

A psicon formed, a handsome man about five-foot-ten, with large violet eyes and a hint of freckles across his nose. Wine-red hair brushed his shoulders. It puzzled Kurj that Eldrinson had silver in his hair; the man was almost twenty years younger than Kurj, who had no trace of gray and expected none for decades. More irritating were his stepfather's spectacles. As far as Kurj was concerned, it was sheer obstinacy on Eldrinson's part to so dislike Imperial technology that he preferred glasses to having his damaged eyes replaced with better ones.

I've spoken with Althor, Kurj said. **I will make the announcement tomorrow.**

Eldrinson nodded. ***Your mother and I will come to Diesha.***

Kurj almost told him it was unnecessary. But in this he relented. Both he and his stepfather had lost a person they loved. He felt Eldrinson's grief in the very fabric of the web.

Roca and I are also having a memorial service on Lyshriol, Eldrinson thought. ***We would like you to come.***

Normally Kurj resisted visiting Lyshriol, his stepfather's

home world. Although pleasant enough in its own rustic way, it was Eldrinson's dominion. However, this was different. **I will attend.**

Your mother will be glad to see you. Eldrinson faded from the grid.

Kurj resumed his walk. At another grid square he thought, **Open,** and once again sank into a bare gray room.

You have 653 messages, Mail Server 1 thought.

That surprised Kurj. It had been less than an hour since he last checked his mail. **Delegate.**

Done. The queue now contains 102 messages.

Prioritize. Relay first on list.

Hieroglyphs appeared on the wall, scrolling downward, a list of who had received this particular message.

Address map, Kurj thought. The list vanished, replaced by a holomap with a network of nodes joined by filaments. It showed every address that had received the message, millions of sites, so dense with lines it was impossible to distinguish individual addresses.

Text of message, Kurj thought.

The map moved to the upper corner. Three-dimensional glyphs appeared on the wall, their height and width containing their primary information, their depth adding shades of meaning. As Server 1 read the glyphs, Kurj studied them, verifying that the server's interpretation matched his own. Although he had fine-tuned its psiware, he still often checked its work.

The message was surprisingly blunt and free of propaganda, given its source: His Exalted Highness, Emperor Ur Qox of the Eubian Concord, declares war on Imperial Skolia.

Kurj snorted. Skolia and the so-called Concord had been having an undeclared war for centuries. This changed nothing. But since it had become known that Emperor Qox's heir had died while a prisoner of ISC, Kurj had expected this.

Who else has received this message? he asked.

Server 1 answered with a metallic thought: All government offices on the planets and habitats of the Eubian Concord, Skolian Imperialate, and Allied Worlds.

Kurj accessed an image of Ur Qox, the Trader emperor. A tall man appeared in front of Kurj, lean and gaunt, with red eyes and shimmering black hair.

You think you grieve, Kurj thought to the image. **Don't come to me with oaths of war over your ill-bred spawn. You will pay for my sister's death, Qox. You will pay, until the blood of the Trader Aristos runs red across the sea of stars.**

3

Jeremiah, stop being provincial. Why do you find it so hard to believe humans have settled 2700 worlds and habitats? Yes, I know, our Allied Worlds have only have 300. But I came to know the Imperialate much better during my studies at their institute on Parthonia. It's true, they have over 900 colonies. And that's nothing compared to the Traders. The Eubian Concord—what we call the Traders—they have nearly 1500, some with billions of people. Think of it! Humanity numbers over 3000 billion people. Only 400 billion live among our Allied Worlds of Earth. Skolians number almost 1000 billion and the Traders a full *1700 billion.*

But here's a sobering thought, Jeremiah. Except for a few hundred Aristos, those 1700 billion Traders are all slaves.

—*From the collected letters of Tiller Smith to his brother*

Soz knelt on the ground in front of the valise-shaped box that contained their computers. She was wearing only the shirt from Jaibriol's prison uniform, which reached to her thighs, but the warmth of the night required nothing more.

Jaibriol had turned off the quasis screen and was standing in the cave entrance, in his trousers, looking out at the night. His presence both soothed and agitated her. He was a beautiful sight, his broad chest smooth with muscles, his classic face in profile as he gazed into the darkness. But he was strange too, unfamiliar, Imperial Space Command's worst nightmare, an Aristo who could power a psiberweb.

He glanced at her. "Did you find anything?"

"Erin left a file in GeoComp."

"Erin? You mean the pilot who brought us here?"

Soz nodded. "According to this, an automated Allied probe discovered this planet a few days ago." Actually, *days* was inaccurate. During their escape, they had never quite managed to engage the stardrives, racing instead on the edge of light speed. It had made their time dilate, eighteen minutes going by for them while almost three months passed for the rest of the settled galaxy.

"The probe transmitted its discovery to the Harvard-Smithsonian Center for Astrophysics on Earth," she said. "No one had yet downloaded the data when President Calloway's routines found it." Reading the file, she whistled. "Calloway must have some system. She got in, copied the data, and then wiped out all trace of it. Aside from us, only she and Erin know this place exists."

"And your father," Jaibriol said.

Soz swallowed, thinking of the tears in her father's eyes as he had bid her good-bye. Loving a Rhon psion himself, her mother, he understood Soz's decision to free Jaibriol. So he had used his hot line to the Allied president to request sanctuary for the lovers.

Her eyes hot with unshed tears, knowing she would probably never see her father or family again, Soz leaned over the computer. "These files have some data on the planet."

Jaibriol gentled his voice. "How about the length of the night?"

Soz flicked her finger through a holicon above the screen, the tiny icon of a world. A much larger holo appeared floating in the air over the computer, showing a star system. "Prism orbits a red dwarf star, which orbits a blue-white star." She paused, studying the data. "This is all referenced to Earth. The red star pulls on Prism with a force more than twenty times that of Earth on its Moon. That ought to drag Prism into a tidal lock, which means it would always keep the same face toward the red sun. But either it isn't locked yet or else it's in some sort of resonance. It rotates three times for every orbit it makes around the red sun."

"Three days per year?" He stared at her. "How long until we see sunlight again?"

Soz brought up more data. "For every three days that pass relative to the red sun, four days pass relative to the blue-white sun. So sometimes we have no suns in the sky, sometimes we have one, and sometimes two." She grimaced. "What a flaming mess."

Jaibriol laughed. "Does that last have a scientific translation?"

She gave him a rueful smile. "Unfortunately, yes. Right now we're at the start of a 135-hour night. We get a long night because we're on the side of the planet facing away from the red star when red is between us and the blue-white star." Peering at the data, she said, "When day comes, it will last 243 hours, with both suns up for 135 of them. Then an 81-hour night. Then a 486-hour day, when Prism passes between the blue-white and the red sun. While red is up, blue-white sets and then later rises again. After both suns go down, we get another 81-hour night, followed by another 243-hour day. Then the whole mess starts over again."

"Gods," Jaibriol said. "Do we get cooked during the days?"

"I don't think so." She studied the glyphs on the screen. "Both suns have to be up for the planet to receive as much light as Sol shines on Earth. We're more in danger from flares on the red star. But the atmosphere offers protection.

It also does a reasonable job holding heat, which is probably why it's warm right now."

She glanced at him standing in the entrance, his chest bare to the balmy night. Distracted by his husbandly attributes, she lost her train of thought. It was a moment before she could refocus on the GeoComp. "We can determine the north celestial pole from how the stars move in the sky."

"How do you know it's north?"

She looked at him, pleasantly distracted again. "It?"

"Why call this the north hemisphere?"

"We have to call it something."

"I just wondered why you picked north instead of south."

"If you want to call it south, that's fine."

"I didn't say I wanted to call it south."

"All right. North."

"That's not—never mind." He looked outside again. "So what is our latitude?"

She hesitated. "We're pretty far north. Or, uh, south."

"North is fine."

"About sixty degrees north of the equator." She squinted at the screen. "This is all relative to Allied standards. 'The same latitude as Sundsvall.' Whatever the hell that means."

"It's in a place on Earth called Sweden." Jaibriol rubbed his palm across his chest. "I guess we'll have to get used to the dark."

Seeing him touch himself, she smiled. "I could get used to long nights."

He glanced at her, then flushed and looked away. Once again he rubbed his chest, this time with a self-conscious motion.

What had she said? They were married, after all. It wasn't as if she were drooling over him in an erotica arcade. Then again, she also found her reaction to him unsettling. She hadn't responded this way to her former fiancé, Rex Blackstone, another Jagernaut. After being injured in combat, he had withdrawn his proposal for fear of what the war would do to their marriage. She had died inside then, for the loss of their newly acknowledged affection. Yet in all the years she had known Rex, she had never felt such an intense passion as Jaibriol had stirred in her from the moment she met him. Like knew like. Rhon.

Jaibriol swatted at his arm. "That's odd."

She flushed, afraid he had picked up her thoughts. "Odd?"

He scratched his arm. "My skin itches."

She stood up and went over to him. "Where?"

"Everywhere." He rubbed his cheek. "It hurts."

Soz drew him back into the cave. "Maybe you should—"

"No!" He jerked away from her. "I can't come in here. If I have something on me, it could hurt you."

"I'm going to turn on the quasis screen." The thought of his being unprotected outside stirred an intense emotion in her. She wasn't sure how to define it, but she knew she wanted him here with her. Safe.

As she reactivated the screen, Jaibriol made a strangled noise. Turning, she saw his face go pale. She grabbed the medkit off a crate and pulled out the diagnostic tape. When she set the flexible strip against his chest, holos formed in front of it, views of a man's body, red and blue veins on one, the nervous system on another, ivory for his skeleton. Glyphs scrolled across the tape.

"Oh, hell," Soz said. "Do you have any allergies?"

He heaved in a strained breath. "None I know of."

"You're having an allergenic reaction." She took an air syringe out of the kit, dialed in the antihistamine recommended by the tape, and injected his neck.

"I can't—" He choked and sagged against the wall.

"Jaibriol!" Soz caught him as he collapsed. His weight knocked them over, but her hydraulics kicked in and she controlled their descent enough to lay him on his back. The red alert icon on the tape gave the story: he was in anaphylactic shock. His larynx had swollen, blocking his respiration, and his blood pressure had dropped far too low. Tipping back his head, she tried to breathe air into his lungs. Without breaking the rhythm of her efforts, she pressed the end of the diagnostic tape against a receptor square on the syringe. When the syringe beeped, she injected his neck again, all the time breathing air into his lungs.

Blow in. Wait. Blow in. Wait. Over and over she tried, praying the swelling would recede enough for him to take in air.

Don't die, Soz thought. **Gods, don't die.**

With a shuddering gasp, Jaibriol heaved in a breath. As Soz jerked up her head, his chest rose again. She watched, ready to resume, but he continued to breathe on his own. His long lashes twitched and his eyes opened.

"Thank you," she whispered, she wasn't sure to whom.

He spoke in an almost inaudible voice. "Soshoni?"

She drew in a shaky breath. "We can call it south. East. West. Anything you want. I promise. Just don't die."

"North," he whispered. "North is up. South is down. North is optimism . . . That's why I wondered why you chose it."

Then he passed out.

After hours of watching Jaibriol sleep, Soz finally let herself doze. When he stirred, she snapped awake, afraid he was having a seizure. But he was only sitting up.

He rubbed his eyes. "How long was I out?"

She didn't know whether to laugh or cry. He looked so normal, just sitting there. "Ten hours."

"What happened?"

"You had some kind of reaction to something."

He smiled. "That's a precise diagnosis."

Soz managed a laugh. "As near as I can tell, some pollen dusted across your skin, nose, and mouth. You know the rest."

His smile faded. "If I have that reaction every time pollen comes along, how will I survive here?"

"I have the computer working on an antidote. It also says you may develop immunities." She indicated the shimmering quasis screen at the entrance. "For now, that will keep you and the pollen apart." Although on a macroscopic scale the screen was a rigid barrier, it didn't actually "freeze" the slice of air it contained. The air molecules continued to rotate, vibrate, and otherwise behave as they had when she activated the screen. What the quasis, or quantum stasis, did was keep the molecules in the same quantum state. Any penetration of the screen, even by one particle, involved a state change. So nothing penetrated. A few hits from a high-energy weapon could break it down, but against pollen it would work just fine.

Of course that created other problems. No air or light could penetrate the screen, either. Fortunately their cave had vents to circulate air. But quasis wasn't meant to be used this way; rather, it protected starfighters and their occupants from the immense accelerations and energies involved in interstellar warfare. The generator required to produce the screen was no minor piece of equipment; only her high security clearance and familiarity with ISC procedures had made it possible to obtain this one.

Soz watched as Jaibriol sagged against the wall. "How are you?"

"All right."

"Jaibriol."

"Yes?"

"Don't be so stoic. I can feel how much you hurt." She slid over to him. "We can't take chances here. There are no hospitals."

He gave her a wry smile. "This business of living with another telepath may be more difficult than I realized."

"Does it bother you?" Growing up in a family of psions, she and her siblings had learned early to keep their minds private, a mental knock expected for personal interactions. With Jaibriol, the doors kept fading, reappearing, fading again, as the two of them danced their awkward waltz of *Who are you?*

"Being near people bothers me," he said. "Their emotions beat on my mind. Solitude seems more natural. It is what I've known most of my life. But I don't like being alone. Solitude—it's not the same as *alone.*" He drew her into his arms. "Now I have someone to share my solitude. Someone like me."

She hesitated. "I had a sense, earlier tonight, that you didn't like it when I, uh—looked at you."

He made an exasperated noise. "I wanted to talk about north and south, hope and despair, new worlds and old empires. You wanted me to take off my clothes and lie down."

"That's not true." When he raised his eyebrows, she amended, "I appreciate your intellect too."

" 'Too'?"

"Ah. Well." She flushed.

His lips quirked up. "Then again, we can't discuss hope and despair all the time. Perhaps we should investigate the other side of this 'too.' "

She smiled. "Perhaps we should."

And so they did, throughout the warm Prism night.

Kurj leaned back in a control chair in his office. The comm in his ear connected him to the team checking security on the pavilion outside. Soon they would begin the ceremony investing Althor with the title of Imperial Heir. Kurj glanced at the group in his office: himself, Althor, their mother, Eldrinson, five bodyguards, and Barcala Tikal, First Counselor of the Assembly.

Althor was standing with his parents. He wore his Jagernaut uniform, not the everyday leathers with gauntlets and boots, but his dress uniform, gold pants with a darker stripe down the outer seam of each leg, gold boots, and a gold pullover with a narrow line across the chest, accenting the breadth of his shoulders. The ISC Public Affairs Office had done an extensive analysis for its design, and Kurj approved the result. The holographic cloth made a gold nimbus around Althor, achieving the planned effect, which was to make him look like an avenging warrior angel.

Eldrinson stood next to his son. He wore civilian clothes, dark blue pants tucked into suede boots. For some bizarre reason he had chosen a shirt that laced up the front, with actual leather thongs, and long sleeves that belled out and then came in at the cuffs. His wine-red hair brushed his shoulders and his spectacles framed his eyes. Kurj thought he made an absurd picture, too rustic by far, but the public loved it. He had to admit his stepfather presented a far more palatable image of the Ruby Dynasty than he did with his own harsh appearance.

His mother, Assembly Councilor Roca, stood with her husband. She looked her heritage, a descendant of the queens who had ruled the Ruby Empire. Tall like her sons, regal and graceful, she riveted attention. Her thick braid fell to her hips, gleaming gold with copper and bronze highlights. Tendrils escaped to curl around her incomparable face. Her jumpsuit covered her from neck to wrist to ankle, in the dark blue of mourning, with no adornment at all, yet still he wished she had worn something more discreet. But in truth he knew it wasn't the clothes. Nothing short of a shapeless sack would hide her spectacular sensual beauty.

Kurj wanted to comfort her, hold her in his arms, soothe her grief. He did nothing. He never touched her. He hadn't since he was a child.

Barcala Tikal, First Councilor of the Assembly, stood near the door, going over his speech on his palmtop computer, his lips moving as he mouthed the words. A gangly man with black hair that he allowed to gray at the temples, he stood taller than Roca and Eldrinson, taller than most people, in fact, though compared to Althor and Kurj he had no great height. As First Councilor, he held the highest civilian title in the Imperialate.

One person was noticeably absent. Dehya. The Ruby Pharaoh. Her absence was one of the few topics on which she, Kurj, and the Assembly concurred; no more than two members of the Triad would ever appear together in public. It was yet another precaution to ensure the survival of the web's power sources.

Kurj wondered where in the web Dehya lurked right now. He had no doubt she was monitoring his office. To all of

Skolia he embodied Imperial power. The Fist of Skolia. None of them knew the shadowy, gossamer Pharaoh, who controlled the web with an intricacy he could never approach.

The bodyguards stood posted around the room, massive and implacable, all Jagernauts with Jumbler guns heavy on their hips. But they weren't the foremost defense for the Ruby Dynasty. That protection was never entrusted solely to humans, even the hybrid machine-humans known as Jagernauts. The most valuable members of the Ruby Dynasty carried their first defense in their brains.

Anyone could have a cyberlock implanted in their cerebral cortex, but few willingly agreed to it. The process required extensive surgery, and attempts to remove it resulted in brain damage. When activated, the lock surrounded its carrier with a distorted quasis field. Unlike normal quasis, this field *changed* the molecular behavior of whatever entered it. At its lowest level it disrupted neural activity in an intruder's brain, enough to stun or knock a person unconscious; on medium it stressed the molecular structure of matter; and at its highest level it tore matter apart atom by atom.

Locks were fine-tuned, of course, to ignore specific quantum states, such as those produced by air, certain sound waves, and visible photons, making it possible for the person within the field to breathe, hear, and see. However, the modifications that allowed a device to recognize different quantum states were prohibitive, to say the least, particularly given that a lock also had to be synchronized with its carrier's brain waves. It made cyberlocks almost impossible to obtain—unless one had the resources of Imperial Space Command at their disposal.

Kurj chose to have a cyberlock; had he decided otherwise the Assembly would have danced a careful waltz of power with him, trying to convince without commanding. Dehya had designed the locks, and as far as he knew she also chose to carry one. Roca, Eldrinson, and Althor were a different matter; the Assembly decreed they take cyberlocks, Kurj agreed, and so it was done.

Eldrinson had refused the lock. So it was implanted against his will, an operation far more sensitive for him than for the others. Kurj's stepfather had epilepsy. Without the aid of modern medicine he would have long ago died from the severity of his convulsions. That he dreaded any treatment he considered invasive, that hospitals made him uncomfortable, that he disliked the cyberlock—none of that deterred the Assembly from protecting him with it.

A comm link on Kurj's desk chimed.

Activate line 18, he thought.

Activated, his office answered.

A voice came out of the comm. "First Councilor Tikal, this is Jak at the pavilion. We're ready down here."

Barcala Tikal looked up. "We will be there in—" He glanced at his palmtop. "Two minutes."

"Very good, sir," Jak said. "Out."

Deactivate line, Kurj thought.

Deactivated, his web answered.

They left the office, two bodyguards in front, followed by Tikal, Eldrinson and Roca, Althor, then Kurj and the Jagernaut with the cyberlock keys, then the last two guards. The maglift took them down two hundred stories, to the skyneedle's third level, and let them out into a foyer. Across the room, beyond fortified doors, history waited for them.

Tikal glanced at Kurj. "We have to activate the locks now."

Kurj nodded and turned to the guard with him, a Jagernaut Primary, one of only fifteen officers in all of ISC who had achieved that rank.

Activate, Kurj thought.

Yes, sir, the Primary answered, his thought strong and well-formed but with less power than Kurj's mental thunder. He lifted his right arm, a cybernetic construct all the way to his elbow, and brushed his natural left finger over his cybernetic palm. Red light glowed as a laser in his machine-hand read the diffraction pattern produced by his fingerprint. It was Kurj who had specified what patterns the picoweb in the Primary's hand would accept, sending the data to his arm via IR and locking it so even the Primary himself had no access to it.

The Primary's picoweb verified his identity, and a panel in his right hand slid open, revealing four wafers.

"No." Eldrinson stiffened. "Not mine."

Councilor Tikal spoke to Eldrinson with a respect that irritated Kurj. "Lord Valdoria, we appreciate the danger inherent to you in the cyberlock. Please be assured we will use the utmost care."

"You only need one field," Eldrinson said. "It can surround us all. It isn't necessary to turn on all four."

"I understand your reluctance," Tikal said. "But with both you and Imperator Skolia appearing in public together, we feel extra precautions are necessary."

Eldrinson exhaled. But he nodded, his face pale. "All right. Proceed."

Kurj wondered if Eldrinson actually believed he had the authority to forbid the procedure. They would activate the cyberlock regardless. Still, given his stepfather's condition, it was better to have his cooperation.

The Primary slid the wafers into a slot on his belt. Kurj felt a familiar disorientation as the cyberlock field activated and spread out from his brain. Althor frowned but otherwise gave no indication he noticed. Their mother paled, reaching for the arm of her bodyguard, Jagernaut Secondary Ko, a husky woman who stood like a rock.

When Eldrinson drew in a breath, everyone froze. He made no other sound, just stood still.

"Lord Valdoria?" Tikal asked. "Are you all right?"

Eldrinson started to answer, then stopped, a blank look dropping across his face.

"Eldri, no!" As Roca grabbed her husband's arm, Althor took a lunging step—and caught his father as he collapsed. Althor laid him on the floor, on his back, while Roca knelt at his head. Secondary Ko knelt on Eldrinson's other side and laid a medical patch on the inside of his arm.

"His face is turning blue!" Tikal said.

"It's all right," Roca said. "It happens this way."

Although his mother's voice was calm, Kurj felt her fear. He suspected Althor also picked it up, but he doubted anyone else did, even the empathic Jagernauts. His mother hid her emotions almost as well as he.

Secondary Ko continued to monitor Eldrinson while Roca smoothed her husband's forehead. The rest of their party stood silent, unsure whether or not the crisis had passed.

Then Eldrinson began to convulse.

His entire body went rigid. Then he spasmed back and forth, his muscles clenched, his entire body jerking like a doll shaken hard by a giant hand, the motions so violent they looked as if they would tear him apart. With a dismay that startled him as much as the convulsion itself, Kurj realized he was seeing a grand mal seizure, a generalized tonic-clonic attack.

Secondary Ko spoke. "Everyone, step back please."

As Kurj and the others moved away, Althor turned his father on his side, his tender motions incongruous with his intimidating size. Ko continued to monitor Eldrinson. Roca made no attempt to touch him, other than to ensure he didn't choke.

Kurj was stunned by the depth of his fear for his stepfather. Med had warned him that Eldrinson's grief could make him more susceptible to seizures, so Kurj had ordered extra precautions. ISC always made sure his stepfather had the best available medical treatment, but this morning they had taken him to Med for additional care, precisely to prevent an incident like this.

Seeing Eldrinson convulse, seeing that frightening loss of control in his stepfather's body, Kurj felt a surge of protective instincts, followed by another sensation, one harder to define, as if a hole opened inside him. A memory came then, one he had buried but never forgotten; he was six years old, playing with his stuffed animals. His mother came to him with tears on her face and took him in her lap, cradling him in her arms, her voice broken as she spoke the words, those impossible words. Gone. His father was gone. Dead. Lost in an accident . . .

Eldrinson suddenly went limp. Roca exhaled and Althor closed his eyes, then opened them again. Secondary Ko's relief showed in the subtle easing of her posture. As Eldrinson's face took on a more normal color, Roca drew his head onto her knees, murmuring to the unconscious man.

"He'll be all right," Ko said. "He just needs sleep."

Roca turned a withering gaze on Tikal. "Are you satisfied with your 'protections'?"

He spoke quietly. "I am truly and deeply sorry, Councilor Roca. I wish there was another way. But better to risk what just happened than his assassination."

Roca's shoulders slumped. She turned back to Eldrinson, murmuring comfort he couldn't hear. Watching them, Kurj felt awkward, as if he intruded on a private moment. Eldrinson rarely spoke of his epilepsy, except to those closest to him, which had never included his stepson.

But Kurj had made it his business to learn about his stepfather's condition. If neurons in Eldrinson's brain became overstimulated, they sent out an abnormal flood of electrical discharges, causing a seizure. Had Eldrinson been other than a Rhon psion, his doctors could probably have cured him. But in Eldrinson that cure would also destroy the magnificent *paras* that made him such a gifted telepath. Now, with the medical care he received, he lived a normal life for the most part. The only times Kurj had seen him have trouble was when he was under extreme stress.

Eldrinson opened his eyes and looked at his wife. "Roca?"

"It's all right," she murmured. "You're fine. Just fine."

"Where—?"

She stroked his forehead. "The ceremony. At the pavilion."

"Oh. Yes. Of course." He sat up, rubbing his eyes, his motions disjointed and fatigued.

Kurj knelt next to Eldrinson and spoke in what, for him, was a gentle voice. "You need not attend the Investment. The guards can take you back to the palace."

His stepfather regarded him. "I am fine."

"What if you can't make it through the ceremony?" From what Kurj understood, Eldrinson often slept after a seizure.

"It won't be a problem," Eldrinson said.

Roca laid her hand on his arm. "Perhaps you should go back, Eldri. You look exhausted."

His face gentled. "I'm fine. Really." Turning to Secondary Ko, he said, "Give me a stimulant.

Ko glanced at Kurj, who shook his head. He had no intention of endangering Eldrinson with drugs that might have side effects.

As Kurj stood up, dwarfing everyone else in the foyer, Roca frowned at Secondary Ko. "Give him the stimulant," she said.

The Jagernaut bit her lip, an odd gesture from the usually placid warrior. Kurj understood her dilemma. She couldn't disobey his orders, but by refusing Roca and Eldrinson, she antagonized another branch of the Imperialate's complicated power structure.

With Althor's help, Eldrinson stood up. He rubbed his hand across his eyes and swayed, then regained his balance. Taking a breath, he turned to First Councilor Tikal. "Shall we proceed?"

Kurj almost swore. Eldrinson intended to go through with the ceremony? Without help to ensure no further incidents occurred while they were on display before the public? Was the man hammerheaded?

Stop it, his mother thought.

Her voice came into his mind, cool and guarded. Private. This communication was only for him. She stood watching him while everyone else spoke in quiet tones, arranging what to do if Eldrinson showed signs of a collapse during the ceremony.

He needs rest, Kurj thought to his mother.

He needs to be with his family. Lines of strain showed on her face. ***Especially now, Kurj. We all need each other.***

Kurj regarded her, knowing his anger at Eldrinson masked his fear for his stepfather. Then he turned to Secondary Ko. "Give him the stimulant."

Ko nodded, relief washing out from her mind. She unhooked an air syringe from her belt and gave Eldrinson a shot, then examined the medical patch inside his elbow. She ran her finger along an edge of the patch, and the silver square became flesh-colored, hiding itself.

Councilor Tikal motioned toward the safe door across the foyer, as if inviting them to dinner. A guard entered security codes into a control panel by the doors, and lights played across everyone's eyes and hands, verifying retinal and fingerprint patterns. Then the doors rolled back to reveal an ornate pair of portals with huge gold handles.

When the guards hefted open the doors, harsh Dieshan sunlight poured into the foyer—along with the murmuring from a sea of people. The crowd's anticipation beat against Kurj's mind like ocean breakers. His mother turned her head, as if that could block the empathic onslaught. Althor remained impassive, but his posture stiffened and Kurj's internal monitors registered a rise in his brother's heart rate.

Outside, a pavilion extended in a semicircular stage. Kurj couldn't see the crowd; the stage cut off the front part of his view, and a banner hanging along the top of the doorway here masked more distant areas. Dignitaries were already out on the pavilion, aglitter in the blazing sunlight, diplomats in gaudy ceremonial dress and military officers in uniform, replete with medals and ribbons. They made a striking contrast to Kurj's group with its somber hues, except for Althor's radiant figure.

Althor had asked permission to wear black, in deference to his sister, but Kurj refused his request. ISC needed a hero now, and Althor, with his powerful physique, strong-jawed good looks, and gold skin, fit the role perfectly. Kurj wore black to accent Althor's appearance rather than put his mourning on display. Although he appreciated Althor's request, for him color made no difference. It wouldn't make Soz live again. Dark colors hardly touched the depths of the loss he felt.

Councilor Tikal's palmtop chimed. He flicked his finger over it and Jak's voice came into the air. "We're all set, sir."

"All right," Tikal said. Then he walked out onto the pavilion, flanked by two bodyguards.

The hum of the crowd swelled into applause: clapping, ringing bells, shouts, the eerie birdcalls of Dieshan natives. As the roar swept into the foyer, both Roca and Eldrinson blanched. Althor maintained his impassive demeanor, but Kurj felt his brother's unease. Few empaths liked crowds. To the Rhon, having so many minds focused on them was excruciating.

With his guards, Tikal went to a podium near the front of the pavilion. The only hint of the extensive security systems focused on him was a faint distortion in the air. The crowd fell silent when he began his speech. They listened to his eulogy for Sauscony and cheered when he spoke of her sacrifice "to rid the stars of the scourge known as the Highton Heir." Kurj found it melodramatic, but it had the desired effect, stirring up the crowd.

Jak's voice came out of Kurj's gauntlet. "Imperator Skolia, we're set for the entrance."

"Very well." Kurj glanced around at his family. "Let's go."

Their guards went first and stood to the side of the doorway like sentries presaging their appearance. Roca and Eldrinson walked out next, followed by Kurj and Althor, all of them surrounded by the rainbow shimmer that marked a cyberlock field on lethal. Integrated with their brains, the locks knew who and what to protect, their four fields combined into one superfield.

Breezes ruffled their hair. The harsh sun, small and white, pierced a sky turned pale red by dust and the reflection of the red deserts that covered so much of the planet. Diesha had been made livable by ISC biosculptors, those gentler cousins of terraformers. They augmented the atmosphere until humans could breathe it, seeded the barren surface with primitive life, and fine-tuned the biosphere until it became more welcoming to Earth's children.

Holovid cameras followed the Ruby Dynasty, recording the ceremony for viewers throughout three civilizations. The news would be transmitted by every method available: starships, electro-optic webs, nanowebs, picowebs, the psiberweb, and even radio.

Finally Kurj saw the crowd that waited for them. People overflowed the city. They filled the quadrangle before the stage in a turbulent sea, clogged every street leading to it, lapped up on buildings and walls. As the Ruby Dynasty appeared, a tidal wave of applause and shouts surged forth, swamping the pavilion with its thunder until the stage shook. As soldiers ran to reinforce the supports, the roar rose even higher, made voiceless by the uncounted voices within it. Eldrinson and Roca froze, staring at the crowd, and Althor paled. Even Kurj was unprepared for the intensity of the response. Was the public truly this starved for a sight of the reclusive Imperial family, a dynasty that, technically, didn't even rule anymore?

Kurj spoke into his comm. "Jak, can security cover this?"

"Yes," Jak answered. "If they lose control, retreat into the foyer. It's a veritable fortress. We also have mag-copters up, which could lift you out if necessary, snipers on the skyneedle, and lasers with EI brains scanning the crowd."

"Good." Kurj nodded to his family to continue. They walked forward, the wind blowing their hair, and stopped by Tikal's podium. The crowd kept applauding, shouting to them. Realizing what they wanted, Kurj motioned to Althor. His half brother swallowed, but he did as Kurj ordered and walked to the edge of the stage. Hands resting on the rail, he looked out at the people who had come to see him.

The roar surged again. People rushed the stage, struggling with the soldiers and robot sentinels. Elastic quasis fields gave under the pressure, then snapped the trespassers back into the crowd. A girl screamed for Althor, extending her arms, and a youth standing on a wall was knocked off into the surging crowd. Althor stood frozen, staring at the scene. Kurj felt Althor's dismay but didn't motion him back. His brother looked the way ISC needed him to look, like a radiant hero come to defend the empire.

It took a long time, but the roar finally faded, ebbed, subsided, and became a murmur. In a low voice, Kurj spoke into his gauntlet. "I'm going up now."

"We're covering you," Jak said.

As Kurj walked to the podium, the crowd waited in silence. He deplored public speaking, which was why he almost never did it, but today a few words were required. Hell, just giving all of Althor's titles was a speech. Kurj preferred only one title. Imperator.

He raised his arm to Althor and spoke. As loudspeakers picked up his words, they rumbled out over the crowd. "I give you Prince Althor Izam-Na Valdoria kya Skolia, Warrior Secondary, Im'Rhon to the Rhon of the Skolias, First Heir to the Imperator, Fifth Heir to the throne of the Ruby Dynasty, once removed from the line of Pharaoh, born of the Rhon, Eighth Heir to the Web Key, Sixth Heir to the Assembly Key." He lowered his arm. "Today I Invest Althor Valdoria as my successor. From this day on, he will be the Imperial Heir."

And the people thundered their approval, for the hope an avenging angel offered against the unending brutality of a war that ground them down, year after year, decade after decade, century after century, until they had no defense except the symbolism they craved from the dynasty of a long vanished empire.

4

Emperor U'jjr Qox, called Ur Cox by those who found the Eubian accent difficult, was a gaunt man. Tall and lean, he maintained his health well. At sixty-six years of age, life had added few lines to his face.

Until three months ago.

Hands clasped behind his back, he stood in a bare room with glossy white walls and watched the scene played out on his wall screen: Kurj Skolia, declaring his heir. Ur Qox clenched his fist. He too had named an heir. Jaibriol II. His son. The man the Ruby Dynasty had killed.

Ur had named his son after his father, Jaibriol I. The elder Jaibriol had been pure Highton, in mind, in appearance, and in his Aristo perfection. But Ur Qox's mother had been a slave.

You tainted my blood, Ur thought to his father's memory. You made me less than perfect. But he understood the necessity. His father had selected his mother for her genetics. And she gave him what he required, a son who carried every mutated gene needed to make a Rhon psion. That those genes were recessive meant Ur Qox manifested none of their traits. He was neither empath nor telepath.

In secret, Qox had continued his father's work, combining forbidden genetic research with the hunt for a slave who could provide the genes he required. And he found her. He paired Camyllia's Rhon genes with his and she gave him a Rhon son. Jaibriol.

All those years, his hopes, his pride in his son, the great sacrifice of contaminating the Qox bloodline—it all came to nothing. Jaibriol would never follow him as emperor.

Ur tried to find consolation. Jaibriol no longer suffered having to hide his Rhon nature. Ur Qox himself had never had trouble with that game of deception. He thrived, in fact, a better Aristo than true Aristos, with their inbred bloodlines. The recessive nature of Rhon genes allowed him to reap the benefits of genetic diversity without the weakness of being an actual psion. Of course no one knew his mother had been a provider. A pleasure slave.

Providers were rare. Those chosen few, whose sweet suffering provided transcendence for their Aristo masters, had to be psions. Ninety-nine percent of the Eubian population were taskmakers, the backbone of civilization. All slaves, of course. They needed owners. Aristos took better care of their slaves than the slaves could themselves. Qox had long ago tired of the hysterical Skolian cries about the so-called sadism of Eube. In their fevered raving, Skolians neglected to mention that Eubian slaves had a higher standard of living, on average, than Skolians. Giving them freedom would only frighten and disorient them.

And of course the Ruby Dynasty objected. They themselves were providers without ownership. The ultimate slaves. They had to be controlled before they destroyed the sublime beauty of the universe the Aristos sought to create.

As they had destroyed his son.

Qox waved his hand. The wall became transparent, letting him gaze out over Upper Qoxire, the city below and beyond the palace, a lofty metropolis of spires and alabaster. Upper Qoxire graced this biosculpted planet called "Eube's Glory," so named for Ur's grandfather, Eube Qox, who had founded the Eubian Concord and designated Glory as its capital world.

A scene of deceptive serenity greeted him, a sunny afternoon of clear air and clear skies. Still a young planet, Glory had a short day, only sixteen hours. She claimed fourteen moons, most of them small, but several of substantial size. Mirella hung in the east, almost full. Named for the first empress, the moon appeared huge in the sky, the size of a giant gem. Eube Qox had ordered her surface altered so it glittered like carnelian. Two tiny moons shared her orbit, one sixty degrees ahead and one sixty degrees behind, each named for a handmaiden of Ix Quellia, the ancient moon goddess of Qox's ancestors.

Mirella caused the major portion of the huge tides that battered Glory. But she wasn't the largest moon. That honor went to Zara, named for the wife of the second emperor, Jaibriol I, who took his sister Zara as his empress. Zara was four times farther from Glory than Mirella, yet appeared more than half Mirella's size in the sky and raised respectable tides. Jaibriol I had sheened the moon gold. She made a gilded crescent now, high in the west.

Viquara, the third largest moon, shone half full in the east. Although she was only about forty percent the size of Mirella in the sky, Viquara was the most agile of the three empress moons, orbiting Glory faster than the planet rotated. So Viquara rose in the west and set in the east. She glittered like diamond, an effect Ur Qox's wife had requested when he named the moon after her.

The dim crescent of Glory's fourth largest moon hung above the far, far horizon. G4. The Unnamed Moon. The choice of what name to bestow on G4 had belonged to Qox's heir, Jaibriol II.

Now it would forever be G4.

Behind Qox, the door opened. He knew no one could enter here without his blessing. His bodyguards stood outside and his defense systems remained in operation. Still, hearing a door open behind his back, he wondered if this, then, would be the day of his death.

Without turning he said, "So."

"My greetings," his wife said.

Qox turned to her. The bare room needed no adornment with the Empress Viquara present. He had chosen her for one thing and one thing alone: sexual beauty. That she also turned out to be intelligent had been an unexpected asset.

Dark lashes framed her red eyes. She had a classic face, with skin as smooth as snow-marble. Her hair shimmered, straight and black, glittering in the cold light. After twenty-six years of marriage, her shape remained perfect. How she maintained her youth he never bothered to ask, but she was even more the epitome of Highton beauty now than the day she had met him, at their wedding twenty-six years ago, when she was fourteen.

He had sterilized her using methods so discreet she never knew it happened. All she understood was that despite prewedding medical reports to the contrary, she was barren.

She urged him to allow her artificial methods to produce his heirs. He refused, of course. It violated Highton beliefs. It was done anyway, but it served him no purpose to grant her the children she craved. He left her one honorable choice, an ancient solution practiced within their highest caste, where the need for heirs outweighed matters such as love. He offered to let her commit suicide.

She begged for clemency, wept, used the many feminine

gifts nature granted her. In the end he "relented." The price of her life was an oath: when he found a woman to produce his heir, Viquara would acknowledge the child as her own and ask no questions. So the empress kept her title and her life, and Ur Qox had his Rhon son. As promised, his wife gave no hint the boy wasn't hers. Ur had hidden Jaibriol until a year ago, and by then Viquara played her role with ease.

Now she murmured her husband's name, *Oojoor*, making it silken, with a glottal stop after the first syllable, a sound shared by Skolian and Eubian languages alike, all derived from an ancient tongue five thousand years old. He went over and took her into his arms, brushing his lips over her hair. He had never determined if she loved him or was even capable of love. It didn't matter. She gave him what he required, as did all people, when he required it, as he required it.

If they didn't, he got rid of them.

Their bodyguards waited outside, four men in the stark midnight uniforms of the Razers, the secret police who served the emperor. Gunmetal collars glinted around their necks, the only outward indication the officers were slaves. Thus guarded, the emperor and empress descended to the ground level of the palace.

Black and gold diamonds tiled the floor, and columns graced the huge, airy halls. The glittering white pillars and walls were made from neither diamond nor snow-marble, but a blend of the two, created atom-by-atom by nanobots. As with all nanotech, the bots were no magic machines, simply molecules capable of one function, in this case docking certain atoms into a crystal lattice.

The group stopped at the great double doors to the Hall of Circles. One of the Razers touched his collar and the doors opened. Inside, high-backed benches ringed the circular hall, glittering white and set with red brocade cushions. Aristos dressed in glistening black clothes filled every bench, hundreds of Aristos, from all three castes: Highton Aristos, who controlled the government and military; Diamond Aristos, who attended to commerce, production, and banks; and Silicate Aristos, who produced the means of pleasure, including providers. All had ruby eyes, shimmering black hair, and perfect faces.

They looked the same.

They moved the same.

They spoke the same.

They thought the same.

They watched their emperor and empress walk up an aisle that radiated like a spoke from a dais in the center of the Hall. Ur Qox mounted the dais with Viquara at his side. Then he sat in the glittering red chair there. The Carnelian Throne.

In unison, three hundred Aristos raised their arms and clicked three hundred cymbals. One blended note rang through the Hall. It was a rare expression of grief, merited only by the highest among them. Today they mourned the Highton Heir. In silence, they swore an oath: the Ruby Dynasty would pay for the loss of Jaibriol II, Eube's shining son.

Soz stopped by a hip-high boulder, the laser carbine slung over her shoulder. Jaibriol sat down on the boulder, holding the valise with their computers.

The sky arched overhead like a pale blue eggshell. To the east, the red dwarf sun gleamed in a molten disk of gold. Although the "red" star was actually hot enough to appear white to the human eye, Prism's atmosphere scattered away enough of its scant blue light that it shone orange instead. To the west, the blue-white sun blazed, intense and white. Soz had named the red dwarf Red and the blue-white sun Blue, at least until Jaibriol thought of something better. Although Blue was well over three times the diameter of Red, it was far enough away that Red's molten disk appeared more than six times as large in the sky, almost three times as big as Sol when seen from Earth.

Forest surrounded Soz and Jaibriol, except for the clear stretch of ground before them. A few meters away, a wide river swelled over fallen trees.

"This is beautiful," Jaibriol said. "The best site so far."

She indicated a hill across the river. "We could build a house up there."

He nodded, absently rubbing his chest through his blue environment suit.

"Is the pollen bothering you?" Soz asked.

"Not since I took MedComp's last concoction." With a grin, he spoke in a nasal twang. "Not even a clogged nose."

At the sight of his smile, Soz sighed. Her mind started imagining him without the environment suit.

He made an exasperated noise. "Saints almighty, you only think about one thing." He put his arms around her waist and drew her between his knees. "You've no respect for my mental facilities, Wife."

She smiled. "I respect all your facilities, Husband. Mental and otherwise."

His face gentled. Then he sighed and let her go. "We should get to work."

Soz would have rather explored his facilities, but she knew he was right. So instead, she said, "All right. You run reconnaissance while I secure the river."

He laughed. "This isn't a military operation."

She grinned and gave him a salute. "Onward."

They chose a spot by the river with a small beach enclosed by palms that chattered when their crackling fronds rubbed together. Across the river, gigantic roots buckled out of the bank. The only candidate for the tree that had been nourished by those monstrous roots was a toppled trunk rotting in the water.

Over the next hour, Jaibriol explored and Soz worked with GeoComp, analyzing the samples Jaibriol brought her. The results agreed with those from the other sites they had investigated. About half the foliage was edible, a quarter mildly poisonous, the rest lethal. The water also tested the same, drinkable if they boiled it, though MedComp predicted they would eventually develop immunities to its odd honeycomb bacteria. The soil had the dark green color they had seen elsewhere, derived from chlorophylls mixed in with the loam. She suspected it would grow good crops, if they could figure out what to plant.

Although Prism was a young world, the age of Precambrian Earth, its life-forms had a sophistication more congruent with Earth's Paleozoic Era. It thrived with primitive flora and, to a lesser extent, with fauna. The animals were unlike anything Soz had seen before. Gold and red fliers hummed through the air, part crustacean, part reptile, and part plant, with chitinous hides that incorporated chlorophyll.

The first scan made by the Earth probe, after it found the planet, had detected what seemed to be a humanoid species. Subsequent scans revealed the "humanoids" were actually bizarre plants that could move by bending over until their crowns touched the ground, sending down roots from their crowns in the new location, then pulling out their original roots and straightening up until their old roots became their new crowns.

Standing on the beach, Soz looked across the river. The forest thinned on the other side, and a loamy green hill swelled up from the bank, peaking after a few hundred meters. If the soil was as good there as here, she and Jaibriol may have found their homestead. She nodded, then leaned down and pulled off her hiking boots.

"What are you doing?" Jaibriol asked.

She straightened up to see him a few meters down the beach. "Going wading."

"How do you know it's safe?"

"Calculated risk." She motioned at the water. "We've found no predators or other dangers. Nothing but slugs and bugs." The "bugs" were actually more like tiny crustacean-plants.

" 'Slugs and bugs' can hurt," Jaibriol said. "What if they sting you or something?"

"MedComp says they have no poison."

"The ones we've checked." He came over to her, holding the carbine at his side. "We can't have analyzed more than a tiny portion of the species here."

She unfastened the collar of her environment suit. "I've

done planetary surveys for ISC. This world fits well within accepted standards."

"That doesn't mean nothing in the water can hurt you."

"I'll take the air syringe. If I get a sting or bite, it can make an antidote."

He frowned. "How? It has no history of this world."

"We've given it one." She indicated the valise with their computers. "Even one sample tells it a lot, and we've given it hundreds, more than enough to map the chemistry here. MedComp is already designing antidotes."

Jaibriol wiped the dusting of pollen on his cheek. "MedComp is effective, I'll grant that. But you shouldn't take chances."

"We have to try sooner or later. We can't avoid risks forever."

Softly he said, "I don't want to have to bury you."

She laid her palm against his cheek. "You won't."

"I'll come with you."

"One of us should stay here. Just in case."

"I'll go then."

"Jaibriol, I'm trained to do this."

He blew out a gust of air. After a moment he said, "I'll cover you from the bank."

She touched his hand. "That would be good."

Soz peeled off her clothes, then strapped on her belt and hung it with the syringe, a knife, her palmtop, a life jacket folded into a palm-sized square, and a cord reinforced with nanotube fibers, making it as thin as spider silk and as strong as steel. Then she waded into the river.

Clear water swirled around her legs. She let it run through the palmtop analyzer, recording more of the rich bacteria life. Spatula leaves floated past her and rocks rolled under her feet. By the time she reached the middle of the river, the water had risen to her waist. Turning, she saw Jaibriol on the beach. She waved and he nodded to her, the carbine gripped in his hand.

Soz tipped her face up to the sky. Sunshine streamed around her, blue and gold mixed together, clear and bright.

Although the human eye wasn't sensitive enough to detect the differences in light intensity when one sun was up as compared to both, her augmented optics registered that Red put out most of its light in the infrared whereas Blue put out most of its in the visible and ultraviolet. Prism's rich atmosphere, a thick ozone layer, and extensive oceans helped protect her fragile human inhabitants, both from Red's rare but powerful flares, which could shine with the light of many suns, and from Blue's UV radiation.

Turning her attention to the river, Soz saw her two shadows rippling in the water, one in front of her and the other behind. All around her, the day chattered with life. Prism was an attractive world, open and free, lonely perhaps, but relatively benign all things considered. She and Jaibriol had been fortunate.

She surveyed the opposite bank, where water gurgled over the half-submerged cage of giant roots. The roots had a red tinge and were mottled with purple moss. Vines grew over them, ropy cables with leaves that resembled red sponges.

Soz waded to the roots. The river ran deeper here, cutting a trench as the gnarled roots funneled its flow. She climbed up on a root that buckled out of the water, a pulpy arch as thick as her waist. Sitting on her perch, she dangled her legs above the river and scraped her finger through a patch of moss, fetching a sample for the analyzer.

Water splashed at her feet. She looked to see ripples in the river, as if a small creature had broken the surface and disappeared.

"Soz?" Jaibriol called. "Are you all right?"

She glanced up at him. "Fine," she called.

He stayed at the water's edge, shifting the carbine from hand to hand. Soz gave her moss sample to the palmtop, then scraped her fingernail along the root for another sample.

Water splashed again.

Her reflexes kicked in and she looked faster this time. It still wasn't enough; whatever had made the splash had already disappeared.

She directed a thought to her spinal node. **Analysis.**

The disturbances suggest a living organism. Or something falling in the water.

Soz looked around. A few roots arched above her head, with smooth surfaces patched by moss. **Could moss be falling?**

Possibly. However, it would probably make a different sound.

She peered at the water. **Maybe something is hiding down there.**

After a pause, it thought, Estimated probability that an organism hides in roots: 72 percent; under rocks: 48 percent; that it jumped out of water: 24 percent; that something dropped into water: 17 percent; that water exhibited random turbulence: 9 percent; that root snapped out of water: 3 percent; that rock jumped out of water: 0.05 percent. Its response came in a normal-speed mode, as words, rather than in the accelerated data dump of a fast-speed battle mode.

She smiled. **Rocks jumping out of water?**

The probability is small, it admitted.

You think something is hiding down there?

This is a reasonable guess. A blue light glowed on her palmtop, indicating it was receiving IR from her node, sent via fiberoptic threads in her body to her wrist socket, which then conveyed the signal to the palmtop. The light turned purple as the palmtop sent data back to her internal biomech web. Then her node said, I suggest analyzing these roots further. The sample you gave the palmtop suggests a chemistry different from other life in this area.

Different how?

Part plant, part crystalline.

That intrigued Soz. **Does it photosyn—**

This splash was much bigger.

The root under her whiplashed, flinging Soz into the river. As she hit the water, a root snapped around her ribs, pinning her right arm, and another circled her waist. Then the roots whipped her out of the water.

Her reflexes responded even before her brain registered what had happened. With her pinned arm she strained against the coil around her torso, pushing outward to keep it from crushing her ribs. She worked her other hand into the coil around her waist, going for her knife.

The root slapped her into the water, down to the riverbed. It scraped her face-first along the rocks and she gulped in water. Nanomeds in her body tried to ferry the water out of her lungs, but it came in too fast for the meds to keep her from drowning.

She managed to get her arm the rest of the way inside the coil around her waist and push outward with both arms. Her hydraulics were working at maximum, and the heat produced by her microfusion reactor dissipated into the water.

With a sudden frenzy, the coils yanked her out of the river and she gasped, choking up water she had swallowed. Trees and sky spun past and a burning stench assailed her senses. She glimpsed Jaibriol sighting across the river with the carbine.

Soz kept working her arm down her side until her fingers brushed the hilt of her knife. She manipulated it free and stabbed the blade up into the root. The response was immediate: the root whipped her back toward the bank. She kept stabbing, struggling to breathe. Black spots danced in her vision. Her biomech could operate for a few moments without her conscious mind to direct it, but she doubted it would be long enough to save her life.

She glimpsed Jaibriol again, sighting on the roots. Then the roots jammed her into the center of their mass and held her there, blocking his shot. Blackened scars showed in the central mass and the stench of scorched pulp saturated the air. Her arm felt numb, but her node kept her hydraulics working and she kept stabbing the coil. The spots of darkness in her vision grew.

With a cracking snap, the root fell away from her waist. Using her freed arm, she hacked at the coil around her ribs with more force, again and again, until it too loosened. As it lost its grip, she tumbled into the water. Other roots thrashed at her, injured now, blind as she wriggled through their seething mess.

A loop of vine caught her ankle. More vines wrapped around her legs and arms, and their spongy red leaves covered her face. They dragged her out of the water, back into the center of the roots. The burning stench was even worse now, and Soz choked on the smell. Jaibriol must have hit the roots again when she was in the water.

As a backup system the vines were less effective than the roots. She sawed at them, snapping one cord, then another, then another. More curled around her body, but they were weakening, moving with erratic jerks. She kept at it, cutting, cutting, cutting, until the weight of her body became more than the vines could hold and she slid into the water. A few loops tangled around her legs, but a good hard kick sent her arrowing out of their grasp.

She reached the center of the river and stood up. Jaibriol was running through the water, sending sprays of liquid into the air. His emotions beat against her, a mix of fear, relief, and fury. She waded toward him and they collided when they met. Sliding his arm around her waist, he pulled her against his side. Together, they stumbled out of the river. Soz collapsed onto the bank and lay on her back, half in and half out of the water, gasping for breath.

He knelt beside her. "Are you all right?"

"Yes." She heaved in a breath. "That thing was *alive.*"

In a voice tight with anger he said, "Obviously."

"I mean sentient." She sat up, grimacing with the effort. "It knew you were causing it harm, so it held me in front of itself to stop you."

His fury washed over her. "You survived." Then he got up and walked away.

"Jaibriol?" Soz climbed to her feet, took a wobbly step, and fell down, catching herself on her hands and knees.

You have three broken ribs, her node informed her.

So fix them, she thought, knowing it couldn't.

Nanomed series G is carrying nutrients to the damaged area, series

H is aiding the breakdown of cellular detritus into usable molecules, series B—

Never mind, Soz thought. **What about my ribs?**

You need to set the bones.

I don't know how.

I will direct you. Put your hands over your rib cage.

Still kneeling, she placed her hands on her ribs and tried to relax. Her hydraulics took over, directed by her node, and moved her hands as she shoved the ribs. Her node had produced a molecule similar to morphine to dull the pain, but she still had to bite her lip to keep from screaming.

Alignment complete, her node thought. I recommend limiting your activity until your repair is sufficient to keep the bones from slipping again. You also have venom in your bloodstream, injected by thorns on the vines. I am synthesizing an antidote, but you must rest. The more you move, the more it circulates the poison.

I can go back to the cave, Soz thought.

You need to find a closer place. It would be to your advantage to have subject Qox's aid in this endeavor.

His name is Jaibriol.

My apologies. My combat routines aren't designed to attach affectionate names to Highton Aristos.

Soz gave an unsteady laugh and rolled onto her back, staring at the patch of sky ringed by treetops. **Why is he mad at me?**

I'm afraid my routines aren't designed to analyze emotional conflicts of humans involved in the intimacy associated with sexual reproduction, either.

Can't you do better than that?

I don't think so. However, I have a request.

Soz frowned. Usually "a request" meant it had calculated she would resist some upgrade it wanted. **What?**

I would like a name.

Say again?

You designate the Highton Heir by a personal name, yet call a node within your own body "node."

You're joking, right?

Have you considered the implications of refusing to name me? It paused. If you cannot handle the emotional issues involved with your capacity as a weapon of war, how do you expect to deal with your current situation?

Soz swore under her breath. **I thought you didn't do psychology.**

A large probability exists that my attempts will be flawed, it admitted.

Soz didn't see how naming the node would solve anything, but what the hell. **I'll think about it.**

Thank you. For now, I recommend you find a secure location in which to commence recuperation.

She stared at the sky. **Not sure I can move, Node-without-a-name.**

Ask Jaibriol for help.

He's gone.

Call him with your mind.

He closed his doors.

If you mean he has deliberately spurred his brain to produce kylatine that blocks the neural receptors assigned to processing signals from your brain, you are correct.

Whatever.

However, the node continued. He has many more psiamine receptors than those his brain dedicates to his interaction with you. Magnify your KEB output and stimulate his KAB so it sends pulses to neural structures with those receptors.

I won't break his doors. It's trespassing.

It is not in your best interest to lie here undefended so near an organism that just attempted to eat you.

Eat me?

The "roots" appear to be a carnivorous plant that feeds on large animals.

I'd rather not be its lunch.

Then call Jaibriol. Worrying about telepathic etiquette at this time is inappropriate.

It's more than etiquette. It's a moral issue. With a groan, Soz made herself sit up. **I'll walk back.**

It would be better—

Node, Soz thought. **No more.**

She climbed to her feet. Jaibriol had left the carbine by her clothes, which meant he was alone and unprotected. She dressed, favoring her ribs, then packed up their supplies and headed into the forest.

A flash of blue in the trees caught her attention. Pushing her way past the bushes, she found a clearing. Several meters away, Jaibriol was sitting on a boulder, watching her.

"I thought you went to the cave," she said.

"Do you want to walk back together?"

"My node says I should stay put. I took some venom."

He sat up straighter. "Will you be all right?"

"Fine. I just need to rest for a while."

He came over, pulling off his pack. "Our rations should last at least a day."

She doubted she needed that much time, given that this day would last 243 hours. "That's more than enough."

He set down his pack and sat on the ground, then stretched out on his back with his hands behind his head.

"You're angry," Soz said.

He continued to watch the sky. "I have made a decision."

"A decision?"

"I am leaving."

Leaving? "For where?"

"It is done."

"What's done?"

"Us."

"Us?"

"Yes."

"Oh." Soz nudged his mind, but if he knew she was knocking, he gave no hint of it. "Why is it ended?"

"I will go south," Jaibriol said. "You can stay here."

"This is crazy." She leaned over him so he had to look at her. "We have to accept the risks of living here. We can't run away every time something bad happens."

He sat up, anger suffusing his emotions, which he let free

with an ease that made her suspect he knew exactly what she was doing when she knocked at his mind. "Why didn't you just let me die in your brother's torture chamber? Why bring me here to make the torture last a lifetime?"

"What do you mean?"

"It doesn't matter."

"It does to me. But I can't read your mind." She could, actually, but that was beside the point. "If you won't tell me what's wrong, how can I fix it?"

"This can't be fixed."

"Jaibriol!"

He leaned back on his hands. "Love is a façade. A literary metaphor created by writers. Never accept it, because it will be taken away. So I saw this afternoon. So you continue to tell me. We will die here." He shrugged. "I prefer to die alone."

She almost said, *How can you think that?* then stopped. She considered *that's absurd* but realized it was no more likely to evoke a positive response. Neither *It isn't that way* nor *You've a distorted view of human relations* seemed right either.

Finally she said, "I would be lonely if you left."

"Loneliness is the human condition."

"It doesn't have to be." Was she making this worse? She had never been good at "relationship" talks. She tended to avoid them, a trait that had contributed to her first husband's decision to leave her sixteen years ago. Her taciturn inclinations hadn't been the trouble so much as her inability to discuss the real problem, which was his fear that her military career would widow him. Given Jaibriol's linguistic bent, she suspected this discussing business was going to be important again, and she feared she would muck it up as much this time as before.

He was sitting cross-legged now, staring at his hands, which he had moved into his lap. As she watched him, his youth struck her. Twenty-three. Heaped on that was his lack of experience with human relationships. She wondered how they would ever make this work.

At least try, her node thought.

Stop eavesdropping.

I have no choice. I'm inside of you.

Thank you for stating the obvious.

Directing sarcasm at me won't solve your current problem.

Soz exhaled. Softly she said, "What happened at the river—that frightened both of us."

Jaibriol continued to study his hands.

"We both knew I could die," she said. When he didn't respond, she tried another tack. "I've lived with the knowledge of my mortality for three decades, ever since I took my ISC commission. I've grown used to the risks. But you haven't."

Jaibriol looked up at her. "I've loved two people in my life. My nurse, Camyllia, who died. And my father." He shrugged. "Now that I know him for what he is, he might as well be dead too."

She knew it hurt him far more than he wanted to show. "Now you think I'll die too? So you want to leave before it happens?"

"Yes."

Gently she said, "I can't promise there's no danger. But we can face it together. Besides," she pointed out, "you can't go south. We haven't decided what to call this hemisphere yet."

A smile quirked his mouth. "Soshoni, you are so literal." With a sigh of capitulation, he pulled her close, wrapping his arms around her. "Maybe I'd better stay here. If I don't, you will start inflicting names on this place like 'River' for the river and 'Plants' for the plants."

Relieved, she leaned against him, giving in to her fatigue. "You're right. We can't let that happen."

So they stayed together, in the north.

II

Year Two

358 ASC on the Imperial Calendar
381 EG on the Eubian Calendar
A.D. 2261 on the Gregorian Calendar
Ie 5264 on the Ruby Calendar
About 6277 on the Iotic Calendar

5

Of course we measure our year according to the orbital period of the planet Raylicon. That world is, after all, the ancestral home to all our peoples. But what of our surprise in learning our year equals that of Earth? A moment's reflection reveals we should have been less startled. The race that moved our ancestors to Raylicon wanted us to survive; otherwise why choose a planet that supported human life? That they found or altered its orbit to ensure its year matched the one programmed into our DNA is a further indication of their intent.

Our honored Imperial Calendar dates from the magnificent founding of the Skolian Imperialate, Year One being denoted 1 ASC, or 1 Ascendant, to honor Skolia's ascendance. Earth still uses her quaint Gregorian Calendar, where A.D. 1904 corresponds to our Year One. Rather predictably, the uninspired Eubian Calendar dates from the birth of Eube, so 1 EG on the Eubian Calendar is 33 DSC on the Imperial Calendar, or thirty-three years prior to the founding of Skolia.

For those who prefer antediluvian measures of time, the Ruby Calendar began with the rise of the Ruby Empire. Our Year One corresponds to Ie 5477 on the Ruby Calendar, where Ie is believed to stand either for "Imperial Era" or "Inner Era." The Iotic Calendar derives from the advent of human life on Raylicon, a date we know with only limited accuracy.

—*From* The Lost Empire, *by Tajjil Bloodstone*

The War Room existed in sharp, gleaming functionality on the space habitat known as the Orbiter. The War Room amphitheater was filled with controls, web consoles, and giant robot arms that carried telops. High above the amphitheater, a power chair hung suspended under a holodome that showed views of space, so that anyone looking up saw the chair silhouetted against a glistening panorama of holographic stars. A hood packed with apparatus formed a cavern for the head of whoever sat in the chair, and its arms were rectangular blocks, fifty centimeters wide, glinting with control lights. Thousands of channels fed the chair's web—and the brain of the man who sat in it.

Kurj became part of his throne. Its exoskeleton inserted prongs into his ankles, wrists, lower spine, and neck. A spiderweb of conduits on his head extended microscopic threads into his scalp. Today he used a virtual reality mode, drifting in space with the battle cruiser *Roca's Pride* and its attendant flotilla, hundreds of ships ranging from single-pilot Jag starfighters to Starslammer destroyers. The ships were spread out through a large volume, millions of cubic kilometers.

A Wasp corvette kept pace with him. He had made his size in the simulation equivalent to his real size, which meant the Wasp dwarfed him. Yet it was one of the flotilla's smaller craft. Its crew of four rode in its two forward sections, the head and thorax. A stalk separated those sections from a detachable abdomen.

Antimatter readout, Kurj thought. The VR simulation produced a display of the abdomen's interior and superimposed it on the Wasp. Luminous red curves highlighted the invisible magnetic fields. They surrounded a Klein containment bottle, essentially a three-dimensional Möbius strip. In normal space, the outer surface of a Klein bottle narrowed into a tube that curved up, looped over the bottle, and joined back into its own body, curving smoothly to form the interior, until it opened out into the mouth, so the inside of the bottle became its outside.

The Klein bottles used on starships had a quirk: when the bottle looped over itself, it also looped out of normal space, its "interior" taking on both real and imaginary parts. The bottle spread the particles it contained through that space by adding imaginary parts to their mass and charge. Varying

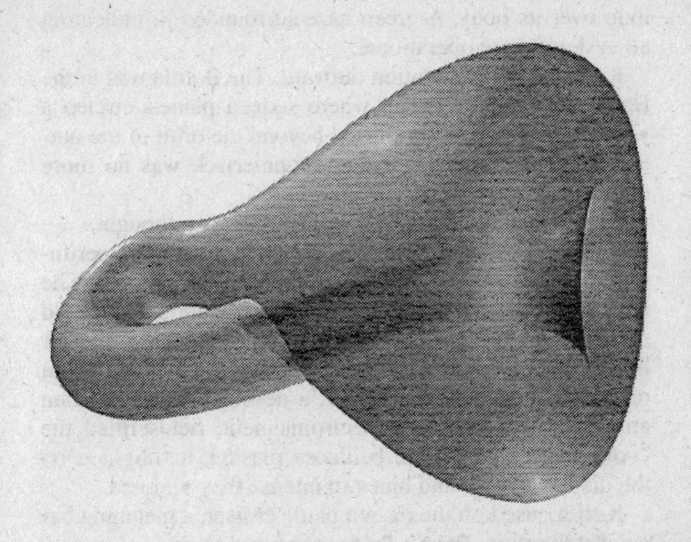

the imaginary parts allowed the bottle to hold far more antimatter than it could have in real space. Klein containment bottles cradled antimatter within a twist of reality.

Most Klein bottles served as fuel tanks. During flight they also collected antimatter from the cosmic ray flux in complex space. A Wasp, however, used its abdomen bottle for less serene purposes. One toggle from the weapons node and the Klein bottle in the abdomen collapsed, dumping a hundred kilometers of antimatter plasma into real space, creating an imbalance the plasma immediately rectified—with explosive force.

Bottle secure, Kurj's node **A** thought. It highlighted the bottle in a spectrum of color, red at the mouth, shading into orange as it narrowed. Then the bottle vanished, looping out of normal space. It reappeared where it intersected itself, now a vibrant purple color that shaded into red as it curved outward to form its mouth.

Show image in complex space, Kurj thought. The rest of the bottle appeared, yellow, green, and blue on the loop over its body. A green haze surrounded it, indicating all systems were operational.

Kurj turned his attention outward. The flotilla was in the Hammerjack star system, where sixteen planets circled a yellow-white sun. They drifted beyond the orbit of the outermost planet, so far out that Hammerjack was no more than a bright star.

Give me a readout of local space, Kurj thought.

The Wasp vanished and a new display formed, superimposed over space, revealing the neighborhood's secrets. The flotilla had taken up position in a disk of debris that ringed the star system, but the chunks of rock were few and far between compared to the ships. Local space claimed about one atom per cubic centimeter, a desolation emptier than any laboratory vacuum. Electromagnetic fields filled the "void" with a turbulent, bellicose plasma, highlighted on the display in reds and blues so intense they vibrated.

Kurj focused on the distant battle cruiser, a gleaming bar against the stars. ***Roca's Pride*, acknowledge.**

Attending, the battle cruiser rumbled.

Location of target? Kurj asked. A spark appeared, a distant asteroid highlighted in white.

The cruiser growled in Kurj's mind. Demonstration primed.

Proceed.

The Wasp arrowed toward the spark, and Kurj went with it, streaming through the vibrant fields of space. The asteroid grew from a speck to a rocky body about 260 kilometers in diameter. The Wasp jettisoned its abdomen and veered away, but Kurj flew on with the abdomen, bearing down on the asteroid.

Show bottle, Kurj thought. The display of the Wasp's abdomen reappeared, its Klein bottle glowing like a ghost. Only seconds from the asteroid now, the abdomen showed no sign of slowing.

Drill extend. That came from the fleeing Wasp.

A massive drill extended from the abdomen. Then the entire abdomen crashed into the asteroid, pulverizing its surface. The drill blasted its way through rock, embedding the abdomen deep within the small planetoid. The VR simulation turned the rocky body into a skeleton representation, showing the Klein bottle glowing within it.

Klein field collapse, the Wasp thought.

The bottle suddenly twisted into real space—along with all its stored antimatter. Unable to confine so much plasma in so small a volume, the abdomen detonated the asteroid, the explosion driven by a plasma that annihilated matter. In majestic silence the asteroid flew apart, most of it annihilated, the remaining debris hurtling in all directions as the void raged with fountains of gamma photons, particle showers, and radiant floods of energy.

Data poured in from the flotilla ships: photon wavelengths, nuclei distributions, energy profiles, plasma pressure, particle densities, time scales, radiation damage, impact trajectories, and so on, every datum examined, sorted, and stored.

Test successful, *Roca's Pride* rumbled.

Kurj sent his thought out to the flotilla. **Good work.**

A sense of satisfaction emanated from the ships.

Proceed with tests, Kurj thought. **Switching out.**

Out, the ships echoed.

As Kurj withdrew his mind from the flotilla psiberweb, space became translucent. He could see the web now, a mesh stretching to infinity. The presence of his mind curved it into a narrow circular hill, and his peripheral thoughts ringed the peak in concentric ridges that spread out in bigger and bigger circles, like the ripples made by dropping a rock into water, or the intensity plot of the diffraction pattern for a circular aperture.

War Room, Kurj thought.

The hill sank into the mesh. His mind re-formed in a new region with many other peaks, indicating the many telops working in this part of the web at tasks similar to his.

Ψ gate, he thought.

Accessed, node **A** thought, and the gate transformed his mind back into spacetime.

Kurj became aware of voices and machines humming

below and holographic starlight from the dome above. He looked out at the War Room, hundreds of light-years from the flotilla war games. Still sensitized from the web, he could actually trace lines of thought in the amphitheater. Subtler tendrils were hard to pick out, but the sturdier cables glowed. They all worked together like a well-ordered machine, tuned by his mind to mathematical precision.

A disruptive cord caught his attention, a sense of ripe innocence and vitality. He focused on it and a holoscreen on his chair activated, showing him the body that went with the mind.

A fine body indeed.

She was a page, one among the group of men and women who served the telops, or telepathic operators, in the War Room. Pages brought water or food, made pleasant conversation, and in general nurtured the telops. Kurj had found it improved performance. When telops surfaced from the web, disoriented and fatigued, they preferred being tended by pleasant humans instead of machines.

This girl wore a green jumpsuit with a sparkling trim on the collar. Curly brown hair floated around her shoulders. Although she wasn't a spectacular beauty, she had a pretty face with a sweet quality.

File on subject, Kurj thought.

Accessing optics, node **E** answered.

Glyphs scrolled alongside the girl's image. She came from the planet Titrate II, in the Imperial Chemical Sector. The orphanage in a shack town there had brought this girl into an immigration center at one of the starports. Unable to support all their children, they were sending the older ones offworld, a questionable practice given that most ships took them as indentured crew. To hide that violation of child labor laws, dock officials called them "wards of the ship," in essence claiming the spacecraft were their guardians.

An ISC major, one G. S. R. Bozner, had been on business at the immigration center that day. Taken by the girl's sweet nature, he arranged for her employment as a page on the Orbiter. She worked hard and did her job well. In fact, an analysis suggested several of the telops were falling in love with her.

Kurj frowned. Pages should be pleasant, yes, but this girl went beyond agreeable. She distracted. It made no difference that she had no idea she created disorder. The mere fact of her presence disrupted the smooth operation of his War Room.

Seeker, he thought.

Attending.

Get me security team p.

Link established. Jagernaut Primary Hirsh waiting.

Give him access.

The Jagernaut who headed Kurj's private security force thought, *Attending, sir.* Although Hirsh had a strong mind, next to Kurj's rumbling power his thought seemed muted.

Hirsh, download the profile in my holomap file.

Downloaded, Hirsh answered.

Have the page described in that profile taken to my quarters, procedure 803.

Yes, sir.

Switching out, Kurj thought. Then he turned his attention to other matters. He still a great deal of work to do.

Cloaks of snow blanketed the long slope from the lake to the house. Inside, Soz and Jaibriol sat huddled within a blanket on their bed. They had built their one-room home three kilometers from the site where, a year ago, they found the carnivorous roots. They named the roots a Prism people trap, in honor of the Venus flytrap, an Earth plant GeoComp claimed resembled it.

A light burned in the corner of the room. To save the charge of their sole remaining motion-sensor lamp, they were using a handmade lamp fueled with oil from the bushes they called triops, for their resemblance to a triceratops.

Jaibriol shifted his arms around Soz's bulk. "How much colder do you think it will get?"

"Today? Or in general?"

"Either. Neither." He exhaled. "I just need to talk. This waiting grinds me down."

She readjusted her weight. "Last time I checked GeoComp's estimate of the year, it was the same. About seven and a half Earth years, and we're at the start of winter." It wasn't a true winter, though, given the way their distance from Blue varied as they orbited Red. "Maybe it will warm up again when we come back into the sunlight." She hoped so. The snow had been falling for ten hours, and seventy hours more remained until dawn.

Soz shifted her weight again, trying to get comfortable. "I need a stardock loading crane to move."

Jaibriol laid his hand on the swell of her abdomen. "Can you feel him kick?"

"Like a smash-ball league."

"Is that normal?"

"I don't know. I've never had a baby before."

A memory came to her, one she had long kept hidden, of her miscarriage seventeen years ago, when she lost the only other child she had ever conceived. She and Jato, her husband, had mourned deeply. But she had been unable to speak of it, leaving him to face his grief in silence. Her inability to share her feelings had been one reason he later divorced her. She blamed herself. Yet with Jaibriol it didn't matter. He understood her without words, which for some reason let her open up to him as she had never done with anyone else.

She felt Jaibriol's mind brush hers and then reach out to their son. The baby's brain hadn't formed enough for conscious thought, but at a more primitive level the three of them already shared a bond.

Jaibriol was watching her. "Are you all right?"

She nodded, then groaned with another contraction. "Except for this."

"Shouldn't you do that breathing MedComp taught us?"

"I can't concentrate on it."

"Maybe you could program your node to make you do it."

It was worth a try. **Attend,** she thought.

Attending, her node answered.

Can you make my body do the breathing business?

I can exert a degree of control over your muscles. However, your natural responses are better suited to delivery.

Jaibriol's forehead creased as he tried to follow the silent conversation. "It won't do it?"

"It wants me to do the work myself. Says I'm better at having babies than it is."

He smiled. "I guess so."

Soz grunted as another contraction hit. It went on forever, though her node claimed it took less than two minutes.

When she relaxed, Jaibriol said, "These are closer together than before."

Time interval between contractions is about two minutes, her node offered.

"I can't tell—what the—?" Soz frowned as a rush of water poured down her thighs and soaked into the bed.

"No!" Jaibriol tightened his arms around her. "What is it? What's wrong?"

Jaibriol needs to calm down, her node thought.

Don't you have anything more helpful that? Soz asked. **Like what the hell just happened? Am I having a problem?**

Your water broke.

Oh. Relief swept over her. **That's normal, isn't it?**

Yes. I had some concern, because it usually breaks before this stage of labor.

How long since my labor started?

Ten hours.

"What's going on?" Jaibriol asked. "What is it saying?"

"It says I'm fine." With a smile, she added, "Except I can't breathe with you squeezing me so hard."

"Oh. Sorry." He relaxed his embrace. "What is all this fluid?"

"My water broke." Another contraction hit, and she blew out a stream of air. "Remember? MedComp says that happens."

"Then everything is all right?"

Node? she asked.

Accessing optical nerve. It produced a display of data showing blood pressure, pulse, respiration, and so on, for both the baby and Soz.

"It looks all right," Soz said.

Jaibriol leaned his head on hers, and she felt the pressure of his mind, gentle against hers, the way they had practiced it.

"Can you see it?" she asked.

"Faintly." He sounded more relaxed. "It does look all right." ***He feels all right too.*** Jaibriol's thought surrounded Soz and their son with a sense of warmth.

Soz smiled. **That he does.**

Jaibriol shifted position, sitting against the wall behind them, drawing her with him. Leaning back with her legs stretched out was one of the few positions that eased her weight.

Another contraction came and she huffed with Med-Comp's vexatious breathing exercises. They sat through several more contractions in silence, except for Soz's breathing.

"This isn't what I expected," Jaibriol finally said. "I thought it would happen much faster, with much commotion."

"That comes later." Soz grinned. "It starts after the birth and gets worse for the next twenty years. Or at least it seemed that way with my younger siblings—ah!" Another contraction came, like a bumpy conveyor belt turning inside her, and she made herself huff and puff. When it eased, she muttered, "I hate these exercises. They don't help."

"Are they really necessary?"

Node? she thought. **Can I stop?**

If you wish, it thought. They are meant to ease labor. If they irritate you, they aren't fulfilling their purpose.

"The node says I can stop if I want," Soz said.

Status report, it thought. Cervical dilation at ten centimeters, effacement at 98 percent, station at +4.

What does that mean? Soz asked.

You are about to give birth. I suggest you drink more water.

Jaibriol was watching her face. "What is it?"

"The node says I'm about to give birth."

"We *know* that. So where is the baby?"

"I don't know. Can you get me some water?"

Jaibriol eased away from her to pick up the jug of purified water they had set on the floor. He unsealed it and filled the wide-mouthed lid with fluid.

Soz drank it all. As she was pouring more, a contraction wracked her body and she dropped the cup, spilling water on the bed.

"Ah!" She heaved in a breath, trying to regain her dignity. "This is worse than running obstacle courses."

Jaibriol managed a smile. "Must be good exercise."

She grunted, then poured more water and drank it. "I'd rather run obstacles. Why don't we quit and finish tomorrow?"

"Soshoni."

"Well, it was just a thought." When he grinned, she tugged him back to sit with her.

"Do you think it will keep getting worse?" he asked.

"I've no idea. I just want to push this guy out."

He sat back up like a shot. "You're going to *push? NOW?*"

"I think so."

Jaibriol scrambled off the bed and crouched by the equipment they had arranged on the floor. He washed his hands with the boiled water from the big thermos, then opened the sterilization box and set its contents on the bed within Soz's reach: air syringe, surgical scissors, forceps, towels, and several blankets he had woven, using yarn he made from the hemp of their oatburl crop. As he got back on the bed, Soz leaned forward and he slid behind her, his legs on either side of her body. Another urge to push hit her and she braced her elbows against his thighs, bearing down hard.

So it went, Soz straining again and again. And again. And again. For one hour.

Two.

Three.

Soz groaned, sweat dripping down her face. "Why doesn't he come out?" From their son she felt a vague agitation, unformed and unfocused.

Jaibriol slid out from behind her, piling pillows around her body. Then he moved between her knees. "Soz! I see him!"

She pushed again, her vision clouded with fatigue, sweat running into her eyes.

"Here's his head," Jaibriol said. She felt his knuckles against her thighs, which meant his palms were touching their son. She groaned and pushed, groaned and pushed—

and screamed as a new pain wracked her, ripping her apart.

"Come on, little boy," he kept saying. "Come on. You can do it. We're right here. Come on—oh, gods, Soz, he's *beautiful!*"

She grunted and pushed again, too exhausted to answer.

"Soz!" Panic rang in Jaibriol's voice. "The umbilical cord is wrapped around his neck—" His voice cut off. Then: "He's not breathing—no! Jai! Baby, *breathe.* Soz, push him out the rest of the way!"

Clenching her teeth, she bore down harder—and felt another release of pressure. She immediately tried to sit up, uncaring of the pain, the blood, or the placenta she had yet to deliver. "Is he breathing? *What's going on?*" Leaning over, she saw a tiny wet, wrinkled baby in her husband's hands.

A breathing baby.

Soz heard a sob, realized it was her own. Jaibriol finished clamping and cutting the umbilical cord. With tears streaming down his face, he lifted their son and gave him to her. Soz felt tears on her own face. She cooed at the infant and made silly noises that she would have never, in a million decades, expected to come out of her mouth. *Cooing,* for saint's sake. The baby looked up at her as if he recognized her voice, and she cried more.

When she turned his mouth to her nipple, he latched on and sucked, good and strong. His contentment suffused her, unmitigated by conscious thought. Cradling him in her arms, she sat back against the wall. Jaibriol had finished washing his hands and was sitting cross-legged in front of her, holding towels, a thermos of warm water, and soap.

Watching their son, Soz said, "Jaibriol the Third." She looked up at her husband, Jaibriol the Second. "I can't believe it."

"You won't regret the name." He wiped his palm across his wet cheek, smearing his tears. "I swear it, Soz. He will grow up worthy of both the Qox and Ruby Dynasties."

She smiled. "Before we have him ruling empires, we ought to clean his bottom."

Jaibriol laughed and bent over their son with a towel.

6

Allied Worlds.

Emperor Ur Qox brooded at his desk, leaning back in his chair, one elbow resting on its arm. His bodyguards stood around the perimeter of his office, more for show than defense, given that his hidden weapons systems could kill far faster than human reflexes. The walls glittered, made from black diamond, a crystal built atom by atom with molecular assemblers. Despite its name, its molecular structure differed from diamond. It absorbed all visible light, creating its distinctive black color. The ceiling curved high above him in a dome of black diamond, with a white diamond sphere shimmering in its center, lit from within. The topaz floor glowed with pinpoint lights in geometric patterns.

The top of his desk consisted of a glossy black holoscreen. At the moment a holomap floated above it, rotating to let Qox view its star systems.

The Allied Worlds. A conundrum.

He wanted them. But he wanted Skolia more. He would have vengeance for his son. He wanted Skolia's people, wealth, resources, telops, psiberweb. All of it. Most of all he wanted the Ruby Dynasty, kneeling to him in chains and slave collars.

So he came back to the same thought. Earth. She had more use as an ally than as an enemy.

The clink of gem against gem came from across the room. Qox looked to see the empress watching him from the doorway, standing *just so,* as if she were about to shut the door again, with the suggestion of delights to follow.

Qox rubbed the bridge of his nose with his thumb and index finger. He knew what she wanted. The Sphinx delegation had arrived last night, headed by his elderly cousin, Corbal Xir, the son of his grandfather's sister. The empress meant to show Xir that she had the emperor's favor, lest Corbal seek to undermine her position in pursuit of improving his own. Qox had no time for their intrigues and ignored her, as he had earlier ignored Corbal. Soon she left.

So Qox worked, planning, plotting, brooding. Finally the cool air of evening breathed over him, sent by conduits in the palace walls. The living lattices used to construct the conduits contained self-replicating nanobots, each carrying a picochip that operated on quantum transitions. Taken all together, they formed a picoweb he programmed to suit himself. When the system let him know, with its wafting air, that evening had come, he put away his work. After the evening meal, however, he would return to his office; like most humans on this world with sixteen hour days, he slept only every other night.

He found Viquara in their personal suite on the top level of the palace. Their huge bedroom was almost the negative of his office, with white diamond walls, gold furniture, gold vases and snow-marble statues around the perimeter of the circular room, and a carpet woven from cloudgold, a plush metal alloy so soft it felt like velvet.

Viquara had settled into an armchair softened by red brocade cushions. She was watching the wall screen, which showed the opulent quarters of a favored provider. Dark curtains draped those walls, purple and heavy, and black marble urns stood in the room. The only light came from an amethyst lamp that shone dimly in one corner. The bed stood on a dais, covered with a spread that matched the somber curtains.

A youth of about twenty lay on the bed, curled into a fetal position, staring at nothing, his arms clutched around a cushion. He had the large eyes, soft curls, and husky build Viquara favored in her pleasure slaves. Qox didn't recognize the boy, but that meant nothing. He didn't recognize all the pieces in her collection of exotic music boxes either.

Qox came up behind her chair. "Is he sick?"

"I don't know." She sighed. "I bought him from the merchants in Corbal's delegation. He's been curled up like that ever since they delivered him."

Judged from the boy's catatonic behavior, Qox suspected he hadn't been born into slavery and was having trouble adjusting to it. One of the frigates that hunted Skolian ships had probably harvested him from a captured vessel. The frigates, what Skolian propagandists called pirates, carried no military identification, of course; to associate them with ESComm, or Eubian Space Command, would be politically inexpedient given the sensitive nature of their work. But they provided a much needed influx of new providers into Eube's limited psion gene pools.

Something about the slave bothered him, though. The fellow looked familiar.

"Where is he from?" Qox asked.

"Onyx Sector." Viquara continued to watch the boy. "He just lies there. I think something is wrong with him."

Qox frowned. The law forbid selling damaged slaves. "Do you have an invoice or warranty?"

"An invoice," she said. "No warranty."

Irritated, he asked, "Why did you buy him without one?"

"I liked him."

He pulled over an armchair and sat next to her. A black diamond table separated them, with a crystal carafe and goblets. He poured himself some wine, tapped his fingernail on the crystal glass to acknowledge Viquara's presence, as etiquette demanded, and then sat back to study the youth. Something tugged at him. Recognition. But why?

"Yale," he said.

Viquara glanced at him. "Yale? Who is that?"

He took a sip of wine. "It was on a shirt. That boy was wearing it." He raised his voice. "Maximilian."

"Attending," his computer said.

"Define the word 'Yale' in conjunction with the following: It is printed on a white shirt that has short sleeves and a round neck. A young man about twenty is wearing it." He paused as more of the memory returned. "He's also wearing those tiresome blue trousers the Allieds export. Jeans. What does 'Yale' mean in this context?"

"Working." After a pause, Maximilian said, "It probably refers to the Earth educational institution of that name."

"Earth." Qox drank his wine, putting together the memory. When it coalesced, he swore out loud.

Viquara tensed. "You are displeased?"

"I've met that boy. At a social function given during my state visit to Earth last year." Qox snorted. "A bizarre thing called a 'picnic and swim.' "

"He was a servant at this function?"

"No. A guest. He's the son of Jack Tarrington, a senator in the Allied Congress."

Viquara's perfect lips curved in a smile. "So the mighty fall, my love. One by one."

She was right, of course. Unfortunately, in this case "right" and political expediency didn't agree. "Maximilian."

"Attending."

"Have Empress Viquara's new provider brought up here."

Viquara gave him a coy smile he knew masked unease. "Whatever for? I would rather be with you."

"You can't have this one, Viquara."

"Why not?" When Qox said nothing, she changed her posture, a subtle pose that promised great pleasures if she had her way. "He can provide for both of us, my beloved."

Qox just shook his head. He continued to sip his wine, contemplating this new situation with the Tarrington boy.

Several minutes later, Maximilian said, "The escort you summoned waits in the foyer."

"Bring them in." Qox turned his chair to face the door and waited while Viquara did the same.

The walls around them glittered like snow laced with ice. A door slid open across the room and four Razers entered with the boy. Someone had dressed him in dark green velvet trousers that clung to his long legs, accenting his muscular build. His shirt was the same material, with belled sleeves and thong laces in the front. Whoever dressed him had left the laces untied, revealing his muscular chest. His curls, the color of loamy earth, spilled over his shirt collar in luxuriant profusion. The collar around his neck glittered with diamonds, like water flashing in the sun, as did the slave cuffs around his wrists and ankles. His bare feet added the final touch, making him look like a wild forest creature the empress had caught.

Viquara drew in a breath. She looked at Qox, earnest now, letting him know how much she wanted this one. He shook his head no, just the barest motion.

The Razers brought the boy to where Qox and Viquara sat. Their prisoner moved like an automaton, his face pale. One of the Razers shoved on his shoulder and the boy dropped to his knees, his eyes downcast. He moved with the awkward grace of an athlete who had only recently learned to kneel to Highton Aristos.

The Razers didn't kneel, of course; it compromised their ability to carry out their function. Qox motioned for three of them to withdraw to posts along the walls. To the fourth, he said, "Bring him a chair."

The Razer brought over a third chair and set it at an angle, facing Qox, then took up position behind it.

Qox spoke in English. "You may sit, Mr. Tarrington."

The boy jerked up his head, perhaps startled by the sound of his language. Or his name. Qox doubted he had heard it since his capture. The merchants would have assigned him a number for their inventory.

The youth got up and sat on the chair, his posture stiff, his gaze shifting between the emperor and empress, his face drawn.

Resting one elbow on the arm of his chair, Qox considered him. "It's Jessie, isn't it? Jack Tarrington's boy?"

Jessie swallowed. "Yes, Your Highness." He stayed on the edge of his chair, leaning neither forward nor back.

After letting the boy wait for several moments, Qox said, "Be assured, you are an honored guest of my household."

Jessie's emotions flooded out: hope, fear, confusion. He literally radiated a quality all empaths possessed to some degree, a promise of *completion* for any Aristo who took him as a provider. Qox strove to dampen the effect. Usually he had more control, but Jessie's unusual empathic strength made it difficult to remain unaffected. He understood now why Viquara had bought the boy even without a warranty. It was a shame they had to give him back to the Allieds.

It finally registered on Jessie that he had been addressed by the emperor of Eube and hadn't responded. His voice came out in a rush. "I—I'm honored, sir. Your Highness."

Qox waited, letting Jessie experience the discomfort of fearing he had offended an emperor. Then he said, "The Empress Viquara tells me that she has rescued you from a deplorable situation. What happened?"

"I was going to visit my uncle over spring break." Jessie foundered. "From school, I mean. But a pirate—" He tensed, remembering his audience. "A Eubian frigate boarded our ship, robbed the passengers, and—" His voice cracked. "And took me. To sell."

Qox played his first game piece. "You are a free man. It is not our practice to hold foreign dignitaries against their will."

Jessie stared at him. "Your Highness?"

"We will return you to your father. Until you leave, you are our honored guest." He glanced at the antique clock on the wall, then shifted his weight in obvious preparation to stand. "Please accept my regrets for what happened. You can be assured that all parties involved will be punished."

Jessie was starting to shake, succumbing to the effects of whatever shock he was suffering. Qox supposed it was difficult on the boy, being brutalized one moment, then made an honored guest of the most powerful man alive the next.

Standing up, Qox glanced at the Razer behind Jessie. "Have the Ambassador's Suite prepared for Mr. Tarrington."

The guard bowed. "Yes, sir."

Qox gave Jessie a nod of dismissal. Glancing at Viquara, he added, "Attend me, Wife."

She blinked at his tone. But she stood up and waited while the guards escorted Jessie out of the room.

As soon as they were alone, Qox said, "Maximilian, get

me everything you have on Senator Jack Tarrington of the Allied Congress. I want in particular to know if he is involved with the current treaty negotiations between Eube and Earth."

"Searching," Maximilian said.

" 'Attend me, Wife'?" Viquara put one hand on her hip. "Attend you where?"

He gave her a slow smile. "You know, my dear, I am a difficult husband to please. Cold. Harsh. Obsessed with work. For a soul as sensitive as yourself it is agony, trapped in this loveless marriage."

Unease flickered across her face. "What are you talking about?" She took her hand off her hip. "No woman could ask for a better—"

He touched his finger to her lips. "You are the loneliest woman alive. Oh you admire me, consider me an inspired leader, a man who foresees a future of peace and prosperity for the Allied Worlds and Eube, our people working together, free of this brutal war brought on by the malice of Imperial Skolia. But my duties leave me no time for you, a sweet blossom trapped by the bleak machinations of the royal court."

She watched him warily. "A sweet blossom indeed."

"And of course I am mortified by the inexcusable treatment that young Tarrington received."

"Of course."

"As emperor I would express these thoughts to the wire I so take for granted." He spread his hands. "But given my many duties, I haven't the time to entertain our Allied guest."

"This sweet blossom of yours does, I take it."

"Of course."

Her expression changed, becoming so convincingly sweet and forlorn she looked like different person. "I've such an austere life, with no friends and a husband who forgets I exist. I should be careful not to spend too much time with that charming young man who suffered so at the hands of those terrible pirates—oh!" She put her hand to her mouth, a lovely flush suffusing her cheeks. "I shouldn't use that word. I might be overheard."

Watching her transformation, Qox wondered how she did it so well. Was she acting like this when she swore her passion for him? "Can you make him believe it?"

Her soft expression vanished, replaced by the savvy Viquara he knew. "I'm not sure. What do you want me to do with him?"

"Consider this," he said. "That devastated young man, vulnerable, in shock, traumatized, his world fallen apart. Who rescues him but the lovely empress herself? He is a ripe fruit, Viquara. Pluck him. Make him fall in love with you."

She stared at him. "Whatever for?"

A chime came from the computer console.

Qox spoke to the air. "Yes?"

"I have the information on Senator Tarrington," Maximilian said. "He has no connection to the treaty negotiations."

Although it disappointed Qox, it wasn't a surprise. "Does he have any involvement with interstellar affairs?" It was perhaps too general a question, but better to throw the net wide and see what he brought up than to cast over too small an area and miss an important catch.

"He is sponsoring an environmental protection bill for the Allied colony Nuevo España," Maximilian said. "He also belongs to the Masonriders Guild. The rest of his work concerns issues specific to Earth."

"What is the Masonriders Guild?" Qox asked.

"A society that performs charitable acts to benefit colonies without sufficient technology to support their populations."

Qox frowned. "Doesn't he do anything useful?"

"That depends on what you consider useful."

"Anything that benefits me."

"Significant correlation exists," Maximilian said, "between membership in the Masonriders and Allied operatives who gather intelligence on the Skolian Imperialate."

That intrigued Qox. "He spies on the Skolians?"

"It is more likely that he directs such an operation. His patterns of travel and his 'hobby' of reading about the Ruby Empire, when sifted in with his general profile, suggest his specialty is the Valdoria branch of the Ruby Dynasty."

"Well done," Qox murmured. A back door into Allied surveillance on the Ruby Dynasty was a playing piece well worth acquiring.

"An interesting development," Viquara said.

He regarded her. "You really must be careful about how much time you spend with young Jessie. Otherwise, by the time he returns home he will be so thoroughly besotted with you he won't be able to think straight."

Her lips curved into an icy perfect smile. "Indeed."

From space the Orbiter looked like a metal ball bristling with antennae, weapons, towers, and cranes. Lights traveled in loops along it, like great radiant necklaces. The habitat was otherwise gray and functional, a craggy ball spinning in space.

Inside was a wonderland.

The Orbiter's rotation axis pierced its north and south poles, and the apparent gravitational force created by the spinning sphere pointed perpendicular to that axis. At the Orbiter's equator, the force was perpendicular to the inner hull, which made the ground flat. Walking away from the equator was like climbing a slope that became steeper as one neared the pole. The surface was terraformed to match, becoming more and more mountainous. But gravity lessened as the slope steepened. Although at the actual poles the slope became vertical, gravity was zero there, so "vertical" lost meaning.

It took the Orbiter ninety seconds for one rotation. With a diameter of four kilometers, its gravity at the equator about equaled that of Earth. Anything moving on the inner surface of the sphere also experienced a Coriolis force that pushed it to the side. The faster its motion, the greater the push. For typical speeds the effect was small, but in the low-gravity regions around the pole it became more of a problem, making hikers drift to the side.

The inner surface had an area about fifty kilometers square, divided into two hemispheres, Sky and Ground. The north and south poles lay on the horizon. Sky was blue, a dimpled luminous surface that changed color according to the time of "day." Every thirty hours a sun rose in a coral-hued dawn, made its way across Sky on an invisible track, and set in a fiery sunset. The huge lamp provided electromagnetic radiation at wavelengths optimal to human life.

Parks and mountains covered the ground hemisphere, with City in its exact center. As coloratura was to song, lyricism to prose, and filigree to metalwork, so City was to other metropolises. Its graceful curves and arches pleased the eye, as did its soft colors, sky blue, rose, lavender, forest green. And City was never still. The ends of bridges floated down to tiled paths. Arches opened in walls, then closed again or drifted to other places. Travel was by foot only, or a small monorail that blended with the scenery.

The horizon separated Ground and Sky, and the north and south poles lay on it. The equator circled the sphere equidistant between the two poles, and crossed the circle of the horizon at right angles. Near the equator, the horizon was no more than the border of a lawn, grass on one side, sky on the other. Away from the equator, approaching the horizon was like moving sideways along a hill—except at the horizon you could keep going, edging with poetic whimsy along the sky just as you had edged along the hill.

Near the poles, the horizon was terraformed into cliffs, to discourage hikers. Airborne robots patrolled the area. The lighter gravity made the cliffs easy to climb, but a misplaced step could cause a fall. Those bemused hikers who fell onto Sky could end up sliding with ever-increasing weight down a two-kilometer-long slope.

Strolling along the equator was like walking on flat ground, with "down" being right under wherever a person happened to be standing. Hikers could start from City, go to the horizon, walk along Sky until City was "above" them, continue to the opposite horizon, step back onto Ground, and cross the parks back to City. With a circumference of only twelve kilometers, the equator could be walked within a day. On holidays the sky filled with people hiking, picnicking, and playing sports.

Command centers honeycombed the Orbiter's hull, including the War Room. About halfway from City to the horizon, the mountains hid an idyllic valley guarded by the Imperialate's best security, sheltering houses where the Ruby Dynasty lived when they were on the Orbiter.

Kurj rode a magrail car to the valley, which in his ever-literal style he had named Valley. Entering Valley required extensive security checks, all of which unobtrusively took place while he sat in the car reading holographs of the last Assembly session. The magrail let him off a few hundred meters from his house, and he walked the rest of the way to the stone mansion on the side of a mountain.

Today he felt heavy.

Kurj knew it made no sense, given that the gravity here was only at about 70 percent. He preferred it that way; he was simply too massive for standard gravity, the volume-to-area ratio of his body too big. But still, today, he felt heavy.

He entered his home by a doorway big enough for three men to walk through together. It had no door. In Valley's controlled environment, the weather was whatever he wanted. So he lived in eternal spring and left his house open to the air.

His living room was five times as large as those built by normal-sized humans. It stretched out, open and airy, all stone surfaces, smooth, polished, gray. When he entered, the dormant walls were drowsing, just the barest line of gold glowing at waist-level. The pressure of his tread woke the house and the glow increased, outlining a desert landscape, sand below the horizon, amber sky above.

Kurj sat on the couch, one of the few furnishings in the sparse room. It molded to his body, easing his muscles, but his fatigue went far deeper than the exhaustion produced by the strain of carrying his large bulk. Leaning forward, with his booted feet planted wide, he rested his elbows on his knees and—in the privacy of his home where no one could see—put his head in his hands.

He had just spent two days monitoring the war machine under his command. Maneuvers, inventories, war games, communications, skirmishes—he oversaw it all. He absorbed data from across the stars and processed it in a web that spread throughout his body and the Orbiter. Every analysis yielded the same result; ISC operated like a well-oiled machine. But within the beauty of that order he saw another pattern, one that added a weight to his step no change in gravity could ever ease.

It wasn't enough.

He had shaped the most powerful war machine ever known by free humanity. The most versatile. The fastest. And it wasn't enough. The Traders wouldn't conquer them today, tomorrow, or next year. But bit by inexorable bit, Eube would wear them down, until Imperial Skolia fell to its relentless force. He had given his life, even his humanity, to prevent that future. And it wasn't enough.

Kurj looked around the empty room. "I'm tired," he said. The room didn't answer.

A, attend, he thought.

Attending.

Access the Ψ gate and link me to the Assembly web on Parthonia.

You aren't jacked into the web.

Use an IR link. Although IR transmissions were less secure than a direct link, little chance existed that anyone could intercept a transmission sent from where he sat to a console across the room.

Link to planet Parthonia established, **A** thought.

Has the Assembly session begun yet?

No. It begins in two hours and six minutes, standard. Will you attend?

Yes. He would rather have slept, but Parthonia time cycles had no connection to the Orbiter. He also needed to finish his preparations for the session. Dehya opposed the proposed ban on trade with the dust merchants who mined Onyx Sector. She claimed the ban would weaken the Onyx economy, but Kurj suspected she had other reasons, such as using the merchants to spy on Onyx Platform, his ISC base in that sector. So he opposed her opposition. Her challenge in the upcoming Assembly session would be subtle. Intricate. Thorough. Of all opponents, Dehya was the most worthy. So he had to work more on his preparations.

He needed sleep, however. His body required only two hours for every twenty of activity, but losing even one of those hours blunted his acuity. If he slept an hour now, that left him one to work on the Onyx material.

Kurj went to his bedroom, entering through a wide opening with no door. Inside, golden desert images softened the walls of the big stone room, their glow more subdued here. His bed stood against one wall, its huge expanse custom-made for his frame.

A girl was sleeping on the bed.

Kurj stopped. At first his fatigued mind couldn't absorb her presence. Then he remembered. The page.

She lay on her side, curled into a ball, her arms wrapped around his pillow. Her jumpsuit was in a style that had become popular after Eldrinson first appeared in public wearing his irritating rustic clothes. It looked much better on her than on his stepfather. The green velvet pants clung to her well-shaped legs. The leather thongs on her bodice had been laced up to her neck in the War Room, but since then someone had loosened them, revealing the curve of her breasts. Her dark brown curls gleamed and her necklace sparkled like water in the sun.

Kurj reevaluated his need for sleep. Sitting on the bed, he smoothed her hair back from her face, then touched the sparkling trim on her collar. He wondered what would happen when she opened her eyes.

The companions he chose reacted in different ways to his attention. Often they feared him, though many tried to hide it, some putting on a show of love that would have fooled a lesser empath. If their fear was too great, he let them go. But many accepted their situation. A few even grew to like him. All sought to use his favor, hoping their charms would soften his heart. And somehow he always found himself giving them what they wanted, wealth, jewels, a new job, a nicer house.

He usually sent his security team for the woman he chose and had them leave her here. Sometimes he took her to a lake hidden in the hills, where they dined on a floating barge with lamps and music and later made love surrounded by the whispering lap of the water. It was, he supposed, romantic. Women seemed to like it, anyway.

Kurj watched the page, whose name he couldn't remember. As far as he could tell, no specters haunted her sleep. It relieved him that as of yet he had picked up no fear on her part. He didn't want to have to let this one go, not now, when he so needed companionship.

An oddity registered. This morning he had left a shirt on his bed when he decided to wear a sweater instead. For some reason the page had wrapped the shirt around the pillow she was holding. Why would she embrace his clothes?

He slid his hand along her side, in to her waist, and out again over the swell of her hips. The girl stirred, then opened her eyes, blinking. With his hand resting on her hip, Kurj leaned down and kissed her.

Her jumble of emotions swept over him: surprise, shyness, uncertainty. Through all that confusion, a vivid thread gleamed. Disconcerted, he stopped kissing her and pulled back. Of all the ridiculous things. This girl thought she was in love with him.

He eased down his mental barriers to see what else he could pick up. Her images vibrated. Although she hadn't been sexually abused in the orphanage, the emotional lacks had done almost as much damage. She didn't perceive herself as a source of disorder; rather, she saw the rest of the universe as chaos. Her gratitude to Bozner for sending her to the Orbiter permeated her thoughts.

But one image stood out. The day she walked into the

War Room and looked up to see Skolia's Imperator in his throne among the stars, she felt safe for the first time in her life. So she fell in love with him. She imagined him as a hero and populated her fantasies with him as an affectionate, gentle suitor. It was an image so far removed from his true personality it might as well have been another man with no connection to him at all.

She watched him like an animal mesmerized by night lamps. For some reason his face relaxed into an unaccustomed expression. A smile. He tugged the pillow out of her arms and lay down next to her. When he drew her into his arms, she tensed, her confusion sweeping over him.

"It's all right," he said. Then he outdid himself in verbosity, adding a second sentence. "I won't hurt you."

She slid her arms around his waist, giving him a tentative smile. "My greetings, Imperator Skolia." Her voice had a rich quality that pleased him.

"What is your name?" he asked.

"Ami."

"Ami." He pulled the laces on her jumpsuit, unfastening them the rest of the way. "A pleasant name, that."

As he undressed her, she stared at his chest, her cheeks red. From her mind, he picked up that she had hardly ever been kissed before, let alone anything else. He knew he was far from most women's choice for their first lover. Yet her thoughts left no doubt. She wanted him and no one else.

He rubbed his thumb along the lacy halter holding her breasts, and she slid her palm over his chest, her curiosity tickling his mind. Then a chime came from the console in the nightstand across the bed.

Kurj swore under his breath. In a louder voice he said, "Skolia here."

A woman's deep-timbered voice came out of the console. "Imperator Skolia, this is Admiral Tahota. We've intercepted a transmission between the office of President Calloway on Earth and the Eubian Trade Ministry on Glory."

He pushed up on his elbow. "How much have you decoded?"

"Most of it," Tahota said. "It concerns an Allied citizen, a boy who ended up in the trade inventory of a Sphinx merchant. Apparently the empress freed the boy and the emperor is arranging his return to Earth."

Kurj frowned. What purpose could Qox have in freeing a slave or having his own people attend to such a minor matter? "Do you have an ID on the boy?"

"Jessie Tarrington," Tahota said. "His father is Senator Jack Tarrington, of the Allied Congress."

So. Politics reared its head. "Where was the boy taken?"

"We aren't sure yet," Tahota said. "It looks like his ship changed its flight plan to deliver emergency supplies to a colony near Onyx Sector. Apparently it crossed into Eube space and a pirate caught them."

"How certain are you that his ship actually left our space?" Kurj asked.

"It's questionable," Tahota said. "In fact, they may not have even been close to the border regions."

"Get me a full analysis," he told her. "I want all records of Onyx raids in our space, the distribution of their raids, and any known interactions they have with the Onyx dust merchants. I need it in time for the upcoming Assembly session."

"You'll have it," Tahota said. "Shall I open a channel so you can monitor the investigation?"

Kurj watched Ami. When she smiled at him, he almost groaned. To Tahota he said, "No. Have my brother Althor take care of it."

"Will do, sir."

"Very good, Admiral. Skolia out."

"Out, sir."

Kurj bent his head and kissed Ami again, stroking his hand over her breast. He didn't have time to make love to her now, not if he intended to take it slow, to avoid hurting her. But for these few minutes he wanted to touch her. For just a few moments he wanted to feel light.

III

Year Four

360 ASC on the Imperial Calendar
383 EG on the Eubian Calendar
A.D. 2263 on the Gregorian Calendar

7

Soz climbed the hill, with the laser carbine slung over her shoulder and a bow and quiver on her back. She followed Jai as he toddled through the spatula grass. Her son's mood matched the weather: happy and bright. When he crouched to examine a broken geode sparkling with purple crystals, Soz stopped and shifted the weight of the baby in a sling on her hip. Lisi. She and Jaibriol had named her Rocalisa, after Soz's mother Roca, but they ended up calling her Lisi.

When Lisi let out with a wail, Soz sighed. Only 250 hours old and already her daughter had a pair of lungs to raise the dead. As Soz lifted the baby out of the sling, Jai looked back at them with concerned eyes. Red eyes.

"Why Leesy cry?" he asked, still unable to pronounce the short "i" sound in his sister's name.

"She's hungry." Soz sat down and tugged up the fur shirt Jaibriol had made for her, then cradled Lisi against her.

Jai toddled over. "Leesy always hungry. I want mum-mum too."

With her free hand Soz tousled his hair. She understood why MedComp wanted her to keep nursing Jai. The immunities and nutrients she gave him were even more important here, where humans maintained so precarious a balance with the environment. It also fulfilled an emotional need for him, creating a contentment that suffused her mind. She had thought she would have to stop when she became pregnant again, but MedComp said it was fine, even when Jai grumbled about the change in the taste of her milk. Still, nursing both children at the same time was too much.

"You can have some after Lisi is done," she said.

"Hungry now," Jai insisted.

"In just a few minutes, Jaibird."

"Want *now!*"

She smiled at him. "Are you practicing to be an emperor or an imperator, hmmm? You wait till Mommy says yes."

"Now," Jai grumbled. He sat down and laid his head in her lap, sucking his thumb. Lisi nestled against her, nursing like the suction tube on a star-dock crane.

"Daddy like mum-mum too," Jai said around his thumb.

Mortified, Soz stared down at him. "Why do you say that?"

"Saw Daddy and Mommy. Daddy hungry too."

Soz flushed. Living in a one-room house had its problems. Apparently Jai hadn't been asleep sometime when they thought he was. "We're going to build you your own room, Jaibird. Special for you. Would you like that?"

"All mine?"

"That's right. All yours."

He considered the proposal. "Jaibird like," he decided.

"Good." Soz shifted Lisi on her arm. "I have to take you back to the house now. Daddy will look after you for a while."

"Don't *want* house." Jai sat up, glaring with an inimitable scowl. "Go with you!"

"Sweetbird—"

"No! Go with you!"

"Jai, don't you know any other word but 'no'?"

"No!"

Soz made a show of sighing. "Well, I'm sorry. I guess only Lisi gets to stay with Daddy today."

Confusion sped across his beautiful face. "No! I go with Leesy."

"Well, I don't know." Soz put on a doubtful look.

"Go with Leesy!"

"Well . . . all right. You can go with Lisi."

"Where Mommy go?" Jai sounded worried and Soz knew her game hadn't fooled him; it just gave him an excuse to give in.

"Hunting," she said. "We need food."

"Mommy catch the tommy-jommy?"

"The what?"

He tried a different pronunciation. "Tummy-jummy."

"I don't know what you mean."

"Big and black. Tastes good."

"Ah." She nodded. "You mean a tomjolt. Yes, I hope so."

Jaibriol had named the animals "tomjolts" because EcoComp claimed they resembled Earth bobcats. Given EcoComp's description, though, Soz suspected one tomjolt could slaughter five bobcats before breakfast. Like the gilded crimson fliers that lived near the river, tomjolts had eight legs and were part crustacean, part reptile, and part plant, with chitinous hides rich in chlorophyll. Jaibriol decreed the animals belonged to their own phylum and christened them chloropods.

Soz had no intention of seeing a tomjolt dine on her family. So she hunted them with the same single-minded ferocity she had once directed against Eubian warriors.

"Hoshpa!" Jai's delighted shout rang out as he scrambled to his feet. Looking up, Soz saw Jaibriol walking up the hill toward them. Still feeling bulky from her recent pregnancy, she climbed to her feet, holding Lisi in the crook of her arm. MedComp insisted she was too thin, but MedComp always complained.

As Soz started down the hill, Lisi made a noise of protest, then resumed nursing. Jai ran toward his father, and Jaibriol crouched down, extending his arms to the boy. Jai promptly tripped on a spiderpouch weed, sprawled face forward on the grass, and let out a wail to split the sky.

Jaibriol jumped up and ran to his son, his smile vanished, replaced by the fear Soz knew well, the one that came every time their son took even the smallest tumble. Here, with only themselves to rely on, a simple injury could be fatal.

When Jaibriol scooped the boy into his arms, Jai sniffled and hugged his father around the neck, mollified. As Soz came up to them, Jaibriol's attention shifted to her.

"You look tired," he said.

"Just a little," Soz answered. Lisi quit nursing and Soz slid her shirt back into place.

"Don't go," Jaibriol said. "Stay here. Rest."

"We can't sit around while tomjolts eat our son's pets."

"Bad tommy-jommy." Jai sniffled. "Ate Puppli."

"We don't know that a tomjolt got Puppli," Jaibriol said.

Soz thought of the remains they had found of Jai's furred pet, a small chloropod with big ears and a long, green tail. "It's the same pattern as with the other jolts." She handed Jaibriol the carbine. "We can't take chances."

He pushed the carbine back at her. "You take it."

"If I shoot it with the laser, there won't be anything left for us to use but charred bones." Quietly she said, "You'll have the children. Better you have our best weapon."

Jaibriol glanced at the boy in his arms, then slung the carbine over his shoulder. When she offered him Lisi, he took her with the same ease Soz had long ago seen in her own father when he held her younger siblings. Who would have thought it, that the Highton Heir, the terror of three empires, would be such a gentle, loving father? She wondered if the emperor or empress had ever held Jaibriol the way Jaibriol held Lisi and Jai. She doubted it.

He spoke in a subdued voice. "My mother is a superb actress."

"You mean Empress Viquara?"

He nodded. "She could convince a rock she loved it. But convincing a Rhon telepath is different." He tried to shrug. "She resented acknowledging another woman's child as her son."

Softly Soz said, "I'm sorry."

"It doesn't matter. I have far more now than my parents will ever have, with all their palaces, slaves, and wealth." He watched her face. "Be careful, Soshoni. I know you think you're invulnerable, with all that hardware inside your body. But you're not."

"I'll be careful." She rose up on her toes and kissed him.

They parted then, Jaibriol headed to the house with the children, and Soz going in the other direction, up the hill.

The walk was easy and the day beautiful. She enjoyed it, except for her unease at even a short separation from Lisi, who so far had no predictable schedule as to when she ate or slept.

Soz felt as if she and Lisi were still one body and mind. Jai's mind was gradually becoming distinct from hers. Lately he asserted his independence with gusto, coming up with more ways to say "no" than she had ever imagined existed. Smiling, she sent a mental caress to her family. The union they all shared as Rhon telepaths was strong enough that even from this far away her loved ones might pick up a sense of her thought.

Her node was running calculations. Combining data on other tomjolts with what they knew of this one, it predicted where she might find the predator. The mountains in this area consisted of open rolling hills covered with light green spatula grass and dotted by clumps of palm trees. She scanned the terrain at various EM wavelengths, cranked up her ears until she could hear spatula fronds fall from trees, and inhaled the pungent scents of a land teeming with flora but scant on fauna. No trace of the tomjolt turned up.

She came to a minicliff a few meters high. At its base, the hill rolled away in ripples of knee-high grass. Soz jumped off the cliff, letting her node calculate her optimum trajectory and her hydraulics move her body. She landed in a crouch, poised like a human tomjolt ready to leap. Then pain twinged in her hip and she fell over.

"Pah," Soz grumbled. So much for being a human tomjolt.

Suggestion, her node thought.

What? Soz stood up, rubbing her sore hip.

Unnecessary physical exertion makes it more difficult for your body to regain strength. You should exert yourself less.

My strength is fine.

That is an inaccurate statement. You are in excellent health given that you gave birth 250 hours ago. However, you are far from your optimum.

"I'm fine," Soz muttered.

Question.

She set off down the slope. **What?**

Have you thought of a name for me yet?

No.

Why?

Because I haven't.

You named your children before they were born.

You aren't my child. You're part of me.

Then my name is Sauscony?

She unslung her bow and nocked an arrow in it. **No, your name is not Sauscony.**

Why are you preparing to shoot?

It's called "a state of readiness," which you well know.

Have you considered that your tension in regards to my name has psychological implications?

No.

I have a suggestion.

Be quiet, Soz thought. She continued down the slope until she reached a forest. Within the trees, the day's brightness became muted and a chatter of spatula leaves surrounded her.

Finally she thought, **So are you going to tell me your suggestion?**

Call me a name for one day. See how it affects you.

Why are you so certain this has some deep, dark significance?

I believe your refusal to name me reflects your inability to make peace with the fact that you are, simultaneously, an empath and a weapon.

That caught her by surprise. It was a long moment before she answered. **Giving you a name won't erase the scars in my heart.**

After a pause, her node thought, I am sorry.

Sorry. Her computer was sorry. The strangeness of that left her with no response.

The trees gave way to a circular clearing. A mat of crystalline grass the color of white jade stretched out ahead of her. She felt a distant tug at her mind, like a call, and wondered if it was time to go back. But she still hadn't found the tomjolt. Jai had been devastated over the death of his pet, and that was minor compared to the tragedy a tomjolt could inflict on humans.

Caught between the decision to go back or continue, Soz touched her boot to the crystal grass. **What is this stuff?**

I have no data on it, her node thought. I need a sample to analyze.

Crouching down, Soz touched a filament. It vibrated in a soft chime. She brushed her palm across the grass, and a shimmer of chimes greeted her. "Hey. It's beautiful." When she stood up and walked onto the grass, it sang like angels.

I would suggest you give me a sample to analyze, her node thought. Wait for the results before you continue.

It sounds so soothing.

Yes. It does.

Soz sat on the grass and it crooned to her, sweet notes in her mind. Lying on her back, she stared at the circle of sky above her. Red was low in the west, hidden by the trees, and Blue blazed overhead, far too bright to look at. She closed her eyes. The grass hummed and chimed, soothing, soothing, soothing . . .

Soshooooooo . . . nnnnn . . . iii . . .

Soz twitched at the intrusion into her bliss. Above her, the evening sky shimmered pink with Red's sunset.

Soshooooonnnnniii . . . Somewhere a baby screamed.

Soz sat bolt upright. *How could it be evening?* She heard nothing, but the sense of a baby's screams filled her mind.

She scrambled to her feet and ran across the clearing. The grass shrieked in protest, its song vicious now. Her stomach clenched in a way that suggested the grass was using frequencies below her hearing range. It had to be all the grass together; a single blade couldn't produce that sound. The effect intensified, became unbearable, she had to make it end, had to stop running—

"Like hell," she muttered, and ran off the grass. **Node! What happened?**

No answer.

Node!

Nothing.

Soz kept running. The trip back seemed to last ages, but she had no idea how much time actually passed. She couldn't access her internal timer. Her node had to be working, though, because she was running with enhanced speed, which meant it was directing her hydraulics. If she used them too much, it strained her skeleton and muscular systems, but right now she didn't care.

Soshoni! The thought burst into her mind.

I'm almost home, she thought.

Jaibriol's relief exploded over her. ***You're alive!***

How long have I been gone?

Ten hours. Lisi won't eat. She's worked herself into a frenzy.

Hoshma! Mommy! Jai's thought was frantic. *Leesy dying!*

Soz could hear Lisi screaming now. She ran down to the house and through the open doorway. Jaibriol was coming toward her, the red-faced infant in his arms. Toddler Jai hovered behind him like an agonized supervisor unsure how to direct the crisis.

"Ai, Babylisi, lisi, lisi." Soz crooned as she took her screaming daughter. She pulled up her shirt and put Lisi to her breast, but the frenzied infant was too worked up to suckle. Standing with her planted feet wide, dressed in a fur shirt and the black leather pants of her Jagernaut uniform, Soz looked down at the baby in her arms and swayed back and forth.

Suddenly Lisi took a choked breath and latched onto Soz's nipple with the vehemence of a stardock crane grasping cargo. She suckled furiously, her tiny body shaking with her exertions.

Jaibriol made a strangled noise. His relief was so intense it felt tangible.

Is Leesy happy now? Jai asked. He was watching with such earnest concern, Soz wanted to scoop him up into her arms too.

Lisi happy, Jaibriol assured him.

"I'm sorry, little hurricane," Soz murmured to her daughter.

"Where you go, Mommy?" Jai toddled forward and put his arms around her leg. "We looked all the places in the world."

Soz smiled at him. "In the whole world?"

"All over," he assured her.

Jaibriol pushed his hand through his hair. "We searched for hours. Where were you?"

"I went out past the minicliff."

"We went through there." His mind crackled with lingering remnants of his fear, and anger too, now that he knew she was all right. "Couldn't you hear us calling? Lisi was screaming loud enough to break the sky."

"I'm not sure what happened," Soz said. "I found a patch of grass. Crystal grass. It *sang* me into a trance, and my node too." Remembering its earsplitting protests when she left, she said, "It may have a rudimentary sentience."

"Where is it?" Jaibriol asked. "I've never seen it."

"In the minicliff woods. It must have only recently grown." Soz went to an armchair Jaibriol had made and sank into it, cradling Lisi, who was nursing more gently now.

Attending, her node announced.

For heaven's sake, Soz thought. **I called you a long time ago.**

I seem to have suffered a disruption in my ability to process your neural impulses.

Why?

The plant you term "crystal grass" apparently creates fields that disrupt neural activity.

What about your overrides? Soz asked. **Safety routines? Emergency toggles? Backups? You've a hundred and one ways to deal with a situation like that.**

This hit 102.

Jaibriol brought over another chair to Soz. As he sat down, Jai crawled into his lap. Holding his son tenderly,

Jaibriol "spoke" in Soz's mind. ***Do you have any idea what this "crystal grass" is?***

Her node answered. A relative of the people trap. Its entranced prey must die of starvation. The decomposing body would provide nutrients for the grass.

That's disgusting, Soz thought.

But efficient. The grass probably secretes chemicals to help break down substances.

We should get rid of it, Jaibriol thought.

It could prove useful, the node answered. Its size suggests it preys on large animals. The largest animal we've seen is the tomjolt. If you can contain the grass and bait it somehow, it might make a tomjolt trap.

Good idea, Soz thought.

Lisi pulled away from her mother's nipple and gave a cry of protest.

"It's all right," Soz murmured. She shifted the baby to the other breast, and Lisi latched back on. When Jaibriol crooned to her, Lisi looked at him, still nursing, then closed her eyes and concentrated on dinner.

With Jai nestled in his lap, Jaibriol watched Soz nurse. "Who would have thought it?" he said. "The warrior turns to mush."

Soz scowled. "What mush? I'm not mush."

He smiled. "Do you know, Soshoni, once I saw a rogue tomjolt try to invade the lair of a female that had just given birth. The mother tomjolt tore the invader to shreds. Then she went back to feeding her cubs."

She squinted at him. "Are you comparing me to a tomjolt?"

"Let's just say I'm glad I'm your love and not your enemy."

Softly she said, "I will always love you. If anyone ever tried to hurt you or the children, I would surely tear them to shreds."

Caged in an exoskeleton of controls, Althor Valdoria, the Imperial Heir, sat at his console. Today he worked in his web chamber, a bare room with nothing but the console and his control chair.

Onyx. Althor doubted he would ever know what had spurred his brother, two years ago, to put him in charge of the situation at Onyx Sector. Usually Kurj kept control of sensitive areas. Whatever the reason, he had loosened his iron grip that day. Fascinated with the puzzle Kurj handed him, Althor had studied every report detailing the encroachment of Trader pirates into the region of Onyx Platform, a major ISC base. Over the last two years he had gained increasing authority in that sector, until now he directed ISC activities there.

Onyx Platform was in Onyx Sector, a crucial territory where Eube, Skolia, and the Allied Worlds intersected in a diffuse region claimed by all three powers. Although Trader pirates raided the ISC outposts there, they no longer harassed Allied holdings. The ISC Public Affairs Office claimed credit for protecting the Allieds, but Althor had no illusions. ESComm no longer sent pirates into Allied space because Emperor Qox wanted a treaty with the Allieds.

What bothered Althor today, however, had little to do with raids. The puzzle he had tracked for over a year was no more than a simple glitch in one inconsequential datum. It concerned a discrepancy he had found for one price listed in a shipment of construction supplies to an Onyx space station. The invoice in ISC Records differed by one centilla, one Imperial cent, from that listed by Onyx Records.

Althor would never have noticed if he hadn't been searching the invoices for another reason, to figure out how his aunt, Dehya Selei, paid her agents among the dust merchants who trawled Onyx Sector. A one-cent difference in a million-dollar shipment? He almost ignored the error.

But the discrepancy tugged at him. He searched it out, to verify it was nothing. What he found puzzled him. Sending the invoice from Onyx to the Orbiter involved no human input. No one to enter the number. Nor did he find any trace of a rip or other problem in the web that could have corrupted the data. It seemed absurd to grow concerned over one cent, but it bothered him that no reason existed for the disagreement.

For a year he tracked it through the web, searching for one cent among daily billions. He found the memory location used to store the invoice. As he followed its history, the search took him farther and farther from Onyx. Today he finally confirmed the source of the discrepancy. Nearly four years ago in HeadQuarters City, the heart of ISC, someone had erased a file. Of course, millions of files were erased at HQ every day. But whoever deleted this one had first hidden it in a private account accessible only to a select handful of people.

Also, an expert erased that file. The only reason anything came up at all was because the hacker had worked from a civilian node. They had eradicated all trace of the work—except for one bit of data removable only from a computer within an ISC control center.

One bit of data.

The hacker apparently even knew about that one inviolable bit. They couldn't reset its value, from one to zero, so they camouflaged it. A tiny problem came up: the hidden bit caused a bit in an adjoining memory location to change from zero to one. The new bit immediately reset to zero, but in the process it changed another bit from zero to one. So the glitch propagated for over a year, after which it disappeared. Somewhere along the line, it altered the value of an invoice by one cent.

Release exoskeleton, Althor thought.

Released. The exoskeleton around his body opened and the psiphon prongs clicked out of the sockets in his spine and neck.

Lost in thought, Althor left the chamber and walked through his office, then through the outer offices where his assistants worked, and out into the corridors that networked the hull. He took the magrail to his apartment in City, where he had chosen to live, instead of in Valley.

City drifted around him as he strode through its plazas and along its boulevards. The sailpath he summoned took him to a blue building with onion towers and shimmering spires. When it set him down on a third-story ledge, a doorway shaped like the keyhole for a giant skeleton key opened in the wall. After Althor went through it, the doorway disappeared, leaving a smooth surface glowing with blue light, like a piece of Sky.

The halls inside also glowed blue, a translucent luminance that extended deep into the walls. At the end of one hall he came to another large horseshoe arch shaped like a keyhole. Purple and silver mosaics bordered the blue door within it. He brushed his finger across a scroll of leaves and the door chimed.

"Come in, Althor," the door said. It shimmered and vanished.

He walked into an airy room with wicker furniture. The door had barely re-formed behind him when an adolescent girl with violet eyes and a wild head of bronze curls stalked through the horseshoe arch of an inner doorway. She stopped when she saw Althor, glared at him, and stalked out again.

Althor blinked. "Eristia?" He started after the girl.

An older woman came through the inner doorway. Tall and willowy, with blue eyes and red hair streaked with silver, Syreen looked every bit the actress she had once been, before she retired to pursue a career in linguistics.

"Althor." She took his hands. "It's good to see you."

He lifted her hands and kissed her knuckles. "What's wrong with Eristia?"

Syreen made an exasperated noise. "She's been like that all afternoon. Maybe you can talk to her."

An irate voice came from the room beyond. "I don't feel like talking."

Syreen frowned. "Eristia, come here and greet your father."

The girl appeared in the archway. "Ultra, Daddy." Then she disappeared back into the inner room.

Althor glanced at Syreen. "Ultra?"

Her mouth quirked up. "As near as I can tell, it has positive connotations."

He smiled, then went into the inner room and found his daughter glaring at a holo-painting on the wall. "Why are you angry?" he asked.

She continued to glare.

He tried again. "Are you mad at me?"

"At you?" She turned to him. "No, of course not."

"You're angry at someone."

"Yes."

Althor waited. When it became clear no more information was forthcoming, he said, "At your mother."

"She never lets me do anything." Eristia crossed her arms. "*Nothing.* Everyone else has fun. Everyone else razzles. But me? No, not me."

It was beginning to make sense. "You want to do something and your mother said 'no'."

"She's the most unreasonable person alive."

Althor grinned. "Alive anywhere?"

"Don't make fun of me."

"What won't she let you do?"

She spread her arms to accent her words. "It was going to be the razzlest. Ultraviolet. Out the galactic *arm*."

He rubbed his chin. "Does that have a translation into normal language?"

"Oh, Daddy."

He looked for help at Syreen, who had come into the doorway.

"She wants to go on a trip with some other children from Academy," Syreen said. "To Blazers Starland."

"Blazers?" Althor frowned at his daughter. "Isn't that the entertainment complex on Sylvia's Moon?"

"Everyone ultra is going," Eristia said. "It will be the firestorm of the year." Her pretty face suffused with hope. "Tell Hoshma it's all right, Daddy. Say I can jopper. Please?"

"Jopper—that means go on a trip, doesn't it?"

"Of course." She regarded him with the sympathy of the enlightened for those less savvy about the universe. "Everyone razzle will be there."

"Everyone?" He liked this less and less. "Just who is everyone? The girls from your school?"

"Girls?" Syreen snorted. "Don't be naive, Althor. Half these 'razzle' personages are boys. None, it seems, are chaperones."

Althor stared at his daughter. "You want me to let a thirteen-year-old girl go to an entertainment complex on a world as wild as Sylvia's Moon, with boys and without chaperones? Absolutely not."

Her frustration rolled out in a wave from her mind. "But why not?"

"It's not safe."

"Yes, it is," she assured him.

"Erista, I'm sorry, but the answer is no."

Her face crumpled in anguish. She swung around to include Syreen. "You're horrible people!" With that, she stalked out of the room.

When they were alone, Althor squinted at Syreen. "Do you think she really means that?"

"Althor, no." Syreen came over to him. "She's just disappointed."

"I can't fathom why people would let their children go on a trip like that."

"I checked with the other parents. Most of them said 'no' too." Her smile crinkled the lines around her eyes. "When Eristia discovers how many of the others had to stay home, they'll have a great time commiserating about their heartless parents."

"I suppose." It didn't make him feel any better about being a source of the commiseration.

"Would you like to stay for dinner?"

He shook his head. "I have plans."

"Oh. Yes. Of course." She paused. "How is Coop?"

"He's fine."

After an awkward silence, she said, "Say good-bye to Eristia before you leave."

He gave her a rueful smile. "I'll try."

He found his daughter lying on her back on a divan in the sunroom, staring at the skylight above her head. When he entered, she scowled and focused harder on the glass.

"I will see you tomorrow," Althor said.

Her disappointment suffused his mind. "I know," she said. "I'll still be here. Everyone galactic will be on Sylvia's."

He came over and sat next to her. "Did you really think we would let you go on that trip, Podkin?"

"Don't call me that baby name."

"All right." He wondered when she had stopped liking the nickname. She continued to stare at the skylight, so he tilted his head to look. All he saw was an unremarkable patch of Sky.

"Not much up there," he commented.

She sighed. "Oh, Daddy. You're so infrared."

He turned back to her. "Infrared?"

"Don't feel bad," she consoled. "Parents are supposed to be that way." She sat up and hugged him around the neck. "Come for dinner tomorrow, all right?"

He hugged her back, relieved she didn't find her taciturn father so horrible after all. "Of course." Softly he said, "Your mother and I love you, Pod—Eristia."

"Me too," she said. "You, I mean."

After he left Syreen's apartment, he walked to his own. He didn't know what to make of Eristia's taste for the fast life of her rich friends. Having grown up on a rural world, he never even knew that kind of life existed until he went offworld at eighteen, to attend military school. At thirteen, he had spent his free time hiking in the countryside around Dalvador, the village where his family lived. His friends were all local boys. Their idea of getting into trouble was sneaking into a tavern to drink watered-down ale.

A voice spoke, sounding like Cobalt, the node that ran his apartment. "Althor, are you coming home?"

He stopped. "Cobalt?"

"The door registered your presence and interpreted your body language as an intent to come home," Cobalt said. "But you kept going."

Althor looked around. He had indeed walked past the turn to his apartment. He retraced his steps to a corridor where the walls glowed in ever-deeper layers of blue. The keyhole arch at the end stood twice his height, with stained glass in its upper curve and a mosaic border of cool geometric designs. The building's beauty was one reason acquiring an apartment here was impossible without connections. Althor had gotten Syreen one when she discovered her unexpected pregnancy after what had been, for both of them, a fling of a few days. They tried to make a go of their relationship, only to discover they did far better as friends than as lovers. But he was glad she had stayed all these years, making him part of Eristia's life.

The door shimmered open and he entered. His apartment had a different feel than Syreen's home. Where she chose wicker, he chose glass and chrome; where she used curves, he used angles. The floor-to-ceiling holopanels on the walls displayed whatever he felt like looking at. Right now, they showed his childhood home, the village of Dalvador. Blue-capped mountains made a backdrop for a town of white-washed houses with purple or blue turreted roofs. Plains of silvery grass rippled in a breeze.

The horseshoe arch across the room had no door. Beyond it, sunshine poured through many windows into the sun-room where Althor often went to relax. As he entered the sun-drenched chamber, a young man came through another archway across the room, a willowy youth, twenty-four years old, about five-ten, with red curls and blue eyes. He could have been Syreen's brother.

The youth froze. Then he remembered himself and said, "My greeting, Prince Althor."

Althor smiled. "Coop, my name is Althor. You don't have to use a title."

Coop managed a more relaxed smile. "Althor."

"How is your painting?"

"I finished the landscape this afternoon."

Althor nodded, pleased. Coop's art had caught his notice when he had wandered into an outdoor exhibit while walking home from the War Room. The work had struck him as close to genius. After learning how much time Coop wasted doing ISC holobanners to support himself, Althor became his patron. He set Coop up in a luxury apartment with a huge studio and gave him a sensible credit line to cover expenses. At least Althor considered it sensible. For some reason Coop thought it extravagant. Tonight he had invited Coop to dinner, to begin introducing him to Orbiter society.

Althor went into the circular alcove that served as a kitchen and bent over the counter, checking its console for messages. "My family should be here soon."

"Cobalt set up dinner." Agitation crackled in Coop's voice.

Althor turned to see him standing in the archway of the alcove. "What's wrong?"

Coop flushed. "Nothing."

"I'm an empath," Althor said. "I can tell you're upset."

"It's just—" Coop exhaled. "Before you, the most important person I ever met was the pilot on the ship that brought me here. And she was just a liner captain."

"You'll like my family," Althor said. Another thought came to him. "You meant my family are the ones that make you nervous, yes? Not me?"

Coop smiled. "You did at first. Not now."

"Althor," Cobalt said. "Your parents and your brother Eldrin are in the hall." The holopanel in the wall next to Coop erased its mountain scene and showed a view of three people. Tonight his parents were the same height. When Althor had been young, his father had often worn boots to make himself taller than his statuesque wife, but he had eventually stopped caring that he was short compared to her family.

Althor's brother Eldrin was their oldest, out of ten children, with Althor coming next in line. Althor had long thought he and Eldrin embodied their parents' differences. Except for his violet eyes, Althor took after their maternal grandfather, with his height, massive physique, and gold coloring. Of the seven Valdoria sons, Eldrin most resembled their father. He had inherited a few Skolia traits, being broader in the shoulders and taller than his sire. But he had their father's wine-red hair, the violet eyes, even the sprinkle of freckles across his nose.

Eldrin's hands were the Lyshriol norm, four thick fingers and a vertical hinge that folded his palm lengthwise. Althor had been born with Lyshriol fingers, but without the hinge that let them oppose each other. Instead, he had a rudimentary thumb. His parents had his hands rebuilt when he was a baby, to match the human norm. It served him well; with Lyshriol hands he would have had trouble making efficient use of ISC technology.

At sixteen, Eldrin's interests were swordplay and girls; fourteen-year-old Althor had wanted to learn engineering and play sports. After he and Eldrin had a knockdown fight over a girl, their parents sent Eldrin offworld, to the Orbiter, an environment they thought more conducive to books than swords. Devastated, Althor hadn't understood why Eldrin picked the fight. Althor hadn't really even liked the girl. It was years before he realized it had nothing do to with her and everything do to with the fact that at fourteen, Althor was bigger, stronger, faster, more advanced in school, and more at ease with Imperial technology than the older brother he worshiped.

On the Orbiter, Eldrin had struggled with a culture where his skill with knives and swords was seen as juvenile delinquency rather than a source of admiration. In working with him, the education specialists began to understand why Lyshriol natives had no written language. Eldrin saw words as pictures; if the pictures weren't identical, he read them as different words. Use five different fonts and he saw five different words. The hieroglyphic languages of Skolia and Eube had so baffled him that the sixteen-year-old warrior had once slammed his broadsword into a web console. Until then, no one had realized the depth of his frustration at being unable to process what came so naturally to his "little" brother.

Nor had Eldrin understood why his stunning looks and singing voice garnered so much more attention on the Orbiter than the soldiering attributes he considered far more worthwhile. But when he realized the genuine value people placed on his musical gifts, he let himself pursue his love of singing. Known now for his spectacular voice, he wrote and sang folk ballads about their home, the village of Dalvador on the planet Lyshriol.

Althor walked into the living room just as Cobalt let in his parents and Eldrin. His mother was wearing a blue dress and her gold hair floated everywhere. His father had on his usual trousers, laced shirt, and knee boots. Eldrin wore Orbiter styles now, simple and elegant, dark pants and a white shirt.

His mother hugged him, her face glowing. "You look wonderful." She held him at arm's length. "But Althor, you need to eat more. Look how thin you are."

Eldrin laughed. "She told me the same thing."

Their father made an exasperated noise. "Roca, these boys are giants already. Make them any bigger and it will throw off the Orbiter gravity."

Laughing, Althor embraced her. "It's good to see you, Hoshma." He grinned at his father over her shoulder. "And you, Hoshpa."

His father nodded, pretending to look gruff. "Are Syreen and Eristia here?"

"Not tonight." Althor glanced at his brother. "Dehya couldn't come with you?"

Eldrin shook his head. "She's working in the web."

It didn't surprise Althor. Dehya's work as Assembly Key

left her little time for a normal life. Eldrin, as her consort, took care of their social obligations.

A rustle came from behind them, accompanied by the tread of shoes on the carpet. Althor's father turned toward the sound—and his genial expression vanished like a doused candle flame.

Coop was standing in the inner doorway. To Althor, the artist looked like a work of art himself, bathed in sunlight, his diamond earring sparkling, his beautiful face radiant.

Eldrinson spoke with stiff formality. "I'm afraid I have work on the web tonight. Please accept my apologies, but unfortunately I will have to miss dinner."

Althor swung around to him. "What? What duties?"

"My apologies." Eldrinson nodded without acknowledging Coop. He simply left the apartment then, the door snicking open for him and sliding shut after he stepped outside.

Althor stared after his father. Then he scowled at his mother. "It never stops, does it?"

"I'm sorry." She sounded stunned. "I don't know why he did that."

"Like hell. We both know why."

She started for the door. "I'll go talk to him."

"No." Althor caught her arm. "I'll do it. This is something he and I have to settle."

Coop came up to them, obviously mortified. "I'm sorry. I should go."

"You aren't going anywhere." Althor discovered he didn't have to feign his anger.

Eldrin glanced at the door, then at Coop, then at his brother. ***Althor?*** he thought. ***Do you want me to talk to Father?***

Althor shook his head. **No. I have to do this myself.**

Roca turned her diplomat's smile on Coop. "So you're the mystery guest Althor wanted us to meet." She motioned to a divan. "Come sit with me. Tell me about yourself."

Glancing back at Althor, Coop let Roca pull him to the

couch. As they sat down, Althor focused on his mother. **Can you play host for a while?**

Of course. She looked up at him. ***I truly am sorry about your father. I didn't expect that.***

Nor I, Althor lied.

So he left the apartment, and the building, and summoned a sailpath. As it carried him through the air, he thought, **Moonstone Park.**

The path landed in a sequestered glade on the outskirts of City. Althor found his father sitting on a bench under an arch of blue moonstone, among trees and flowers. A fountain gurgled nearby, but the area was empty of people, as Althor had arranged earlier this afternoon.

Eldrinson frowned at him. "You could have warned us."

Althor sat next to him. "I wasn't sure you would come." He sent a thought to his spinal node. **Basalt, verify security.**

Verification complete. Area is secure.

"Basalt checked security," Althor said. "No one can monitor us here."

"Fine." Eldrinson still sounded angry. "So no one can spy on us. Perhaps now you will tell me what is so sensitive you had to play this charade with that boy? He has no idea it was a setup, no more than your mother or brother do. They think I believe he is your lover and I'm angry because of it."

"Would you be?" For Coop's sake, Althor didn't want that scene repeated in earnest. Although he had hoped his father could get out here without arousing suspicion, he hadn't expected him to use Coop.

"Would I be what?" his father asked.

"Angry if he were my lover?"

"I would like to think I would see the best in any companion you chose." Squinting at his son, he asked, "Is he, ah—your lover?"

"He's an artist." In truth, Althor didn't know yet where he stood with Coop. So all he said was, "I'm his patron."

"Then what is this about?" Eldrinson spread his hands. "I couldn't make sense of that convoluted message you had

Basalt send me. I had to guess what you wanted. Give you an excuse to meet in private, yes? Without arousing the suspicion of all the monitors that watch us?"

"Yes." Althor stood up and paced across the glade. "What happened that night Soz tried to recapture Jaibriol Qox?"

His father blinked. "What?"

"The night Qox escaped." He turned to his father. "What happened?"

Eldrinson's puzzlement intensified, shaded by old grief. "You've seen my statement about your sister's death. Why dredge it up now?"

"I want to know why Soz was at the palace."

"I was alone there. She came up as my bodyguard."

"Why? That palace has the best security available."

Eldrinson shrugged. "Kurj ordered it. Ask him."

"When did Qox show up at the palace?"

"You're more in a position to know those details than me."

Althor kept his voice cold. "I want to hear your version."

"Why does this sound like an interrogation?"

"Just tell me."

Eldrinson watched him with a baffled look. "Apparently an ESComm special forces team freed Qox. But something went wrong. I don't know how he ended up at the palace. He got to a flier on the roof. To escape the planetary cordon, he activated the ship's stardrive. Your sister went after him and they vanished."

"How did he penetrate palace security?"

"I don't know."

"Soz must have said something." Althor tried to decipher his father's closed expression. "Security is her expertise."

"I really can't say. You know how I am with computers."

Althor understood what he meant. Eldrinson came from a world that had been isolated for millennia after the fall of the Ruby Empire. The dependence of the settlers on their ancient psiberweb proved disastrous when their technology decayed. They lost everything, even their memory of the Ruby Empire. Their focus on breeding psions went awry as the gene pool mutated and they ended up with an inability to process written language. Eldrinson was illiterate, not only with language, but with computers as well. However, psiberspace was his universe. He had no need to understand the technology. All he had to do was think. And so he did, with a facility in the web greater than anyone else alive.

"Did you work in the web the night Soz died?" Althor asked.

"No." Eldrinson studied him. "What is it you're after?"

"What about Soz?"

"What about her?"

"Did she perform any web operations that night?"

"Of course. I don't know what."

"I think you do."

Quietly Eldrinson said, "Perhaps you better tell me what this is about."

Althor came back and sat on the bench. "I want to know why Soz erased a data file on your Prime account that night."

When Eldrinson's face paled, Althor felt as if the ground dropped out from his feet. Until that moment he had, deep within himself, believed in his father's innocence. Now he knew otherwise—and it gave him an impossible choice. He loved his father more than his life. But he had a duty to ISC and the empire that depended on its protection. Why would his father have used his Prime—his hot line to the Allied president—only hours before Soz went to her death? And why would Soz, a top-ranking ISC intelligence agent, have tried to erase all trace of that communication?

Althor suddenly remembered the epileptic seizure his father had suffered four years ago, prior to the Investment ceremony. The doctors had called it a stress response brought on by his grief over Soz's death. But what if it came from some other source? Then the precautions they took to protect him against grief would have been more likely to fail.

As they had.

Althor realized he was clenching his fists on his knees. He exhaled, making his hands relax. "What could you have possibly had to say to the Allied president when Soz and Jaibriol Qox were both at the palace? Father, *what?*"

"I never spoke to President Calloway," Eldrinson said.

"You're lying."

"Althor, don't."

"Why?" He spread his hands, no longer able to maintain his impassive façade. "Gods, give me a reason *not* to."

His father said nothing. After waiting, Althor said, "The night Soz went to her death, someone used your Prime account." He stood up. "I have to take this to Kurj."

"Althor, *no*."

"I have no choice."

Eldrinson took a breath. "She's still alive."

"What?"

"Sauscony is alive."

Althor slowly sat down again. "That's impossible."

"No. It isn't."

Althor couldn't absorb the words. They refused to register. All he could think to say was, "You went through the funeral, the memorial services, my own Investment, thinking that Soz was alive?"

Eldrinson swallowed. "Yes."

"Why?"

"President Calloway helped a Skolian and a Trader go into exile together."

"What does this have to do with Soz?"

"The Trader was Jaibriol Qox." Softly he added, "The Skolian was your sister."

Althor froze. Breezes rustled the glade and a bird chirped in a tree. For the first time he realized how much more gray had appeared in his father's hair these last few years.

When Althor could finally speak, he said, "No."

Eldrinson was watching him like a man awaiting execution. "What are you going to do?"

"Father, tell me this is a joke." Althor struggled to keep his voice even. "An elaborate game. You're angry about Coop. It stirred up our old arguments and now you're doing this."

"I would never do such a thing. You know that."

"You want me to believe my sister went into exile with *Jaibriol Qox?* That you committed treason at a level so profound it undermines every principle we live by?"

"It isn't that way."

"Then tell me what way it *is*."

Eldrinson exhaled. "Qox and your sister wanted to marry."

"You're insane."

"No. Quite sane."

"Soz is incapable of loving a Highton."

"He isn't Highton."

Althor felt as if he had missed a beat in the tempo of their conversation. "What?"

"He's only one-quarter Highton," Eldrinson said. "Jaibriol Qox is a Rhon psion. The Qox Dynasty bred itself an answer to us. But he wanted nothing to do with them. Jaibriol and Soz met someplace, I don't know how. On Delos, I think."

Althor wondered if he had a problem with his hearing. "Jaibriol Qox is Rhon?"

"Yes."

"The heir to the Carnelian Throne. He is Rhon."

"Yes."

"The man destined to rule our enemies."

"Yes."

"The enemies we manage to hold off only because we are Rhon and they aren't."

"Yes."

"And you freed him."

"Yes."

"Father, I can't believe this."

"I trust him."

"Then you truly have gone mad."

Eldrinson spread his hands. "I made the best decision I could."

"How did Qox really get into the palace?"

"Soz brought him. She's the one who freed him. His

escape was detected before they could get offworld, so she took him to the last place she thought ISC would look."

It made sense, in its own horrifying way. "Surely they knew that sooner or later someone would discover them." Althor didn't add the obvious: *and execute them.*

"They knew. They thought they were going to die. I made it possible for them to live." Eldrinson swallowed. "Will you go to Kurj with this?"

Althor knew full well what would happen if Kurj learned the truth. "He'll throw you in prison for life. Maybe execute you. Then he'll find Qox and Soz and execute them."

"Yes, I think so."

"Gods." Althor got up and paced across the glade, back and forth. "I don't know what to do."

"Don't do anything."

He stopped. "The Highton Heir is out there making babies with my sister and you want me to do *nothing*?"

"Yes."

Althor shook his head. "The data isn't secured."

"Sauscony erased it."

"If you mean the session on your Prime, yes, she did. If I hadn't known so much about it because I'm your son, even I wouldn't have found it." He tapped his temple. "I mean it isn't secured here. You have information that could tear apart three empires. Unprotected information. What if someone captures you? How will you keep them from extracting what you know?"

"That's a risk we all live with."

Althor knew he could be court-martialed for what he was about to tell his father. "If I'm interrogated, my spinal node triggers my biomech web to release chemicals that block certain receptors in my brain. It prevents me from speaking. Other triggers can disrupt neural pathways, to erase my memories. I can't reveal what I don't remember."

Eldrinson blanched. "You let ISC do that to you?"

Softly Althor said, "They did it to you too. When they implanted your cyberlock."

His father stared at him. "That's obscene."

"Is it? Do you know what those triggers protect? In my case military secrets, but more than that. The Ruby Dynasty. Mother. You. All of us. If you're captured, you can't betray the people you love."

Eldrinson took a moment to assimilate it. In a quieter voice, he said, "If it protects your mother and you children, I can live with it."

Althor felt as if he were breaking. How could he betray this man who had taught him loyalty and integrity? Yet the very strengths that Eldrinson had imparted to him, through his example and guidance, now demanded he turn his father over to ISC.

Slowly Althor said, "I have, all my life, admired you."

"I'm sorry if I've destroyed that."

"You haven't, Father." Althor paused. "You say you made the best decision you could. I must do the same."

Eldrinson tensed. "And?"

Althor exhaled. "We never discussed this. Jaibriol Qox and Sauscony Valdoria are dead."

Color returned to Eldrinson's face. "Thank you."

Althor thought of the first time he had gone into battle. At sixteen, before he went offworld to attend military school, he rode once with his father's army. In addition to his Lyshrioli weapons, a sword and lance, Althor had also taken a laser carbine.

And so he had ended war on Lyshriol.

One carbine destroyed the balance of power among the peoples of the entire continent. No Lyshrioli weapon could stand against it. His father had become a legend then, the man who wed a golden woman from the stars and sired giants who commanded the lightning. People came from all over to honor him.

As they had done then, so now Althor knelt to his father. He swore his loyalty and his silence, but this time in doing so he committed treason against the empire he was destined to rule.

8

In the gazebo at the top of the tall tower, an arched opening in one wall stretched from floor to ceiling. Ur Qox stood in front of the archway, gazing out at the Jaizire Mountains of Glory. His Razer bodyguards were posted around the gazebo and a quasis field shimmered in the open space before him. Outside, mist hung over the tangled hills, eerily quiet, with a hint of mystery. It was a lush scene, richly green and wild, with tendrils of luminescent fog curling in the air and around the foliage.

A rustle sounded behind him. Turning, he saw Lieutenant Varque, a member of the ESComm unit that had accompanied him to this mountain retreat. Varque wore a gray uniform with blue stripes down the trousers, crimson braid on his sleeves, and a gunmetal slave collar. He knelt on one knee, his forearm resting on his thigh, his head bowed.

"You may rise," Qox said.

Varque stood and bowed. "My honor at your esteemed presence, Your Highness."

"Is Senator Tarrington waiting in the guardroom?" Qox asked.

"Yes, sir."

"Very well. Bring him up."

After Varque left, Qox turned back to watch the veils of mist.

A muffled tread of feet behind him soon interrupted the silence. After several minutes, Qox turned. Senator Jack Tarrington was waiting in the center of the gazebo, flanked by four ESComm soldiers. A tall man with gray-streaked dark hair, Tarrington was a huskier, older version of his son.

He wore a dark suit, drawing no attention to himself, and he knelt to the emperor with far more grace than had his son three years ago.

Qox spoke in Highton. "You may rise."

Tarrington stood and bowed, with the subtle flourish of his left fist placed at his waist, thumb pointing to the right to indicate optimism. Qox noted the detail. This Allied politician had taken the time to learn nuances of Eubian protocol.

"Attend me," the emperor said.

Tarrington came over and they stood side by side, watching the mists. "I hope your accommodations are sufficient," Qox said.

"Superb, Your Highness." Tarrington spoke Highton with a lilting accent. "Your hospitality has no equal."

It was the usual flattery, and expected, but still, this senator had enough savvy to learn Highton protocol, which was more than could be said for most Allied or Imperial citizens.

"What think you of the treaty negotiations so far?" Qox asked.

Only the barest stiffening in Tarrington's posture betrayed his reaction. He was here to observe the Eubian-Allied treaty discussions being conducted in Qox's luxurious hunting lodge. Given the inauspicious state of the stalled negotiations, it would be interesting to see how the senator responded: say too little and he offended an emperor; say too much and he compromised the negotiating position of his people; choose a poor turn of phrase and he compromised himself.

"We have optimism," Tarrington said. "Particularly in the auspicious grace of Glory."

Qox almost smiled. *We have optimism;* the traditional Aristo phrase had many meanings, depending on context. Here it was shorthand for an older and more baroque phrase: *I honor your authority, esteem your name, stand in awe of your magnificence, and will say no more.* What it really meant was *I won't tell you a thing, but I'll do it in language ornate enough for an emperor.* The praise of

Glory, ancestral home of the Qox Dynasty, was an unnecessary but well-chosen diplomatic note.

"How is your son, Jessie?" Qox asked.

"He does well, Your Highness, thanks to your benevolence." Genuine gratitude showed on Tarrington's face. "He graduated from Yale this year. With honors."

Qox nodded. The informal *thanks* didn't translate well into Highton and the *with honors* could have been omitted; he had no interest in the little awards the Allieds bestowed on their children. But the senator otherwise spoke well, his flattery predictable but with an attention to protocol that showed his respect more eloquently than the clichéd words themselves.

According to Qox's informants, Tarrington's son had taken a year off from his studies and spent it in therapy, recovering from his "trauma." Qox had ordered the "pirates" sentenced to prison after a well publicized trial presided over by the High Judge herself, Calope Muze, one of Qox's distant cousins. In private, Qox commuted the sentences and compensated the crew for their trouble. Having met Jessie, he understood why the frigate officers had acted as they did, even if they had tried to cover it up later. They were half Aristo. That they felt the need for a provider was a natural result of the elevated blood in their veins. And Jessie was practically shouting for Aristo attention, with the way he exuded such empathic strength.

Qox clasped his hands behind his back and looked out at the mist-shrouded hills. "I can appreciate the joy in seeing one's son thrive."

"Our children are our immortality," Tarrington said.

An interesting response. Immortality. Qox would have thought it more a Eubian concept. Allieds and Skolians exhibited little urgency in keeping their bloodlines true. They tore themselves apart with their differences while Hightons grew ever stronger in their uniformity. Odd to think that the Ruby Dynasty came closest among them to attaining a true bloodline, with their desperate attempts to produce viable Rhon psions by inbreeding. But such matings only further weakened them.

Qox knew what most Hightons refused to acknowledge, that inbreeding also sapped the Hightons of their vitality. He had long suspected that his superior acuity derived from his more varied genetic makeup. An irony indeed, if what gave him the edge to conquer the Ruby Dynasty came from the same source as their treasured Rhon traits. It was fitting that they should, in that manner, participate in their own subjugation.

He considered the senator. Tarrington was a politician and politicians had agendas. However, he was proving himself reasonably adept at the intricacies of Highton interaction.

"Your son is an impressive young man," Qox said. The boy had certainly impressed Viquara.

Tarrington inclined his head at the compliment. "Jessie admires you."

Qox read far more than Tarrington realized he revealed with that comment. Subtexts of gesture, face, and body accompanied his words. Tarrington had recognized his son's hopeless passion for the empress. He also saw that Jessie respected Ur Qox despite his unrequited desire for the man's wife. That Jessie admired a man he had every reason to hate, in both personal and general terms, impressed Tarrington far more than any accolades.

Qox wondered what Tarrington would think had he known that same emperor had monitored every "private" walk Jessie took with the empress, every meal they shared, every moment they spent reading insipid poetry. He had watched Jessie bid the empress good-bye, watched him embrace her and swear his undying love. Viquara wept prettily in his arms, vowing to treasure his memory even though they could never see each other again. Qox suspected she hadn't even been acting all that much. She did want the boy, though her idea of what to do with his charms rather differed from what he envisioned.

So Jessie returned home, with a far different story of Eube than the malice spewed by the Skolian propaganda machine.

"I like your son," the emperor said, which was true, in its

own way. "And I know what it is like to lose such a joy in one's life." That too was true. "If I played some small role in sparing another that knowledge, I am pleased."

Quietly Tarrington said, "And in that, you have my deepest gratitude."

Qox watched the mist. "We have a saying among my people: 'Mutual appreciation paves the road of knowledge.' "

"As well it should," the senator said.

So. Tarrington was willing to trade. Although the Allied intelligence agencies were less efficient than their ESComm counterparts, the Allieds had a different relationship with Skolia and so acquired different data on the Skolians. Valuable data. As Tarrington well knew.

"It is unfortunate the negotiations stalled on the question of Allied trade autonomy," Tarrington said.

"Indeed," Qox said. An interesting change of subject. The terms the Allieds wanted on trade autonomy were absurd. Freedom to export to Eube, with no taxes? It brought to mind the maxim that wars were fought more by banks than by armies. If this was the price for whatever intelligence Tarrington offered, the senator wanted a treaty concession far greater than any the Allieds had so far extracted from Eube.

"The worth of paving a road depends on where the road leads," Qox said. He had no intention of making concessions until he knew what Tarrington offered, just as he knew Tarrington had no intention of giving him data without a guarantee that any bargain they made would be upheld. So they had a dilemma.

The senator considered him. "I've been encouraged by the progress the teams have made in the mediation of property rights in Onyx Sector."

Another interesting change of subject. The question of what belonged to who in Onyx Sector was one Eube wanted settled more than the Allieds, who had few holdings there. The negotiators were close to an agreement, but a well-placed word from Tarrington could destroy the accord. So he offered a solution to their dilemma: Qox agreed to the export concession, Tarrington gave him the information, Qox honored their agreement, Tarrington stayed out of the Onyx Accord. If Qox reneged, Tarrington destroyed the Accord.

"Perhaps my people have been too stubborn on this matter of export," Qox said. "Together with the Onyx Accord, a new export treaty will benefit both our governments."

"Indeed it would." Although Tarrington hid his triumph, Qox detected it. The senator had driven a hard bargain and won.

They were both silent for a while. Then Tarrington said, "My son requested I bring you a letter."

"It is charming of him to write," Qox said. When Tarrington pulled a computer ring out of his coat and gave it to him, Qox added, "I am glad we were able to meet, Senator."

Tarrington bowed, recognizing the dismissal. "I am honored by this audience, Your Highness."

So you should be, Qox thought. Still, the man had handled himself better than Qox expected.

After the guards escorted Tarrington from the tower, Qox sent for his Trade Minister, Kryx Quaelen. Then the emperor took out his palmtop. Tarrington had taken into consideration the difference in Eubian and Skolian standardization, providing a ring that fit a Eubian palmtop.

The letter from Jessie came up on the screen. It was short, a well-phrased greeting to the emperor and empress. Qox easily ferreted out the hidden files and read them with far more interest than he had read Jessie's letter.

A rustle came from the entrance. As Qox looked up, a tall man entered, a Highton with broad shoulders and eyes as cold as red ice. He bowed, fist at waist, thumb extended.

"My greeting, Kryx," Qox said.

"My honor at your presence, Your Highness," Kryx Quaelen said.

The emperor considered him. Quaelen was the one who would actually sign the export agreement with the Allieds. As Trade Minister, he oversaw the merchant guilds run by the Diamond Aristo castes. Qox knew many Hightons questioned his appointing Quaelen to a position of such power. Quaelen's great-grandfather had married a Silicate Aristo instead of a Highton, a scandal that reverberated for decades. Although the Quaelen family had since maintained an impeccable bloodline, the stain remained. Privately, Qox suspected it was why Quaelen did his job well. Just as forbidden Rhon genes enhanced Qox's abilities, so forbidden Silicate genes enhanced Quaelen.

Qox motioned the minister forward. "I had an interesting meeting with Senator Tarrington."

Quaelen joined him. "A taciturn man."

"His son sent me a letter."

Dryly Quaelen said, "How charming."

Qox gave a slight smile. "It seems Skolians like Mozart."

"Who is Mozart?"

"An ancient Earth composer." Qox paused. "I learned a most interesting fact, just before you came in. You can use the works of Mozart to define transformation maps for sequences of time-varying complex variable functions."

Quaelen snorted. "A game for mathematicians."

"Indeed." Qox lifted the palmtop, as if testing its weight. "Think of the possibilities it offers for encryption."

"An encryption scheme without encrypted messages to translate has little use."

"True," Qox said. "Just as intercepting encrypted messages without a key to unlock them has little use." ISC changed their codes often, almost always before ESComm broke the code. Whether or not ISC would ever use the Mozart Code remained to be seen. For that matter, it may have already been retired. But if they did use it, and ESComm picked it up, the pirated data would be available in a timely manner.

Only the future would tell them if the sweet strains of Mozart were worth their price.

The halls beneath the Wilderness Palace were smooth black glass, tunnels far underground in the Jaizire Mountains. Antique lamps shed dim light on the severe Razers who walked with Qox. In his black uniform and military boots, the emperor became an austere shadow in the dark hours of the night.

Qox knew he had earned the reward he allowed himself now. His work with Tarrington had ramifications beyond their bargain; it helped counter ISC propaganda. Each such success further established the truth for the Allieds, that Aristos were nothing like the monstrous caricatures imagined by Skolia. Each success further revealed the hysteria behind the Ruby Dynasty's fevered crusade to destroy Eube.

Qox stopped before an obsidian door. It opened into darkness. When he touched the gauntlet around his wrist, a signal went to sensors within the room. In one corner, a dim light appeared, making a glint on the floor. As the light spread, the glint resolved into a metal chain stretched across the stone. A rodent ran across the links and disappeared into the gloom.

Dampness saturated the air. Moisture collected on the walls and formed drops that ran down the stone. The expanding sphere of light reached a rectangular steel frame, half a meter high. The chain ran over the frame to a steel ring embedded in it.

Two hands took form out of the shadows.

The wrists were chained to the ring, palms facing outward. The expanding light revealed slender arms and a length of yellow hair looped over one elbow. Then the head came into view. The girl was lying on her back, unclothed, her arms pulled over her head. Yellow curls surrounded her face, a beautiful face, delicate and sweet, with gigantic eyes. A gag covered her mouth.

The frame pushed her upper back into an arch, then angled down to put her hips level with his. Chains secured her neck and long legs to the steel struts. His bodysculptors had further refined her exquisite shape, augmenting here, cinching there, rounding as needed.

The emperor closed the door of the dungeon and motioned his guards to posts around the walls. He walked to the frame, the martial clip of his boots echoing in the cell. When he stopped by the girl's shoulder, she stared up at him with sapphire eyes. He had selected the unusually intense color himself, from the palette offered by the Silicate pavilion where he bought her.

"Don't be afraid, Cirrus." He had named her after the wispy clouds. "Reassure yourself with the knowledge that by raising me to a higher state of existence, so you elevate yourself."

A tear leaked out of her eye and ran down her temple, where it soaked into her hair. Qox touched the dampness, then raised his finger to his lips and tasted it. "To reach elevation is never easy, love. That is what makes it worth attaining."

A table stood next to the framework, with tools laid out for him. He chose a leather-handled quirt. When he snapped the whip across Cirrus's torso, she gave a muffled cry and her pain surged out from her mind, magnified by her empathic strength. His Aristo brain picked it up and sought to increase his pain tolerance by directing the neural impulses to his pleasure centers. Transcendence swept over him. Ah yes, his choice of Cirrus had been inspired tonight. He had barely begun on her and already she was providing for his needs.

The emperor felt at peace, knowing that today he had taken another step in establishing the truth for the Allieds, that the Hightons of Eube formed an honorable people of good character, rather than the monsters hallucinated by the Ruby Dynasty.

IV

Year Fifteen

371 ASC on the Imperial Calendar
394 EG on the Eubian Calendar
A.D. 2274 on the Gregorian Calendar

9

Everyone helped build the orchard fence. They climbed the green and azure hill, wading through spatula grass, beneath a blue-violet sky with only Blue shining in its arched dome. Up this high, Jai could look out over the mountains that plunged and rose in great folds, in every direction, as far as he could see.

Jai watched the procession wind up the hill. Six-year-old Vitar led them all, carrying a big rock and running around his exasperated sister. At the mature age of eleven, Lisi considered herself too dignified to give in to her brother's antics. Finally Vitar took off up the hill, hair streaming out behind him, black curls that turned wine-red and ended in gold tips. He glanced back, laughing, his face classic in its Highton bone structure.

Lisi chose a more sedate pace, carrying her bigger rock. Her hair fell around her shoulders, a glossy mane of red-gold curls much like that of the grandmother she was named for. She had their mother's green eyes.

At fourteen, Jai was almost as tall as his father and still growing. Across his broadening shoulders, he carried a wooden staff he had carved himself. Nets filled with rocks hung from each end.

His full name was Jaibriol Valdoria Qox Skolia. Jaibriol III. He preferred "Jai," having outgrown the "Jaibird" that his parents, in their more annoying moments, still used. He had the red eyes and classic features of a Highton Aristo. His hair, however, had a normal healthy sheen, rather than the Highton glitter. When he spent time in the sun, the tips turned gold.

Vitar reached the top of the hill and dropped his rock on

the pile there, then spun around and made faces at Lisi. She clunked down her own rock and took off after him, laughing as they ran. When Jai reached the pile, he eased his staff onto the ground. As he unloaded the boulders, his father came up next to him. Jaibriol II carried a similar load to his son, but with a heavier staff and bigger nets that held more stones. He smiled at Jai, his pride in his son's work obvious in the tilt of his head, in his thoughts, in the crinkle of lines around his eyes.

Their mother came into view, hiking up the hill, her hair blowing in the breeze, all the way to her waist now. She wore a fur skirt, fur boots crisscrossed with thongs, and a spiderpouch silk shirt their father had made for her birthday. Jai thought it silly to have birthdays set by a "standard" calendar with no relation to the real year, but he liked the celebrations.

She carried the carbine slung over one shoulder and a bow and quiver on her back. Instead of balancing a staff on her shoulders, she pulled a sled loaded with rocks, its towing cables attached to a halter around her torso. In the worn sling resting on her hip, del-Kelric slept with his thumb in his mouth.

Jai's father finished unloading his boulders and turned to his wife, his face gentling as she handed him the baby. Del-Kelric gurgled at his father and went back to sleep, content in his father's arms. While Jai helped his mother unload the sled, Vitar ran around them and Lisi ran after Vitar, both shrieking with laughter.

"Enough already!" their father said.

Soz laughed. Then Vitar plowed into her and almost knocked her over. Watching her regain her balance with enhanced speed, Jai wondered again if he would ever become that fast. His mother said no, it was something she had done before they came here, out in the universe he had read about in EdComp's holotexts.

It was hard to believe anything existed "out there." EdComp insisted it was teaching him different languages:

Iotic, the ancient tongue of the Ruby Empire, spoken by almost no one now but the Ruby Dynasty; Highton, spoken by Highton Aristos and their providers; Skolian Flag, a universal tongue designed for an empire with as many languages as it had peoples; Eubian, or Eubic, the Trader equivalent of Skolian Flag; and the Allied languages English, Spanish, and Japanese. It all seemed one big language to Jai, easy to learn.

His mother stretched her arms, then walked over to examine the site where they intended to build the fence, about twenty meters away. The forever chattering Lisi and forever running Vitar went with her.

Jai's father glanced at him. "Shall we sit?" He settled down on the pile of rocks, holding del-Kelric in his lap. As Jai sat down by his father, del-Kelric opened his eyes and drowsily contemplated his big brother.

"I enjoyed reading your essay on Aroclean philosophy," Jaibriol said.

Pleased, Jai sat up straighter. "I spent a long time on it."

"It shows." Jaibriol smiled. "EdComp tells me you're doing university-level work now."

Jai felt his shoulders tense. *But I'll never see a university.*

It was a moment before Jaibriol answered. ***Your mother and I have discussed this.***

Jai didn't like the sound of that. *Your mother and I have discussed this* usually meant unwelcome changes, such as when they decided he had to study music composition. *Discussed what?*

What to do now that your children are growing older. You need companionship.

Relief touched Jai. He had harbored doubts his parents would understand how he felt. *Will we leave here to find more people?*

Your mother and I must stay. But if you children are careful, we think you can go.

That caught Jai by surprise. His family was part of his mind. They couldn't separate. *I don't want that.*

Nor do we. Ours is one of the only Rhon communities in existence. He paused. ***Perhaps, when you are older, you could leave to find a wife. If you wished, you could return here with her.***

A Rhon wife.

Regret shaded his father's thoughts. ***The chance of your finding a Rhon woman is almost nonexistent. But you can find someone to love.***

How will I look?

We can use the neutrino transmitter. A ship might pick up the signal and come here.

Might?

We have no guarantees.

What if they won't help? Jai paused. *What if they want to do harm?*

That risk always exists. His father glanced at his mother, who was pacing out an area for the fence while Lisi and Vitar ran around her. Smiling, he turned back to Jai. ***If I were them, though, I wouldn't wish to anger your mother.***

Jai grinned. *She'd make them study music composition.*

His father's face gentled. ***If that is the worst you can imagine, you are a fortunate fellow.***

I read, Hoshpa. Jai frowned. *I know what books say people do. It makes no sense. Why would people hurt each other? Do you think it is stories? "Literary devices"? I have been studying this with EdComp.*

Literary devices? Jaibriol swallowed. ***I pray, my son, that the universe will always seem so gentle to you.***

Del-Kelric started to fuss. When he reached out his pudgy arms to his brother, Jai laughed and hefted him into the air. "You're turning into a giant, Kelli." He set the boy on his knees and thumped his legs up and down, making the delighted del-Kelric bounce. Then Jai grinned at his father. "I'll bring back a wife and we'll make babies. We'll have a whole community. All psions."

Jaibriol smiled. "It is a nice dream."

"It's not a dream. Even Hoshma is optimistic. She's decided to name her spinal node."

His father stared at him. Then his face gentled. "That is indeed good news."

Jai looked at his mother. She was lying in the grass now, with Vitar climbing on her as if she were a pile of logs and Lisi sitting next to her, talking, talking, talking. Jai wondered where his sister found so much to talk about. It didn't matter. He liked watching them. He would leave Prism to find someone to share this. Then he would bring her home and life would go on as it always had, the days and nights, the crops and livestock, and the people he loved.

Barcala Tikal, First Councilor of the Assembly, stood by the wall of polarized glass in Kurj's office. A few meters away, Kurj leaned against the glass with his massive arms crossed.

"When President Calloway was in office, we knew where we stood," Tikal said. "Ever since the Allieds elected this new president, everything has shifted. The Allieds openly express doubts as to the stability of the Ruby Dynasty. They even question whether Trader pirates exist anymore. They think ESComm cleaned them all up."

Kurj snorted. "Then they're fools."

"The Traders are fighting this war with propaganda." Tikal pushed his hand through his hair. "Earth isn't about to jump into bed with Eube, but we're beginning to look like an even worse choice for an ally, an unstable government doomed to fall. We have to change our approach. No more dire prophecies. We must woo them."

"Diplomacy is an Assembly function," Kurj said. "Talk to my mother. She's the expert."

Tikal cleared his throat. "The Assembly has, ah, spoken with Councilor Roca."

Kurj frowned. What was this? The Assembly had met without his knowledge? He needed new web monitors. Barcala and his cronies must have figured out how to outwit the ones Kurj had spying on them. Tikal had to be up to something; otherwise he wouldn't be hiding his mind with such strong mental barriers right now.

"We've set up a program of reforms," Tikal continued. "Most of the changes we can implement ourselves. There are, however, a few matters that we, ah—need your cooperation on."

Kurj kept his arms crossed. "What?"

"It has to do with your image."

"What image?"

"Your public image."

"I don't have a public image."

"I'm afraid you do. We would like to soften it."

Kurj scowled. "I don't have time for 'image.' "

"We will take care of everything for you."

"Take care of what?"

Tikal spoke in a rush, as if to get it all out before Kurj stopped him. "We want you to marry. We have several candidates in mind, all lovely women. Charismatic. Beautiful. The type of woman who will capture the hearts of people everywhere." Hastily he added, "And yours too, I'm sure."

Kurj stared at him. "This is a joke, right?"

"Not at all."

"The answer is no."

"The Assembly passed it as a resolution. You can't say no."

"What, you voted to force me into an arranged marriage?" Kurj made an incredulous noise. "The last time you all tried that, it ended in disaster."

"What disaster? The Iceland Treaty is still in effect."

Kurj had no wish to repeat the history. The Iceland Treaty had been established 135 years ago by the arranged marriage of Dehya and Seth Rockworth, an Allied naval officer chosen for his high rating as a psion. Earth wanted an alliance and marriages were how Skolians made alliances, so Seth became Dehya's consort. After years of grappling with the intrigues of the Imperial court, Seth said "enough," went home to Earth, and divorced his Pharaoh wife. Given that the treaty was tied to the marriage, neither government acknowledged the divorce, even after Seth remarried and Dehya gave in to the Assembly's demands that she take Eldrin as her consort. It left them with the bizarre situation of having two major interstellar figures living in apparent violation of accepted social custom.

As far as Kurj was concerned, the treaty wasn't worth the trouble it caused. For all its many volumes, the closest it came to a pledge of military support from the Allieds was a promise to help protect the Ruby Dynasty during times of war.

"We don't need another Iceland Treaty," he said.

"This isn't." Tikal walked over to him. "The Allieds are listening to ESComm propaganda. They think the Ruby Dynasty is a mess." When Kurj glowered at him, he held up his hands. "I'm just telling you what they think. Everyone knows the survival of the Imperialate is tied up with your family. We have to convince the Allieds that the dynasty is stable."

"So tell them the truth. ESComm is lying."

"It isn't working. We sound shrill. We need a positive approach. Allieds look at *image.* Give them a good show and half the battle is won."

"For gods' sake, Barcala. I'm not an entertainer."

Tikal launched into an obviously prepared spiel. "We will take care of everything. A full Imperial wedding, all the pomp, flourishes, and splendor. A great show. We'll find you a bride who exudes charm and glamour. Someone to, ah, polish your image. We play up the fantasy, the dream, the romance. Afterward we ease her into position as spokeswoman for you. You and she will have beautiful children, of course, and she will be a wonderful mother. The Allieds love this sort of thing."

Kurj stared at him. "You're out of your flaming mind."

"All our research points to this as a more effective means of dealing with the Allieds than our current propaganda against the Traders. You needn't do anything. We will do it all."

"I choose my own women."

Tikal spoke carefully. "The woman you marry will know this is a political arrangement. Your, uh, intimate preferences remain your choice. In private of course."

Kurj scowled. "In other words, I can cheat on this bride all I want as long as I keep it secret?"

"What you do in your private life is your business."

"My marriage isn't my private life?"

"Take some time. Think about it."

Dryly Kurj said, "I'm afraid to ask what you have in mind for Dehya's 'image.' "

Tikal squinted at him. "Actually—we can't find her."

"What do you mean, you can't find her?"

"No one knows where she is."

The conversation was becoming more surreal every moment. "She's on the Orbiter."

"No one there has seen her," Tikal said. "When we send her web mail, we only get automated responses."

"You see her in Assembly all the time."

"Only as a holographic simulacrum."

Kurj snorted. "Maybe she doesn't want to see you." At the moment, he didn't blame her.

"I don't think you understand," Tikal said. "She isn't *anywhere.*"

"Then have a spy monitor locate her." He knew the Assembly had less chance of spying on Dehya than smoke in the wind. Even he couldn't do it.

"Our monitors can't find her either," Tikal admitted.

Kurj regarded him curiously. "So what you're telling me is that you and all the Assembly can't find the Assembly Key."

"Well, yes. That about sums it up."

He laughed. "She'll get in touch. When she wants to."

"Kurj, this is serious. No one has seen her in three years."

It occurred to Kurj that he hadn't seen Dehya in a while either. "She's a shadow, Barcala. You can't manipulate a shadow. It has no substance."

"Can you contact her? In person, I mean."

"Maybe." All he had to do was go to the Orbiter and walk the few hundred meters from his house to hers. At the moment, however, he felt disinclined to help the Assembly on anything. "Why do you want to talk to her?"

Tikal made an exasperated noise. "She's the Ruby Pharaoh, for gods' sake. Our hereditary leader. The position may be titular now, but she has a responsibility to let the people know she *exists.*"

Kurj wondered if the Assembly had any idea how thoroughly Dehya had infiltrated the web. She ruled in ways the Assembly never knew, playing the strands that tied together an empire. Shadow Pharaoh.

"If I see her, I'll relay your message," Kurj said.

"I appreciate it."

After Tikal left, Kurj sat at his desk and entered the psiberweb. Thousands of messages waited for him. His routines were dealing with most of it, responding according to macros lengthier than many of the actual messages. The queue marked for his personal attention only contained ten letters.

Mail server, attend, he thought.

Server 1 attending.

Send mail to Assembly Key Selei. "Icon is Sophocles." End.

Message sent.

Good. Kurj turned to his personal queue. The first message was from Admiral Starjack Tahota, now in command of Onyx Platform, the massive ISC base in Onyx Sector. She wanted him to speak at a ceremony honoring a group of soldiers for their bravery. Although Kurj liked to attend such ceremonies, he rarely had time. Normally his aides dispatched an ISC officer to stand in for him. If Tahota herself requested his presence, though, this must be an impressive group. He still couldn't go; it was scheduled at a time when he had other commitments. But he could send Althor, his heir, as his representative.

Kurj wrote Althor a note and attached a proposed itinerary. Then he sent it off, scrambling it with the Fling cipher.

I have a response from Assembly Key Selei, Server 1 thought. Shall I read?

Go ahead. Kurj thought.

Message is: "Sophocles wrote the icon."

Sophocles? He and Dehya had been at this for fifteen years and he had yet to figure out what icon she meant. He had no doubt she changed the target from time to time, either because he was getting too close or because her interpretation of whatever she was getting at changed. Kurj didn't really expect to uncover the answer. The communication served more use in giving him insights into the current workings of her mind.

Send message, he thought. He searched his memory for characters in plays of Sophocles and picked a name at random. **"Jocasta is the icon." End.**

Message sent, Server 1 thought.

Cirrus lay on a padded table, listening to the murmur of voices as Qox and his ministers worked across the emperor's office. They had pulled several divans around a table and holographs lay scattered on the furniture. Several ministers had gold dinner platters balanced on their knees.

The chill on Cirrus's bare skin made her shiver. Izar Vitrex, the Minister of Intelligence, had returned to the divan and now sat with his head leaning back, his eyes closed. The others were deep in their meeting, intent on their files and palmtops, planning strategies against the Allieds.

Qox glanced at Vitrex with a hint of a smile. Then he turned to Trade Minister Kryx Quaelen. "Your pleasure, Lord Kryx?"

Quaelen looked up. "My honor at your hospitality, Your Highness." He set his platter on the table, moved his shoulders to work out kinks, then stood and bowed to the others.

Then he walked across the room to Cirrus.

Alone in the privacy of the emperor's personal suite, after a luxurious bath, with her hair washed and a soft wrap around her body, Cirrus felt relief. The worst was over. All she had to do now was report, a far easier task than keeping her mind open while the emperor's advisers occupied themselves with her.

If a Highton offered the hospitality of his possessions to his guests, then political expediency disguised as etiquette required they treat his property well. So Cirrus wasn't physically hurt. But she hated them all.

When she had been the emperor's favored provider, she had taken refuge from him in her mind, creating a mental sanctuary where she wandered among gleaming white columns near a lavender sea, talking with ephemeral beings. Eventually Qox lost interest in her. After that she lived a quiet life in her small house on the palace grounds, imagining her sanctuary.

One day she realized that as she talked to her imagined beings, she was also talking to herself, out loud. She stopped doing it, and after that she began to recover. For the first time in her life she actually enjoyed being alive. She began to visit with the elderly slave who lived on the other side of the garden, a woman who had provided for Qox's father and now lived in peace, ignored by the current emperor.

Then Qox called for her again, this time because he wanted a child. Eventually she gave birth to a son. Qox came every ten days to visit them, a formal and distant emperor who spoke to his son with adult words the boy rarely understood. Qox still sent Cirrus to the bodysculptors to keep her appearance the way he liked it, but he otherwise ignored her. Her next seven years were spent in contentment, raising her son.

Then Qox wanted her for yet another reason. She was one of his most powerful psions, rated eight on the Kyle Scale. Only one person in every hundred million had a mind as strong as hers. So now she waited in his suite, curled into a fetal position on his sofa.

After a while, Qox came in and strode over to her. He sat down, then pulled her into his arms and slid his hands inside her wrap, over her washed and perfumed body.

"You feel warm," he said.

Cirrus made herself smile.

He leaned his head back on the couch. "What do you have for me tonight?"

"Minister Vitrex's baby son."

Qox yawned. "Everyone knows Vitrex has an heir."

"He doesn't." She hesitated. "Have an heir, I mean."

That got his attention. He lifted his head. "Meaning?"

"The boy isn't his son. It was sired on his wife by one of her providers. She didn't want her baby to be a slave so she bribed the genetics team to lie." Cirrus was unsure about the bribe; like all Hightons, Vitrex knew how to fog his thoughts when he was with a provider. "She had the boy altered to look like a Highton."

"So." Qox gave her an appraising look. "This could be useful. If it bears out."

Cirrus flushed. "I swear I would never make up—"

"I know." He set his fingers against her lips. "You've done well."

"There's more."

"Yes?"

"It's Trade Minister Quaelen." She hesitated, knowing useful information would be rewarded but afraid to stir his anger. Even if his ire was against someone else, she was the one here. "What he thinks and the way he acts have great differences in them."

Dryly he said, "If you find this a revelation about people, you have lived an even more sheltered life than I thought."

"It's his thoughts about you, Your Highness."

"Indeed?"

"He—well, he only pretends to honor you."

"And inside he loathes me. I've known this for years." Qox tugged down her wrap, pushing it to her waist. "Quaelen does a good job as Trade Minister. He remains loyal because I have always ignored the stain on his name." Bending his head, he kissed her, his hand on her breast. "But he hates us all, knowing we are pure Highton and he is not."

"He considers himself pure Highton."

"I suppose." Qox bit at her ear. "Anything else?"

"Minister Quaelen still thinks about your heir."

The emperor froze. "Jaibriol?"

"Yes." She could mean no one else. The empress had yet to produce another heir. Whispers in the palace claimed she was barren, that the deceased Jaibriol II would be her only child.

"What exactly does Minister Quaelen think?" Qox asked.

"I'm not sure," she admitted. "It was fuzzy. Old memories. I reminded him of Lord Jaibriol for some reason."

"Ah, Cirrus." Qox sat back from her. "I am sorry to hear you say that. Truly sorry. I have been fond of you."

As soon as she saw his face and felt his emotions, her world stopped. She had just signed her death warrant. But *why?* What had she done?

One mistake showed itself immediately. She had told the emperor that one of his ministers had compared the Highton Heir to a slave. It was a deep insult to the Heir's esteemed memory. But to kill her for that?

It hit her like ice water. If Minister Quaelen compared Jaibriol Qox to a provider, it implied the Highton Heir had the blood of a slave. That such a suggestion was false made no difference. If it became known that one of Qox's powerful ministers believed it, it could start rumors no sane emperor dared risk.

And if it were true?

Qox walked to the nightstand by the bed and took a syringe gun out of its top drawer. Desperation swept Cirrus. Minister Quaelen was Highton, one having proven use to the emperor, an Aristo with his own political machine, the most powerful after the palace. She was nothing, only a provider, easy to dispense with.

As Qox came back to her, Cirrus grew frantic. "Please. I'll never tell anyone."

"I'm sorry." Qox looked genuinely troubled. But he sat next to her and set the syringe against her neck.

She talked fast. "What about the next provider you use to spy on your advisers? What if she isn't as loyal as I am, if she doesn't tell you what she learns, but repeats it to others? How can you ever again risk using a provider to learn Quaelen's secrets? At least you and I know this now. You know you can trust me." She willed him to believe her. "You can trust me."

"I doubt it," Qox said. But he lowered the syringe. "Very well. You will continue to watch Quaelen for me. But you will stay here with your son, in a room off my suite, and see no one."

"Thank you, Your Highness." Her voice shook. "You have my loyalty and my gratitude forever." She knew he still might eventually kill her. But she had given herself time, enough to think of new ways to extend her life.

10

Kurj's shuttle slowed on approach to the Orbiter, matching velocity and acceleration to the metal world. With one rotation every ninety seconds and a diameter of four kilometers, the sphere's hull moved at eight kilometers per minute. For a conventional habitat, cylindrical or wheel-shaped, the shuttle could have come in at a center hub that didn't rotate. For the Orbiter, no "hub" existed, so ships docked in the outer hull.

Kurj wondered why the Ruby Empire engineers had chosen a less conventional form for the Orbiter. The ancient habitat had survived many millennia since the fall of the empire, but the reason for its design was lost. After ISC found the ruined habitat drifting in space, they worked long and hard to remake it—for the Orbiter contained the First Lock.

Without Locks, the psiberweb would cease to exist. Telops, the telepathic operators trained to use the psiberweb, could access the web from any console, if it had the correct equipment, but the web's creation and maintenance required the Locks. Three existed. Kurj had used the Orbiter Lock to join the Triad. The Second Lock was on Raylicon, ancestral home of the Ruby Empire, one of the best protected planets in the Imperialate. The Third Lock was a space station currently at Onyx Platform. To protect the Lock, the Onyx military complex had grown to twenty-three stations, becoming the largest ISC base—which was why ESComm had turned its interest to Onyx Sector, pushing its boundaries.

The huge door of a docking bay in the Orbiter hull rolled open. The shuttle pilot fired a burst from the rockets, using chemical fuel to maneuver, rather than the antimatter drives adapted for more open space or the inversion stardrive.

After the shuttle moved into the bay, robot arms clamped around it, anchoring the ship in place while the great door closed. As soon as an atmosphere tube fastened onto the shuttle air lock, the craft emitted its only passenger: Kurj Skolia. The Imperator had boarded the Orbiter.

Kurj found the Assembly councilor he sought in a lodge shaded among a grove of trees within Valley, the private mountain retreat of the Ruby Dynasty. Silent and unobserved, he stood on the wooden balcony that bordered the second level inside the building. The room below was also wood, mellow and gold, with an antique quality to it, a luxury here where they used almost no wood. Bars lined one wall and mirrors another. A golden woman in a blue leotard, pink tights, and a filmy blue dance skirt was spinning across the room in pointe shoes, her movements as light and graceful as the tendrils of hair that had escaped her bun.

Kurj had always loved to watch his mother dance. A memory came to him; he was five, going with his father to see her perform with the Imperial Ballet under the stage name Cya Liessa. It had been a magical night, with a small boy enthralled by his beautiful, beloved parents. Strange how he had forgotten that.

Roca stopped in midspin and looked at the balcony. "My greetings, Kurj."

"Mother." He went down the wooden steps that descended from the balcony. "You dance better than ever."

A smile gentled her face. "You're being kind." She wiped her face with a towel she took from a wooden chair near the wall. "I never have time to practice anymore, with my Assembly duties."

His voice cooled. "And when did your Assembly duties extend to my private life?"

She stopped toweling herself. "Barcala talked to you about the wedding."

"You knew about it?"

"Only after they made the decision. They wanted me to tell you." She sat down and began untying her toe shoe. "I told them it was their decision and their funeral, so they could flaming well tell you themselves."

Kurj rather enjoyed the image of his diplomat mother, usually the essence of tact, cussing at Barcala Tikal. He settled in the chair next to her and stretched out his legs. "Have you talked to Dehya recently?"

"This morning." She pulled off the shoe and began winding its ribbons around it. "In web mail."

"I mean in person."

"It's been a while." Roca stopped winding her ribbons. "A long time, actually."

"How long?"

"Months?" She stared at him. "That can't be right."

"What do you think she's doing?"

Dryly she said, "With all those *paras* of hers, who knows?"

Kurj understood the reference. Some schools of thought in neuroscience held that the greater density of neural structures in a psion's brain could enhance intellect. It depended on the structure and distribution of the *paras*. Dehya's brain apparently maximized the effect. No one knew the full extent of her intelligence. The last tests, done in her adolescence 150 years ago, had put her into the genius range. Since then her mind had continued to evolve.

"She sent me a strange message," Kurj said.

"Strange how?"

"It said, 'You are right.' "

Roca laughed. "From Dehya to you, that is strange."

"She meant I finally picked the right icon."

His mother took off her other shoe and began wrapping its ribbons. "What icon?"

"She's trying to tell me something." He blew out a gust of air. "For all we know, she's dead and she left an EI running on the web to simulate herself."

Roca nearly dropped her shoe. "You think she's *dead?*"

Before he realized what he was doing, he had laid his hand on her arm, the first time he had touched her in years. It felt like an electric shock. She went rigid, then pulled away from him.

Disconcerted, Kurj withdrew his hand. "She's not dead."

Roca spoke uneasily. "What is all this about icons?"

He tried to frame an answer for something he wasn't sure he understood himself. "Making peace. I think."

"With ESComm?"

"No. Myself." Kurj stared across the room. For a century he had focused his existence on building ISC. He had given up all semblance of a normal life, hardened his mind, crippled his capacity to love, all to make ISC what it was today. And it wasn't enough. Even the Assembly wanted more from him.

"Do you remember the ruins we used to visit with Father when I was a boy? Before he—" The word *died* stopped on his tongue. "Before he was gone?"

"SunsReach? I remember."

"I had the entire planet classified as a wilderness sector."

"Whatever for?"

"To keep it untouched. No one can go there without my permission." He made himself turn to face Roca. "You and I have too many ghosts. We need to make peace before it's too late. But I can't here. Too much history lives in this place."

She watched him as if he were a cipher. "I've never heard you talk like this."

"Come to SunsReach with me. Help me settle the ghosts while we still can."

"Kurj, don't."

"Don't what?"

"Talk like you're about to die."

"I've no intention of dying, I assure you."

She looked at her shoe, turning it over and over, watching its ribbons flutter. "I don't think it wise I go alone with you to such a remote place."

"I won't—trespass against you. You have my word." It was the closest he had ever come to acknowledging the labyrinth of emotions he negotiated where she was concerned.

"Eldri will object," she said.

Kurj suspected that for his stepfather Eldrinson, "object" would be a mild word for his reaction to Kurj's request. "I will swear your safety to your husband as well as to you."

She looked up at him. "I need to talk to him."

"Of course." He stood up. "I leave for SunsReach tomorrow. If you decide to come, I will be in the Skyhammer ruins." He bowed to her and left the studio.

The sun was setting as Kurj walked out into the rustling glades of Valley. It took only a few minutes to reach Dehya's home. Built into a hillside, the house stood shaded within a grove of trees. Colors from the sunset glowed on the pale door, like a soap bubble film.

Kurj touched a gilded leaf on the door and a bell chimed within the house. After several moments he tried again, with no more success. But as he was about to leave, the door opened. His half brother Eldrin stood in the archway, rubbing his eyes.

"Kurj?" Eldrin blinked at him. "My greetings."

"Did I wake you?" Kurj asked. "I can come back later."

Eldrin smiled. "Don't do that." He stood to the side. "Come in."

Goldwood furniture set with white satin cushions graced the airy living room. Sunshine sifted in through the windows, dappled by the trees outside.

Eldrin went to a faceted crystal cabinet in one corner. "Would you like a drink? Rum?"

"No. Just water." Kurj knew how Eldrin had wrestled

with alcohol in his youth, during his troubles adjusting to life on the Orbiter. Eldrin never drank now, a choice Kurj respected.

His brother poured water into two crystal goblets and brought one to Kurj. Sitting on the couch, Eldrin studied his face. "You look tired."

"A little."

Are you all right? Eldrin asked.

"Fine." Kurj didn't want to shut him out, but he couldn't relax his barriers.

Even so, his half brother's presence soothed him. Roca and Eldrinson had named Eldrin for his father, dropping the "son" rather than inflicting "Eldrinsonson" on him. For the first year of Eldrin's life, Roca had lived on the Orbiter without her husband. So Kurj had watched Eldrin grow. He had rocked his brother to sleep in his arms, comforted him when he cried, fed him, even cleaned him. In one of the more painful ironies of his life, it was his love for Eldrin that had finally convinced Roca it was safe to return to her husband, that Kurj would never harm the father when doing so would harm the son.

Tonight they talked about a ballad Eldrin was working on, improvements to the house, and a letter from his son Taquinil, an economics professor at Imperial University on Parthonia.

"He talks 'meta' this and 'micro' that," Eldrin said. "I've no idea what he's saying. Dehya seems to understand, though."

"She saw the letter?" Kurj asked.

"Well, yes. Of course."

"Then you've talked to her?"

Eldrin smiled. "I hope so. I live with her, after all."

"When was the last time you saw her? In person, I mean."

"This morning."

Tension eased out of Kurj's muscles. Until this moment he hadn't realized the doubts he harbored about Dehya's life. "Is she all right?"

"Well, yes." Eldrin looked puzzled. "Why wouldn't she be?"

"No one else has seen her for months. Years, even."

His brother laughed. "That can't be true."

"She's always in the web," Kurj pointed out. "What is she doing?"

"I'm not sure, actually. Lately she's been talking about mathematics and precognition." Eldrin rubbed his chin. "She claims it's impossible to tell where mathematical extrapolations of the future leave off and precognition starts. Then she told me that she would always find an escape route for us."

Kurj went very still. "An escape from what?"

He shrugged. "When I asked, she laughed and said it meant nothing, really, that she just thought I might like to write a song about that theme."

"That doesn't sound like what you write." Most of Eldrin's songs were folk ballads about his homeland.

"When she's ready, she'll tell me what she means."

"Let me know what she says," Kurj said.

Eldrin gave him a dry smile. "If it makes sense?"

"Even if it doesn't." Over the years Kurj had become adept at deciphering the often cryptic results of Dehya's accelerated thought processes.

Eldrin regarded him curiously. "Any news with you?"

"It seems I am getting married," Kurj said.

"What! Who is she?"

Kurj scowled. "The Assembly has several candidates in mind, women of the appropriate style, diplomacy, and charisma, none of which it seems I have, according to our esteemed governing body. My input isn't required."

Eldrin's smile faded. "Oh."

"Yes. My reaction."

"Perhaps she will please you."

"Perhaps I won't do it."

Eldrin spoke carefully. "Legally, you have no power to refuse the Assembly. Their law is the law of the Imperialate."

"So they say."

Eldrin paused. "Have you decided what you will do?"

"Perhaps." Kurj left it at that.

After their visit, Kurj walked through the growing dusk to the magrail station. It was dark when his magcar reached his destination, one of the less upscale apartment complexes in City, if any building in that architectural work of art could be called anything but upscale. He went to a bronze door graced by delicate gold leaves. When he touched the bell, a chime came from inside. He waited, then tried again.

No response.

"Steel acknowledge," Kurj said.

"Attending." The voice belonged to a City-wide computer that answered only to him, that indeed no one else knew existed, except probably Dehya.

"Open this door," Kurj said.

The door slid open. Kurj entered a living room decorated in gold and bronze, all in shadow except for light sifting through the open doorway.

"Shall I turn on the lamps?" Steel asked.

"No. Just close the door."

The bedroom was small, filled by the bed, with a wardrobe crammed against one wall and a console in one corner. The shadowed form of a small person made a mound in the big bed.

Kurj sat on the bed and touched the woman's shoulder. She stirred, and sighed in her sleep. He removed his boots, then undressed and set his clothes in an ordered pile on the floor. Then he slid under the covers and drew the woman into his arms. Her filmy nightdress felt soft under his hands. As he took it off, she spoke sleepily. "My greetings, Kurj."

"And mine, Ami."

Her face had matured in the eleven years since he had first seen her as a page in the War Room, but it had never stopped mirroring her gentle nature. It wasn't beauty that kept him coming back to her, long after he usually forgot his favorites. If that had been all he wanted, there were far more spectacular women he could have taken to his bed. Ami was the only person he knew who liked him exactly as he was. She wasn't a politician, an actress, a highborn noblewoman, or a diplomacy adept. She was simply a page who loved him with uncomplicated affection.

They made love in the bronzed shadows. When they finished, the Imperator of Skolia asked his sometimes mistress, an orphan with the most common birth imaginable, to be his wife.

Althor met Syreen and their daughter Eristia in Syreen's apartment. They all stood in the airy living room, drinking cider and making small talk. Eristia gleamed in her silver jumpsuit, with the Dalmer Shipping logo emblazoned in blue on her shoulder.

"So, Captain Valdoria." Althor heard the catch in his voice and took a swallow of cider to hide it. "How does it feel to have your own ship?"

Eristia laughed, her eyes as green as a forest. "It only has a two-person crew."

"Only?" Syreen waved her hand. "Twenty-four years old and already she has her own ship. And she says 'only.' "

"Oh, Hoshma," Eristia said.

Althor smiled at the familiar *Oh, fill-in-title-of-parent* phrase. But he was breaking inside. For twenty-four years his daughter had lived only a few hundred meters away from him. True, in the past few years her duties with the shipping line had taken her on extended trips. But always she came back. Today ended that. Today she became captain of her own ship and left home forever, to make her way in a universe she wasn't ready for.

Actually, in his more candid moments, he had to admit his daughter was perfectly capable of taking care of herself. If anything, the universe wasn't ready for Eristia Leirol Valdoria. He had given her the Valdoria name, acknowledging his paternity, never really understanding that part of his paternal duty meant letting her go when the time came.

After they finished the cider, they walked to the magrail and rode out to the Orbiter hull. Eristia and Syreen chatted and Althor listened, afraid that if he joined in his voice would catch again. He had never been good at small talk anyway. Syreen and Eristia had never seemed to mind his taciturn inclinations, as if they knew the affection he felt even if he couldn't express it well.

In an observation module above the docking bay, he and Syreen waited while Eristia donned her environment suit. It fit her like a skin, with a power module in the belt. Then she grinned and saluted them. "Captain Valdoria reporting for duty."

Althor smiled. "I used to be Captain Valdoria."

"Not anymore." She gave him a hug. "Come ride on my ship sometime, Hoshpa."

"I will." His voice caught, despite his efforts to stop it.

"Oh, Daddy," she murmured, her eyes filling with tears. "I love you."

"And I you, Podkin." Realizing what he had said, he added, "I mean Eristia."

"That's all right," she said. "You can call me Podkin."

Eristia hugged Syreen next. And then it was time for her to go.

As they watched their daughter stride out to her ship, Syreen spoke gently. "She's like you were at that age, Althor."

He swallowed, hit again with a familiar surge of relief that his daughter had chosen a civilian route to her dreams. How had his own parents endured it, knowing that every time he went out he could die in combat or be captured? More than ever he understood their relief when Kurj put him behind a desk.

After Eristia's ship left, Althor and Syreen rode the magrail back to City. They were quiet for most of the ride, but toward the end Syreen said, "She turned out well."

"Yes," Althor agreed. "She did." He could hardly contain his swell of pride.

After another stretch of silence, he asked, "Will you stay in the building?" With Eristia gone, Syreen was free to go where she pleased. As much as Althor had wanted them to live near him, he had made clear from the start that he would never force Syreen to remain in City against her will or use his influence to take Eristia away from her if she left.

That she had chosen to stay for so many years meant more than to him than he knew how to say.

Her face gentled. "It's a good building. Besides, Eristia will come home for visits."

Althor grinned. "Then we'll have to listen to her say, 'Oh, Hoshma,' and, 'Oh, Daddy.' "

Syreen laughed. "That we will."

They parted at City, having affirmed that their friendship remained strong even without the glue of a daughter. Althor rode to the other side of the Orbiter and went to his office within the hull. He strode through the spacious outer rooms, nodding to his multitude of assistants, crossed the expanse of his own office, and entered his private web chamber. As he settled into the control chair, its exoskeleton folded around his body and snicked psiphon prongs into his spine and neck, through pores in his uniform. Then he entered psiberspace.

The web spread around him in hills and valleys made from a grid, the crisscrossed strands varying from cables of intense activity to filaments on the periphery of his awareness.

Today the atmosphere glowed with vibrancy. **Father?** he thought.

The "air" answered him. ***My greetings, Althor. Did Eristia leave?***

Yes. Althor let his joy and sadness suffuse the web.

Ah, well. She will always be with you. Just as you are with us.

Father, did I ever say, "Oh, Hoshpa," to you?

Puzzlement tinged the atmosphere. ***I don't think so. Why do you ask?***

Althor smiled. **I just wondered if it was hereditary.**

His father sent him a sense of laughter. Then his awareness faded as he returned to his work.

As a psicon, Althor lay down on his back and called up his mail on the "sky." Web traffic was heavy now, slowing response with what telops called bytelock. So it took his mail a while to appear. It formed in an unexpected font, the headers made from glistening ice that split the virtual sunshine into rainbows. Bemused, Althor smiled. Coop had been designing new fonts for him again. Althor generally chose a more utilitarian style, but he discovered he liked this one. In the years since Coop had moved in with him, the artist had often enhanced his life in these small ways.

Programmed macros had dealt with most of his messages, but one from Kurj waited for attention, a revised itinerary for his visit to Onyx Platform. He approved the schedule, scrambled the message with the Fling Code, and sent it to Kurj.

Warning. That came from an ISC security monitor. Fling Code no longer secure.

That gave Althor pause. *No longer secure* meant evidence existed that someone had broken the code or compromised its security. **Cancel Fling. What else do you have?**

Recommend Wagon Code, the monitor thought.

Wagon isn't complete.

You would be the first to use it.

Will the receiver have the keys to decode it?

Probability is 62 percent.

Do you have anything with a higher reliability?

One of the banked codes.

Give me a list. Banked codes were a select few that had never been used, the intent being to keep a reserve for situations such as this.

A list of psicons appeared in the air, including one of a man bent over a page of music. The Mozart Code. The description intrigued Althor. To scramble a message, the code dismantled glyphs into their constituent lines and transformed each line according to a random set of complex variable functions that varied with time. Once every microsecond, the code produced microkeys that specified the functions needed to convert the hodgepodge back into a message. It sent those keys to memory cells within the ISC web, the locations specified by a master key of complex functions. The master key required yet another key, the Mozart Key, to decode it. That key consisted of a selection of music and was what the web actually transmitted into space.

Unless someone knew how to look, finding a Mozartcoded message was almost impossible. Too many billion renditions of his music graced interstellar space, sent by everyone from professors to lovers to ad agencies to corporations. Add to that the arcane form of the code and its intricate hierarchy of keys, and it produced an almost unbreakable cipher.

Use Mozart, Althor thought.

Scrambling, the monitor answered. Message sent.

Satisfied, Althor turned his attention to his other work.

11

First Councilor Barcala Tikal threw the holographic printout on the table. "It is utterly, undeniably, without question, *unacceptable.*"

Four of the eleven Inner Assembly councilors were sitting at the conference table in the Strategy Room on the Orbiter: Stars, a vibrant woman with silver-dusted hair, the councilor concerned with transportation; Nature, a former physics professor who now served as a science and technology councilor; Industry, a man of dark hair and immense energy; and Judiciary, an iron-haired woman in dark trousers and shirt, a former judge known for her rigid adherence to Imperial law. The blocky oval table where they sat was made from transparent plastiglass and packed with web components made from precious metals and jewels.

The other councilors preferred to stand. Slender and graceful in her middle years, Protocol leaned against a gleaming goldwood wall of the room with her arms crossed. Life stood by another wall, a hale man with a strapping physique who oversaw health, human services, and education. Planetary Development was next to him, her dark eyes scanning the others. Finance paced up and down the room. Tall and thin, he had a mind as sharp as the profile of his face and a mechanical left arm packed with implants he used to monitor the economic state of an empire. Domestic Affairs was sitting on the edge of the table. Youngest of the Inner Assembly, she oversaw the office that dealt with relations among Imperialate worlds.

Standing by a web console near one wall was the councilor for Foreign Affairs—also known as Roca Skolia.

So they made up the powerful Inner Circle of the Imperial Assembly, the civilian body that governed Skolia.

"Unacceptable it may be," Judiciary said. "But it's legal."

"The hell it's legal," Tikal said. "Annul it."

"On what grounds?" Judiciary asked. "We have no law that says we can dissolve the Imperator's marriage against his will."

Tikal scowled. "Then make one."

"And after we set this precedent of creating arbitrary retroactive laws designed solely to suit our purpose?" Judiciary said. "Then what?"

Stars made an incredulous noise. "Our decision was anything but arbitrary."

"I've spoken to the woman, Ami," Protocol said. "She is perfectly willing to help us."

"I don't see that we've grounds to annul it," Life said. "They've apparently, ah, completed the requirements."

Domestic Affairs snorted. "If you mean consummation, they completed that requirement years ago."

"She's too common and too inarticulate," Finance said.

"We can augment her education," Planetary Development said. "Terraform her intellect, so to speak."

"Talk to her sometime," Domestic Affairs said. "She's so sweet you could make candy with her. That's what we're looking for, isn't it?"

"She's too short," Tikal said. "She'll look ridiculous next to Imperator Skolia. He's two feet taller, for gods' sake."

"So we'll put her in high heels," Protocol said.

"You'll need stilts," Judiciary muttered.

"This all could have been avoided if he had cooperated with us." Tikal walked over to Roca. "Does the phrase 'the greater good' have no meaning to him?"

Roca met his gaze. "Don't tell me that my son hasn't acted in 'the greater good.' " She looked around at the others. "When even one of you can say you've done half as much as Kurj for 'the greater good' of Skolia, then you can come to me with your complaints."

Nature spoke quietly. "No one wishes to disparage your son, Councilor Roca. But he has left us in a quandary."

"So I see," Roca said.

"Why did he marry her?" Tikal demanded. "To make a point?"

"Maybe he loves her," Roca said.

Silence greeted her words. The councilors, however, had the prudence to keep private their thoughts concerning the Imperator's ability to love, or lack thereof.

Industry spoke. "If we take this as an accomplished deed, our next step is to work with this woman, prepare her for her future role."

"She's willing to go through with whatever wedding ceremonies we want," Protocol said. "I rather had the impression she was looking forward to it."

Tikal considered Roca. "Can you bring her to us?"

"She's staying with my sister Dehya and my son Eldrin," Roca said. "Until Kurj returns. After that, you can talk to them both."

"Returns?" Stars frowned. "From where?"

"He's gone on retreat," Tikal said. "On SunsReach."

Domestic Affairs stared at him. "The day after his marriage?"

"Who is running ISC?" Stars said.

"Starjack Tahota," Tikal said. "And the Imperial Heir is on his way to Onyx Platform. But the Imperator isn't in seclusion. Both Admiral Tahota and Prince Althor are in contact with him on SunsReach."

"Even so," Industry said. "This strikes me as an ill-chosen time for a retreat."

Roca made an incredulous noise. "All he asks is a few days. This is one of the only breaks he's taken in *decades.* Just when *is* a well-chosen time?"

No one had an answer.

Ur Qox sat at his desk frowning over the request from Intelligence Minister Vitrex for an audience. It wasn't the request that surprised Ur Qox, but rather its form:

> Weep softly for the lord
> Who weaves his love like vines;
> Where tendrils all curled,
> With the Heart intertwine.

What was Vitrex up to? With subtle innuendo, Qox had been hinting to Vitrex that he knew the truth: the Vitrex "heir" was a bastard fathered by a provider who belonged to Vitrex's wife, Sharla Azer, a doctor and geneticist. Qox suspected Vitrex had given in to Sharla more for her well-placed Azer connections than for any passions in his heart.

Establishing the boy's parentage had proved difficult. Cirrus had been wrong about how Azer falsified it; rather than fabricating test results, Azer had tampered with his DNA. She couldn't change it enough to make him into Vitrex's genetic son; such would require more alterations than the child could survive. She would have more luck cloning Vitrex, as other Aristos had cloned themselves to secure what they considered the best heir. But clones or near-clones lacked the diversity needed among a people already plagued by inbreeding. Which Sharla Azer probably well knew.

So instead she altered only those DNA sequences needed for the tests that would verify him as a Highton Aristo. Those were no few in number, however. If Qox hadn't known where to look, he doubted he would have uncovered the truth. But he knew—for he had done the same for his own son, as his father had done for him.

The emperor paged his security lieutenant. "Bring Minister Vitrex to my office." Qox had summoned Vitrex to the palace earlier, and the minister had since been waiting on the emperor's call.

Vitrex soon arrived, escorted by Razers. His narrow face was composed, but his excitement coiled in the room, ready to snap.

Qox dismissed the guards and motioned Vitrex to a ruby chair. Usually brocade cushions softened its hard surfaces, but today Qox had removed them. After Vitrex was settled and the office secured, Qox raised the parchment with its calligraphic rendering of Vitrex's message. "Poetry, Izar?"

"I've always appreciated the discretion of verse," Vitrex said.

The emperor considered him. "As I appreciate the discretion of my office." Vitrex must know no one could eavesdrop on them here.

Softly Vitrex said, "They call his father the Heart of Skolia."

Qox tensed. The Heart of Skolia could mean only one person. Eldrinson Valdoria. The Web Key. "Go on."

"The tendrils of love," Vitrex said. "What father wouldn't weep at the loss of his son?"

As far as Qox knew, Valdoria had lost none in his herd of oversize sons lately. The only dead one was Prince Kelric, who had disappeared sixteen years ago. "Do you refer to any son in particular?"

Vitrex leaned forward. "Althor Valdoria."

"Yes?"

"Mozart, sir."

The room suddenly seemed quiet to Qox. Waiting. Poised. "I know of a code by that name. It unscrambles messages."

"Indeed it does." A slow smile spread across Vitrex's face. "Including the itineraries of Imperial Heirs."

Qox took his time absorbing that. The Intelligence Minister had just given him reason to let Vitrex keep the secret of his false son.

The emperor spoke quietly. "Bring me Althor Valdoria, Izar, and your line will forever remain esteemed among Hightons."

Kurj sat with his back against a tower and gazed across the plaza at the remains of another tower. Not all the lost Ruby colonies had survived their isolation. Only ruins remained on SunsReach, including these at Skyhammer, which had finished its decline by about Ie 1400 on the Ruby Calendar, 2200 B.C. on Earth, six centuries after the collapse of the Ruby Empire.

Skyhammer's architecture went up rather than out, in crooked towers, narrow and asymmetrical, or stems topped by great bulbous heads, or towers with rooms on the outside rather than in. Plazas separated them, paved with stones that had cracked and crumbled over the centuries, giving way to yellow grass.

The orange sun shone in a dark blue sky and warmth suffused the day. With an almost circular orbit and no tilt to its axis, SunsReach would have enjoyed an eternal spring had it belonged only to the star Topaz. But Topaz was part of a binary system, two stars that took centuries to go around their center of mass. At the closest approach of Topaz and its companion Amber, SunsReach became inhabitable to human life. Skyhammer had fallen into ruin because it had lost access to the fragile Ruby technology that protected it from the ravages of its parent stars.

Although on human time scales the world had a stable orbit, eventually it would decay, perturbed into destruction by its parent stars. SunsReach had probably been put into its orbit by Ruby planetary engineers, for an arcane purpose long since forgotten. Ruby technology had enriched the oxygen-thin atmosphere, but over the millennia the oxygen concentration had gradually been decreasing again. Days were short, only fourteen hours total.

Alone in the ruins, Kurj waited for introspection to occur.

When it didn't, he went back to work. He spent most of his first two days inside the tower where he had laid out his bedroll, reading reports and web mail on his palmtop.

On the afternoon of his third day, he decided to try introspecting again. Perhaps it would work this time. So now he sat and stared at the towers across the plaza. His parents had brought him here when he was five, and they had all climbed the bent tower together, running up its stairs, laughing the whole time.

"Father."

Kurj said the word. *Father.* He had loved Tokaba Ryestar, a scout who pushed back the boundaries of known space. Then one day Tokaba pushed too hard and the boundaries pushed back. He died in the blazing crash of his ship on an uncharted planet.

Kurj had been six. Held in his mother's arms, he had cried until he felt broken. As a boy, he knew only that he loved his father; as an adult, he recognized the integrity, strength, and emotional depth of the man who had inspired that love.

When Kurj was eight his mother married Darr Hammerjackson, an athlete of great fame. Kurj had seen Darr as a powerful hero. But that wondrous exterior masked a rage neither Kurj nor his mother expected, one made all the more painful by Darr's ability to twist the emotions of others with his empathic skills. Kurj once grew so enraged by the emotional manipulation that he beat the walls in his bedroom until he broke his fist.

Now, after a century of dealing with the Traders, he better understood what he and his mother had faced. With Darr they had lived, on a far smaller scale, the abusive relationship Skolia now suffered with Eube.

Kurj's mother Roca was a daughter of the Ruby Dynasty, descended from towering warrior queens who owned and often outmassed their husbands. When only she faced the violence she hid it, shamed by her situation. She hoped to change Darr, believing if only she tried hard enough, he would love his wife and stepson the way Tokaba had loved them.

Then came the day when Darr turned his anger against Kurj. At ten years of age, growing at a phenomenal rate, Kurj had been almost as tall as Darr, with a build that already showed signs of the monstrous physique he would have as a man. When Darr beat him, Kurj fought back, driven by the fury of so many nights spent lying in bed, forbidden to leave his room, forced to listen to his stepfather's violence against his mother.

He and Darr nearly killed each other.

Unlike the Skolian-Eube war, their situation had a solution. Roca pressed charges and Darr went to prison. Kurj's physical wounds healed, but even empathy couldn't bridge the silence that grew around mother and son. In the cruelty of his rage, Darr had accused Kurj of coveting his own mother; in the confusion of a youth torn by loss and grief, Kurj feared he spoke the truth. Hating Darr Hammerjackson, he hated himself, and in doing so he withdrew from everyone who loved him.

Now in the ruins of SunsReach, he acknowledged for the first time why he so often ran war games in the Hammerjack star system, blasting apart its planetoids. As the sun sank below the too-close horizon, he realized he had brooded the entire afternoon. If this was introspection, he could do without it. For decades he had banished Darr from his thoughts. Now the memories refused to stop. Was that what drove him so hard against the Traders—the fury of being forced to relieve the nightmare of his youth on a galactic scale?

"Enough," Kurj said. He returned to the tower and ordered his biomech web to put him to sleep.

In the morning he communicated with Starjack Tahota on the Orbiter, sent a message to Althor en route to Onyx Platform, and worked on his palmtop. When Kurj realized he had reorganized the same files four times, he quit and went to sit outside again.

So. Had he made peace yet? Apparently not; he felt worse than yesterday.

Peace indeed. How the flaming hell could he make peace? For the first thirty-five years of his life he had kept the image of Tokaba in his mind, admired and beloved, a man who earned respect simply by being himself. When the urge to grasp for power lured Kurj, he denied it, thinking of Tokaba's example.

In those days, a Dyad had powered the web: Lahaylia Selei, the Ruby Pharaoh who founded the Imperialate, and her husband, Kurj's grandfather Jarac, a giant that Kurj so resembled they could have been brothers. It wasn't coincidence that Jarac and Lahaylia had minds dramatically different from each other, just as did Kurj and Dehya. If the psions in the powerlink were too similar it set up a resonance like a driven oscillator, forcing their minds into greater and greater fluctuations until the link shattered.

So Kurj denied his drive to join the powerlink and focused his energy on ISC, until he commanded the Imperial military in all but name. Yet still he coveted his grandfather's title. Yes, he coveted it, with a passion he found difficult to admit even now. But he remembered Tokaba and controlled his ambition.

Kurj knew by heart the histories detailing Tokaba's life for the public. He had read every overwritten, melodramatic word, how the Assembly searched for a Rhon man suitable to marry the beauteous Roca Skolia, a hero who together with the golden lady would produce golden Rhon children. Fodder for the web, though none of the histories put it so bluntly.

No Rhon candidate turned up, so the Assembly chose Tokaba instead, a suitably heroic figure who carried all the Rhon genes, but most unpaired. Left to chance, it was unlikely his Rhon genes would all pair with those Roca carried. So the geneticists helped matters along. Never mind that Rhon psions were so sensitive to genetic manipulation that even clones died. Never mind the vanishing probability of finding a man like Tokaba or the even smaller probability that he could produce a viable Rhon heir. History offered Kurj as living proof it had worked.

History lied.

Kurj wished he had never come to SunsReach. Once begun, the damned introspection refused to stop. As the sun descended in the sky, he relived the day in his thirty-fifth year when he had found and restored a lost cache of files in the Orbiter web. It had been erased by experts decades before, but a buried trace remained, enough for him to get back the files.

It was all there. All of it. Medical records. Fertility analysis. Genetic maps. Tokaba's DNA came nowhere near a full set of Rhon genes. The Assembly had nothing to do with his marriage to Roca. Her parents arranged it because they knew Tokaba would make a good husband. The hoped-for source of Rhon children? Not Roca and Tokaba, but Roca's parents, Lahaylia and Jarac, the Ruby Pharaoh and Imperator, their extended youth giving them a faint hope of fertility beyond what nature granted.

Roca and Tokaba couldn't have children, Rhon or otherwise. It was common among couples where the people came from colonies that had been isolated for millennia. Fertility declined.

The hidden truth of Kurj's conception turned out to be far less benign than the public histories. Desperate for more Rhon children, the Assembly had sent an agent to the clinic that both Kurj's parents and his grandparents were using in their waning hopes for children. Unknown and unseen in the night, that agent fertilized Roca's egg with Jarac's seed and labeled it with Tokaba's name. The next day, the unsuspecting doctors implanted the egg in Roca's womb. Everyone rejoiced when the pregnancy took. Roca thrived and delivered a healthy baby.

A Rhon baby. Kurj.

In his thirty-fifth year of life, Kurj learned the truth. Tokaba Ryestar had almost no Rhon genes. He couldn't be Kurj's father.

Jarac had sired him. Kurj was his grandfather's son.

His world shattered. His memory of Tokaba became a sham. Already wracked with the legacy of Darr's accusations, Kurj saw his true parentage as the ultimate betrayal. He had refused to believe his grandfather committed no crime, that none of the parties involved even knew what had happened.

Blinded by a sense of betrayal so overwhelming it was drowning him, he went to the Orbiter Lock and forced himself into the link that powered the web. He turned the Dyad into a Triad.

Kurj's life had made him a harsher man than his grandfather. But they were matched in the quality of their thought processes: power without nuance, pragmatic, taciturn, literal, blunt. The Triad couldn't support them both.

The link imploded, tearing itself apart from within. Rather than see Kurj die, Jarac gave his own life to the web. On an isolated observation deck of the Orbiter, holding Jarac's head in his arms, Kurj wept while his father died.

Now Kurj sat in silence. It was dark, only a faint line of light on the horizon to mark the day's end. Tears dampened his face. He cried for all of them, for the beloved father he had lost, for the father who had betrayed his love, for the father whose love he had betrayed, and for the father now who would have loved him, given the chance, but instead paid the price of his stepson's ravaged heart.

12

The ISC *Destrier* rode through space. The destroyer carried an array of weapons: Annihilators, tau cannons, Impactors, Dusters, lighter artillery. A flotilla escorted it, eight Wasp corvettes, four Cobra frigates, four Leo dreadnoughts, and eight Jag starfighters. Humans crewed ten of the ships and Evolving Intelligence computers commanded the rest.

The ships all inverted in formation, circumventing the speed of light by adding imaginary components to their velocities. They thus avoided the light speed singularity, where mass became infinite compared to slower objects, length shrank to nothing, and time stopped. Light speed blocked sublight ships from the superluminal universe the way an infinitely tall tree blocked a road. So the flotilla left the road and went around the tree.

Faster-than-light travel did allow ships to travel pastward relative to the sublight universe, but it made a poor time machine. Ships going that fast ended up a long way from home by the time they reached their destination in the past, and coming back in space also sent them to yet another time. The paradoxes about a pilot going back to stop his own birth turned out to be red herrings. The Lorentz transformations of special relativity linked *all* reference frames; an event in one frame had to be consistent with observations of it in every frame, as specified by the equations. That included everything in the pilot's rest frame. If his current self had killed his earlier self, he would have already experienced it.

As it turned out, ships that tried to reenter normal space earlier than when they left it either failed or vanished, perhaps into an alternate universe where they couldn't tamper with their time line. *Within* the superluminal universe, however, a ship could go pastward or futureward. It played havoc with communications. A fleet that inverted in formation came out of superluminal space with its ships spread out in both space and time.

Enter the web.

Before *Destrier* inverted, its telops linked to the psiberweb. It let them communicate in superluminal space, making it possible for the flotilla to reenter normal space in perfect formation. Shrouds hid the ships; films on their hulls created illusory star fields, scramblers deceived electromagnetic probes, and shadow generators confused neutrino probes. Moving at constant speed, using thrusters only to correct course, and communicating only through telops, they sailed on, silent and invisible.

Althor Valdoria sat in the command chair suspended in

the stardome above *Destrier*'s bridge. The officers below worked at consoles, running checks. It was standard procedure to drop into normal space during long voyages and clean up errors that had accumulated during superluminal travel.

Incoming message via the web, *Destrier* thought.

Receive, Althor answered. The message downloaded into his spinal node, a note from Kurj at Skyhammer verifying a change in training maneuvers Althor would conduct at Onyx.

A warning entered his mind: **J** frigate emerging from inversion, starboard. **Q** frigate to port.

Stats on the ships poured into Basalt, Althor's primary spinal node. A second later a voice on the comm in his ear said, "**Q** frigate to port and **J** frigate to starboard."

Althor spoke into the microphone that extended to his mouth. "Web chatter on Node 11." It identified the channel that would print a log of the flotilla's psiberweb communications, for crew members who couldn't access psiberspace.

Prime Annihilators, Althor thought.

Primed, *Destrier* answered.

"Node 11 active." That came over his ear comm, verifying that the *Prime Annihilators* command had appeared on the computer log. *Destrier* identified the speaker as Major Hooklore, Althor's first officer.

Althor's communication with the *Destrier*'s EI brain took only a fraction of a second. It went by so fast his mind perceived the communication as numbers and verbal symbols rather than as full words. The log of the entire exchange appeared to flash into existence all at once on Node 11:

Tau cannons loaded, *Destrier* thought. Dusters primed.

Backup 6, Althor thought.

Impactors primed as backup.

Fire pattern G8 now.

Annihilators fired.

An accelerated beam of antiprotons hurtled through

Destrier's focusing chambers, picking up positrons, and shot into space, seeking matter to annihilate. Both *Destrier* and the **J** were traveling close to light speed, so *Destrier* aimed for the expected intersection of its beam with the frigate's path rather than at the frigate itself. Beam weapons were easier to evade than missiles, but made a better offense against quasis shields. A ship in quasis couldn't change its quantum state, not even by one particle, so ideally weapons fire couldn't affect it. But quasis collapsed after a few hits, and annihilating matter in quasis was easier than exploding it with missiles.

Annihilator hit on **J**, *Destrier* thought. No damage. Then: Impactor hit on ISC Wasp One.

The **J** frigate fired its Annihilator at *Destrier*—

Quasis jump, *Destrier* thought. Annihilator hit on deck 47. To shield against the hit, *Destrier* had gone into quasis for two seconds. To Althor, it seemed as if no time elapsed; hence the "jump."

Damage report, he thought.

Basalt linked him to *Destrier*'s EI brain, which linked then to picowebs in other ships, all at light speed. With a direct connection to his brain, the simulation provided sensory input so authentic it felt real. He moved alongside a Wasp and touched its hull, rubbing its pitted surface.

Wasp One, he thought. **Report.** It was one of his crewed ships.

Fine, Commander, its telop answered. *We lost an inversion engine, but we've two left. Releasing abdomen.* His human thoughts had more life and character to them than the communications from the EI brains in the ships, but he came across with less power than did Althor, who wielded the mental force of a Rhon psion.

Barely more than two seconds after the frigate attacked, the Wasp's abdomen hurtled after the fleeing **J** at relativistic speed. It caught the frigate and drilled through its buckling quasis fields. Then its Klein bottle collapsed and its antimatter plasma exploded outward, taking the frigate with it. Debris hurtled in all directions. The **J**'s fuel bottles collapsed and pieces of the ship vanished with the bizarre *gulped-away* effect of real matter sucked into complex space.

J frigate destroyed, *Destrier* thought. During the explosion, *Destrier* had gone into quasis for one second.

Don't destroy the Q, Althor thought. **Capture it.** He wanted to know how the hell the frigates had found them.

Annihilators fired—

Quasis jump, *Destrier* thought. **Q** frigate damaged.

Both the **Q** and *Destrier* came out of quasis in the same instant—and rather than be captured, the crippled frigate blew itself up in a blast of silent energy.

Quasis jump, *Destrier* thought. **Q** frigate destroyed.

Althor swore. Now he would never know how the frigates had found them. They may have been pirates who happened upon the flotilla and had the bad judgment to attack. But if a breach in ISC security had occurred, they could be part of a larger ESComm force. Without a web to coordinate reentry into real space, the ESComm ships would be spread out in time and space—which meant more could be coming.

Prepare to invert, Althor thought. **Randomize course.** Once they inverted into superluminal space, they would be almost impossible to locate, particularly by ESComm ships with no psiberweb access. As the flotilla accelerated toward the speed needed to invert, Althor thought, **All ships: damage and status reports.**

Data poured into his mind. The quasis shields had provided more than physical protection during the battle; they also shielded the telops, who otherwise experienced the deaths of their enemies as their own. Military telops learned to block their empathic reception, but if they muted it too much they ceased to function as telops. However, in quasis nothing could change quantum state, including neurons, which meant telops could neither think nor receive thoughts. Quasis thus protected them, indeed, was vital to their survival. A crucial balance existed: if a ship came out of quasis too soon its telops suffered, but if it stayed too long it became easy prey for ESComm ships, which could come out of quasis earlier, having no empaths to temper their lust for death.

Jag starfighters were the swiftest, most maneuverable ISC ships, with the most weaponry per cubic centimeter. Jagernauts, the Jag pilots, became part of their ships in both mind and body. That symbiosis created a weapon of unsurpassed versatility, which was why Jags were assigned to protect the other ships and came out of quasis first. However, it also required Jagernauts be strong psions. They were chosen for their ability to endure empathic backlash as well as for their military expertise.

Crewed frigates and Wasps carried telops with low Kyle ratings, making them less vulnerable to backlash. They usually came out of quasis right after the Jags, followed by the bigger ships. It was only a few seconds' difference, but in battles fought at relativistic speeds by computers, a few seconds could be eternity.

In Althor's case, it became even more crucial. As commander of the flotilla he formed its central node and made full use of his immense Rhon capacity. His training and biomech web gave him formidable defenses against telepathic backlash, but the potential for damage remained.

As the smaller flotilla ships reached inversion speed, Althor thought, **Activate inversion engines—**

Quasis jump, *Destrier* thought. A flood of data followed:

ESComm Wasps incoming—

Quasis jump.

Four ESComm frigates to starboard. Coordinates—

Quasis jump.

Two ESComm destroyers to port.

Quasis jump.

Dreadnought to port—Oh, hell. That last from a dismayed telop. *Firestorm battle cruiser to starboard.*

Althor swore. Given the lack of cohesion suffered by ESComm forces during reentry into normal space, the appearance of this many Trader ships at once implied a much larger total fleet, one that far outnumbered the flotilla. Had the trader ships burst out of inversion just seconds later, his flotilla would have already escaped into superluminal space.

Fire Impactors, Althor thought.

Firing, *Destrier* thought.

More ESComm ships appeared, firing as they hurtled past the flotilla. The entire battle moved almost at light speed, in an eerie realm where ships moving at different relative velocities contracted as they raced past each other like relativistic knights jousting with high-energy lances. At such velocities, differences in speed caused time dilation to play havoc with firing times. The smaller ships, which could accelerate more easily, attacked and then inverted into superluminal space, using quasis to protect them from the crushing accelerations while they came around for a second try. The ESComm ships cut down isolated ISC craft, herding the flotilla into a wedge as it shot through space. The constant barrage forced the *Destrier* into continual quasis jumps and so prevented it from reaching inversion speed.

Warning, Basalt thought. Althor, your body is sustaining damage at a rate beyond the capacity of your biomech web to repair.

Nausea gripped Althor. If his environment underwent drastic changes while he was in quasis—such as his ship exploding—then when he came out of it, the new forces could tear him apart. The changes weren't that extreme, yet, but *Destrier* was dropping in and out of quasis too fast. His command chair released a cocoon of foam to protect him against the buffeting, but it wasn't enough.

Fire tau missiles, he thought.

Fired.

Miniature starships themselves, the six taus flashed in and out of quasis, unhampered by the need to protect a crew. Five hit their targets, turning their immense kinetic energy into explosions, along with their warheads. The sixth inverted into superluminal space, its path controlled by a telop on *Destrier* who was linked to the tau's EI brain. The tau punched a hole into real space, coming out right "on top" an ESComm Wasp, and the resulting explosion sucked both tau and Wasp out of real space.

Quasis jump, *Destrier* thought.

Althor's vision blurred. But his starscape remained clear, and he saw a weak spot in the Trader formation. It was an intuitive judgment on his part, one *Destrier* wouldn't have made, but as soon as his mind formed the idea, *Destrier* calculated the firing pattern and sent smart missiles rocketing at the weak—

Quasis j—

Quasis jum—

Quasis jump, *Destrier* thought a third time.

Althor swallowed his bile, hit by both telepathic and quasis backlash. Death reverberated around him. The flotilla's human component numbered fifty-eight: thirty on the destroyer, one each on the eight Jags, and twenty others spread throughout the other ships. Even without the incoming data, he would have known that over half his people had died; their deaths tore through his mind in an agony of silent screams.

He recognized the ESComm strategy. *Extract and eliminate:* pull out the desired prisoner and kill everyone else. The Halstaad Code of War had established rules for taking prisoners, but ESComm found them inconvenient. Althor had no intention of surrendering anyway. If any of his telops survived, they would be interrogated and then sold as providers. According to *Destrier*'s files, every telop in the flotilla had gone on record as preferring death to capture. ESComm would execute the rest of his people. Except for slaves of great rarity, such as providers, the Traders had no intention of letting ISC warriors contaminate the slave populations they had manipulated, coerced, and brainwashed into submission.

Quasis jump, *Destrier* thought.

Althor saw another opening, one *Destrier* had ignored in favor of better targets. In response to his shift in concentration, *Destrier* made the necessary calculations.

Firing, it thought. Smart-dust rolled out from the cruiser and entered the bores of tau cannons on three ESComm frigates. The few seconds the dust was active coincided with the moment all three frigates fired their cannons. Attacked by the microwarheads within the dust, the tau missiles detonated *inside* their bores—

Quasis jump, *Destrier* thought.

Althor struggled to focus on his disintegrating starscape. All three frigates had exploded. He gave a ragged laugh, realizing his hyperextended Rhon awareness had given him a hint that the commanders on the frigates intended to fire in synchronization an instant before they did it.

Quasis jump, *Destrier* thought.

Althor groaned with the strain on his body. Basalt tried to activate his hydraulics to support him, but they no longer responded. He hung onto consciousness, refusing to give in to the encroaching darkness.

Quasis jump, *Destrier* thought. Decks 6 and 29 destroyed.

Major Hooklore, Althor thought. No answer came from his first officer. The flotilla was nothing but debris, the jagged pieces moving at near light speed. Only *Destrier*'s bridge remained intact, leaving little doubt ESComm knew who was onboard.

Althor wet his lips. ***Destrier*, initiate self-destruct macro 1101.** He transmitted the secured codes. He would never have wanted to end this way, but it was better than becoming an ESComm prisoner.

After a pause, *Destrier* thought, ESComm has inserted quasis generators into my hull. Apparently they put the generators in some of their tau missiles, instead of warheads. When the taus hit, they deposited the generators, which then produced rogue quasis fields. Those fields are interfering with my self-destruct by freezing key systems.

What the hell? Althor had never heard of the technique.

It seemed impossible. How had ESComm kept the taus from destroying themselves and their targets on impact? Swallowing, he thought, **Basalt, engage my internal self-destruct.**

Engaged, Basalt answered.

Destrier, Althor thought. **Crash any of your remaining web nodes and erase any files that haven't already been destroyed.**

Working. *Destrier*'s response crackled with static. Its next thought came faint and garbled: I am being boarded.

Slam your hatches on them. Closed with enough force, the hatches could slow an armored warrior and cut an unarmored invader in two. It was like trying to stop a flood with a bucket, but it was better than nothing. Looking over the bridge below, where his people lay dead in their chairs, he gritted his teeth. **Open and slam them as fast as you can.**

Done . . . Even dying, *Destrier* continued to fight, like a drum in his mind, keeping time with the pulse in his body.

Basalt, he thought. **Why aren't I dead?**

The self-destruct toggle in your biomech web is inactive.

No! How?

0.0056 seconds before you gave the self-destruct order, you went into quasis. I calculate a 98% probability it was produced by ESComm generators and used to sabotage your self-destruct.

A chill went up his back. **Kill me. I don't care how you do it. Just do it. They're almost here.**

The quasis is blocking my systems.

Althor fought the protective cocoon around his body until he pulled free. He grabbed a section of the chair arm and yanked with normal strength, unable to activate his hydraulics. The panel resisted, then buckled and ripped in a jagged edge. He couldn't get it off, so he jerked his wrist across the edge, over and over, until blood covered his arm and stained the cocoon.

Loss of blood has reached critical stage, Basalt thought.

Althor sagged back in his chair. **Good-bye, Basalt.**

Regret came to him from the node. *Good-bye, Althor.* Then: *Bridge penetrated.*

In a daze, Althor saw ESComm soldiers floating toward him through the stardome, the human fortresses called waroids, their mirrored armor reflecting the bloodred warning lights. "Too late," he whispered. "I'm dead."

He was conscious when the first waroid reached him, but then the universe went dark.

13

Snow fell softly through the night, piling drifts against the shuttered windows. A single oil lamp on the wall shed yellow light over the room. Soz sat curled on the bed with Jaibriol, a woven blanket over their knees as they watched their children sleep. Jai and Vitar were in the bedroom, but had left the door open. Jai was lying on his back, one long leg off the bed, one arm over his head. Vitar's bed was half-hidden by the wall so only his head and shoulders showed. He slept with a six-year-old's blissful peace, on his side, his hands tucked under his head.

In the main room, Lisi was sleeping in a bed across from where Soz and Jaibriol sat, and del-Kelric lay in his cradle, his face angelic in the dim light.

"They look so peaceful," Jaibriol said.

"That's because they're asleep," Soz replied.

He laughed. "It's the only time they're all quiet at once."

Soz grinned. "Just wait another few months." She took his hand and laid it on the swell of her abdomen. "You'd think that at the doddering age of sixty-four I would know better than to keep doing this."

"You aren't sixty-four. I'd say early thirties. Younger than me."

"Really? How did I manage this remarkable feat of halving my age?"

"You know what I mean." Drowsily Jaibriol added, "All those little nanobugs we have in our bodies that make us age slower."

She tilted her head. "I'm glad they really delay aging instead of just making me look young."

"There's a difference?"

"If it was only cosmetic, I couldn't have children at this age."

Jaibriol rubbed her stomach. ***She's definitely in there.***

That she is. With the ease of long familiarity, they melded minds and reached out to their child, suffusing her with affection. Her brain hadn't developed enough to comprehend love on a conscious level, but she responded with an innate sense of comfort more primal than thought.

Jaibriol lifted Soz's chin and bent his head to kiss her. As their lips met, a giggle came from the bedroom.

"Saints almighty," Soz grumbled. They looked to see Vitar smirking at them. He laughed and yanked the covers over his head.

"One wonders," Jaibriol said dryly, "how we ever found the privacy to make a second, let alone a fifth."

Soz smiled. "I seem to remember a patch of crystal grass." Penned and contained, the singing crystals created an effective trap for tomjolts. If people didn't get too close to the grass, they could enjoy the singing without going into a trance. The effect was rather like that of drinking a fine wine, and inspired certain sensual activities that went with the mixture of good spirits and good companionship.

"Ah, yes," Jaibriol murmured. "I remember."

Soz sighed, content. "This is a good life. I don't think I would want to go back even if we could."

He kissed the top of her head. "Nor I."

Dawn suffused the Skyhammer ruins, slanting in the doorway of the tower. Bathed in that light, Kurj sat on his bedroll and broke his fast. While he ate, his palmtop read him his mail, sent down by telops on *Anvil,* the ISC dreadnought that had brought him to SunsReach.

A footstep rustled outside. Looking up, he saw a woman in the doorway with gold hair drifting around her body, the hip-length curls haloed by the dawn's radiance.

Startled, Kurj stood up. "Mother."

"My greetings." Roca smiled. "You look rested."

"It's quiet here." He motioned toward the plaza behind her. "Just me, sky, and grass. Nothing else on the entire planet."

"Come outside with me," she said. "It's beautiful."

"All right." Kurj picked up his palmtop. A red light glowed on it, notifying him of mail marked *urgent.* He brought the message up on the screen. "That's odd."

"What is it?" Roca asked.

"Dehya is shouting at me."

"Dehya?" She laughed. "I've never heard her raise her voice in her life."

"Look at this." He showed her the message:

KURJ, DON'T LEAVE SKYHAMMER. STAY THERE.

"Are you sure she wrote it?" Roca asked. "That's hardly her style."

"It's probably a shell." When working on the web, Dehya often started up shell processes that ran off her mind and performed routine functions while she concentrated on more intricate tasks. Kurj suspected she had imparted urgency to this one, and shouting at him was its unsubtle rendering of her undoubtedly more nuanced intent.

He moved his finger through the response holicon, a bird floating above the screen. When the palmtop prompted for his message, he wrote: Why? and sent it to the *Anvil,* marked for transmission to Dehya. Then he clipped the palmtop to his belt.

He and Roca walked together into the dawn. Crisp air surrounded them. No hint of insects, birds, or trees touched the landscape on this aging biosculpted world where nothing survived now but fields of bronzed grass that stretched to the horizon. Three towers stood across the plaza. In unspoken agreement, they went to the leftmost tower. Its door had long ago disintegrated, but the tower remained intact, built from a stone hardened by ancient molecular bonders. The building had deliberate crooks, leaning right, then left, then right. The staircase inside climbed in an asymmetric spiral that had grown more uneven over the ages.

Kurj followed Roca up the narrow stairs, four levels in all, to a drafty chamber at the top. In its entrance they could stand up straight, but a few paces away the floor rose in a shelf, to within a meter of the ceiling. The doors to their right and left had been made by an ISC officer stationed here a while back who had nothing much to do. No trees grew on SunsReach, so Kurj had allowed him to import the wood. Kurj leaned past Roca and pushed open the right-hand door, revealing a stone bridge that crossed from this tower to another one only meters away.

Roca eyed the bridge. "Do you think it's safe? It's been a century since we last used it."

"I think so. But I'll go first." Kurj went out onto the bridge. Its sides came up to his elbows and were a good two hand spans thick, but its width was so narrow he had to turn sideways. The last time he had been here, as a small boy, he had run across the bridge without a thought for its dimensions.

He eased his way along the span until he reached the landing on its far end, a narrow terrace that circled the tower. The crown of the structure curved up and over his head in the shape of a huge angular flower. This second tower had no entrance; its "stem" was solid stone, sculpted to resemble a plant, though time had erased details of the artistry.

Turning to face the first tower, Kurj beckoned to Roca. She came across the bridge, watching him as she walked, as if his presence alone could prevent the bridge from crumbling. When she reached the landing, her relief filtered past her mental barriers and touched his mind.

So they stood together, gazing out at the rippling ocean of yellow-gold grass that lapped at the bases of the towers and stretched to the horizon, undulating in the breezes, its surface unbroken by other plants, structures, or hills. Silence surrounded them, embodying the unspoken words that shadowed their lives.

Kurj's palmtop chimed. Pulling his attention in from the horizon, he unhooked the palmtop and brought up the new message:

I don't know why.

"Is that from Dehya?" Roca asked.

"More likely one of her shells." He sent a response: Can you find out? Then he put away the palmtop and extended his left arm, inviting Roca to proceed along the terrace that circled the tower. The stone ledge was just barely wide enough for them to walk side by side, but no rail protected its edges, so Roca went first and Kurj followed.

As they rounded the other side, the third tower came into view. With a sturdy fluted stem and bulbous head, it resembled an ash-gray water tank, except for its flattened top, which had a diameter of about fifty meters. Three meters of open space separated it from the terrace where Kurj stood with Roca.

"The bridge is gone," Roca said.

Standing at the edge of the terrace, Kurj stared down at the ground far below. The remains of a bridge lay half-buried in the grass. Scanning the terrace, he saw only one possible replacement, a plank of wood leaning against the central column of the tower, probably left by the carpenter who had built the doors.

As Kurj went to the plank, Roca said, "That won't support you."

Node C, attend, he thought. **Will the plank hold my weight?**

Estimated probability of support is 64 percent, **C** answered.

"It should be fine," he said. With his nodes calculating

trajectories and his hydraulics guiding his motion, he hefted the plank into the air. Its far end landed with a *smack* on the other tower.

His palmtop chimed. Curious, Kurj brought up the message:

Please stand by.

Roca peered over his arm. "What does that mean?"

"She must be running one hell of a calculation." He sent back: I'm almost ready to come home. I have a war to win, an Assembly to pacify, and a bride waiting. If you want me to stay, you have to give me a reason.

Roca smiled. "Which do you think is easier, pacifying the Assembly or winning the war?"

He laughed and put away his palmtop. "Good question."

Her face gentled. "You hardly ever laugh that way anymore."

"What way?"

"As if you genuinely feel like it."

That caught Kurj off guard. At a loss for a response, he started across the plank. It was only wide enough for one of his feet, which made balance difficult, but his biomech web determined the forces needed to keep him steady, down to every gesture and weight shift. Soon he was stepping onto the rounded edge of the third tower.

He turned to Roca. "Come on."

"I'll fall," she called. "I don't know how you did that."

"You're a dancer. Far more graceful than me."

"You have biomech."

That gave him pause. He took his biomech for granted, but she had far less than he. Kurj was about to start back when she stepped onto the plank.

"Never mind," he said. "I'm coming back."

Roca ignored him, placing her feet with care. Kurj tensed, suddenly aware of how fragile she looked, suspended high above the sea of grasses, breezes ruffling her glorious cloak of hair. As he watched, antiqued memories came to his mind. Decades ago, for the short span of time when he and his grandfather Jarac had both been in the Triad, before Jarac died, their minds had overlapped. Kurj knew Jarac's memories. Seeing Roca now, he recalled her as a child, balanced on a log above a stream. Daughter. Sister. Mother.

She reached the end of the bridge with no mishaps. As she stepped onto the tower, Kurj's palmtop chimed. Roca looked up with a start—and lost her balance.

Kurj lunged for her and clamped his arm around her waist, moving with enhanced reflexes and speed. Normally a man his size moving so fast would have gone over the edge. But his hydraulics took over, helping him control his momentum, and he stumbled back on the tower. The plank rattled, jumped, and skittered off the edge, and slowly fell to the ground far below.

They sat down hard, Kurj holding Roca in both arms now. She stared up at him like a captured bird, and they froze, watching each other, only a meter from where the tower curved down under itself.

Embedded in that instant of time, like gold flies in amber, they stared at each other. Then the moment cracked open and Kurj let her go. They stood up, the wind blowing her hair around them.

"It didn't seem this precarious last time," she said.

"No. It didn't."

They went to a sunken area in the center of the tower that had been the bottom of a room. Kurj jumped into the cavity, surprised by how much smaller it looked. The walls that had loomed over him when he was five only came to his shoulders now. The room was about six by ten paces, its near side longer than the far. Its only roof had consisted of two arches, one that spanned the longer sides and one that spanned the shorter. The arches had met overhead in the room's center, but all that remained of them now were their bases.

As Roca climbed over the edge, he realized she had no comm or palmtop. "What ship brought you here?" he asked.

She jumped down next to him. "The *Bayshore.*"

"Edyth Klo is the commander, yes?"

"That's right."

"Why did she let you down here without a comm?"

"I didn't want one."

"She should have made you take it."

Roca shrugged. "If I need one, I can use yours. Besides, you know they're monitoring everything we do."

"I have a shadowmaker in my cyberlock." The technology was classified, but his staff all knew he carried it. The shadowmaker hid him in a sphere of shadow space about four meters in diameter. "When it's activated, like now, no one can monitor me. Or you, if you're within two meters of me."

"If I'm within two meters of you, I can use your palmtop."

He spoke softly. "Suppose I won't allow it?"

She took a moment to absorb that. Then she said, "You gave me a promise on the Orbiter. I trust it." Watching him, she asked, "Must I spend my life fearing my own son?"

Startled by the blunt question, Kurj turned away and walked to the opposite wall. He sat on a stone ledge there, facing her again. In the quiet air of SunsReach he could hear her breathing.

"You love your children too much," he said.

"I've always thought it wasn't enough." She leaned against the wall, her palms flat on the stone. "Maybe if I had I done a better job, you would be happier."

"What makes you think I'm not happy?"

"Are you?"

"I don't know."

"Why do you think I love you too much?"

"I didn't specify myself."

"It's what you meant, isn't it?"

"You see your children through a filter," he said. "It distorts the truth."

"And what is the truth you think I refuse to see?"

"What I am."

"What is that?"

Bitterness edged his voice. "A tyrant. A military dictator. A murderer. A rapist."

She stared at him. "Saints almighty, what have you been doing out here, locked away with your thoughts?"

Dryly he said, "Introspection. It is profoundly unpleasant." He leaned forward, his booted feet planted wide, his elbows on his knees. "Darr was right."

She stiffened. "Darr Hammerjackson is our past."

"The past never goes away." He tilted his head. "Have you ever compared an organic memory with one you've stored in a node file? It is amazing the distortions time creates. Give a man long enough and he can convince himself of his innocence in anything."

Roca came over and sat next to him, within the shadow field. "You should take more care with your words."

He stared at her, his fist clenching. "Even now, what is your first impulse? Put yourself in danger to protect me, lest someone overhear my words and use them against me. You didn't leave Darr when he beat you. Only when he turned on me." A long buried anger crackled in his voice. "Didn't it ever occur to you that knowing he hurt you was killing me?"

Her voice caught. "I'm sorry."

He had to make a conscious effort not to grit his teeth. "When I was a Jagernaut, every time I killed an Aristo in battle, in my mind I was killing Darr."

Quietly she said, "I'm sorry, Kurj. I made the best choices I knew how."

He looked at the stone floor. Cracks made a web of lines across it, but only a few wisps of grass had taken root. "I can't handle your loving me."

"Why?"

"Because if you hated me, it wouldn't matter what I did to you."

Roca swallowed. "And what would you do?"

His palmtop chimed again. He jerked at the interruption,

then pulled it off with a yank. This message was in Dehya's personal font:

Kurj, I'm not sure why you have to stay on Skyhammer. I'm running extrapolations. And to be honest, part of this is intuition. Is precognition a Rhon trait? I doubt we can even define the line between extrapolation and precognition. All I know is that you must stay there. It's the only model that doesn't diverge or zero out.

Roca concentrated on the palmtop, as if reading it could shield her against hearing an answer to her last question. "Zero out? What does she mean?"

"It sounds like she's trying to calculate the future," Kurj said. "We do it all the time in ISC."

"To predict the outcome of combat?"

"That's right. But it doesn't work. Too many variables." He sent the message: I can stay two more days.

"What did she mean by 'icon'?"

He hung the palmtop on his belt. "Icon?"

"You said you came here because you guessed the icon Dehya had in mind."

Kurj pushed his hand across the short brush of hair on his head. "It was Jocasta."

"Who is Jocasta?"

"You don't know the Allied classics? *Oedipus Rex*, by Sophocles?"

"Not really." She studied his face, in lieu of reaching his mind, which he had closed to her. "What are you trying to tell me?"

"Dehya thinks I have problems relating to you. She's trying to fix it, in her own convoluted way."

Roca exhaled, a soft sound. "You didn't know your entering the Triad would kill him."

He stiffened. "We weren't talking about Jarac."

"Weren't we?"

It was a long moment before he answered. "When he was

my grandfather I admired him. When he was my father I hated him. But he was the same man. I knew that, finally." In a quiet voice he added, "After it was too late."

"The Assembly ruled his death an accident."

"What did you expect them to do? I was out of control. They were terrified. With good reason."

"If you were truly the monster you claim," Roca said, "you wouldn't worry about this."

"It is a man's actions that define him. Not his capacity for guilt."

"You think so?" She watched his face. "If Ur Qox convinces the Allieds, through his actions, that he is a decent human being, does that make it a fact?"

"If his actions toward all humanity mirrored his propaganda, then yes, it would make it fact." Tiredly Kurj said, "Then we could quit fighting this gods forsaken war."

His palmtop chimed. Kurj swore, then brought up the message. "She thinks two days isn't enough. She wants ten." He sent back: Ten is too many, but I'll see what I can do.

Roca spoke carefully. "I don't think you should brood here for even two more days, alone like this."

"I'm not alone."

"I promised Eldri I wouldn't stay too long."

Softly he asked, "And what is too long?"

Unease flickered on her face. "I don't know."

"Maybe it is already too late."

"Kurj, don't."

He touched her face, his fingers lingering on her cheek. She had come at his request, trusting his promise. He regretted that promise now, for fear he couldn't keep it. If he acknowledged what brooded in his heart, would that release its power over him—or would he lose control of it forever and destroy what he loved?

His palmtop chimed again and Kurj hit it with his fist, deactivating the summoner. Dehya could wait.

"What are you doing?" Roca asked.

He brushed her curls, his hand so large that it folded around her head. Then he trailed his finger along her jaw.

"Kurj, stop."

"I have to know." He clenched a length of her hair in his fist. "I have to know what will happen if I look into the darkness."

She searched his face as if it held a means of escape. Yet he still felt her trust. Even now, she believed he would honor his promise. She sat watching him. Waiting. Waiting for him to stop. Waiting for him to justify her trust. Refusing to acknowledge she had been wrong.

A breeze laid a strand of hair across her mouth. He touched his finger to it, brushing her lips. For a long moment they sat that way, Kurj holding her hair clenched in one fist, Roca staring up at him, frozen. Waiting. Vulnerable. His.

Then he let go of her.

Kurj released the breath he hadn't realized he was holding. "How did you know?"

Her voice shook. "Know?"

"That you could trust me?"

The color was coming back into her face. "Because at heart, Kurj, you are a man of honor." She motioned at the sky. "The people out there, all of them, they want us to be everything to everyone, keepers of the web, symbols of an empire, saviors of their freedom, strong, beautiful, perfect. They want us to be more than human and curse us when we aren't. Is it any wonder we bend under the strain?"

"You offer me excuses where I deserve none."

"You condemn yourself for an evil you don't possess."

"You're wrong." His expression gentled. "But I thank you for believing it." He felt a curious lightening, as if the gravity of SunsReach had decreased.

An engine rumbled over them. Looking up, Kurj saw a shuttle stark against the sky. He stood up, pulling off his palmtop. The waiting message came not from Dehya, but from *Anvil*'s captain:

Code Two. Am sending shuttle.

Kurj stared at the display. Code Two. It meant a crisis only one step down from full-scale invasion.

The shuttle landed on the tower. As he and Roca ran to it, the hatch opened, framing Major Coalson, a member of Kurj's staff. Kurj paused while Roca boarded the shuttle, then stepped up after her.

"What is the situation?" he asked Coalson.

"The message came from HQ." Coalson glanced at Roca.

"Go ahead," Kurj said. "My mother has the clearance."

"It concerns Commander Valdoria, sir."

"You mean Althor?" Roca asked. "My son?"

The major shifted his feet. "Yes, ma'am."

Kurj waited a heartbeat. "Go on, Major."

"He's been captured, sir. By ESComm."

"No." Roca stared at the major. *"No."*

Coalson flushed. "Ma'am, I'm sorry."

In a gentler voice, Kurj said, "Report, Major."

"The flotilla was destroyed," Coalson said. "We aren't sure what happened to Prince Althor. His control chair was covered—" He paused, glancing at Roca. "With evidence of a struggle."

"What evidence?" Roca asked.

When Coalson hesitated, Kurj said, "Go ahead."

"Blood," Coalson said. "All over it."

"Althor's blood?" Kurj asked.

"Yes, sir."

Roca's voice cracked. "Did he lose too much to survive?"

"We aren't sure," Coalson said.

"How long will it take for *Anvil* to rendezvous with the *Bayshore?*" Kurj asked.

"About half of one orbit," Coalson said.

"That's too long," Kurj said. "Councilor Roca and I will both go on *Anvil.*"

"Kurj." Roca shook her head. "What about Dehya's warning?"

He suddenly felt tired. And heavy. "Future extrapolations aren't accurate at all. I can't stay here on that basis alone." He looked up at the sky. "Not now."

* * *

Ur Qox stood in the high observation lounge, a pleasant room with lacquered tables and vases made from diamond. The window in front of him stretched the length and upper half of one wall. On this side it afforded a view of the transition room below; on the other side it was opaque.

In the transition room, sterilization vents puckered the ceiling and environment suits hung on one wall. Equipment lined another wall: limblocks, collars, cuffs. Slave restraints. Waroid soldiers filled the room, fortresses eight feet tall, with mirrored armor that reflected the harsh lights. Only one man had no armor. Althor Valdoria stood in numb silence as a waroid fastened a slave collar around his neck.

The Imperial Heir still wore his ISC uniform, black pants and a pullover sweater, with two gold rings on each of his upper arms indicating his Jagernaut rank of Secondary. His arms had been twisted behind his back, the lower arms crossed on top of each other and bound together by a mesh. Half-hidden under the mesh, a bandage showed on his right wrist.

Qox had read the reports. Soldiers from the ESComm cruiser *Viquara's Glory,* named in honor of the empress, had captured Althor as he was dying. The doctors on the cruiser saved his life, aided by his own hale constitution. He stood on his own now, dark circles under his eyes and a hollowed look to his face.

A reflection in the window showed one of Qox's secret police approaching him from behind. The Razer stopped a few paces away. When Qox turned, the man bowed.

"Yes?" Qox asked.

"A Lieutenant Xirson from *Viquara's Glory* waits outside, Your Highness."

"Bring him."

Xirson turned out to be a tall man with Highton features, red eyes, and dull black hair. He knelt before the emperor, his head bowed. His gunmetal collar identified him as a taskmaker who had earned the honor of serving as an ESComm officer. His name indicated he was the son of an

Aristo called Xir, possibly Qox's own cousin, Corbal Xir. Qox made a mental note to ask Corbal about the fellow. He needed more Razers and preferred to use relatives.

"You may rise," Qox stated. As the lieutenant stood, Qox said, "You have a message for me?"

"Yes, Your Highness." Xirson's voice had the rumble of a slave bred from the Hardacol line, a sturdy stock. "Admiral Ajaks requests an audience."

"You may inform him it is granted," Qox said.

After Xirson left, Qox turned back to watch the room below. The waroids were still installing Althor's collar, inserting its prongs into the socket in his neck. Picotech packed the metal collar, ready to assail the security protecting Althor's biomech web. It was a tricky form of invasion, given that a Jagernaut's nodes were set to erase when subjected to tampering.

Seeing the reflection of his bodyguard approach again, Qox spoke without turning. "Is Admiral Ajaks here?"

"Yes, sir," the Razer said.

"Good." He continued to look out the window. "Bring him."

In the reflection, Qox saw Ajaks enter. Razers escorted the admiral, who came with none of his own bodyguards, as did anyone granted an audience with Qox. The only guards allowed in the emperor's presence belonged to the emperor.

Like most Hightons, Lassar Ajaks was tall and classic of feature, without a white hair on his head. He was also heavily built, even with a few pounds of fat, a rare sight on an Aristo. He wore a severe uniform and military boots, all black except for red piping on the sleeves.

Qox had granted him command of *Viquara's Glory* because Ajaks coveted only riches, as opposed to power. The political situation now was too volatile to take chances. Qox had spread rumors of another Highton Heir, again hidden from assassins, a story that carried weight given Jaibriol's death. But he had no heir. He had sired a boy on Cirrus, trying for another Rhon psion, with no success.

In the transition room, the waroids had removed the

binding on Althor's arms and were fastening cuffs around his wrists, each restraint networked with picotech that would monitor his activities and provide various means of control.

Qox turned to Ajaks. "My greetings, Lassar."

The admiral bowed, his fist at his waist and his thumb pointing upward to indicate success. "My honor at your esteemed presence, Your Highness."

Qox tilted his head toward the transition room. "I am pleased with what you brought me."

Ajaks straightened, puffing out his chest. "It is my great joy to bring you this result of our glorious engagement against the malice of Imperial Skolia."

Qox almost smiled. Ajaks had always had a florid way with words. He was useful on news broadcasts, which required the kind of hackneyed expressions Ajaks produced with such versatility.

"A glorious engagement indeed," Qox said.

"There is more, sir. A matter of intelligence." He spoke with distaste, as if to suggest intelligence had been mishandled until he, Lassar Ajaks, rectified the situation. It didn't surprise Qox. Intelligence Minister Vitrex had attained great prestige since Althor's capture. So other Hightons sought the minister's downfall. Qox encouraged the intrigues, as it diverted attention from him.

But the admiral's attitude today suggested more than simple intrigues. Ajaks could barely contain his excitement. "Your Highness. Sir. Your Most Exalted Honor."

Amused, Qox said, "Yes, Lassar?"

Ajaks unhooked his palmtop and offered it to Qox. In his side vision Qox saw his Razers stiffen, hands dropping to their weapons. The room's security systems would also have just notched up their defense readiness. Even so, he took the palmtop. And when he read its screen, the room suddenly seemed very quiet.

He looked at Ajaks. "You have done well. I won't forget."

The admiral bowed. "It is my joy to bring you the final stroke in uniting the universe under Highton benevolence."

"Indeed." If this information proved as useful as it looked, Ajaks's histrionic prose might have truth in it.

The message summarized the efforts of the admiral's people to crack the *Destrier* web. Most of the ship's nodes had been erased, but the web wizards had managed to cull a few files—including a message from the Imperator. Kurj Skolia was on SunsReach, of all places. An attack on SunsReach offered little chance of success; the planet was far too well guarded. But who would have expected him to be there? Given the proximity of SunsReach to the Orbiter, it would make more sense for him to return to the Orbiter when he learned of his heir's capture, rather than ISC headquarters on Diesha.

And where was one most vulnerable? En route to his destination. In space.

Songbell flowers chimed in the clear night air, adding soft music to the parklands of Upper Qoxire. Rosy light from the moon Mirella bathed the lawns, her luminence silvered by five smaller moons, all at least half full, including the Sisters, Ilina and Tarquine, which gleamed like gibbous silver coins. Named for the sisters of Eube Qox, they circled Glory in orbits separated by barely fifty kilometers. The lower, faster moon never managed to pass her sister. As the lower moon approached the upper, the upper moon's gravity slowed her down and pulled her toward the higher orbit, whereas the lower moon's gravity sped up the upper moon and pulled her down toward the lower orbit, until finally they swapped orbits and the new lower moon sped away from her sister. Seen from the surface of Glory, they appeared to bounce off each other in the sky. Tonight they were so close, they almost seemed to touch.

Izar Vitrex, Minister of Intelligence, waited among the diffuse carnelian shadows.

A rustle came from a path on his left. Then Kryx Quaelen appeared.

"My greetings, Minister Vitrex," Quaelen said.

"My greetings, Minister Quaelen," Vitrex said.

"A lovely night."

"So it is." Vitrex nodded toward the palace, which glowed on a distant hill, radiant and graceful. "It honors our emperor."

Quaelen watched him with a hooded gaze. "May the House of Qox bless our people." He paused. "And our sons."

"A noble sentiment." The implication wasn't lost on Vitrex. How Quaelen had discovered that Vitrex's "heir" wasn't his true son, Vitrex had no idea. Apparently the Trade Minister wielded a more formidable intelligence force than Vitrex had realized. Quaelen had used subtle innuendo to express sympathy, indicating he knew how it felt to endure a stigma on the Highton bloodline. Vitrex didn't believe for an instant that Quaelen gave a kiss in hell about his dilemma. The Trade Minister intended to blackmail him.

Even worse, the emperor knew. In an impressive dance of innuendo, Qox had assured Vitrex his secret was safe, a reward for his role in the *Destrier* triumph. But Vitrex had no illusions. By letting his wife Sharla talk him into this deception, he had compromised his standing with the emperor and given Qox a means to control him.

It was all the fault of that girl Cirrus. H...ng providers spy was nothing new, and Vitrex had b...careful when he was with her, using the same ment...cking techniques ISC telops used to protect their...in battle. He had believed himself protected w...enjoyed himself with the emperor's pretty little t...ad been wrong.

He considered denou...arla, playing the appalled husband to the disc...r deception. But even if it disassociated him...ess, it still would stir rumors that he knew...claimed. It would also earn the enmity of...ople, a powerful Highton line. Beside...Sharla, who played the ice princess in p...re of his dreams in private.

...far better than he at politics. Left on his ...ave settled into obscurity. But now was a good time for moves to power. Somehow he had to make this mess work to his benefit.

Quaelen gazed at the moon-swept garden, silent. Such silences used to agitate Vitrex, spurring him to babble. Then Sharla told him it was a technique meant to have exactly that effect. After that, he learned to employ the technique himself.

When the silence became tiresome, serving no purpose for either of them, Quaelen said, "A son for a son. Bless the emperor's good fortune. And your esteemed role in it."

"Indeed," Vitrex said. Quaelen obviously referred to Althor Valdoria. Still, this business about sons made him uneasy.

"A son." Quaelen paused. "A brother."

"A brother?"

"Who descends from the sky like a hammer."

"A hammer?"

"Skyhammer."

"Skyhammer?" Vitrex couldn't see where this was going.

Quaelen rubbed the bridge of his nose between his thumb and index finger. "On SunsReach. You do know the place, don't you?"

His tone irritated Vitrex. Of course he knew SunsReach, the Ruby D[illegible]sty retreat. It was, after all, the intelligence work of his ow[illegible]eople that had led to Althor Valdoria's capture and the reve[illegible]n of the Imperator's location. He almost snapped at Quae[illegible]en caught himself and simply said, "Indeed."

"It is a shame it's [illegible]ch farther from SunsReach to ISC headquarters than [illegible]biter," Quaelen commented.

"Indeed," Vitrex said, [illegible]now. "Although shame or lack thereof depends on y[illegible]f view."

"True. Humiliation for In[illegible]ia may be a blessing for Eube. One worth the atte[illegible]mperor himself."

"As well it should be," Vitr[illegible]rently Quaelen knew the emperor planned to [illegible] *Viquara's Glory* in the cruiser *Meg*[illegible]attle cruiser [illegible]ouldn't go into combat, of course. But if ESComm located and captured the Imperator, Qox would have the glory of taking him prisoner. Vitrex himself had seen to the preparations for the additional fleet required to secure Qox's safety. Actually, his people had seen to them. He had little talent for intelligence or any other profession. His gifts lay in an ability to identify people who could do what he couldn't and then take credit for their work.

Of course they had no guarantee ESComm would find Kurj Skolia. Still, Vitrex imagined a triumphant Ur Qox facing the captured Imperator. What a scene! Splendid material for the news broadcasts. As Intelligence Minister, he was well placed to shape what went into those broadcasts, making sure the glory reflected on him.

Quaelen was watching his face. "It will be a great moment when our esteemed emperor returns from his perilous mission."

Perilous? Vitrex stiffened. What did Quaelen imply? That he, Izar Vitrex, couldn't ensure the emperor's safety? It was an insult. Peril, indeed.

Then a new angle occurred to him. The people didn't need to *know* Qox was in no danger. It wouldn't hurt Vitrex's growing base of support to be lauded as the minister who had helped their courageous emperor return home from his daring mission.

"The people will rejoice in his safe return," Vitrex said.

"As indeed they should." Quaelen waited several heartbeats. "Assuming he does."

Vitrex froze, finally comprehending Quaelen's intent. The Trade Minister was looking far beyond public relations coups. Vitrex could ensure the emperor returned in triumph—

Or didn't return at all.

Saying the idea held risk was like saying a sea held water. Vitrex could dare no more than to make the *chance* of a disaster possible. If any evidence came forward that he had even an infinitesimal part in it, he would suffer a long, ugly death. If Qox died, it would plunge Eube into chaos, particularly with no acting Highton Heir.

But chaos also provided opportunity for Hightons of intelligence to increase their power.

Was it worth the risk?

14

The ISC *Anvil* dropped out of inversion, hurtling through space in the distorted universe of time dilation and space contraction. Within seconds it slowed to more mundane speeds, along with its escort, the flotilla that had accompanied it to SunsReach plus an additional ten Starslammer destroyers taken off the SunsReach orbital defense system.

Ten seconds later the ISC *Rampart,* a Firestorm battle cruiser, burst into real space. With it came two thousand craft, in perfect formation, including Starslammers, Leos, Asps, Cobras, Wasps, and Jags. The void suddenly thrived with ships. Most were drones piloted by EI brains; one in ten carried a human crew.

The *Anvil* and *Rampart* armadas began their intricate dance of maneuvers as the two fleets rendezvoused. Roca waited in the stardome above the bridge of *Anvil,* next to the command chair where Kurj sat, the nanohooks in the soles of her boots holding her to the catwalk by grasping complementary hooks in the walk.

With one hand to his ear, listening to his comm, Kurj turned to Roca. "We're ready to transfer."

Her voice caught. "Bring him home, Kurj."

Gently he said, "I will." He thought of Dehya's warning to stay on SunsReach. The noise in future calculations was so large that in general it swamped the predictions themselves, making them useless. On rare occasions, a strong enough correlation existed to rise above the noise. Dehya believed she had found one. But what? She thought it could be anything from his death to a victory so great it altered history and his role in it, until he no longer resembled his former self enough to remain consistent in her calculations. Or her findings could be an artifact, with no meaning at all.

He regarded his mother. "If you see Ami before I do, will you tell her something for me?"

She nodded, her eyes glimmering with moisture. They both knew that with Roca headed to the planet Parthonia and he to the Orbiter, where Ami lived, no reason existed for her to see Ami first, unless something happened to him.

Tell her that I love her, he thought.

Her face gentled. *I will.*

Over the next ten minutes Kurj disembarked from *Anvil* and boarded *Rampart*. He installed himself in the command chair above the huge bridge, with its consoles, weapons grids, and comm stations crewed by his best officers. *Anvil,* now accompanied by a thousand ships from *Rampart*'s complement, inverted into superluminal space, taking Roca to safety on Parthonia.

Kurj extended his mind throughout *Rampart*. **Prepare to invert.**

Accelerating. *Rampart*'s voice rumbled in his mind like the booming vibrations of a massive metal plate.

An ESComm Stinger hurtled out of inversion, its passing hardly more than a wisp of ions in space.

INVERT! Kurj shouted.

Wasps could reach inversion speed in seconds, using quasis to protect them from the crushing accelerations. Frigates took longer, destroyers even longer. The *Rampart* needed three minutes. On an astronomical scale, three minutes was nothing.

On the scale of interstellar warfare, it was eternity.

Within the first second after the ESComm Stinger appeared, two more Stingers flashed into real space and released warheads. One exploded an ISC Wasp and the other impacted a frigate in quasis, to no effect. During the next few seconds, fourteen more ESComm drones appeared and engaged the ISC craft.

Within fifty seconds, a Trader fleet nearly a thousand strong had burst out of inversion, preceded by waves of MIRVs, multiple independently targeted reentry vehicles that went after their prey with single-minded ferocity. Most of the ships only had the chance to fire one shot as they raced past their targets. Faster ships had time to reinvert into superluminal space, if they survived the first volley, and come back for another pass.

The entire battle hurtled through space. The larger ISC ships continued to accelerate to inversion speed, the smaller craft remaining behind to defend them. Annihilators turned the void into a maelstrom of gamma radiation and high energy particles. Impactors released swarms of smart missiles that fused on impact, adding to the plasma. The battle expanded in a cone millions of kilometers long and thousands wide. Relative to the native dust floating in space at mundane speeds, the ships were squashed into flat coin shapes, their crews moving in slow motion.

The quasis shields on the ships began to fail. Klein fuel bottles collapsed, sucking the smaller ships that carried them out of real space and crippling larger ones. Schematics showed a chaos of wildly oscillating fields in space as it became a raging sea of debris and plasma.

Initially far outnumbered by the ISC ships, the ESComm drones died by the hundreds. But they kept coming, wave after wave, their sheer numbers compensating for their lack of cohesion as a fighting force.

Embedded in his command chair, Kurj became part of *Rampart.* His mind extended throughout the web of a thousand-ship fleet. Indistinguishable from the web itself, he analyzed and responded at speeds far beyond normal human thought, the words becoming rapid-fire numbers and sounds that flashed like sparks in his mind.

Estimate size of ESComm force, he thought. **Including ships still in superluminal space.**

3,000–10,000 ships, *Rampart* answered.

Then *Viquara's Glory* blasted out of inversion.

Kurj turned his vast array of sensors on the battle cruiser. He "saw" in every wavelength of the EM spectrum, from languid radio waves to killing gammas. **Fire Impactors. Dagger patterns 2–6.**

Rampart and *Glory* engaged, two giants flooding each other with enough energy to sterilize a continent. In a fraction of a second, the barrage of missiles from *Rampart* took out over forty drones attending *Glory,* forcing *Rampart* into quasis jump after quasis jump to protect itself. Ions spiraled in a mad dance along magnetic field lines.

Quasis shield on *Glory* penetrated, *Rampart* thought. 10 of its 48 inversion engines destroyed.

Fire Impactors, dagger patterns 7–15, Kurj thought.

Quasis jump, *Rampart* thought. I've lost 12 decks.

Kurj absorbed the damage reports and sent out his commands. Within seconds the breach in the hull was sealed and recovery teams dispatched to the damaged area.

Fire tau cannons 26–38, he thought. **Whip patterns 1–4.**

The taus rocketed out of their cannons. Two of them hit ESComm frigates, exploding one while the other went into quasis. Four taus accelerated to near light speed and detonated against *Glory*'s shields, weakening the quasis. One tau blew up when its own quasis failed, and the last three taus inverted out of real space. Two of the inverted taus reappeared "on top" their target, an ESComm destroyer guarding *Glory*'s flank. The combined force of their explosions collapsed the destroyer's shields and all three craft disappeared in a burst of radiation and debris.

The last tau dropped back into real space *within* the *Glory* quasis field. For one millisecond the quasis remained coherent, holding the tau frozen in space only meters above the cruiser. Then the relativistic force of the tau broke the quasis and the missile hit *Glory*'s bridge at 96 percent of light speed. With a fountain of spewing debris, energy, and particles, explosions ripped through the battle cruiser.

Glory command web damaged, *Rampart* thought.

How many ships left? Kurj thought. **For both fleets.**

ISC fleet at 306, *Rampart* answered. ESComm at 298.

Kurj exhaled. He had lost seven hundred ships in less than three minutes, most of them unscrewed drones. **Estimate the probability of successful completion of this engagement in favor of ISC.**

Probability is 79–88%.

Kurj controlled his wave of triumph. **Activate auxiliary Impactors and Annihilators.** They needed victory fast. The longer the battle drew out, the more it favored ESComm, which could leak ships out of superluminal space for hours.

Quasis jump, *Rampart* thought. Tau hit on my starboard docking bays. At 159 seconds after the battle began, it added: ISC fleet at 228. ESComm at 140. Probability of successful engagement in favor of ISC at 83–94%. Rampart inversion possible in 21 seconds.

Then the *Megapolis* blasted out of inversion.

The ESComm battle cruiser hurtled into real space with its Annihilators and Impactors firing, a cloud of smart dust and MIRV missiles racing before it, and an antimatter Wasp the size of a Starslammer destroyer.

At 175 seconds into the battle, five seconds before *Rampart* could invert, it thought, Quasis jump, followed by: Imperator Skolia, the attack from the *Megapolis* destroyed over 80% of my body and systems. The ESComm ships have also planted quasis generators within my hull, using doctored tau missiles.

Kurj absorbed the disaster: all that remained of *Rampart* was the bridge, several decks, one inversion engine, and a few Klein containment bottles. The deaths of his people tore through his mind, leaving an agonizing sensation of amputation.

Quasis jump, *Rampart* thought. ISC fleet at 82. ESComm at 265. Probability of ISC success at 37%.

Kurj focused on his displays. Thirty-seven percent. Still a better than a one-in-three chance. Embedded in his command chair, he was a force unlike any ESComm would have met in other battles, both in the Rhon strength of his mind and in the sheer depth of his military experience. Reaching out with a mental power unmatched by anyone alive, even within his own family, he literally grabbed *Megapolis* with his mind and submerged into the mammoth cruiser, radiating his consciousness along its conduits and pathways, taking *Rampart*'s awareness with him.

Fire the remaining 6 tau cannons in whip pattern 7, he thought.

At 182 seconds, two seconds after *Rampart* could have inverted had all its engines survived, five of its last six tau missiles exploded without effect against the *Megapolis* quasis shield. The sixth tau penetrated a flaw in the shield and destroyed seven decks on the cruiser. In the process, it destabilized the fields of nine out of the cruiser's 462 Klein fuel bottles.

Quasis jump, *Rampart* thought. ISC fleet at 35. ESComm at 253. Then: I have new information. Ur Qox is aboard the *Megapolis*.

Kurj froze. **How do you know that?**

The *Megapolis* web has been sabotaged. Qox wasn't supposed to go into battle. Combined with the amplification I am receiving from your mind, that damage has made it possible to penetrate their security.

Fools, Kurj thought. The Traders were so busy stabbing each other in the back, they sabotaged their own war effort.

The emperor intends to board this craft, *Rampart* thought.

Kurj gritted his teeth. **Can we invert with only one engine?**

At our rate of acceleration, we will reach sufficient speed in 6 seconds.

What is the probability that in 6 seconds we will still be alive, free, and in a condition to invert?

17%, *Rampart* thought.

Why so low?

Rampart showed him a display of itself, or what remained, highlighting several areas in red. Continued acceleration or inversion may cause structural collapse in these areas.

What about the ESComm quasis generators in the hull? Kurj asked. **Won't they stop your collapse?**

They have frozen my self-destruct systems, but there aren't enough to stop a full collapse.

So they still had an out. **Can you invert sooner?**

Any sooner and probability of collapse jumps to over 90%.

Kurj exhaled. A 17 percent chance they could invert. One-in-six odds that he would survive to seek vengeance another day.

One in six.

It meant a five-in-six chance of failure. A five-in-six chance he would die for nothing.

Nor was it likely he would ever be this close to Qox again.

How many Klein containment bottles do you have intact? he asked.

41, *Rampart* answered.

Kurj considered. Since the attack on Althor's flotilla, ISC had scrambled to counter this new technique of implanting rogue quasis generators. On such short notice, the best the engineers had been able to do was modify the quasis generators for the Klein fuel bottles on *Rampart* so their fields interfered with the rogue fields. They hoped to make it appear the bottles were under ESComm direction when, in fact, *Rampart* still controlled them. But it was a crisis fix, untested, with no guarantee it would work.

Can you operate any of the bottles? Kurj asked.

18, *Rampart* thought.

Kurj made his decision. **Cut the engine. Play dead.**

Four seconds before they could have tried to invert, *Rampart* cut power. It shot through space at constant speed and *Megapolis* kept pace, maneuvering into position.

Then came the long process of the hunter taking control of its captured prey.

As soon as *Megapolis* gained entry into *Rampart*'s ravaged web, the ESComm cruiser began its captive's deceleration, dumping *Rampart*'s velocity over a huge region of space, gently, to preserve the remains of a ship held together by little more than quasis fields. *Megapolis* used its rogue quasis generators to block the self-destruct toggles in Kurj's biomech web. Intending to take no chance this time that their prize would try to kill himself, ESComm put Kurj to sleep.

Or so they thought.

ESComm had no real sense of what they faced in Kurj. He watched from every section of *Rampart,* submerged even into the picoweb of nanobots that repaired the hull. His spinal nodes put him in a trance state that resembled sleep. But he knew all that happened. Saw it all. Heard it all.

The battle took three minutes; deceleration took three hours. After the cruisers came to a sedate drift, *Megapolis* took another two hours to secure *Rampart.* Quasis fields, hull integrity, inversion engine, chemical fuel, fusion engines, antimatter drives, navigation, weapons, science stations, consoles, thrusters, shrouds—*Megapolis* tested it all, verifying the death of its foe. Again and again its probes passed over the Klein bottles, without a blip of warning.

The time came to take possession. *Megapolis* positioned its great underbelly only meters from *Rampart.* The ponderous door of a docking bay rolled open, a ten-meter-thick section of hull. Cranes the size of city towers unfolded, lights running along their extent. They closed around *Rampart* like claws and drew it into the bay.

It took another hour to secure *Rampart* within *Megapolis.* Probes locked the quiescent Kurj into his chair, fastening his arms, legs, and neck. By now his mind permeated the very molecular structure of the ship. He checked *Rampart*'s Klein bottles, smoothed flaws here, fortified camouflage there.

The ESComm probes passed over the bottles.

Ten hours after the battle began, Ur Qox, Emperor of

Eube, High Commander of ESComm, boarded *Rampart.* In magnetized boots, he walked, surrounded by mammoth waroids, along the catwalk to the command chair.

Kurj watched from everywhere.

"Revive him," Qox said.

With a stimulant applied, Kurj's biomech web pretended to awake, resuming activities ESComm could monitor. Kurj opened his eyes, watching Qox from his own body now as well as from the rest of the bridge. He saw a metal giant locked into the command chair, his face a metal mask with featureless gold shields where a normal man had eyes.

So Imperator and Emperor met.

Qox nodded. "Imperator Skolia."

Kurj's voice rumbled. "Emperor Qox." Then he thought: **NOW.**

Rampart collapsed its Klein bottles. Every particle in every one of eighteen bottles converted to the real universe—

And two metric tons of antimatter dumped onto *Rampart.*

The plasma exploded, tearing apart the ship from within, annihilating everything it touched. Gamma radiation ripped through *Rampart* and into *Megapolis.* Brutally energetic reactions cascaded everywhere, setting off more reactions. The eight destabilized Klein bottles on *Megapolis* collapsed, adding to the storm. The chaos destroyed the protective shields on the remaining *Megapolis* fuel bottles—and over 450 Klein bottles dropped their contents into real space.

The ensuing maelstrom blasted across space, obliterating all trace of the ISC and ESComm fleets. It took with it the two most powerful war leaders known in the history of the human race, one who died as the unrepentant tormentor of humanity and the other who died having finally made peace with the torments that ravaged his heart.

V

The Radiance War

15

Viquara, Empress of Eube, walked through the Hall of Circles. The Aristos of Glory filled the seats, rank upon rank. Silent. Watching. An escort of Razer bodyguards surrounded her, those select few she had best reason to believe remained faithful to the Carnelian Throne. In the silence of the watching Circles, she walked to the dais, tall and silent, wearing a gown made from threads of black diamond, her hair falling to her waist in a glittering sheet like spun black diamond.

She reached the dais and stood by the throne, looking out at the Aristos. Snow-marble, ruby, diamond. Jewels. Hard, chill, and silent. Do jewels have a soul? she wondered. Did it matter?

In the outer Circles, where the lowest ranked Aristos sat, she recognized almost no one. The inner Circles told a different story: here sat High Judge Calope, of the Line of Muze, the grieving wife of Admiral Ajaks, in glittering black mourning; here sat Izar Vitrex, Minister of Intelligence, he too in black; his wife Sharla, with her snow-marble face, red eyes, and black diamond gown; Kryx Quaelen, tall, broad-shouldered, contaminated.

As one, the Aristos of the Circles raised their hands, each with a black diamond cymbal on their thumb and forefinger. As one they clicked the cymbals. The hundreds of chimes combined into a single resonant note. Again they clicked and again the resonant note rang out. The double click had been heard only two other times in Eube history, at the death of Jaibriol I, father to Ur Qox, and at the death of Eube, grandfather to Ur Qox.

Viquara spoke in a voice as cold as the empty space in

her heart. "The Line of Qox acknowledges the honor you bestow."

They continued to watch her. Silent. She knew the question they had come to hear answered. By what right did she claim the Carnelian Throne? She had no Qox blood.

Two of those seated before her carried that blood in their veins: Corbal Xir, firstborn son of Eube Qox's sister Ilina; and Calope Muze, last and only living child of Eube's youngest sister Tarquine. Many would claim they had more right to the throne. Viquara knew she needed a better tie to the Qox bloodline than marriage.

She laid her hand on the glittering throne. "My husband once sat here." Her voice carried throughout the Hall. "His son will do the same."

A whisper of cymbals came from the Circles. With the Razers at her back, always alert, Viquara waited. She neither heard nor expected a challenge now. When those came—and come they would—they would be silent and hidden.

She spoke again. "Rumor has claimed that Emperor Qox, whose esteemed memory we revere, hid our son to protect him from ISC malevolence. Those rumors were true, but in a way none may expect." She touched her abdomen, where the lie had begun its life. "Years ago Ur Qox and I fertilized my eggs with his sperm and froze them. I now carry one of those eggs."

The Aristos waited. Highton, Diamond, Silicate. All waited to hear more. Viquara let them wait. She had said enough. The situation required she speak and she had done so. Let them bring challenge now if they dared.

In life, Ur had refused her pleas to heal her barren womb. He monitored her every move, blocked her every turn. But he was dead now, and she, Viquara, wielded the power of the throne. Those doctors who had refused to help now jumped to her bidding.

She had formulated this plan the day Ur told her another Highton woman had borne him a child, an heir he would name Jaibriol, to fill the barren void Viquara had left in his life. Over the years Viquara had stolen samples from Jaibriol: a lock of hair, a nail clipping, a scrape of skin, a drop of saliva. With exacting care she stored those precious cells.

Now, when the time had come to harvest them, many of the cells inexplicably failed her. But her geneticist spurred three into healthy totipotence, reawakening their full genetic code, so that each offered a full blueprint of Jaibriol Qox.

The doctor removed three of Viquara's eggs and fertilized them with sperm from one of her providers. She then replaced the nucleus in each fertilized egg with a nucleus from one of Jaibriol's three reawakened cells. One egg died, but the other two survived. So Viquara created two clones of Jaibriol.

Next the doctor repaired Viquara's womb and implanted one egg, leaving the second in storage as a backup. Thus would Viquara make the abiding lie of Jaibriol's birth into truth. She carried a clone of her "son." Genetic tests done on it would match those for Jaibriol and verify the child as the son of Ur Qox.

Highton bloodlines meant strength. Aristos weren't like psions, whose genetic weakness made them almost impossible to clone. Highton clones thrived.

So she ensured her claim to the Carnelian Throne.

Izar Vitrex, Minister of Intelligence, came to observe his people at work. Equipment filled the laboratory: huge machines crouched against the ceiling, silver gurneys whispered by on wheels, consoles flickered with light.

Today the technicians had Althor in a chair. Its back was part of the wall, embedded with conduits. Metal bands fastened Althor's upper arms to the wall, his wrists to the arms of the chair, and his ankles to its legs. Two technicians stood in front of him and two more watched from a few paces back. Someone had folded his clothes into a pile on a nearby stool. His gold head hung to his chest, though whether he was unconscious or simply exhausted Vitrex couldn't tell.

Oq Vitrexson was leaning over Althor. A gaunt taskmaster

with glittering hair and rusty eyes, Oq had distinguished himself as one of Vitrex's best techs. Oq was also his half brother, a son of Vitrex's late father by one of his providers.

Taking a handful of Althor's hair, Oq pulled up the Ruby prince's head and spoke in a pleasant tone. "Let's go back to our earlier conversation. Onyx Platform."

Althor stared at him with drug-bleared eyes.

"Onyx," Oq repeated. "You have a number of weapons platforms there. You want to tell me about it."

"I can't," Althor rasped.

"No?" Oq struck Althor, knocking his head against the wall.

As Althor groaned, a wave of transcendence swept over Vitrex. He stiffened, trying to smother it. Transcendence, what an Aristo shared with a provider, was a private experience, inappropriate in this situation.

A specialized series of nanomeds in his body could damp his reaction to providers, by making kylatine blockers that muffled his reception of an empath's mind. He activated the meds through a sequence of neural firing patterns. It was easy to produce the sequence; all he had to do was think a key phrase. For his key, he drew on one of Eube's best-known poets, Carzalan Kri, who centuries ago had written verses for his favored provider:

> You glimmer in my darkling sight,
> With your tender golden fears.
> Sing shadows from the glist'ning light;
> Sing shimmering sensual tears.
>
> Lie starless in your beauty bound,
> So tremulous in the night.
> Lie softly in my thundering arms,
> Beneath my darkening might.

Almost all Aristos used such techniques. Those few who let their need for providers filter into their public lives became pariahs.

As Vitrex joined the lab technicians, Oq bowed. "My honor at your presence, Minister Vitrex."

Vitrex nodded absently, his gaze on Althor. The Ruby prince watched him with no sign of recognition. Given Althor's drugged state, Vitrex doubted the man would recognize himself. But even with inadvisably high doses, the truth serums so far had achieved nothing.

"My greetings, Prince Althor," Vitrex said.

Althor moistened his cracked lips. "My greetings."

"I understand you've been chatting with my people," Vitrex said.

Althor just looked at him. A muscle twitched under his eye.

"I believe you and Oq were discussing Onyx Sector," Vitrex continued. "Weapons deployment, wasn't it?"

Althor spoke in a hoarse voice. "I couldn't tell you anything even if I wanted to. You know that."

"But you do want to, don't you?" Vitrex gentled his voice. "It would make life so much easier. Think of the rewards. A nice meal, a soft bed, a carafe of wine."

"I can't," Althor rasped.

Vitrex sighed. "That is unfortunate." He glanced at Oq. "Continue."

Oq entered commands on his palmtop. Vitrex knew the process. The palmtop would send instructions to IR receivers in Althor's collar, wrist, and ankle restraints. Oq's team had linked the picotech in the slave restraints to Althor's internal biomech system, using the sockets in his neck, wrists, and ankles. The restraints also extended neural fibers into his body. At Oq's command, those fibers would stimulate Althor's nerves while other signals impeded attempts by his biomech web to muffle the effect.

Althor's body went rigid and he made a choked sound. Then he screamed. Vitrex struggled to remain detached. He considered himself a compassionate man. Even knowing providers were less than human, he allowed that they could earn elevation of a sort. He regretted their pain but consoled himself with the knowledge that by allowing providers to elevate themselves, through their suffering, Aristos granted them a gift they would never earn on their own, as they were too weak to accept the price it exacted.

Vitrex saw Althor as an abomination, a provider who sought to elevate himself to the level of a Highton, an exaltation forbidden slaves. Even worse, he expected to take it without paying any price at all. Vitrex felt neither sympathy nor joy for Althor's agony, only a relief that the universe as he understood it had been made right again.

Roca sat in the dark. Across the room, a gold button glowed on the web console, the only light in the living room.

A rustle came from the archway that led into the bedroom. "Roca?" Eldrinson asked.

She kept staring at the darkness.

"Come back to bed," her husband said.

"I can't." Lying in bed without sleeping was even worse than sitting out here without sleeping. She spoke softly. "I wonder where Dehya is."

"She will come back."

"Maybe she no longer exists." Roca felt numb. "At least before all this happened, Eldrin had seen her. Now she's vanished. Into the web. Drifting forever."

"Roca, don't." Her husband came over and sat next to her. He pulled her into his arms, resting his head against hers. "Althor will come home. You will see."

Her protective numbness disintegrated. "I can't . . . I—Eldri, I can't bear this. They killed Kurj. They killed Soz. They killed Kelric. I can't stand to think what they're doing to Althor." Her voice broke. "How many of our children do they *want?*" Tears slid down her face. "Kurj was finally healing. Finally, after so long."

"He died the way he would have wanted. In battle."

"A great battle," she said bitterly.

Softly Eldrinson said, "He sent me a message after you two left Skyhammer."

"What did it say?"

"Just this: 'Father, the Skyhammer biology web node is down. We need to fix it.' "

It took Roca several heartbeats to absorb what was unusual about the message. "He called you Father?"

His voice caught. "Yes. It was the last thing he ever said to me."

16

Viquara surveyed the office: black diamond walls, topaz floor, ruby furniture. The emperor's office. Her office. But for how long? She clung to power by a spider thread, the promise of the Qox heir she carried. Ur had no close relatives, both his sister and brother having died long ago. Accidents of course. That those accidents happened soon after he discovered they coveted the Carnelian Throne was a lesson Viquara had noted.

Who now most threatened her claim? Her spies brought four names: Calope Muze and Corbal Xir, both of the Qox bloodline, old even by Highton standards, the only Aristos with white hair; Intelligence Minister Izar Vitrex, whose name-plus-title was an oxymoron if ever she had heard one, besides which he was married to the irritating Sharla Azer; and Kryx Quaelen, who had no basis for a claim to the Carnelian Throne but might very well be the most dangerous of her opponents.

So the empress held an auction.

Viquara flicked her finger through the holicon of a file that floated above the desk, bringing up the record of her late husband's estate. She was selling most of his providers at public auctions, but the best would go in private auctions. An invitation to such an auction from the palace was an esteemed honor. And she had known exactly whom to honor.

She flicked another holicon and the wall to her right activated, showing a vibrant image of the Sky Pavilion with its hanging silk panels dyed in blue, gold, or rose. Breezes from the palace gardens rippled the silks and sunshine filtered through them. At a low table in one room, three men reclined in loungers: Izar Vitrex, Kryx Quaelen, and Corbal Xir. The slave girl Cirrus was kneeling by Quaelen, pouring red wine into his goblet.

Although the "girl" looked in her teens, her file listed her as almost thirty. She had perfect skin, blushed with color. The proportions of her voluptuous body were such that both Vitrex and Quaelen had challenged the veracity of the specifications sent prior to the auction. But they could see for themselves now. Cirrus wore a halter made from soft gold. Metal blossoms covered her nipples, but the halter was otherwise little more than gold strips tooled into vine patterns. Her only other garment was a skirt of rose gauze, midthigh in length and slung low on her hips, held in place by a gold belt. Her attire nicely matched the pavilion decor, as Viquara had intended. One had to conduct a palace auction with style, after all.

She had included Cirrus's accessories in the sale, the wrist and ankle cuffs and the matching collar, all made of a diamond-steel alloy. Packed with picotech, the slave restraints not only monitored Cirrus, they also spied on everyone around her. Of course, if the buyer kept the accessories, he would undoubtedly reprogram them. But Viquara knew her spytech. She felt confident that at least some of her hidden routines would remain operational.

The delicate gold circlet on Cirrus's upper arm monitored her health and could be removed only with proper equipment. If anything endangered her, it alerted her owner and had a limited capacity to inject nanomeds. Her glossy hip-length yellow hair had enhanced body and softness, her angel's face glowed with a creamy enhanced complexion, and her gigantic eyes were enhanced to an intense blue. All in all a package well worth the floor bid of a million Viquara had set.

As Cirrus poured wine for the bidders, they debated a recent trade agreement. Although Viquara recorded the conversation, she doubted it contained anything useful. The bidders knew they were being monitored and would guard their words.

After Cirrus finished pouring the wine, she stayed by Corbal Xir. The elderly Highton played with her hair, running his fingers through it. His gestures looked absent-minded, but Viquara knew he was examining the merchandise.

Viquara had never liked Corbal Xir. He smiled too much. He also had strange ideas. She once heard him argue that Hightons, as a higher form of life, had a duty to resist transcendence. Izar Vitrex, now, he made sense. He came from an old line, well esteemed, a paragon of Highton values, his line so inbred that they all looked the same, even by Aristo standards. A gangly bunch of polestorks if there ever was one.

Kryx Quaelen was as aberrant as Cobal, but in the opposite direction. He didn't give a kiss in hell about what his providers suffered. And he was too smart. He sat sprawled in his lounge, his muscular body stretched out, broad shoulders held with the ease of a man who came by them naturally rather than through bodysculpting. Viquara noticed his height, his long legs, the sheen of his hair, the strong cast of his features. Then she flushed.

Pah, Viquara thought. She flicked a long finger through another holicon floating above her desk, the tiny image of a ledger. The latest tally immediately appeared on the glossy black surface. Corbal had upped his bid to 1.8 million, topping Quaelen's 1.7 million. In the Sky Pavilion, Vitrex brushed his finger across his palmtop and his bid of 1.9 million appeared on the tally.

Quaelen motioned to Cirrus. She rose gracefully and went to kneel in front of him. Lifting her chin, he turned her face from side to side. Then he ran his fingertip over a blossom on her halter. Before long he and Vitrex were engaged in a debate about whether or not her endowments would succumb to gravity enough to hold a lightpen under them if their means of support were removed. Quaelen unfastened her halter and took it off, revealing her attributes in all their glory. Her physical charms did nothing for Viquara, but then, she supposed her preferences in pleasure youths probably wouldn't do much for the bidders either.

Corbal produced a pen and handed it to Vitrex, who handed it to Quaelen, who placed it under the mammary in question. The pen fell down Cirrus's torso, evoking a ripple of amusement from the bidders. They launched into a discussion of recent advances in suspension engineering, incorporating so many innuendos to Cirrus that Viquara had to smile. The girl sat motionless, her gaze averted. Only Viquara noticed her frozen expression and clenched jaw. The bids rose at a rapid rate, up to 2.8 million.

So Viquara watched, alternately entertained and bored. When the bidders finished their meal, they took Cirrus into the silk-draped bedroom and Viquara found herself aroused as well. Corbal held less interest for her, being her great-grandfather's age, and Vitrex wasn't her type. But Kryx Quaelen—ah no, she had to resist that lure to his contaminated line.

Corbal seemed to offer Cirrus genuine affection. Vitrex soon grew bored with her lack of enthusiasm and his bids fell off. It irked Viquara. He had known ahead of time Cirrus came from a stock of providers bred for passivity. Quaelen took the girl with a powerful virility that Viquara didn't notice. Not at all. She had no interest in the way his big hands moved on a woman's body, no interest in how his well-developed muscles flexed and tensed as he moved, no interest in how he wrapped his hand in Cirrus's hair and pulled back her head to kiss her, or in the way he handled a woman with such self-assurance. No, Viquara most certainly had no interest in any of it at all.

It wasn't until evening spread its shadows over Glory that

the three Hightons took their leave of the pavilion. Their bids continued to rise, topped by 8.4 million from Quaelen.

Viquara glanced around her office. Her Razer bodyguards all stood at their posts, severe in midnight blue uniforms. She paged Security and another Razer soon appeared, Lieutenant Xirson, a recent addition to the force. Impressed with Xirson's military record, Ur had bought him from Corbal Xir and added him to the palace secret police.

Xirson bowed. "My honor at your presence, Your Highness."

"Bring me the girl," Viquara said.

After Xirson left, she checked the auction tally. The bids were coming in slower now, as they reached levels that strained even the immense financial resources of their makers. Corbal put in one for 9.6 million and no others followed.

Xirson reappeared with Cirrus, the girl once again dressed in her halter and translucent skirt. As Cirrus knelt in the center of the room, Viquara dismissed the Razers, including her bodyguards. Then she closed the door and went to her desk to check her security systems. Finally she turned to Cirrus. Still kneeling, with her head bowed, the girl shivered in the chill air.

"You may rise," Viquara said. As Cirrus got up, her arms hugging her torso, Viquara motioned to a velvet cloth on a table. "You may warm yourself."

The girl's arms shook as she took the cloth and wrapped it around her body. She spoke in a soft voice. "You honor me far beyond what I deserve, Your Esteemed Highness."

True, Viquara thought. She settled herself into the big chair behind her desk. "What do you have for me?"

"Minister Vitrex wonders if you know about his son."

Good. Let Izar sweat. No proof existed that he had contributed to Ur's death, but she had her suspicions. "What else is he up to?"

"He is planting suggestions that your child is the bastard of another man rather than your husband's heir."

It didn't surprise Viquara. Originality had never been one of Vitrex's strengths. His timeworn techniques would be easy to counter with her network of far more subtle mudslingers.

"Anything else?" she asked.

Cirrus nodded. "Lord Corbal has finance problems. A long time ago he invested money in guilds that bought from frigates working Allied territory. Since the frigates have been forbidden to harvest providers from Allied ships, he has lost a lot of wealth."

That intrigued Viquara. Based on the size of Corbal's bids, she would never have guessed he suffered financial trouble. The besotted old Highton must really want Cirrus. She checked the tally. Only one more bid had come in, 9.8 million from Quaelen.

"What about Minister Quaelen?" she asked.

Cirrus tensed, her face turning red.

"Out with it," Viquara said.

The girl wouldn't look at her. "While he was with me, he was thinking of someone else."

"Really?" Viquara smiled, fascinated. "Who might that be?"

"He, um, he—I mean . . ."

"Come on, girl. Speak up."

"You, Your Highness."

Viquara blinked. Quaelen had fantasized he was making love to her? This was unexpected.

Cirrus had no more to offer on that, but she provided many other useful tidbits. The girl's ability to extract information impressed Viquara. Ur had done good work with this one. But then, Ur always did well. Viquara swallowed, remembering his laugh, his hooded eyes, his powerful voice. Gone. All gone.

One more bid came in, 10.1 million from Vitrex. She put out a call for final bids, but neither Quaelen nor Corbal responded. So she closed the auction and regarded Cirrus. "You will go to Vitrex."

Cirrus nodded, huddled in her blanket.

"You understand our arrangement?" Viquara asked.

"Yes, Your Highness."

Viquara wondered if the girl could actually carry it through. "Repeat it to me."

"I'm to send psion transmissions about the Vitrex household to your provider Cayson. I should only do it when I'm secluded from other people, especially other providers. So nobody can eavesdrop." She paused. "And only at the times you said, so Cayson is also prepared."

Viquara waited. Then she prompted, "What about distance?"

"Oh. Yes." Cirrus flushed. "I'm to try no matter how far away I am."

"Good." The interactions fell off rapidly with distance, so Viquara doubted Cirrus would get much through. But any little bit might help. "As long as you please the Throne, your son will be raised as befits a wellborn taskmaker. He will have an education and a home here."

Cirrus's voice caught. "Thank you, Your Highness. You are the most kind and benevolent of all human beings."

Well, of course, Viquara thought. "It is only fitting. He is the son of an emperor, after all."

A tear rolled down Cirrus's face. "Much to my honor."

"Come." Viquara stood up. "You may tell the boy goodbye. Then we will get you delivered to Vitrex."

They all sat at the conference table in the Strategy Room on the Orbiter: Web Key Eldrinson Valdoria, his son Eldrin Valdoria, First Councilor of the Assembly Barcala Tikal, and the rest of the Inner Assembly: Stars, Industry, Nature, Judiciary, Protocol, Life, Planetary Development, Finance, and Domestic Affairs. And Roca, the Councilor for Foreign Affairs.

"I understand your objections," Tikal told Roca. "But you're the only choice."

Judiciary leaned forward. "Councilor Roca, surely you see this."

Roca felt trapped. Kurj had chosen three heirs to follow

him as Imperator, and all were gone now, two dead and the third a prisoner of war. The Triad needed an Imperator. Roca knew she was no war leader, but who else in the Ruby Dynasty could assume the title?

As First Heir to the Web Key, her son Eldrin had trained to follow his father and had even less experience than she with ISC. The twins Del and Chaniece, her next children after Eldrin and Althor, still lived on their home world Lyshriol. They watched over their father's farm in his absence and carried out his duties as the Dalvador Bard. At one time those duties included commanding the Dalvador regiment of the Rillian army, but after Althor had ended warfare on Lyshriol, the position became titular. Not that it mattered. Chaniece had no interest in warfare and Del's experience with sword and lance hardly qualified him to lead Imperial Space Command.

Havyrl, born after the twins, had a doctorate in agriculture. He had earned his degrees from Royal College on the planet Metropoli, without ever leaving home, by attending through the web as a holographic simulacrum, a method possible only to those who could access psiberspace. Content to leave politics to his siblings, he spent the next fifty years farming and making babies with his wife. Soz had been born the year after Havyrl, and then Denric, who taught school to disadvantaged children on the planet Sandstorm. Deni's gentle nature worked wonders with his students but hardly qualified him to run ISC. Shannon ran off at sixteen with a band of Rillian archers, and Aniece had become the child bride of Lord Rillia by seducing him when she was far too young to know about such things. Kelric, their youngest, had died in combat sixteen years ago.

The only other choice was Taquinil, Dehya and Eldrin's son. A brilliant economist, he had once calculated futures with such uncanny accuracy that the dismayed Office of Finance actually passed a law forbidding him to work the stock market. But he was already Crown Prince to the Ruby Throne, besides which he had no military experience. And a more serious problem existed.

When Dehya and Eldrin finally gave in to the demands of the Assembly and had a child, their son Taquinil suffered the price of inbreeding. Born of two psions already at the limit of what humans could endure in empathic sensitivity, he couldn't block *any* empathic input. As a boy, he lived in an unending onslaught of emotions, until finally his personality shattered. Confused and terrified, he hid his many personalities from everyone, including other telepaths, even himself. He was in his teens by the time his condition became too severe to hide any longer. So began his long healing. Fixing his defective genes would have destroyed his Rhon ability, so instead he took biomech in his body, to synthesize the kylatine and neurotransmitters his brain lacked. With help he eventually reintegrated his personalities, but he was in no position to assume command of ISC.

Nor were military and emotional suitability the only factors to consider. Whoever joined the Triad as Imperator needed a mind having the least possible overlap with Dehya and Eldrinson. Roca's sons Eldrin, Del, and Havyrl were too much like their father. Taquinil and Aniece were too much like Dehya. Chaniece was more like Kurj, but neither Del nor Chaniece could even read and write. Roca didn't know about her sons Denric or Shannon; they had always been different, Denric with his sweet nature and penchant for books, and Shannon as the fey archer with white-gold hair. She suspected they were throwbacks to more distant ancestors, with no telling what would happen if either went into the Triad.

Which left her. She resembled Kurj not only in physical aspects such as her gold coloring, but also in her mind.

Roca spoke quietly. "For a decision like this, Dehya should be here."

"She sent me a message this morning," Eldrinson said. "She agrees with the Assembly that you should become Imperator."

"How could she agree with us this morning?" Tikal asked. "We just made the decision."

No one answered. Roca suspected they had given up trying to fathom Dehya. She pushed her hand through her hair. "I'll let you know soon, Barcala. I need time to think."

But she saw no good answer.

17

Cirrus stood at the glass doors in her bedroom and gazed out at her garden, with its neat lawns and flower beds, and the tangled woods beyond. The crescent of G4, the Unnamed Moon, graced the portion of the afternoon sky visible from where she stood. She wished her son Kai could be with her to see this beautiful place. She missed him. Kai had given her a family, something she never had before.

She had been raised by Silicate Aristos, in a crèche designed to produce human merchandise. Her education consisted of learning how to serve Hightons. The Silicates also taught her how to look aesthetic while kneeling in a corner for long periods of time, a pastime that topped her list of stupid tasks.

When she reached physical maturity, they sent her to a pavilion, where she spent all her time learning what she would do for as long as genes and technology made her beautiful, which was giving Aristos pleasure. Before the Silicates sold her, they cheated and made her back into a virgin. They did it so well that the palace bodysculptors verified it and Emperor Qox paid a great deal more for her. So she lost her virginity three times: once just before she went to the pavilion, when a Silicate boy pulled her into a closet; once just after she went to the pavilion, in a ceremony with her instructors; and once when the emperor laid her across his glacial bed.

She never learned to read, write, or do numbers. She was never allowed to play as a child. She had no friends. She knew the word "love" only in reference to her training in the pavilion. Aristos decreed she should be grateful to them, but as far as she was concerned they could all fester with the plague.

At first she had thought her pregnancy was a bizarre new phase in the bodysculpting they were always doing on her body. Then she realized what was going on. She liked being fat. She had always wanted to be huge and wear hideous clothes.

The bodysculptors put her breasts back to normal. After Kai's birth, she saw why; the first thing he did was suckle, which he could never have managed with her enlarged nipples. Perhaps the emperor felt put out by the changes. She hoped so. For months he left her alone, except to visit the baby, who tended to spit up on him, which amused Cirrus no end, though she never let on.

As Kai grew, he pushed her parenting. She was unsure how to respond. He was the emperor's child, after all. When he yelled, "No!" did she give in? She soon discovered that such an approach made life miserable. So she set limits, and no lightning struck her for scolding a child with Highton blood. As had uncounted empaths before her, she reached in instinct for his mind, using empathy to love and understand him. That he grew into such a well-adjusted child at first puzzled her, seeing him so different from herself at that age. Then she decided, so what? He was happy and so was she.

But as Kai grew, she sensed a lack in his life. More and more he asked about his father. She wished he had someone other than Ur Qox to model his behavior on, but she had no way to offer or even define "more."

Kai knew when his father died. He cried while Cirrus rocked him in her arms. Then Empress Viquara separated them, much as she might sell one of two exotic vases in a matched set.

So Cirrus went to Vitrex. As it turned out, she bored him witless in bed. Not that she would ever suggest such a condition applied even when he was vertical. The nights he "allowed" her to provide for him were inescapable. After he satiated himself with her screams, he murmured endearments and fell asleep embracing her, a travesty of affection that left her emotions in an echoing place of emptiness.

What inspired him to pay so much in the auction, though, had as much to do with her abilities as a spy as anything else. So today he came to her suite.

"It is simple," he said as he folded his lanky body into a soft white lounger. "You do the same with Althor as with anyone else."

"But I don't know anything about interrogation," she said.

"You don't need to." He sprawled in his seat with his legs stretched long across the white carpet. "Bring me wine and I will explain."

So Cirrus brought a carafe and knelt at the lacquered table, where she filled his diamond goblet with red wine.

"Althor has neural blocks in his brain that keep us from finding out what he knows." Vitrex took the goblet and sipped from it. "He can't help us even when he tries."

She sat back on her heels. "What would you like me to do?"

With a smile, he cupped his hand under her chin. "What you do best, my love."

A panel glowed high in the cell, shedding dim light over the prisoner who lay sleeping on the cot, on his stomach, his fists clenched at his sides.

Softly Cirrus said, "Wake up, beautiful gold man."

He jerked, then lashed out with his fist as his eyes snapped open. The blow was brought up short by the chain that stretched from his wrist cuff to a ring in the wall. Vitrex had warned her about how Althor woke up, so she had stood out of range, a few paces from his cot.

He stared at her, his eyes bleared with sleep, and spoke in a hoarse voice, his throat torn raw. "Who are you?"

"Cirrus." She twisted the sash on her thigh-length robe of yellow Hesterian silk. "Minister Vitrex sent me to you."

He pushed up on his elbow. "Why?"

"As a reward. Because you are trying to cooperate."

"I doubt that."

"It's true." She hesitated. "May I come closer?"

He jerked on his chain. "How do you know I won't try to strangle you with this?"

She lowered her gaze. Apparently Skolians weren't so different from Hightons after all.

"Ai. Don't look like that," he rasped. "I didn't mean it. Come here if you want."

Wary, she went over and sat next to him. Up close, she saw that he was drugged, in a daze. Feeling his hazed pain, both physical and emotional, she wanted to reach out to him. But she also felt the coiled danger in his massive body.

He was lying on his side, propped up on his elbow. "I know why you're here," he muttered. "Won't work. The more you try to steal, the less there is to take."

"To take?"

"Memories. My web is erasing them."

"Good memories or bad?" She had many of her own she wished to lose.

The question seemed to confuse him. "Neither. Just data."

"Are you sorry to lose them?"

He lay down on his back. "Do you really want to do something for me?"

"Yes." She set her palm on his chest, feeling the rough weave of his shirt and the powerful muscles under it. "Whatever you would like."

"Slit my wrists. Better yet my throat. That works faster."

"Ai, don't say that, beautiful man."

I can't give you what you came for, he thought.

She nearly screamed. His thoughts rumbled in her mind, deep and resonant, without the torn quality of his voice. She scrambled off the cot and retreated to the far wall.

Althor sat up. **Come back,** he thought. That had a lonely edge to it, muffled from drugs and fatigue.

Cirrus knew the cell was monitored. What would the guards think of her huddling against the wall for no reason? Nothing good, of that she had no doubt. So she made herself walk back to Althor, three paces across the floor, metal under her bare feet. Hugging her robe tight around her body, she sat next to him and waited to see what he would do.

He brushed his hand over her hair, then nudged apart her arms and tugged on her sash. As it came undone, her robe fell open, revealing her body. In a husky voice he said, "You are so very beautiful, did you know that?"

"Emperor Qox said so."

He cupped his palms around her face. "I would take you away from all this if I could, to a land where the sun always shines." His voice drifted off and he dropped his arms. "I lived once in a place like that. Day for half the year. Because of the axial tilt . . . It was on . . . I don't remember."

"What would you like me to do for you?" Cirrus asked.

"Here . . ." He lay on his back, pulling her with him. She stretched out along his side and put her head on his shoulder, waiting for him to continue. But he just lay with his arms around her. So she closed her eyes. She picked up almost nothing from his mind, but that "nothing" came far more vividly than from any Highton. His mind was a place of gleams and columns, air and radiance, an open plaza framed by a circular building.

Locked doors showed in the building. She tried them all, with no success. Then she noticed a discreet door hidden in a recess behind a much heavier portal. Unlike the other barriers, this door had weakened under the onslaught of drugs and interrogation. It stayed hidden only because the larger portal shadowed it.

She opened it and walked inside. And there he was.

Jaibriol Qox.

He was sitting alone. Or was he alone? She couldn't see the entire room. On her left, it blended into a haze that separated this chamber from whatever hid behind the larger door.

Why are you here? Cirrus asked him.

I'm not here, he said, in Althor's voice.

Where are you?

I don't know. In exile. On an Allied World.

Her pulse raced. *You are alive?*

Yes. His answer echoed. **Yes.**

Althor stirred at her side, oblivious to her spying. "You smell wonderful." He nudged her onto her back, pushing aside her robe as he stroked her belly. "Tell me," he murmured. "Tell me what you like."

"Like?"

"How do you like to be touched?"

She hated to be touched. But she could never say that.

You can to me, Althor thought. He sighed, his hand stilling as his lashes drooped closed over his eyes.

That caught Cirrus by surprise. No one had ever cared what she wanted before. They took as they pleased. She knew what Vitrex wanted. If she uncovered useful secrets from Althor, it would elevate Vitrex among the Hightons. And now she owned a priceless secret. Jaibriol Qox was alive. Vitrex would reward her. If she told the empress, the reward could be even better. The empress might reunite Cirrus with her son Kai.

But what about Althor? She had seen his mental places, so much cleaner in spirit than a Highton mind. And it mattered to him what she wanted. Or didn't want.

She tried an experiment. *Althor?*

Yes?

She blinked, startled at how easily it had worked. He looked like he was still asleep. *I must tell them.*

Tell what?

That Jaibriol Qox is alive.

His eyes snapped open. **No! He's dead.**

It's in your mind.

NO. You're wrong.

I saw it.

He made a choked sound. **You must never reveal it.**

You can't begin to understand the damage it would do.

Saying nothing will do worse. To you. She touched his cheek, wishing the caress could heal him. *You are dying inside your mind. You must tell. Then they will stop hurting you.*

If you say anything, they'll try that much harder with me, knowing they're close to something big. Desperation edged his words. **I'm barely holding on now. If they push any harder, I—I don't think I can withstand it.**

She felt as if walls were closing around her. As an empath, she knew he told the truth, as he saw it; besides which, he was too drugged to lie. *I don't want to be the cause of them hurting you more.* But what of her son?

Many people will be hurt if you tell. Maybe killed.

Cirrus stiffened. If she caused suffering or death, that made her like a Highton. But still she resisted, thinking of Kai.

He watched her face. **Cirrus, please.**

Again he caught her off guard. Hightons never said "please" to a slave. They gave orders. Althor needed something more important from her than any Aristo had ever wanted and he *asked.*

Cirrus, don't tell anyone. It could destroy my people.

She swallowed. *I will keep your secret.*

He thought, simply, **Thank you,** but the gratitude he projected almost overwhelmed her.

She thought of Cayson, the provider she sent information to at the palace. *But how do I hide what I know?*

They don't train you to block your telepathic responses, do they?

If they think I'm trying to hide, they punish me.

Cirrus, I truly am sorry. If I could take away what you know, I would. He watched her face. **Imagine the secret is locked behind a door. The better you lock it up, the harder it is to find.**

I will try. She lay with her head on his shoulder and

remembered the good times with her son Kai, how he had run laughing to her, or learned a new game, or given a flower to old Azzi in the house across from theirs. She tried to forget that she may have just given up her only chance ever to see him again.

And she tried to forget Kai's brother, the man who could rule an empire.

18

Viquara stood in the hospital room staring at Doctor Tecozil, a gaunt Diamond Aristo with sharp features. "You are mistaken," the empress said. *Mistaken.* It had to be a mistake.

Tecozil offered her a holograph. "This shows it, Your Highness."

"No." Viquara took the graph and set it on the bed next to her. "It must be wrong." The words echoed in her mind. "The child lives."

Softly Tecozil said, "I am truly, deeply sorry."

How could it be? How could *both* clones of Jaibriol be unviable, not only the one she carried but also the second stored in reserve?

"I gave you many cells to work with." Viquara heard the chill in her voice. "How is it that you couldn't make one clone? Not *one?* You expect me to believe that?"

Tecozil spoke carefully. "Someone tampered with the cells."

Viquara didn't believe it. She had been too careful. "Indeed. And just how did they 'tamper'?"

"Those aren't Highton cells," Tecozil said. "They read that way in the tests, but when I realized even the last two clones failed, I did much more intensive exams." She took a breath. "Someone replaced your samples with contaminated specimens, ma'am. Cells from a provider. From a psion. The genetic mutations that create a psion are notoriously sensitive to manipulation. The more of the genes a person carries, the harder it is to clone them." She indicated the holograph on the bed. "He's a telepath, Your Highness. It's all there."

Viquara picked up the graph. She knew how to read it, having recently gone over a similar profile proving Vitrex's son was a slave. This one was even more damning.

Tecozil shook her head, in both denial and wonderment. "The rating suggested by that profile is so high I can't quantify it. I've never seen one like it."

Viquara had seen one very much like it. The profile was in her office right now, part of the genetic workup on Althor Valdoria. This one had the same signature. It belonged to a Rhon psion.

It was all becoming clear. Yes, now she saw. Tecozil was right. There had been a betrayal. But its magnitude went far beyond the doctor's imagining. Her late husband's protective attitude toward his son, the way he had hidden him—oh yes, it all suddenly made horrible, sick sense.

Jaibriol II had been Rhon.

A Rhon Highton Heir. It was brilliant. It also violated every standard of Highton decency. And that could only be the tip of the betrayal. Jaibriol's Rhon genes had to come from both parents. *Both.* Either Ur Qox hadn't been his father, which meant the Highton Heir had no Qox blood, a true abomination—

Or else Ur had been a slave.

Her husband, the man who had sat on the Carnelian Throne, who shared her bed, who even now she mourned beyond all Highton custom and expectation—he, a *slave?*

Viquara saw the fear in Tecozil's face. She modulated her voice to indicate an approval she didn't feel. "You have done well."

The doctor's shoulders relaxed. "It is my great honor to serve the Carnelian Throne."

"I have a suspicion as to who exchanged this specimen with the authentic sample," Viquara said. "I will send another sample later today. I want to know if the father is the same as the father of—" She lifted the graph. "Of this abomination."

"I will give it my utmost attention, Your Highness."

You had better, Viquara thought.

Viquara's bodyguards were waiting outside, as were a number of advisers wishing to talk to her. She sent them all back to the palace, even the guard captain who dared protest. Then she went to the well-guarded parks behind the palace, the living area for the late emperor's favored providers. She found the boy Kai studying in the house he shared with the old woman who took care of him now. He glanced up as Viquara entered, then scrambled to his feet and dropped on his knees before her with his head bowed.

She stared down at the tousled head. Black hair. The boy had red eyes too. Were they real? Cirrus had yellow hair and blue eyes. But Viquara had no doubt this child belonged to her late husband. Otherwise Ur would never have let him live at the palace. Now came time to see what genes Ur had contributed to him.

She took a lock of Kai's hair, a scrape of skin, and clippings from his nails. Then she locked the frightened child in a suite within the palace and delivered the samples to Tecozil herself, in secret.

Viquara was meeting in her office with several ESComm officers, going over their reports on the quelling of the civil unrest in Sapphire Sector, when Tecozil sent a slave to request an audience. Within the hour, Viquara had arranged to meet the doctor in a garden she knew was unmonitored.

"The father is the same," Tecozil said. "A different mother, though, one with a lower psi rating, about eight on the Kyle scale. The child is probably a nine, perhaps even ten. The father matched every Rhon gene the mother carried, including some she had unpaired."

"I see," Viquara murmured. She wanted to scream. "You have done well."

After Tecozil left, Viquara contemplated suicide. That impulse lasted all of a second. She had never had patience with this "Highton honor above life" business. She walked back to the palace, knowing only her anger. Ur Qox had been half *Rhon.* She had nowhere to turn her rage. He and the people who had created him were all dead, safe from repercussions.

Lieutenant Xirson and her bodyguards waited at her office. After the usual honorifics, which she barely noticed, Xirson said, "The provider Cayson humbly requests the honor of an audience."

"Bring him up," the empress said. This was the time Cayson picked up messages from Cirrus. Viquara gritted her teeth. Cirrus, who had given birth to an emperor's child, something the empress would never do.

She understood now why no record existed of Kai's parentage. She had assumed Ur considered the boy too inconsequential to acknowledge. But he had been protecting his son. And himself. If she had any sense, she would rid herself of that scrap of genetic evidence. But she hesitated to kill Kai, who was all she had left of her husband. Damn Ur Qox to a Skolian hell. She still cared about him, even now.

The matter of Tecozil was more serious. The doctor knew far too much. Viquara called in another contingent of Razers. Her orders were concise: make it look like an accident.

As the Razers were leaving, Xirson returned with Cayson. Viquara watched Cayson kneel to her with his familiar athletic grace. She sent her guards outside and closed the door, then stood considering Cayson. He was her favorite provider, a beautiful youth with curly hair, huge brown eyes fringed by lashes so long she would have envied him, had she cared about such things, and a body sculpted to masculine perfection. He was kneeling on one knee, his head bowed and his elbow resting on his other knee.

"You may rise," she said. It surprised her how calm she sounded.

Cayson stood. "I being honored by your lovely presence, Empress Viquara."

That was rather flowery for Cayson, who had a less than overwhelming grasp of language. Literacy had never been a trait she bothered with in providers.

"You have a message for me?" she asked.

Excitement flushed his face. "Cirrus has news of your son."

Her son. A fist of pain tightened inside her. She had looked forward to motherhood, an experience denied her for decades, one that should have been hers now, as well as her insurance for the throne. "I see nothing Cirrus can tell me I don't already know." Such as: *Your son is dead in your womb.* How did she make the hurt stop?

"Not the *baby.*" For Cayson, he was positively enthusing. "Your first! Jaibriol II."

Viquara stiffened. "My firstborn is dead. Do you speak ill of his name?"

"Your Highness, no!" Fear subdued his voice. "Never."

"Then what can you tell me of a man fifteen years dead?"

"Althor Valdoria is knowing something about his death," Cayson said. "Minister Vitrex sent Cirrus to spy on the prince. She's hiding something. Something important. It upsets her. That came through most strongest. The prince knows something important and Cirrus hides it for him."

Had the Skolians discovered the truth? The magnitude of it went beyond imagining. If they made such news public—no, it was unthinkable. She ought to just commit suicide now and get it over with.

Pah. If the Skolians knew about Jaibriol, they would have already shouted it to the stars. They had no reason to hide the secret when they had so much to gain by revealing it. Still, she had better find out if Valdoria knew anything useful.

"Thank you, Cayson." Her thoughts moved to other matters. "I'm having a guest dine at the palace tonight. You will serve us." She smiled. "I will have new clothes sent over for you. Green velvet." It was her favorite color and cloth.

"Yes, ma'am." He knelt to her again, waiting for her to call his escort.

Absently laying her hand on his head, Viquara stood lost in thought. She would miscarry soon. It meant she had to fortify her defenses even more now. She had surveillance on Vitrex, via Cirrus and Cayson, and other operatives working on Corbal Xir and Kryx Quaelen. Now came time to consider High Judge Calope Muze.

She looked down at Cayson. His pants caressed his long legs, the dark velvet clinging to his muscles. His shirt was white velvet with belled sleeves, unlaced, open to reveal his muscled chest. Inside his beautiful body, he had a biomech web and hydraulics. They conferred neither strength nor speed; rather, they ensured his actions remained appropriate toward whoever owned him, particularly if that person had less physical strength than Cayson. His body also carried specialized nanomeds that spurred intimate responses, according to various stimuli, as set out in the specifications that came with him.

Viquara smiled, stroking his hair while he stared at the floor. He would serve well when she dined with the aging judge tonight. Indeed. Hospitality to one's guest was always important.

"Tell me something, Caysi," she said.

"Yes, Your Highness?"

"Have you ever done spy work?"

"I don't think so." He sounded confused. "I'm sorry."

"That's all right," she said. "I will explain it to you."

High in the Jaizire Mountains, the Wilderness Palace retreat stood alone, shrouded with mist. Tonight Viquara walked its obsidian underground tunnels, shadowed by her Razers in their midnight blue uniforms. When they opened the dungeon, blackness greeted her. She activated her light, revealing a new framework that occupied the cell, this one heavier than the previous, a necessary precaution given the large size of the slave chained to it, on his back with his arms pulled over his head.

Viquara walked to Althor. She wasted no words. "You know something about my son. Jaibriol II." When he shook his head, she said, "Listen to me well, Ruby prince. My expert is going to work on you. He is a Razer now, but he used to be an ESComm major. Interrogation was his specialty. Once every ten minutes I will, in my great benevolence, allow you a respite. You will have one minute then to give me information. If you do, I will reward you. If you don't, my expert goes back to work."

His voice rasped. "I don't know anything about your son."

"Forty-seven seconds," she said.

"How can I tell you what I don't know?"

"Thirty-eight."

Desperation flashed on his face. "Jaibriol Qox died escaping from Diesha."

"I am aware of that. Twenty-three seconds."

"My sister died trying to catch him."

"Tell me what I don't already know. Eight seconds."

"That's all I know."

Viquara motioned forward a gaunt Razer waiting in the shadows.

She expected Althor to break right away. He was obviously pushed to his limits. Yet as the night progressed, despite the best work of her interrogator, Althor told her nothing. More and more she doubted Cayson's information. Telepathic transmission was tricky at best, more so over distance. Althor couldn't have held out this long if he actually knew something. No one was that strong, not even a Highton, certainly not a Ruby prince.

Finally she held up her hand for a stop. As the Razer stepped back into the shadows, Althor's chest heaved in ragged breaths. Viquara leaned over him, to tell him it was done, but before she could do so he spoke in a barely audible voice.

She bent her head more. "Again?"

"Gods grant me forgiveness," he whispered.

"Why?" she asked.

And then he told her.

Jaibriol II was alive.

19

Soz sat against a tree, watching twelve-year-old Lisi and fourteen-year-old Jai bring up water from the well a few paces away. Antiqued sunshine from the solitary Red streamed over the landscape, enough dimmer than the combined radiance of the two suns that the day looked dull to her. She shifted the dozing del-Kelric in her arms, trying to find a comfortable way to hold the toddler. She was so big now. This pregnancy tired her, prodding her to wonder if she was too old for making babies. Her sleep had been ragged lately, her dreams filled with vague horrors of interrogation and Traders.

Del-Kelric wriggled in her arms, then let out a wail. Jai glanced over, scowling at the boy. Then Lisi took the bucket from him, and he swung back around to her.

"Stop it!" he snapped.

She stiffened. "You don't have be a jolt-ass!"

"Quit shouting, you two," Soz growled. What ailed them today, that they flared so easily—

A scream cut through air.

Soz was up and moving toward the children before her mind even registered that her hydraulics had kicked in. She thrust del-Kelric at Jai, then ran toward the scream as fast as her bulk would allow. She recognized that terrified sound, knew that voice all too well. Vitar.

The six-year-old raced out of the forest, his short legs pumping faster than Soz had ever seen them go. She blocked his way and hauled the terrified boy up into her arms.

"Mama!" He kept screaming, flailing his fists at an unseen monster, blind to who held him. *"Hoshpa!"*

"Vitar! It's me. Hoshma!" Soz tried to break his panic. **I'm here! You're all right!**

He gave a ragged sob and threw his arms around her neck, burying his face in her hair.

"Careful, careful," Soz murmured. "What is it? What scared you? Where is your father, honey? Where is Hoshpa?"

"Dead," the boy sobbed. "All dead and gone."

"Vitar, no." Soz struggled to rein in her fear. "He can't be dead. We would feel it." She was aware of Jai and Lisi behind her, their minds hyperextended now, as was hers, reaching, reaching for Jaibriol.

Finding nothing.

Somehow she kept her voice calm. "Vitar, what happened?"

"Big silver bird came." He was almost incoherent. "Bad people in it." He lifted his head to look at her. "Shot Hoshpa. Shot at me. I ran away. They put Hoshpa into the bird and went into the sky."

Soz whirled to Jai and Lisi. "Get in the shelter *now.*"

Lisi hesitated. "But Father—"

"NOW!" Soz shoved them toward their house, which was on the other side of the well. She took off running, Vitar in her arms, with Lisi and Jai running at her side, Jai still carrying del-Kelric. They raced into the house, making a thunder of noise as they ran across the main room.

Soz yanked up the trapdoor in a corner. "Get down there. *Fast.*"

Lisi went first, followed by Jai, with del-Kelric. As they clambered down the wooden ladder, Soz knocked over a nearby shelf and swept everything she could reach into the hole. Trinkets and toys clattered in the darkness, pelting her children. She helped Vitar down after them, then lowered herself into the hole and pulled the trapdoor shut above them.

A deep rumble sounded in the distance.

"Get down!" she shouted. From Vitar's mind she picked up that he had reached the bottom and moved aside. She let go of the ladder and dropped the last two meters, landing with a jolt that made her fall to one knee. Del-Kelric wailed, his fear as tangible as a fog.

Soz lunged through the darkness, reaching out with her hands. As her fingers scraped the console, the rumbling outside grew louder. She stabbed at panels she knew by heart, from the libraries in her node and the drills she had made the family perform.

"Quasis field activated," the comp said.

The rumbling swept above them.

It was as if a giant picked up the world and shook it in a huge fist. It slammed Soz against the rigid quasis shield. Del-Kelric screamed and Lisi cried out, then called his name.

The shaking kept on, relentless, the world convulsing in an enraged frenzy. It threw them into each other, smashed them against the quasis shield again and again, and churned up dirt until it uncovered the curve of the bubble beneath them.

Soz managed to get her arms around del-Kelric. Mercifully, he was still screaming, which meant he was alive and conscious. More frightening, Lisi and Jai had gone silent. Soz curled her body around del-Kelric, trying to protect him and her unborn child while the tumult threw her around like a ball within a ball.

Her node timed the wild shaking for twelve minutes, but to Soz it seemed forever. Finally the world tremored to a standstill. She lay on her side, gasping for breath, her arms still around the sobbing del-Kelric.

"Lisi?" she whispered. "Jai?"

No answer.

Soz dragged herself forward. When her elbow hit a shoulder, she reached out and touched strands of long hair.

Her fingers brushed a face she knew well. Jai. The whisper of his breath on her hand made tears well in her eyes.

Lisi was crumpled against Jai, both children folded around Vitar, protecting the boy. Lisi groaned when Soz touched her and Vitar cried softly. Tears ran down Soz's face. Alive. All four of them were alive.

"Hoshma?" Vitar whispered.

"I'm here, honey." Sitting up, Soz drew him into her lap, with the whimpering del-Kelric. "Jai?" she asked. "Lisi?"

"I'm all right," Lisi said.

"Does anything hurt?" Soz asked.

"All over," Lisi said. "But not bad. Like falling out of a tree."

"Jai?" Soz asked.

Silence.

"Jai?" She touched his shoulder.

"Ahhh." He stirred. "My arm . . ."

"It's all right," Soz said. "Don't move." She patted the ground, searching for the medkit—and a contraction caught her.

Soz cried out and fell back, releasing the children. Del-Kelric started to wail again and Vitar gave a startled cry.

"Hoshma?" Panic touched Lisi's voice. "I don't feel the baby's mind anymore."

Soz lay still until the contraction finished. Somehow she managed to speak without her voice cracking. "Don't worry about that now. I need you all to help me."

"How?" Lisi's fear permeated the darkness.

"Lisi, find the medkit," Soz said. "Vitar, see what else is in here. A lamp would be good."

Vitar sniffled. "I'll try."

As Lisi and Vitar searched, Soz spoke in a low voice to Jai. "How bad is your arm?"

"It's all right." The strain in his voice belied his words.

"I found the medkit," Lisi said. "The laser carbine and the neutrino transmitter too."

Soz reached for the kit, then groaned as another contraction hit her.

"Hoshma?" Vitar's voice shook. "Why are you crying?"

"She's not crying," Lisi said. "The baby is coming."

"Baby can't come," Vitar said. "Baby gone."

"Vitar, don't!" Lisi sounded ready to cry herself.

"Children, don't fight," Soz said. "The baby has to come. Even if—" She shook her head, unable to say it.

"Bad people killed Hoshpa," Vitar said. "Killed baby."

"Father isn't dead!" Lisi shouted.

"Shhh," Soz whispered. "Please." She closed her eyes as the contraction finished. "Gods, not now."

Jai laid his hand on her arm. "It will be all right."

She swallowed. "Yes. It will."

Lisi pressed the medkit in her hands. "What should I do?"

Soz fumbled in the kit until she found the diagnostic strip. Feeling along it, she scraped the edge, activating its textural display. Holos had little use in the dark.

"I found the heat-sensor lamp," Vitar said. "It's all broken. There's an oil lamp too. Do you want me to light it?"

"Not the oil lamp," Soz said. "It would use up our oxygen." She pressed the diagnostic strip into Lisi's hands. "Do you remember how to read the textures?"

"I think so," Lisi said. With something definite to do, the tremor left her voice.

"Jai, help her hold the strip on your arm," Soz said. "Lisi, you have to read what . . . how bad the break . . . ah—" She moaned with another contraction.

"Hoshma?" Vitar's voice shook. "Mommy, don't die."

"I'm fine, honey." She schooled her voice to calm. "This always happens when mothers have babies. Don't be scared."

"We've got the strip working," Jai said.

"His left arm is broken," Lisi said. "It says . . . his ulna has a greenstick fracture."

Soz recognized the term from her paramedic training. It meant he had an oblique crack on one side of the bone. "Is the bone displaced? Has it punctured the skin?"

"No," Lisi said. "Neither."

Relief swept Soz. It could have been a lot worse. "Jai, I'll have to put on a splint. It doesn't sound like it will need much repositioning, but it might hurt. Do you want something to knock you out?"

"No." His voice sounded strained. "Don't do that."

She felt the emotions behind his answer. He feared if he went to sleep, he would wake to find his family dead.

Soz grunted as another contraction came. **Attend,** she thought.

Based on your previous history, these contractions suggest birth within the next hour, her node answered, anticipating her inquiry.

She didn't ask the other question. She didn't want to know, didn't want to understand the void where once she and Jaibriol had nurtured a growing mind. As long she didn't ask, she could cling to the hope that her baby still lived.

Rustles came from nearby. Then Vitar pressed a slat of wood in her hand. "Will this help Jai?"

Soz recognized it as a piece of a construction set Jaibriol had carved for Vitar, good now for a splint. She gave Vitar a hug. "You're a smart boy. How did you know I needed it?"

He touched his finger to her temple. "In here."

With Jai guiding her, Soz found the break in his arm. She submerged her consciousness into his and linked to the picoweb in his body. Soz carried top-of-the-line nanomeds in her body, the type that could pass from mother to child. During her pregnancies, they had crossed the placenta and replicated in her children, giving them the same immunities and health she carried. They also made it possible now for her to link her biomech web to her son's less extensive picoweb, which would help direct her actions as she splinted his bone.

A contraction hit her and she almost lost contact with Jai. When the pain eased, she clenched her teeth, then set the bone and splinted Jai's arm. He remained silent, crying out only once, when she nudged the bone into place.

"Is Jaibird going to be happy again?" Vitar asked.

"I'm happy now," Jai said. "And quit calling me Jaibird."

Soz spoke gently. "Vitar? Can you answer some questions?"

"Don't know," Vitar said.

"It's about what happened to Daddy."

"Bad people shot him."

"Was he still breathing after they shot him?"

"Didn't see."

"Did you feel him get hurt?"

"No hurt," Vitar said.

Soz exhaled. Surely Vitar would have known if anything hurt his father. At great distances, it was less certain they would know, but with Vitar right there, she doubted Jaibriol could have died without his Rhon son knowing it.

"What did the people look like who took him?" she asked.

"Bad people," Vitar said.

"I know, honey. Can you tell me what they looked like?"

"Black hair. Sparkly. Like Hoshpa. Eyes like Jai."

"How like Jai?"

"Red."

Soz felt ice inside her. "And their clothes?"

"Gray. Little pieces of color on the sleeves."

She closed her eyes. It sounded like an ESComm uniform.

"The silver bird had a picture on it too," Vitar said.

"Silver bird?" Soz took a breath. "You mean a spaceship?"

"I think so."

"What was the picture?"

"Big black tomjolt."

No. She bit back her cry of protest. To Vitar, who had never seen a Eubian puma, the Trader insignia would look like a tomjolt. She groaned as another contraction hit her.

"Hoshma?" Lisi said. "Is the baby coming?"

"I think so."

The children found blankets and spread them under her. She braced herself against the wall as the labor progressed and tried not to cry out, though the pain was worse than with any of the other births. Maybe knowing what waited at the end made this one harder, turning her anguish into physical pain. The children huddled in the dark, silent while she struggled not to scream.

And when the child finally came, helped by Lisi, Soz's node answered the question she had never asked. Dead. Her baby was dead.

They wrapped the tiny body in a blanket. Lisi used soap and gauze from the medkit to clean her mother while Soz lay in a crumpled heap, exhausted, her heart aching, her breasts full of milk her baby would never need. She keened to herself, arms wrapped around her body as if she held an infant.

Somewhere a baby wailed and Soz wept for the ghost sound.

"Here, Hoshma." Lisi put a fussing bundle in her arms. The baby cried again and Soz held him close. Lifting her shirt, she put him to her breast and he suckled heartily, squirming to get comfortable. She knew a newborn could never be so adept, but it didn't matter. She hugged him and a bit of the grief in her heart receded.

She must have slept. When she woke, del-Kelric was drowsing in her arms, finished with his nursing. "Sweet Kelli," she murmured. "Thank you."

"Mother?" Jai asked. "Are you all right?"

She sat up slowly, aching and tired. "Yes."

"I'm hungry," Vitar said.

Soz rubbed her neck. "There's food down here."

"We ate it all," Lisi said.

Uneasy, Soz said, "There should be supplies for many weeks."

"The quasis field cut through the cache," Jai told her.

"There's still water," Lisi said. "Would you like some?"

"Yes." Soz wet her lips, suddenly aware of her thirst.

Rustles came from the dark. Then Lisi put a canteen in her hands and Soz drank, the warm liquid running down her throat like a benediction.

"I want to go home," Vitar said. "Dead baby scares me."

"It's all right," Soz soothed. "The baby went into the sky. She's happy there." In her mind, she thought: **Node, how long have we been down here?**

Fifty-six hours. Her node answered in the same manner she had addressed it, a normal-speed mode, which she perceived as words rather than accelerated abstract sounds and numbers.

So long? **Estimate outside temperature, assuming heatbar sterilization fifty-six hours ago.**

Normal temperature, it thought. However, I suggest waiting twenty more hours, to ensure meteorological effects have stabilized and hostile forces have left orbit.

Soz grimaced. **We have no way to ensure either.**

This is true. But based on my data of ESComm operations, the probability the vessels will have left orbit rises to 85 percent in another twenty hours. It will also be morning by then.

Do we have enough air to last?

Yes. EcoComp is recycling it. I recommend rationing the water.

"Mother?" Jai asked. "Can we leave?"

"Not yet." She took a breath. "Try to sleep. We have to stay here a lot longer."

"No!" Vitar's voice broke. "I don't want to! We have to put the baby in the ground or ghosts will come."

"It's all right," Soz murmured. "Come keep me company, Vitar. Ghosts are scared of your hoshma."

A scrabbling sound came from the darkness. Then Vitar was at her side, hugging her as if he feared she would disappear.

None of them slept well. Vitar cried, so softly Soz barely heard. Del-Kelric fussed, only quieting when she nursed him. Both Lisi and Jai were silent. For a while they tried telling stories, but their voices trailed off into the darkness.

When it finally came time to leave, Soz spoke to them all, trying to infuse her voice with a confidence she didn't feel. "As soon as I collapse the quasis field, the dirt around us will fall, if there is any left. Don't be scared. It won't be enough to bury us." Quietly she added, "When we get out, don't expect to see the house. Everything will be gone."

"Gone?" Lisi asked. "Why?"

"Heat," Soz said. "I think the rumbling we heard was something called heatbar sterilization. A ship in orbit uses a wide-beam laser to burn the region under attack."

"We didn't burn," Lisi said.

"The only way heat could come in here is through the quasis shield," Soz said. "The molecules within the field can't change state, so heat can't flow in." *Flow* seemed such a mild word for what she feared had taken place.

"Then why did we feel the shaking?" Jai asked.

Soz grimaced. "The ground can throw around the bubble. It just can't change the bubble itself."

"Why did the bad people want to burn our house?" Vitar asked.

Soz shifted him in her arms, relieved to hear him using more normal sentences. "They didn't know we were here," she lied.

"Yes, they did." Jai's voice was hard. "They tried to kill us."

"Jai, don't," Lisi said.

"Why? You heard what Vitar said. He was describing ESComm soldiers. They took Father away and tried to get rid of us."

"*Stop* it!" Lisi shouted.

"Don't yell." Soz gentled her voice, realizing she couldn't protect them from truths they might need for their survival. "I think Jai is right. They probably believe we're dead. Only a quasis screen could have protected us and they're hard to come by."

"We had one," Lisi said.

Soz nodded, then realized they couldn't see it in the dark. "When your father and I were preparing to come here, I used my security clearance to get us a quasis generator."

"I'm hungry," Vitar said.

"I know," Soz murmured. She was starving, having given her food to the children.

"Are we going to another mountain?" Lisi asked.

"Another world," Soz said.

A long silence greeted her. Then Jai said, "You're going to use the neutrino transmitter. To call in a ship."

"Yes."

"No!" Panic suffused Vitar. "Bad people!"

"It's all right," Soz murmured. "They'll probably think we're the bad people, when we steal their ship."

"If the planet is burned, won't they die?" Jai said.

"We won't leave them here," Soz said. "We'll put them somewhere unaffected by the sterilization, where they can survive. And maybe we can come back." She doubted it, but she didn't want to tell the children.

"Can't they come with us?" Lisi asked.

"No!" Soz took a deep breath. "Listen to me, all of you. We've talked about this, what would happen if you ever left here. *No one can know who you are.* Anyone who sees what you children look like, half Highton and half Skolian, anyone with any clue you are related to me, is dangerous to us. Do you understand?"

Silence greeted her. Then Jai said, "Yes," followed by less confident murmurs of assent from Lisi and Vitar.

"All right. Let's get out of here." Soz tried to exude confidence. "Lisi, do you have the laser carbine?"

"Here it is." Lisi reached out until her hands bumped Soz and gave her the carbine.

"Vitar, I'm going to stand up now," Soz said. "Lisi, here's del-Kelric."

As her daughter took the toddler, Vitar let go of Soz. She pulled herself to her feet, grimacing from the pain of birthing. She tried not to dwell on the bundle wrapped in a blanket so near them in the dark.

"I can collapse the quasis," Jai said. "I'm by the comp."

"When I give the word," Soz said, "everyone put your arms over your head. Jai, protect the equipment. Roca and Vitar, cover del-Kelric."

"All set," Jai said.

"I'm ready," Lisi said.

"Me too," Vitar said.

Shielding her head with one arm, Soz stretched the other upward. "All right. Collapse the field."

Nothing happened.

Soz probed the darkness above her head. Her fingers scraped a smooth surface hollowed out by the quasis bubble.

"When are you going to turn off the quasis?" Lisi asked.

"I already did," Jai said.

"I think we're glassed in," Soz said. "Keep your heads down." She thrust the carbine up as hard as she could, with enhanced strength and speed. The stock slammed into a barrier, sending vibrations down her arm. She hammered at the barrier again, and again, fast and hard, until bits of fused rock rained around them.

Suddenly the roof caved in, with a blast of air and light.

"Ai!" Vitar shouted. "We're free!"

Soz exhaled, silent with gratitude. She looked around the cavity, brightened now by sunlight. Four dirty, frightened faces stared back at her. Jai was huddled over the comp, his broken arm held against his chest. Lisi and Vitar had curled around del-Kelric, who was trying to crawl free. Only the toddler seemed unconcerned, too young to understand what had happened.

Most of the ladder was intact, having been protected by the quasis. Soz went up it, pulling herself the last bit over a glassy lip of stone. She climbed out into sunlight and a fierce wind.

And desolation.

As far as she could see, in every direction, their world had become barren. The mountains were slagged, their soil and forest vaporized, the rock melted. No trace of green remained. Ravaged land spread out beneath a harsh blue sky seared of moisture. On a distant mountain a pillar of rock the size of a city tower broke away and crashed down the naked peak. The thunder of its descent echoed through the world, the only sound except for the wind.

"Gods almighty," Soz whispered.

Lisi climbed up next to her, followed by Vitar. Jai came last, pulling himself with one arm. Vitar put his arms around Soz's waist, and Lisi stood on her other side, holding del-Kelric. Even the toddler's gurgles were silenced by the immensity of what they viewed. Jai stood next to them, his broken arm cradled against his chest. In silence, they stared at the remains of their home.

The coals of anger that had seethed within Soz during their long refuge, during the birth of her murdered baby, ignited now. This was no hot flare of energy that vanished as fast as it came, burning itself out.

No, this blaze would endure.

Viquara, Empress of Eube, stopped before the closed door and rested her hand against it. A new era of Highton triumphs waited for her on the other side.

No one knew. Doctor Tecozil was dead. Ur Qox was dead. Jaibriol I was dead. Only she and the man beyond this door knew the truth. Monstrous yet inspired, unthinkable yet brilliant, that truth would finally let Eube sweep the stars in triumph.

The emperor was Rhon.

"Open," Viquara said. Set to obey only her voice, the door slid aside.

He was staring out a window at the grounds of the palace. He turned as she entered, and she knew him in a glance, knew his face, his eyes, his features, his grace. He was older now, a man in his late thirties rather than the youth she remembered. He still had on the rough trousers and shirt he had been wearing when they found him. His hair fell over his shoulders and down his back, barbaric in its length.

He stared at her as if she were a ghost. The irony wasn't lost on Viquara, who had so long thought him dead. Yet here he stood. None could deny this man—Jaibriol the Second—the title of emperor. The proof lived in his genes. But faced with the threat of that other heinous truth revealed, his Rhon heritage, and the horror it would make of his life, he would keep his silence.

And through him she would rule Eube.

Softly Viquara said, "Welcome home, my beloved son."

20

William Seth Rockworth III was the oldest man alive. Good health, good genes, and a careful lifestyle had extended his life span enough to reach the fledgling era of nanotech and life prolongation. At 173, hale and fit, with a few extra pounds on his frame and gray streaks in his black hair, the retired admiral had outlived all his peers.

One other person came near his age: the Ruby Pharaoh, 155 years old, a woman Seth had once called wife. Time softened the edges of his memories. He recalled Dehya as a lithe young woman with a gentle smile. He had never regretted leaving behind the Imperial court, but even so, he valued the Rhon bonds he had formed during that time of his life. Before then he hadn't known he had a Kyle rating of ten, a psionic strength claimed by no more than one in every ten billion humans. Although he left Dehya, he had sworn her an oath on that day he departed the Orbiter to return to Earth. A Rhon oath. If ever she needed help, she could ask it of him. In the seven decades since, she had never invoked it.

Until now.

Her message was simple. Meet my ship, *Tailors Needle,* at Logan Starport. Rhon Oath. He stood in his study reading the words on his console, wondering what had spurred her to contact him after so long.

It was three in the morning when Seth drove his hovercar into the parking lot at Logan. *Tailors Needle* was arriving at a domestic terminal, which meant it came from Allied space, another conundrum. Why would Dehya's ship have an Allied ID?

He found the gate in an out-of-the-way concourse emptied by the late hour. Only vessels that couldn't afford better berths used these areas. He had to walk out onto the tarmac to meet the pitted two-person scout ship that sat in an old docking bay.

The hatch opened and Dehya jumped down to the tarmac. Seth couldn't see her well in the shadows by the ship, but he recognized the heart shape of her face, the length of her hair, and her innate grace. Except she was too tall.

In the instant before she left the shadows, he realized it wasn't Dehya. Like a ghost come to haunt, the woman stalked into the light.

"Soz?" Seth asked. This couldn't be Dehya's niece. Soz had died fifteen years ago.

"You gave Dyhianna Selei an oath when you were her husband," she said. "Rhon Oath. Do you still honor it?"

That sounded like Soz: to the point, wasting no words. "Yes," he said, wondering what he had gotten himself into. *Soz?* he asked. *Is it you?*

She kept her mind closed. She was holding a laser carbine she must have smuggled past the port's at-a-distance sensors, not a difficult task for someone who knew how. "Do you honor the oath?" she repeated.

"Yes." He paused. "I made it to Dehya, though."

"Rhon Oath."

He understood her meaning. Given the Rhon's interwoven relationships and merged minds, it was impossible to give an oath to one without impacting the others. "I will honor it also to you."

Her hands relaxed their white-knuckled grip on the carbine. In an unexpectedly gentle voice she said, "Then I have four miracles for your keeping. Protect them for me."

"Miracles?"

She motioned—and four children climbed down from the ship. At first he saw only their general forms: a boy about six-foot-one, gangly with youth, probably still growing, his left arm in a sling and a toddler cradled in his right;

and an adolescent girl with long hair, her arm around a boy hanging onto her waist.

Then they came into the light and he saw them better, the tall youth's red eyes, the glitter in the younger boy's hair, the trace of red in the baby's eyes. The older boy's features were unmistakable. Highton. But Seth also saw the multi-color streaks, wine-red and gold, in the children's hair, and the green eyes on the girl and the middle boy.

"My children," Soz said.

"How?" he asked. Had she been a prisoner all these years, the provider of a Highton?

She didn't answer. Instead she said, "You can never reveal their identity or let anyone know they're psions. Say they're refugees from Eube, that you became their sponsor, anything. Can you promise this? I can't leave them with you unless you do."

Psions? Their father couldn't be Highton then. Seth decided to trust her, not based on any profound analysis, but because it was Soz, whom he had always liked, though he hardly knew her. It was also the middle of the night, she was a ghost, and nothing this interesting had happened to him in decades.

"I will promise." He hesitated. "Were you caught by the Traders? Your children look like they have Highton blood."

"My husband is one-quarter Highton."

"Your husband?" He would have thought it inconceivable that a member of the Ruby Dynasty would marry anyone with even a modicum of Highton blood. "Why?"

"He's Rhon."

Seth wasn't sure what response he had expected, but that wasn't it. Rhon? *Rhon?* Just like that, simple as you please, *my husband is one-quarter Highton and he's Rhon.* The implications staggered. During the time Seth had lived on the Orbiter, he saw enough of Highton attitudes toward the Ruby Dynasty, and Skolians in general, to know how grievously Allied authorities erred when they discounted ISC claims of Trader atrocities. He had no wish to live in an age when ESComm had access to a psiberweb, which they soon would if they were making Rhon psions.

"Who is your husband?" Seth asked.

"Jaibriol Qox."

He waited for her to laugh. When she didn't, all he could think to say was, "The First or the Second?" It was an absurd question, given that both were dead, but it was far less absurd than what she had just said. Then again, she was dead too.

"Second," she said, with her usual verbosity.

When it became clear no explanation was coming, he tried to put it all together. "You say Jaibriol II is alive, that he's Rhon, that you two have these children—come to think of it, they must all be Rhon if both you and Qox are. And you're married to him?" When she nodded, he said, "Then these children are your legitimate heirs. That would mean they are heirs to both the Ruby and Carnelian Thrones."

"That about sums it up," she said.

"Good Lord, Soz." What hit him most wasn't the interstellar implications, the prospect of empires in upheaval. It was that she chose to entrust her miracles to him. He looked at them and they looked back, their faith in their mother suffusing his mind. If she said he would do right by them, they believed her.

"Earth is the best place for them," Soz said. "You're the only person I can trust on Earth."

"But why? You hardly know me. Dehya and I split up before you were born."

"She trusted you," Soz said. "I trust her. We're Rhon. You can't hide in a family of telepaths as close-knit as ours. She knew your mind; I knew her mind."

Dehya trusted him? Had anyone asked, Seth would have said he had neither right nor reason to believe such. Oddly enough, though, had he ever needed to hide his children, he would have thought first of Dehya. Of course his children were all grown, and his grandchildren, and on down the generations. They had less time now for the old man in the

Appalachians. It would be nice to have young people filling his empty mansion again.

He felt the minds of the children. They weren't trying to reach him; it just hadn't occurred to them that he was someone they should protect against. Their emotions surrounded him in a sea of warmth.

"I'll do my best," he told them. The six-year-old smiled and the baby gurgled.

Soz's voice gentled. "I know."

He turned to her. "What will you do now?"

Her eyes glinted in the dark. "Get my husband."

The War Room on the Orbiter slumbered. In the stardome, the command chair was empty. Although telops worked in the amphitheater, many consoles were dark, unable to sustain peak efficiency without the power provided by the Triad. Stillness lay over the area like a blanket.

On a dais at one edge of the amphitheater, a group of civilians sat at a table: Roca, her husband Eldrinson, their son Eldrin, Kurj's widow Ami, First Councilor of the Assembly Barcala Tikal, and the other councilors of the Inner Assembly. An archway opened in the wall there, on the dais, and a corridor stretched from it into the guts of the Orbiter. Translucent columns bordered the corridor, made from an ancient composite that modern science had yet to reproduce. Lights spiraled around the machinery within the columns, scintillating, flashing, sparkling. The corridor extended back so far that its perspective converged to a point, drawing the eye to infinity.

The First Lock waited at the end of the corridor.

Roca looked around at the others. "If I do this, it can't be undone." Once she used the Lock to join the Triad, her mind would become too interwoven with the web ever to extract it. If she tried, it would disrupt the multitude of Lock-formed changes in her brain and leave her brain dead.

Fatigue showed on Eldrinson's face, the exhaustion of

trying to operate a Triad with only two people. "We need you, Roca."

Barcala Tikal looked around the table. "Any of you has a right to object."

"Kurj would want it," Ami said.

Eldrin nodded. "I agree."

"Does anyone disagree?" Tikal asked.

Silence answered him.

Tikal started to speak, then stopped, his gaze shifting to a point behind Roca in the amphitheater. Then he closed his mouth and rose to his feet. Eldrin looked and started, then stood with a sudden, powerful motion. Eldrinson turned his gaze that way, and he also stood, followed by everyone else at the table.

Puzzled, Roca got up and turned around.

The woman stood in the cup at the end of a massive crane suspended a few meters above the amphitheater. Everyone in the War Room had stopped working and was watching her. Among the colossal machinery, she looked as fragile as a soap bubble, her delicate face gaunt with exhaustion, her skin pale almost to translucence, the circles under her eyes as dark as bruises. Gray streaked the braid of black hair that hung over her shoulder to her hips. She had lost weight, become so thin she seemed ready to drift away. Fragile and vulnerable, she stood before them, this woman Kurj had called the most powerful human being alive.

"I agree that Roca should join the Triad," Dehya Selei said.

Eldrin's relief bathed Roca. Until that moment, she hadn't realized that not even her son had seen Dehya, his wife, since the death of Kurj.

The robot arm lowered Dehya to the ground, and she stepped out into the amphitheater. A telop jumped to clear a carton from her path. Pages stepped back and bowed as she passed. They were all bowing, throughout the War Room, telops, ISC officers, soldiers, pilots, citizens from every stripe and seed of the Imperialate, bowing to their Pharaoh.

Dehya came up onto the dais. "The Traders are about to make an announcement."

It was Tikal who found his voice first. "How do you know?"

"I know." Her voice was shadows. She looked around at them, her gaze coming again and again to Eldrinson, as if he were a puzzle she had to solve. She indicated a great screen above the archway of the Lock corridor. "Listen."

Tikal spoke into the control band on his wrist. "Activate the dais holoscreen in the War Room."

The screen shimmered and the image of a black puma formed, more than life-size. The Trader anthem drifted into the air, a haunting work of art that Roca had never reconciled with its Aristo composers. So much Eubian music had an incomparable yet grief-stricken beauty, as if its creators lamented their own existence. The puma reached out an arm with its claws extended. Then it faded, replaced by the Hall of Circles in the Qox palace on Glory, filled with tier after tier of glittering Aristos.

Five Hightons walked down an aisle of the Hall, accompanied by the palace secret police, the brutal Razers feared throughout Eube. Roca recognized four of the Hightons: Empress Viquara, the Qox heirs Corbal Xir and Calope Muze, and the Eubian Trade Minister Kryx Quaelen.

Then she saw who walked with them and her heart froze.

Tall and unsmiling, his hair shimmering, his ruby eyes cold, his stride like the beat of a drum no one could hear, he walked through the Circles. Jaibriol Qox.

They reached the dais in the center of the Hall, where a chair waited. Made from solid carnelian, the throne stood as an inanimate reflection of its creators. Jaibriol II mounted the dais and looked out at the assembled Aristos. Gone was the vibrant youth Roca remembered from fifteen years ago, the young hero adored by Aristos and hated by everyone else alive. This man stood gaunt and silent, in unrelieved black.

Then he sat on the Carnelian Throne.

As one, the Aristos of Glory lifted their arms. As one they snapped their fingers. It was the only sound they made. In the Hall of Circles, it was an unsurpassed accolade.

Here, in the Orbiter War Room, the Councilor for Life said, "Gods almighty. This we didn't need."

"He must be an imposter," Judiciary said.

Barcala Tikal looked tired. "It has to be him. They would never tolerate an imposter on the Carnelian Throne."

"It can't be," Eldrinson whispered.

Roca glanced at her husband. Eldrinson was staring at the screen as if he had seen a nightmare. She didn't blame him. With the son of Ur Qox returned from the dead to rally his empire, the Traders would surge in morale while Skolia stumbled.

A voice spoke behind Roca. "Ma'am? Do we report to you?"

Roca turned to see a telop, a woman in an ISC uniform. Whom *did* they report to? The lines of command had grown tangled since Kurj's death. She had to find the resources to take charge, with an assurance she didn't feel, lest her lack of experience damage her people's already subdued morale. Solid leadership was even more important now, with a strong young emperor suddenly on the Carnelian Throne.

"Yes," she said. "Go ahead."

"We had a power surge in a conduit feeding a generator in the Strategy Room," the telop said.

That puzzled Roca. Why would they seek her attention over so trivial a matter? "Can't you fix it?"

"It's the conduit to the Command Chair, ma'am."

Then Roca understood. She looked up at the chair in the dome high over their heads. The Imperator would have to go up there to activate the controls.

"That's odd," Tikal said. He was peering at a screen in the table that showed a display of schematics. He pointed out several lines, threads of green on a diagram. "These just activated."

Roca scanned the display. "They should be active. That

system controls the backup for node seven of the War Room web."

"That entire node has been down for days," Tikal said.

"Councilor Roca," the telop said, her hand to her ear as she listened on her comm. "We're getting a report from the SCAD air defense nodes. They're activating."

"What?" Roca frowned at Tikal. "When did you order that?"

He straightened up. "I didn't."

Behind them, Roca heard the bell of a telop summoning a page. The rumble of a crane growled through the growing hum of sound in the amphitheater. Voices came from consoles relaying reports and from the councilors here on the dais, talking into their wrist comms or gauntlets.

Dehya walked away from them all, to the entrance of Lock corridor on the other side of the table. Roca watched her sister. Had Dehya provoked this web activity? If anyone had the resources for it, she did. Or was the Pharaoh simply lost in thought, pacing the intricate labyrinth of her mind?

A clang sounded, followed by a surge in the hum of power. Roca turned to see a crane swing to the floor. She knew telops often sat in the cranes that moved through the War Room, using all levels of the amphitheater. But they did it only when the room was fully energized; otherwise it took needed resources from other systems. And the War Room had been at low power for days.

"Councilor Skolia!" The summons came from the band around her wrist.

She spoke into her comm. "What's the problem?"

"This is Lieutenant Dalero in High Energy. The Impactor data banks are coming back on-line!"

The telop in front of Roca said, "Ma'am, I'm getting another report. Web nodes four and eighteen are activating in Armaments. We've also got a power surge in the Assembly chamber that houses console links to the War Room."

"Look," Eldrin said. He pointed at the stardome above them.

Roca looked to where her son pointed. Beads of light were racing along the catwalks that stretched to the Command Chair. A crane swung up to the chair and stopped as if waiting for an Imperator to step out of the empty throne. Below in the amphitheater, static crackled as consoles came on-line. Many voices were coming from speakers now, both human and machine-born, growing in volume as the great sleeping nerve center awoke.

"What the hell is going on?" Tikal said into his wrist comm. On the dais around him, the other councilors were also speaking into their comms, more urgently now, receiving reports from their offices. What bits and pieces Roca heard gave the same story; all over the Orbiter, dormant power centers were waking from their slumber.

She looked across the table, past the councilors, to where Dehya stood at the entrance to the Lock corridor. Her sister regarded her, green eyes glazed with the sunset. Their father had called Dehya's eyes "sunrise eyes," for the sheen of gold and rose hues that shimmered on them, the only trace of his inner lids she had inherited.

Did you do this? Roca asked.

No, Dehya thought. She turned to the Lock corridor. The scintillating columns of light gave it an endless appearance, as if it stretched back into infinity. She spoke in a soft voice that should have carried to no one, given the level of sound in the amphitheater, but that cut through the noise like a knife.

"Look," the Pharaoh said.

They all looked. Roca saw nothing in the corridor. She had an eerie sense then, one that came from Eldrinson, a chill that stepped up her back like icy fingers. Glancing at her husband, she saw him form the words, *Gods forgive me.*

Tikal suddenly said, "Quiet! Listen."

Voices ebbed into silence as councilors and telops paused to find out what he meant. Then Roca heard it too. The clang of boots. A figure was taking form out of the point of perspective far down the Lock corridor, coming forward from infinity.

One voice continued to speak in the amphitheater. It came from above them, on the holoscreen. A Highton voice. Jaibriol II was standing now, speaking his first words as emperor: *On this day, the glory of our ancestors comes full circle.* Despite his resonant words, he sounded numb. If Roca hadn't known better, she would have thought he was drugged.

The clang of boots grew louder. The approaching figure in the Lock corridor looked like a Jagernaut, but Roca wasn't sure. The pants were right but not the shirt. Whoever it was had mental barriers so strong they hid any hint of identity. But within seconds Roca recognized her.

Jaibriol Qox continued to speak, his words echoing through the Hall of Circles, through the War Room, through three empires: *So will Eube rise to greater heights than ever before.*

The Jagernaut in the corridor came closer, more visible now. She wore the black pants and knee boots of a uniform fifteen years out of date, and a shirt made from fur. The carbine clenched in her fist was an old model, none the less deadly for it. Her hair fell to her hips in a wild mane of curls that swung around her body as she walked. She came without pause, her stride long, her boots ringing on the floor.

Our triumph will be complete, Jaibriol Qox said.

She reached the end of the corridor and stood watching them. On her wrists she wore the massive leather-and-metal gauntlets, packed with web tech, that only the Imperator could claim. The archway framed her wild form, lights flashing and racing around her in spirals. Above her, on the holoscreen, Kryx Quaelen was standing next to his emperor, his arm raised. His voice boomed to the Circles, to the multitude of peoples spread across the stars: *Let it be known! From this day on, the Concord of Eube is reborn.*

And in the Lock corridor, Sauscony Lahaylia Valdoria Skolia, Imperator of the Skolian Imperialate, said, "Like hell it is."

21

Soz strode into the Strategy Room just off the amphitheater, surrounded by Inner Assembly councilors, voices swirling around her. She could barely contain the waves of information that beat at her. Her mind was hyperextending through web space, making link after link after link. How did her father and Dehya endure this madness? How had Kurj organized his mind around this chaos?

Her memories of the past few days tossed like leaves in a whirlpool. The emergency beacon that brought *Tailors Needle* to Prism, the dismay of the captain and mate when they realized their ship was being hijacked, the lush countryside where she set them down, her children's tears as they left—it blended into a collage of images tumbling through her mind.

She had come to the Orbiter through a back door set up for the Rhon, one hidden in the web of security that protected the space habitat. Without the Rhon signature of her brain, she would have been killed within the first second of her approach.

Voices came at her from everywhere, telops humming in her mind, EI brains, people talking. She had no chance to embrace the parents and brother she hadn't seen for fifteen years. The Orbiter demanded her attention. Didn't any of them feel it, the intelligence of this giant space habitat? The Orbiter roared, voracious in its need, striving to awake from a slumber forced on it by the death of its central processing unit.

"How?" Barcala Tikal kept pace with her. "Where have you been? Why now, just when Qox reappears from the dead?"

She stopped in the middle of the Strategy Room and everyone stopped with her. "I've been tracking Jaibriol Qox."

"Tracking him where?" Tikal asked.

"On a world with a name I never knew. For fifteen years. We crashed there, on different continents. A few days ago his people found him. I searched out his neutrino transmitter and summoned help." Soz regarded Tikal with a steady gaze. "I want my parents transferred to Earth."

"What?" He looked like a bull that had run into a wall.

"You have all three members of the Triad on the Orbiter." She motioned at where Dehya, Eldrin, and her parents stood watching them from inside the doorway. "In the same flaming *room,* for gods' sake. Contact the Allied president. Invoke the protection clause of the Iceland Treaty and have the Allieds transfer my parents to protective custody."

He put up his hand. "I think we need to slow down."

"Send my brother's widow too," Soz said. Ami stood half-hidden behind Roca, with Judiciary towering on her other side, like a protector. "She can have her baby on Earth. It will be safer there."

"Her *what?*" That came from Planetary Development, who was standing next to Tikal.

By the wall, Domestic Affairs, the youngest Inner Assembly councilor, bent her head to an ISC telop and spoke in a low enough voice that normally Soz wouldn't have overheard. But with her mind hypersensitive from her entry into the Triad, the councilor's voice thundered in her ears.

"Excuse me," Domestic said. "But who is this person?"

"Sauscony Valdoria," the officer said. "Ruby Dynasty."

Almost at the same time, Judiciary spoke to Ami. "Is it true? You carry Kurj Skolia's child?" When Ami nodded, Judiciary looked up at Soz. "How did you know?"

"Can't you feel it?" Soz asked. Ami radiated Kyle strength and her baby glowed as well. Aching from the death of her own child, Soz could have no more missed Ami's pregnancy than she could have missed a nova.

She turned to Protocol, who stood on her left. "We need a Councilor for Foreign Affairs. You're appointed."

Protocol blinked. "Councilor Roca is Foreign Affairs."

"Councilor Roca is going to Earth," Soz said.

Tikal scowled. "You have no authority to appoint or remove Assembly councilors."

"Right now we need Foreign Affairs," Soz said. "Protocol knows the Inner Assembly. We don't have time to train someone new." She focused on the councilor. "I need you as Protocol too. I need you to put me through to Jaibriol Qox."

Protocol stared at her. "You want to contact Glory?"

Judiciary came over to them. "You can't just call up the emperor of Eube."

"Why not?" Soz said.

"It's not how these things are done."

"It is now."

"Imperator Skolia." Tikal took a breath. "Slow down."

Soz froze at the title. Imperator Skolia. *Imperator.* She couldn't slow down. The Orbiter demanded her attention. The web demanded. ISC demanded. Her mind was going into overload and she had barely skimmed the outermost edges of the storm.

Soshoni.

The voice cut through the chaos like a rumble of stability. Quiet. Deep.

Father? she asked.

Let us help, he thought.

Soz. That sparkling rill came from Dehya. *You need seclusion. Solitude. Time to absorb what is happening to you.*

I can't, Soz thought. **I have no time.** She spoke to Protocol. "Arrange the call. Do whatever is necessary, but get me a link to Glory."

"I will do what I can." The councilor bowed and then left the Strategy Room.

Soshoni. Her father's thought rumbled. **There is a problem.**

She looked at him across the room. **Problem?**

Dehya answered. *Your mind and mine have many similarities. A Triad link with both of us in it may be unstable.*

Soz felt as if an abyss had just opened. Would she repeat history, killing another Triad member to become Imperator?

We aren't as similar as were Kurj and Jarac, Dehya thought. *The link is holding.*

Soz concentrated on them and the chaos receded. She became more attuned to their minds and those of her mother and brother. She felt their shock at seeing her. She also felt the unease of everyone in the Strategy Room. She had come out of nowhere, and no one knew what she would do.

The Assembly councilors and ISC personnel were all watching her. Turning to Tikal, she spoke in a quieter voice. "How long will it take to arrange passage for my parents and my brother's widow to Earth?"

"Why Earth?"

Soz motioned for an officer standing near the wall. Her node identified him as Lieutenant Coalson, an expert on orbital defense systems, but that data was fifteen years out of date. He wore a major's uniform now.

Coalson came forward and saluted her. "Ma'am."

"What centers are currently as well defended as Earth?" Soz asked.

He gave her the five she already knew: Parthonia, Diesha, Lyshriol, Glory, and Platinum Sector. Parthonia was the capitol planet of the Imperialiate, Diesha was ISC headquarters, Lyshriol was home to most of Soz's family, Glory was the Eubian capital, and Platinum Sector was the nerve "center" of ESComm, its equipment and personnel dispersed throughout a huge volume of space.

Soz considered the options. "I would rather they went to Earth," she told Tikal. "If hostilities between Eube and Skolia increase, ESComm will focus on the Imperialate. They haven't the resources to go after both us and Earth."

"It's a good point." Standing on Soz's right, the Inner Assembly Councilor of Finance, a civilian, was reading a display on his cyberarm. "Our markets are plunging, as Imperialate centers receive Emperor Qox's broadcast. The Allieds are less affected."

"Qox sounded like a robot," Planetary Development said.

Dryly Judiciary said, "Maybe he is."

"On the Carnelian Throne?" Tikal snorted. "Not with this obsession of theirs for 'perfect' bloodlines."

As the others debated, Soz listened. She motioned over staff officers from the War Room, and they all migrated to the Strategy Table, an oval made from the same translucent composite as the columns in the Lock corridor. Lights from the reactivating web flashed within it, chasing each other like trains of glowing beads across gold, copper, brass, silver, and platinum components, like the gleaming innards of an antique clock.

Using screens in the table, they brought up ISC records for her: troop deployments, bases, weapons, reports, manifests, logs, and more. The longer she spent leaning over the table with them, the more she realized how many gaps her fifteen years' absence had created in her knowledge of ISC.

Sometime during that session Dehya vanished. Soz felt her in the web, felt Dehya's mental dance as the web tried to incorporate its new Military Key in places already occupied by its Assembly Key. Again and again Dehya *shifted* Soz, rebraiding the strands that wove the Triad together. Her touch was light, ethereal, whispers over the water, but beneath that delicacy ran cables of steel. Soz's father was a sea of infinite depth and extent, supporting the web.

Then Protocol returned. As Soz straightened up, surrounded by her advisers, Protocol bowed to her. "I have a line to the Office of the Ministry of Foreign Affairs within the Palace Protocol Division on Glory. They should be online in about a minute. Do you have instructions?"

Soz almost grimaced. Her years on Prism had mercifully let her forget the convolutions of bureaucracy. The Traders were masters at it, but it was by no means confined to them. The Imperialate had an Office for the Councilor of Foreign Affairs within the Assembly Protocol Division and an

Office of the Councilor for Protocol within the Assembly Foreign Affairs Division.

She indicated a holoscreen on the wall. "If you can switch the link to this room, I'll talk to them here."

Tikal straightened up from a manifest he had been discussing with Coalson. "Not to their Ministry."

"Why not?" Soz asked.

Quietly he said, "You are the Imperator. You talk only to Emperor Qox."

Emperor Qox. Preprogrammed routines in Soz's node kicked in, activating neural firing patterns in her brain that simulated a calm response. Somehow she presented an unruffled exterior, hiding her surge of emotion. She had no illusions. If her marriage to Jaibriol and the reasons for it became known, it would create an interstellar crisis of a magnitude neither he nor she was likely to survive. And then what of their children?

She nodded to Protocol. "Let me know when the emperor is on-line."

"Yes, ma'am." Protocol bowed and left again.

Soz nodded to the other councilors. "If you need me, I'll be in the Solitude Room."

Tikal bowed. "As you wish."

When Soz walked to the doorway, two Jagernauts fell into step with her. She stopped, looking from one to the other, a man and a woman, both huge, looming over her. Then she turned to Tikal.

"Your bodyguards," he said.

She wanted to refuse. She disliked having people follow her around and had managed to avoid it for most of her life. But technically she answered to Tikal. The situation with Kurj and the First Councilor had never been clear, but she knew Tikal had walked with care around the Fist of Skolia. Soz had yet to establish her relationship with the Assembly and knew her choices now were important to their perception of her. Balking at a logical precaution, however much she disliked it, would serve no useful purpose. So she left the room flanked by the two giants.

During the walk to the Solitude Room, Soz remained silent. When they reached the chamber, she said, "Wait outside," to the Jagernauts.

The woman spoke. "We have orders to remain with you at all times, Imperator Skolia."

Soz considered her. "What squad are you attached to?"

If the unexpected question startled the officer, she didn't show it. "Eight, ma'am."

"And who commands that squadron?"

"Secondary Ko."

"Who commands Ko's division?" Soz asked.

"Primary Chaser, ma'am."

"I see. And who is Chase's CO?"

After a pause, the woman said, "That would be Commandant Primary Tapperhaven."

"Tapperhaven." Soz watched her face. "And who would Tapperhaven's commanding officer be?"

The Jagernaut spoke quietly. "You."

"Me." Soz regarded them. "As I said, you will remain outside the Solitude Room."

"Yes, ma'am."

The officers saluted, raising their arms to chest height, outstretched with fists clenched, crossing their wrists with the snap of muscled skin hitting muscled skin.

Soz nodded and entered the Solitude Room. The door hissed shut, leaving her in an unadorned chamber with low gravity. One curving wall was made from dichromesh glass, giving a window onto space. With the chamber located so near the north pole, the window sloped upward like a steep hill. A blocky control chair faced it, one much simpler than the War Room throne, but still connected to the First Lock, the only other control center anywhere with that distinction.

Only starlight lit the chamber. Soz sat in the chair and gazed out at space. A fragment of a poem drifted through her mind: *Magnificent sea forever bright, forever cold and forever night.*

The comm chimed. Soz touched a response button in the

arm of the chair. "Skolia here." It felt odd to call herself by the dynastic title that named the Imperialate.

Her male bodyguard said, "Councilor Roca wishes to see you, Imperator Skolia."

"Let her in."

She turned as the door opened. Her mother came into the chamber, gold and radiant as she walked to the chair. The moment the door closed, Roca stretched her arms across the arm of the chair and folded Soz into in an embrace. Her voice caught, husky with a mother's love. "Gods, Soshoni. It really is you."

Soz hugged her back, surprised at how natural it felt, as if it had only been months instead of fifteen years. "Ai, Hoshma." She kept her mind barricaded, though she ached to respond with her thoughts as well. That such a simple expression of affection had been taken from them was yet another scar left by a never-ending war.

When they released each other, Roca gave her a shaky smile, tears gleaming in her eyes. "I knew it was you in that corridor. You always had this way of holding yourself, even when you were small. Gods help anyone who tried to stop you."

Soz's voice caught. "I've missed you and Hoshpa." It felt odd to say that name for her own father now, after hearing her children use it so long for Jaibriol. How could she think of Jaibriol now, trapped and alone? He probably didn't even know his wife and children had survived. Was he dying inside, trapped in a jeweled carnelian prison with no release for his grief?

The comm chimed again. Soz touched the panel. "Yes?"

"Prince Eldrin is here," the Jagernaut said.

"Let him in."

Eldrin walked in, tall and handsome, his gaze focused on her as if he didn't yet believe she actually existed. He sat on the edge of the console in front of her, watching her intently. "So."

" 'So'?" She managed a grin and somehow spoke around

the catch in her voice. "That's it? That's all I get after my dramatic entrance?"

Softly he said, "Ai, Soshoni. It is good to see you."

His mind nudged hers, and she kept up her barriers, aching from the necessity that forced her to do it. She didn't know what to say. All she came up with was the absurdly ordinary, "How have you been?"

"Still writing ballads," he said.

"I've missed your singing." His spectacular voice had been one of her joys.

"Come to dinner," he said. "We can all sing."

"You don't want me to sing," she said. "Not if you value your eardrums." The small talk sounded strange to her ears. Strange and wonderful.

Her mother smiled. "I have to admit, it was never one of your strong points."

"No." Bitterly Soz said, "I'm great at killing, though."

They both looked at her, silent. After a moment Soz said, "I'm sorry. That was unnecessary."

Roca spoke in a soft voice. "What happened out there? What is it that's tearing you up inside?"

"Nothing." Soz fortified her barriers.

Eldrin spoke quietly. "Do you remember when I was sixteen and I rode with Father's army for the first time?"

"I remember." Soz had been ten. She could still see him swinging up onto his mount, surrounded by older men, seasoned warriors, preparing to ride against the Tyroll army. While girls from the village jockeyed for his attention, Soz had simply wondered why he carried only a sword. She would have taken an electromagnetic pulse rifle.

Two years later her brother Althor had carried a laser carbine into battle—and slaughtered more Tyroll soldiers in five minutes than had died in the previous decade. It ended war on Lyshriol.

As Soz matured, she had come to understand Eldrin's choice. His decision to forgo ISC technology when fighting soldiers armed with swords had been a matter of honor for him. Who had made the better choice, he or Althor, was a question she had never answered.

Eldrin was watching her face. "I killed several men during that engagement."

"Father spoke well of your courage," she said.

He snorted. "Did he boast about how I was sick afterward? About my nightmares? That I cried?"

"You were only sixteen," Roca said. "You have no reason to feel shame."

"But that's just it," Eldrin answered. "Why must I assure myself no shame exists to my remorse? The ability to make moral judgments is what puts sentient beings above other animals. So why do we consider it weakness to show remorse?"

"Because," Soz said, "otherwise we couldn't go to war."

"Perhaps we shouldn't," her mother said.

"That's naive," Soz said.

"Don't misunderstand me," Roca said. "I would rather die than submit to Eube. But does that make it the more moral choice? Does the suffering of one person negate killing another? We claim Hightons are so reprehensible they're less than human. Who defines human? By Highton standards, none of us qualifies."

"Hightons are scum," Soz said. "I'm going to purge the universe of their wretched little souls."

"Ah, Soz." Eldrin smiled. "You are still, as ever, the soul of subtle insight." His teasing sounded as it always had, but a sadness shadowed his words.

Her comm buzzed. Raising her wrist, she said, "Skolia here."

Protocol spoke. "I have a line to the emperor's office."

Soz glanced at her mother. "His office? Not him?"

"The two of you must engage the link simultaneously," Roca said. "So neither of you waits for the other."

Soz nodded and spoke into the comm. "I'm coming down."

When they reached the Strategy Room, they found the table swiveled apart, uncovering a dais. A control chair had been set up there and holoscreens arranged around the half of the dais cupped by the table. The open side faced a similar dais rimmed by holoscreens, but without a chair.

Tikal, Protocol, and Major Coalson accompanied Soz to the dais. "You sit facing the other holobooth," Tikal said.

"We're transmitting through the psiberweb," Major Coalson said. "The signals will go to a console at the palace on Glory."

"How can they pick up psiberweb signals?" Soz asked.

"They have a psiberweb console now," Tikal said.

Protocol nodded. "They arranged with us to install it precisely for this purpose, to minimize time delays in conversations such as the one you are about to have."

"But they can't transmit back via the web," Coalson said. "Their providers are their only psions and they have no training as telops."

"They must have captured Skolian telops," Soz said.

Tikal grimaced. "Usually they sell them as providers. It's not unheard of for ESComm to use one, but it's unlikely."

Cruelty over common sense, ever the Aristo way, Soz thought. "What happens if they don't use a telop?"

"Qox's response goes to a ship in orbit at Glory," Coalson said. "The ship leaves, inverts into superluminal space, and proceeds to an ISC base on the perimeter of Eubian space, which receives the message and transmits it here, via the psiberweb."

Soz mounted the dais. "How long does all that take?"

Protocol answered. "Your brother Kurj spoke with Ur Qox during negotiations for the Halstaad Code of War. Responses took anywhere from thirty minutes to several hours."

"A difficult mode of communication," Soz said. Fitting, though, for two empires locked in such a difficult war. She sat in the chair, where an aide waited with a headset.

"If they use a telop," Major Coalson said, "it will be almost instantaneous."

"Pray they don't," Tikal said.

Soz looked at him while the aide settled the headset over her hair. "Why?"

"If they're employing telops," he said, "that means they're willing to acknowledge providers have a military use."

She didn't like the sound of it. Fifteen years ago it wouldn't have mattered. Telops were of little use without psiberweb access and ESComm had no psiberweb. But her earlier briefing indicated ESComm had became more proficient at cannibalizing the Skolian web. Using a captured telop to hack a Skolian node was tricky, in that it required coercing thought rather than action, but Aristos had honed the art of coercion to a fine edge.

Protocol was speaking. "When you start transmission, you will have full control of the line."

"What line?" Soz asked.

"We've set up a Prime for you," Tikal said. "From here to Glory. We had to do it fast, so we don't have details worked out yet, but it should work."

"You control the transmission," Coalson said. "No one can tamper with it while you speak to the emperor."

The aide working on the headset inserted a comm probe into Soz's ear. "Can you read me, Imperator Skolia?" an unfamiliar voice on the comm asked. Her spinal node identified it as a monitor in Ops, below the War Room.

Soz waited until the aide adjusted the comm in front of her mouth, then said, "Yes."

A telop sitting at a console across the room looked up. "We're ready to open the link."

Protocol spoke into her wristband. "We're set here."

Yet another voice, this on from a comm in the arm of Soz's chair, said, "Same here." Her node labeled this speaker as a lieutenant monitoring the transmission from the War Room.

"Ready?" Protocol asked.

"Ready," the monitor in Ops said.

"Ready," the lieutenant in the War Room said.

"Ready," the telop across the room said.

"Clear the dais," Protocol said. As everyone withdrew, Protocol spoke into her wrist comm. "Activate."

The telop spoke into a comm on his console. "Sauscony Lahaylia Valdoria kya Skolia, Imperator of Skolia, Seventh Heir to the throne of the Ruby Dynasty, once removed from the line of Pharaoh, born of the Rhon."

In the same instant, a voice rumbled from speakers on the dais across from Soz: "His Esteemed Highness, Jaibriol the Second, Emperor of Eube, descended from the Line of Qox, son of Ur, grandson of Jaibriol the First, great-grandson of Eube."

The holoscreens behind Soz hummed and the ones across from her swirled with lines and speckles. An image appeared on the dais, a man seated on a chair similar to her own. He was resting his elbow on its arm and leaning slightly to the side with the same regal posture immortalized in images of his father, grandfather, and great-grandfather. With his glittering hair, cut short now, his severe black uniform, and his Highton features, he looked almost the perfect emperor. Only the dark circles under his eyes marred the effect.

It was almost too much. Seeing him, Soz feared she would lose the control she had clamped over her mind. She wanted to reach out to him, take him into her arms, rejoice that he lived, rage at his capture, even knowing she saw only a representation of digitized data created on Glory from the interference of laser light and sent through the web to a receiver here. *Ah, Jaibriol, my love. Will I ever hold you again?*

So they watched each other across a few meters and a hundred light-years. Finally Protocol spoke over the comm in Soz's ear. "Imperator Skolia, you initiated the link. You go first."

Soz regarded her husband. "The Imperial Dynasty of Skolia acknowledges the ascension of Jaibriol the Second to the Carnelian Throne."

He spoke in a husky voice. "The Line of Qox acknowledges the ascension of Sauscony Valdoria to the Imperial Triad."

An explosion of breath came from Protocol. Soz saw

Tikal swear, his lips moving without sound. So. Instantaneous transmission. The Traders were using their captive telops.

Jaibriol's image wavered, then vanished. A new holo formed, a tall man with broad shoulders and a strong face, classic in its Highton lines. He stood in the center of the dais watching her.

Protocol spoke in Soz's ear. "That's Trade Minister Kryx Quaelen. I don't know what they're trying to pull here. His rank is below yours. Suggest you switch the link to me."

Soz didn't switch anything. Instead she rose to her feet, her gaze hard on the Trade Minister. She had business with this particular Highton. So this was the Aristo who had dared to abuse her husband, to use him as a provider under the guise of being his "mentor."

Quaelen watched her with chillingly perfect arrogance. "The Ministry of Trade greets the Imperator of Skolia."

Protocol spoke over Soz's comm. "This is a severe break with procedure! Switch the line to me. Either break the link or leave the dais."

Soz stayed put, intent on Quaelen. "This Office hasn't acknowledged you as the voice of Qox, Minister Quaelen." In her side vision, she saw Tikal freeze, his gaze fixed on her now.

Quaelen spoke with smug arrogance. "As Imperator, you appear to be acknowledging it quite well."

"Imperator Skolia," Protocol said. "Leave the dais!"

Soz smiled at Quaelen. "I'm coming after you, little Trade Minister. All you Hightons. Take warning. Your days are numbered."

Quaelen stiffened. "Indeed. Your efforts at diplomacy leave rather much to be desired."

Tikal was gesturing at his aides, saying something, swearing, it looked like. In her ear she heard someone say, "I don't care if the line is secured. Cut the damn transmission."

"Diplomacy has to be earned," Soz told Quaelen.

His hand jerked at his side, just barely, as if he intended to strike her. " 'Earned'? You should be groveling at my feet."

"Saints almighty," a voice in Soz's ear said. Tikal looked as if he were going apoplectic. Then Roca's voice came over her ear comm. "Soz, are you out of your flaming mind? *Cut the line.*"

"Got it!" the telop across the room called. The hum of the screens around Soz stopped, cutting her off from Quaelen. She heard a buzz of voices as Protocol replaced her in the link.

Tikal was striding across the room, surrounded by aides. A telop rattled off data in her ear, something about simulations predicting the effect of what had just transpired. As she left the dais, Tikal intercepted her.

"What the hell was the purpose of that?" He almost shouted it at her. "Quaelen is the one who broke protocol. All you had to do was *walk away.*"

Soz kept going. "I wanted to hear what he had to say."

Protocol strode through the doorway, intercepting them. "At what price? Our relations with Eube are already strained enough."

"Strained?" Soz stopped in the doorway, flanked by her bodyguards. "We're at war, Councilor."

"All the more reason for tact," Tikal said.

"What?" Soz said. "You want me to say, 'Excuse me, do you mind if I kill you today'?"

Tikal scowled. "It would have been a hell of a lot better than that slugfest back there."

"He pushed," Soz said. "I pushed back."

"To what purpose?"

" 'Know thine enemy.' "

"Marvelous," Tikal growled. "And now what do you know?"

"Kryx Quaelen has a weak point," Soz said. "He's afraid of losing position within the Aristo hierarchy."

"Right," Tikal said. "You exchange five sentences with him and you're an expert on his psychology."

"Their position is ensured by their caste," Protocol said. "It's inviolable."

"That may be," Soz said. "But he has a problem with it." She paused. "I will be in the Solitude Room if you need me."

Tikal clenched one fist, then made himself relax it. "Very well."

She found the Solitude Room already occupied. Her father was sitting in the chair. She came up to him, and he watched her, his face guarded. "I wondered if you would come," he said.

"I remembered how much you liked it here." She ached at the sight of him. She could tell he wanted to hug her, but she also felt his uncertainty with this daughter he hadn't seen for so long. As a child, she had always been generous with affection, but adulthood had brought distances that became harder to bridge as their lives grew ever more complex. She hesitated now, trapped in her own reserve.

Then she thought of the fragility of their lives, and she reached out to him, across the blocky arm of the chair.

"Ai, Soshoni." He embraced her then, his love and relief enfolding her mind. When they let each other go, he spoke in a subdued voice. "Emperor Qox looked exhausted."

"We did our best." Her voice caught. "Sometimes that's not enough."

"What will you do now?"

Activate shadowmaker, Soz thought.

Activated, her node answered. Vertigo swept over her, the same sensation that came with her cyberlock. She didn't care. She had much to protect.

"I'm going to get him," she said.

"How?" her father asked. "Short of full-scale invasion, there is no way to penetrate to Glory."

"I know that." Her words sounded muffled. Subdued. Belying their import.

He watched her for a long time, absorbing that. Then he said, "ISC hasn't the resources."

"ISC has more than it knows." Softly she said, "I'm going to get him, Father. Whatever it takes."

* * *

"You let her needle you." Viquara walked with Quaelen along a glittering diamond hall in the emperor's wing of the palace.

"She's angry," Quaelen said. "It's useful to know. Anger can impair judgment."

"It's no wonder she's angry, if what my operatives say is true, that she's been pursuing him for fifteen years."

"A compelling scenario," Quaelen commented.

Compelling indeed, Viquara thought. That a Ruby Dynasty heir would pursue the Highton Heir with fanatical obsession for fifteen years—this was a tale the Hightons could believe, revel in even, given how their emperor had triumphed in the end. It sounded too convenient to Viquara. She alone knew the rest. Jaibriol and Soz Valdoria were both Rhon. On the same planet? And Jaibriol had at least one child? It didn't take a genius to put the pieces together.

Viquara had used her best people to find Jaibriol. After a massive search among the Eubian, Skolian, and Allied webs, one of her hackers discovered a brief note deleted from an Allied network fifteen years ago, a cryptic mention of "Gamma IV." Her people followed up the lead, as she had them follow every lead, however small. And this one bore fruit. An ESComm dreadnought found Jaibriol—and the child. Jaibriol's bastard son? That the boy wasn't Aristo made it an inconsequential matter, earning heatbar sterilization as a routine precaution. When Viquara ordered them to go back to the planet and do it again, she knew her command appeared excessive. She didn't care. Let them think she was obsessed with Jaibriol's safety. It was, after all, acceptable for an empress overwhelmed by the return of her long-lost son.

Could anyone have escaped that inferno? No. Yet Sauscony Valdoria had been on the planet. If she had been searching for Jaibriol in another region, the sterilization would have missed her. Then who was the boy's mother? Although the reports said the child had yellow hair, the monitors hadn't recorded a good image of him. Sauscony Valdoria had dark hair, only yellow at the tips, but her mother and brothers had gold hair.

Then again, billions of people had yellow hair. And Valdoria was part of the Ruby Dynasty, for gods' sake. Hardly a candidate for mistress to the Trader emperor, even if he was Rhon. If that boy had been her spawn, why wasn't she with him? Of course the woman could have been on a trip or might have left Jaibriol. The only other protection would have been a quasis field, and Jaibriol had no access to a generator. As an ISC Primary, Valdoria did, but stealing one from ISC was no simple matter.

What wore on Viquara was not knowing. The story could be exactly as it appeared. Or not.

She and Quaelen stopped at the emperor's suite. Security verified their identities and then slid the door open. Inside, Jaibriol was sitting at a marble table, his head bowed. As they entered, he looked up, a drop of water on his cheek.

Viquara spoke softly. "Tears, my son? Whatever for?"

He didn't answer, just wiped away the betraying moisture. At one time Viquara would have had little patience for such weakness. Now that she understood his true nature, she felt more sympathy. What must it be like for a provider to find himself on the Carnelian Throne? It was no wonder he had needed protection as a child. But did he weep for grief—or because he had just learned that his Rhon mistress, the mother of his son, was alive?

Quaelen bowed to the emperor. "My honor at your presence, Your Highness."

Jaibriol regarded him, then stood up and walked to a window across the room. Seeing him there, Viquara tensed, even knowing he had no way to escape. It had been easy to modify the defense systems that made the room impregnable from the outside. Now Jaibriol could no more go out the window than an intruder could come in. The emperor was firmly secured within this suite that constituted his universe.

A muscle twitched in Quaelen's cheek when Jaibriol ignored him. "Concerns have been expressed in regards to your safety, Your Highness."

The emperor continued to stare out the window. The moon G5 made a crescent high in the late afternoon sky, with the slightly smaller crescent of G7 below it. Two moons without names, fourth and fifth largest in the satellites that attended Eube's Glory, numbered for their distance from the planet, waiting to honor the fourth and fifth Eubian empresses.

Jaibriol pushed against the glimmering quasis screen overlaying the pane, and the tip of his finger flattened. "My safety from whom?" He turned to them. "My enemies, my allies, or my family?"

Quaelen gave him an odd smile, almost hungry in its aspect. It made Viquara uneasy. He reacted to Jaibriol much as he had to the slave girl Cirrus. When he joined Jaibriol at the window, her son faced him without even the twitch of an eyelid. But something in Jaibriol's posture reminded Viquara of the way her provider Cayson flinched if she startled him. Was Jaibriol's tension simply a response to his circumstances, or did it reveal something more about his relationship with Quaelen?

As Jaibriol's mentor, Quaelen was the only one besides Viquara who, fifteen years ago, had known Jaibriol as more than a distant acquaintance. In private, with accomplished innuendo, Quaelen had revealed to her that he knew Jaibriol was now a prisoner, rather than a reclusive emperor who chose his seclusion. Faced with exposure, Viquara became his uneasy ally. As it turned out, he offered sound advice. He had been right about putting the slave cuffs on Jaibriol; in addition to monitoring the emperor, they provided a means of control via the neural threads they extended into his body. That and the drugs they used worked well in convincing the emperor of the wisdom in their suggestions as to how he should behave.

Quaelen pushed up Jaibriol's sleeve, revealing the sparkling cuff. "It is for security, you understand," he said.

"The closer we monitor you, the better we are assured of your continued well-being."

Sarcasm grated in Jaibriol's voice. "I'm touched by your concern."

Quaelen removed a needle from a tube on his belt, clicked it into the cuff, twisted it around, and pulled it out again. When he slid the needle back into its tube, lights blinked on his palmtop.

Viquara joined him. "Any problems?"

Quaelen studied his palmtop. "Nothing at all." He glanced at Jaibriol with a subtle condescension Viquara saw only because she was looking now for irregularities. Jaibriol watched him as if they were fighting a battle, one where they both knew Quaelen assumed he had the superior position. Viquara was beginning to fear she had a more serious problem with Quaelen than she had realized. Just what did he know?

Jaibriol wouldn't meet her eyes. So beautiful, this son of hers. Except he wasn't really her son. With his eyes downcast and his cuffs glittering, he looked the truth of his heritage. A beautiful slave. Her slave. It disquieted her that she reacted to him as if he were Highton, but it troubled her even more that Quaelen reacted as if he were a provider.

She touched Jaibriol's arm. "Kryx and I have business to attend. We will check on you later."

Jaibriol just nodded, with the same ambiguous response he always had to her, as if he wasn't sure whether to hate or love his own mother. Quaelen raised his eyebrows. He knew he and Viquara had no business they hadn't already scheduled. But he bowed to Jaibriol and they took their leave of the emperor.

Viquara was silent as they walked through the halls. Quaelen paced at her side, hands clasped behind his back. Four of her Razers and four of his secret police accompanied them, two in front, two behind, and two at each side.

Viquara and Qualen withdrew into her office, leaving the guards outside. She went to the window and gazed out at the gardens with their marble columns, trimmed lawns, and weeping-star trees, all bathed in glittering cold light from her namesake, Viquara, the Diamond Moon.

Quaelen came up behind her, standing too close. "You wanted to talk in private." He stated rather than asked it.

"A thought has occurred to me. In regards to Hightons. And Silicates." Viquara paused. "And providers." She waited, letting implications occur to him. Highton and Silicate: it was his own heritage. Highton and provider: she would see what he made of that.

"An interesting combination." Quaelen rubbed her hair between his fingers, his hand just below her ear, his knuckles brushing her skin. "Some combinations condemn more than others."

"I have found it prudent to take care in offering condemnation."

"Prudence is always wise." He trailed his fingers along her jaw. "Such beauty," he murmured. "Highton beauty."

"Yes. Highton." Whatever you sense in Jaibriol, she thought, did not come from me.

With night darkening beyond the window, she could see their reflections in the glass. He looked down at her hair. "Imagine what a travesty it would be if a Highton—particularly one of intelligence—tried to pass a taskmaker child as his own."

Gods. Quaelen knew about Intelligence Minister Vitrex's bastard son? What *didn't* he know? She kept her voice cool. "It would indeed be a travesty if he, or his wife, attempted such a deception."

"Indeed." Quaelen had both hands on her now, letting them slide down her arms. "I can think of no greater crime." He bent his head and spoke against her ear, his breath stirring her hair. "Except a provider on the Carnelian Throne."

Viquara closed her eyes. He knew. Quaelen knew.

Opening her eyes, she watched his reflection. "Tell me, Kryx. Have you ever heard the tale of the Diamond Prince?"

"A child's tale." He slid his hands up her arm, brushing her breasts. "Stories of beautiful women and handsome men."

"Ah, but that is only glitter on the surface. The real story is the moral. The Diamond Prince fell to the Hightons, as was right and proper." She paused. "But he was mistreated and so the spirits avenged him."

"I have wondered about the telling of such stories to children. The idea of vengeance for a slave has a subversive cast."

"Hightons protect their slaves." She tried to ignore the way he was stroking her arms.

He moved his hands to her neckline. "So we do."

"Care for them even. As a mother would care for a son."

"A son." He undid the catches at her neckline, and the velvet gown fell open, revealing the black lace camisole she wore under it. He drew her gown off her shoulders, pulling the sleeves down her arms. She wanted to tear away from him, but she feared to move.

Softly he asked, "Do you wonder, Empress Viquara, why I have never taken a wife?"

After a deliberate pause, she said, "A man of your esteem must be selective." She knew the true reason: he wanted only the highest of the highborn for his bed, a woman to counteract the stain on his line. Many Highton women would honor the chance to join a man of such power, but they came from lesser lines, more concerned with their own elevation than the taint to his name.

"Selective." He peeled off her camisole and dropped it on the floor. Her reflection showed a woman with a velvet skirt draped from her hips to the ground, clinging to her classic form. Her upper body was bare, marble smooth, like a statue. Her breasts gleamed, not the exaggerated charms of a provider, but the subtle sculpted perfection of a Highton.

Quaelen slid his hands over her breasts. "A man deserves a wife who is his equal."

Viquara tried to ignore the beat of her pulse, the

unwanted response Quaelen evoked from her. "As does a woman, with her husband." And he wasn't. Never would she call Kryx Quaelen consort.

He unfastened her skirt. One tug and it slid to the ground, leaving her in a floor-length underskirt of black silk. "There are many forms of elevation, my lovely empress," he murmured, sliding his arms around her waist. "And many forms of debasement as well. Can you imagine? Someday Vitrex's son will marry. His wife will call him Highton, lay with him, bear his children."

She forced out a platitude. "The Line of Vitrex is an old and powerful one. It has great honor."

Quaelen kissed her neck. "Great honor." His tongue tickled the ridges of her ear. "Few houses have greater. Except the Line of Qox. Or it once did."

"The Line of Qox has risen again," Viquara whispered.

"Can you imagine the horror it would create should that line show itself as false? A line of *slaves?*" He set his hands on her waist. "Imagine the shame."

Desperation touched Viquara. If Quaelen revealed Jaibriol, it would destroy everything. "No."

"No?" He tugged her slip and the lace slid off her body, pooling around her feet, baring her snow-marble body. "I wonder what one might expect in return for keeping the secret of such shame."

She forced out the words, her voice barely more than a whisper. "One might expect much."

"Indeed." Lifting her by the waist, he set her toes on the sill at the bottom of the window, forcing her to stand on tiptoe, bringing her hips level with his. "You are beautiful, my empress," he murmured. "As your consort, I will honor you."

So they merged forces, gazing into a darkened garden, their passion reflected in a pane of glass, both of them facing outward, a woman with the sculpted perfection of heartless marble and the dark shade behind her, a power forever in shadows and forever implacable.

22

"Klein bottles," Soz said.

Admiral Jon Casestar walked with her along a corridor in the Orbiter. He was a man of average height and features, with graying hair, but there was nothing average about his intellect. Although Soz knew little about him, she could see why Kurj had appointed him as an adviser. Casestar was no yes-man; he spoke his mind, with insight, a trait she valued. How well they would work together, however, remained to be seen.

The admiral was also evaluating her. Although he had the usual mental defenses up, she caught traces of his thoughts. He was undecided as to his opinion of her command style, but considered that it might be invigorating.

"Our ships already have Klein fuel bottles," he said.

"Too small," she replied.

"We've improved the design over the past decade," he said. "They vary in size now, depending on how much antimatter fuel a ship needs."

"I was thinking much bigger. Big enough to carry ships."

Casestar drew her to a halt. "You want to put a starship in a Klein fuel bottle?"

"That's right. Crewed ships."

"Imperator Skolia, that's impossible."

"Is it?" She considered him. "I've looked at the work they're doing at the Advanced Theory Institute at Glenmarrow. In theory, we can make bottles that size."

"In theory, maybe. But the engineering is another story." He shook his head. "It isn't only the size. I doubt you can put human beings in a Klein bottle."

"Why not?"

He studied her face, obviously trying to fathom her. "What happens to people if you spread the charge and mass of their bodies throughout complex space? I've no idea."

"We do it every time we invert," Soz said.

"Only for an instant. And it's only our speed that becomes complex. Even that's too much for some. There are people who never travel in space because they can't tolerate inversion. To my knowledge, no one has ever existed in complex space for more than a few seconds and returned alive."

"I have."

That obviously caught him off guard. "How?"

"When I went after Jaibriol Qox fifteen years ago. To escape ISC, he tried to made his ship invert from zero speed. I followed him." In truth, it had been her idea. Jaibriol had actually been on her ship while she "chased" a decoy.

Casestar stared at her. "I thought inversion was only possible from relativistic speeds."

"We never did manage to invert," she admitted. "But we did go into complex space. That's how we got through the cordon."

His curiosity brushed her mind. "What was it like?"

"It's hard to describe." She tilted her head. "Reality became—well, liquid almost. There was a sense of twisting too, I assume as different parts of the ship took on different imaginary values."

"But did you actually experience that? Or was it just how you perceived whatever happened?"

Soz considered. "I'm not sure. We felt like we were melting. But when we dropped back into real space we were solid. We never 'completed' the twist, though. We never inverted."

Casestar gave her an odd look. " 'We'?"

Careful, Soz warned herself. "Myself and the pilot."

"What happened to the pilot?"

"She died when we crashed." As far as Soz knew, the

pilot had actually gone to Earth. Prior to that, Erin O'Neill had been an Allied operative working undercover in an ISC hospital, with the alias Lyra Merzon. O'Neill was also the one who had married Soz and Jaibriol. Somewhere on Earth, known only to O'Neill and the former Allied president, proof existed that the Skolian Imperator and Eubian Emperor were husband and wife.

Casestar started to walk with her again. "A Klein bottle stores only a fraction of its contents in real space. With a big enough bottle, you could hide a lot of ships."

Soz gave a feral smile. "ESComm would have no idea what hit them."

"We would have the advantage of surprise only once."

"They've lost the advantage of surprise with the quasis-in-a-tau trick, but it still works."

He rubbed his chin. "We'll need to know what happens to the mental state of the crews in this complex limbo."

"I kept my anchor with reality by linking to the ship's EI." She studied the thought, turning it around in her mind. "We could have telops link to the psiberweb. The rest of the crew could go into quasis for short periods. ESComm won't be able to duplicate the technique, because it requires a full psiberweb."

"It would be effective, I'll grant that." He spread his hands. "But the questions involved, just with the engineering alone, aren't trivial."

Soz paused at the entrance to a catwalk above the War Room. "That's why I've put you in charge. I've faith in your abilities, Admiral. Make it work and we'll have a weapon the Traders can't match."

He nodded, still cautious. But she felt his mind tackling the challenge, looking at it from different sides. It intrigued him, as she had hoped it would.

After they parted, Soz walked onto the catwalk. The amphitheater below hummed with activity: telops working, aides running errands, pages soothing, cranes swinging through the air or poised above control panels. The stardome arched over her, with its holographic panorama of stars.

As she walked to the Command Chair, a few people below glanced up, then returned to their work. No one realized the significance of the moment. That was how Soz wanted it, with no fanfare. She simply sat in the chair. So it was done: she had taken her place as Imperator.

The exoskeleton closed around her, clicking prongs into her ankles, wrists, spine, and neck. The chaos in her mind had receded as she learned to control it, but now it surged again, flooding her with ISC data while her lone spinal node struggled to sort the deluge. She needed more nodes. Fifteen years ago she had possessed the most advanced biomech web a human body could take; today it was nowhere near the best available.

She started with a survey of her forces. Four components existed to Imperial Space Command. The Imperial Fleet was the largest, having grown out of the navy that had existed on Raylicon prior to space travel. The Advance Services Corps had begun with the naval units that went ashore as advance scouts or foot soldiers. When Raylicon regained air and space travel about 430 years ago, the ASC became an interstellar force independent of the navy, the advance scouts for planetary landings. The Pharaoh's Army had the longest history of any branch in the military. Established by the Ruby Dynasty, it claimed five millennia of service to the empires birthed by Raylicon. Although primarily concerned with planetary warfare, it also maintained deep space divisions.

The J-Force consisted of Jag starfighters and their Jagernaut pilots, both enhanced by biomech and psibertech until the line between machine and human blurred. Rank was defined relative to the navy, with Jagernaut Quaternary about equal to lieutenant junior grade, Tertiary to commander, Secondary to commodore, and Primary to full admiral. The J-Force was analogous to an air force, however, in that it followed the development of space travel similar to the way air forces followed air travel. One branch specialized in covert operations; Imperial Messengers were Jagernauts assigned to the ISC Intelligence Tasking Office, a job Soz knew well, having been a Messenger Secondary in her thirties. She had become a Primary and squad commander in her forties.

ISC had several nerve centers. The Orbiter, named in Kurj's ever-literal style, orbited the Imperialate on a variable route known only to ISC security. From this chair, linked to the First Lock, she could monitor most of the giant ISC war machine. The Onyx military complex, which protected the Third Lock, had grown into a city of space stations with a combined population of two billion. The planet Diesha served as ISC headquarters. Its personnel were concentrated in the city Kurj had of course named HeadQuarters City, but many other installations riddled the planet, most underground. Fifteen years ago, Jaibriol had been imprisoned in Block Three, a complex far out in the Dieshan desert.

The years had brought few changes in ISC strategy. Although the Eube-Skolia conflict had escalated, it remained a shadow war fought in deep space, using a guess-and-attack mode of estimating where an enemy would drop out of superluminal space and then staging an ambush. Space war had gone beyond the ability of unenhanced soldiers to fight it; the split-second response times it required far exceeded normal human capabilities, and the accelerations involved would pulverize anyone without quasis protection. Some battles involved only robot drones, a form of combat where chunks of metal slagged each other while humans monitored the engagement from distant stand-off weapons platforms.

Superluminal combat didn't really exist. Sublight ships had no way to detect faster-than-light craft, and the sheer speed of FTL ships made detection by other superluminal ships difficult. If an ESComm sentry did locate a superluminal ISC force, it had almost no way to warn sublight forces in any reasonable amount of time. ISC fared better with the psiberweb. The term *web extractors* had come into use for telops who located superluminal ESComm forces and coordinated their capture or destruction through the web. Despite low detection rates, extraction proved useful. It was, in fact, how ISC had caught Jaibriol's ship fifteen years ago.

Settled planets were better protected than deep space, secured by ground, orbital, and systemwide defenses. Engagements on civilian worlds were rare. Although interstellar space was harder to protect, regions of heavy traffic were well monitored and rarely saw combat. However, Soz found a disquieting trend. Civilian casualties had been increasing, as skirmishes spilled into higher population areas, affecting commercial carriers and private spacecraft.

She recognized many names on the roster of her top officers. General Dayamar Stone, commandant of the ASC, had trained her at the Dieshan Military Academy, which commissioned Jagernauts but drew its faculty from all the services. Stone had given her no quarter—and in the decades since she had thanked him for it a hundred times over.

It didn't surprise her to see Starjack Tahota in command of the Imperial Fleet. The admiral had an unparalleled record. Soz remembered the towering Tahota, bronzed and muscled, a throwback to the ancient warrior queens of the Ruby Empire. Seeing her and Kurj walk together had been like watching two giants stride out of mythology.

Primary Brant Tapperhaven was top man in the J-Force. Soz had heard of him fifteen years ago, as a brash young officer, but their paths rarely crossed. His profile revealed a leader aggressive to the point of abrasiveness, but with a record that showed he had good reason for his high opinion of his abilities. It didn't surprise her; Jagernauts were notorious for their fierce independence, a quality needed to survive the demands of a job that isolated them from ISC. They faced ESComm one on one, without the mental static of crewed ships to interfere with their Kyle-intensive operations.

Naaj Majda was General of the Pharaoh's Army. She came from an old family, one of the few that could trace its lineage to Ruby Empire nobility. Ties between the Ruby Dynasty and House of Majda had always been strong.

When Soz's brother Kelric had been young, a test pilot, one of the J-Force's glamour boys, he had married Naaj's older sister, Admiral Corey Majda, then commander of the battle cruiser *Roca's Pride*. Corey died a few years later, leaving her husband a widower at twenty-four.

Soz bit her lip as the memories flooded her. A decade after Corey's death Kelric had also become a casualty, dying alone in space. ISC never found more than a few slagged bits of his ambushed Jag.

"Ai." Soz blinked at the moisture in her eyes. She had to stop this, lest she drown in the memories of what this war had taken from her family.

She focused on her work, trying to pull her thoughts in line. What she found disturbed her. It was true that ISC claimed millions of ships, dwarfing the Allied forces and every military in past history. But they lagged far behind Eube. Estimates of ESComm forces ranged from two to six times that of ISC, depending on the accuracy of ISC intelligence and whether pirates were included. Numbers were deceptive, though, in that ISC had better tech. ESComm inventories dwarfed ISC, but ISC could outmaneuver, outcalculate, and outcommunicate ESComm. Eube lumbered; Skolia sailed.

The ISC focus on new technology made sense to Soz, given their greater capacity for invention compared to ESComm. But they needed more ships and bases. She set up committees to reorganize resource allocations and encourage research by the civilian sector, shifting the funding burden for research away from the military without losing the benefits of new work. She did earmark ISC funds for several areas, however, including web extraction and quasis-tau missiles. She also set up the top-secret Klein bottle program, dubbing it the Radiance Project.

Soz soon came to the same conclusion as Kurj had before her: ISC was losing the shadow war. Extrapolations into the future, by both ISC strategists and Dehya, suggested that the longer ISC drew out the war, the greater the probability that unforeseen advances in technology would provide the edge they needed to prevail. Kurj's strategy had been to wear down ESComm with skirmishes and raids, eroding the monolith to gain time while ISC worked on research. The plan was Kurj at his best: solid, ordered, designed to last centuries, with relentless attention to detail.

Soz had a different plan.

She wanted new ideas, the joker in the deck, the random jump of unpredictable genius. The wild card. ISC needed it. She had looked at the cost in human terms of a drawn-out war and found it too high.

There was also Jaibriol.

No more shadow war. She intended to invade Eube.

Solid and black, the obsidian walls and ceiling of the Lava Chamber curved around to make a circular room. The solid topaz floor glittered with geometric patterns of pinpoint lights. Ruby had been used to make the furniture, including the table where the Eubian War Cabinet sat: General Taratus and Admiral Kaliga, the joint commanders of ESComm; Izar Vitrex and Kryx Quaelen, from the two ministries that were military in nature rather than civilian; High Judge Calope Muze, the conduit for communication among the branches of ESComm; and Empress Viquara, representative for the reclusive emperor.

General Taratus sat sprawled in his chair, a large man even for a Highton, with a blocky face and thick eyebrows. Compared to the massive Taratus, Admiral Kaliga looked, at first glance, like a shadow, with his gaunt frame, lesser height, and narrow face. But within that shadow brooded an intellect as keen as a honed knife.

"We must go ahead with this," Taratus said. "ISC wears us down like hail on stone."

"Assign telops to our ships and you create chaos," Kaliga said. "All our officers are Aristos or have Aristo blood. Put them in contact with providers while they are on duty and you court disaster."

Taratus snorted. "Officers without self-control don't belong in an ESComm uniform."

"The question is academic," Calope said. The oldest member of the cabinet, over a century in age, she had a full head of glittering white hair. "Our only trained telops are those we've captured from Skolian ships. That isn't enough."

"We can train others," Taratus said.

"Train providers?" Kaliga leaned back in his chair. "I hardly think so. Even if they could learn, which I doubt, they will panic during combat."

Viquara spoke. "Having telops on ships is no guarantee they can hack the psiberweb. We also need Kyle-capable consoles."

"We're making good progress in the Kyle tech," Vitrex said. "We have more to work with now that we've found a way to stop captured Skolian vessels from self-destructing."

Kaliga nodded. "The quasis taus work well."

Quaelen spoke in a shadowed voice. "And already ISC finds ways to counteract them."

Silence answered him. They all knew his meaning. Had ISC been slower in learning to counter the quasis trick, Ur Qox would still be alive and Kurj Skolia would be an ESComm prisoner.

Viquara exhaled. "They are creative, these Skolians."

Dryly Kaliga said, "Creativity, in the wrong places, is a recipe for turmoil."

Taratus tapped his lightpen against his fingers. "I suggest a limited experiment. Assign one squad to carry telops and see what happens. Perhaps the Hawkracer Squadron."

Viquara glanced around the table. When the other cabinet members indicated their agreement, she said, "I will take your proposal to the emperor."

Starlight silvered the Solitude Room. Eldrinson Valdoria, Key to the Web, sat in the chair staring at the stars. He heard the door slide open, with no warning from his bodyguards. Then Dehya appeared, like a wraith, her long hair drifting around her body. She sat on the edge of the console in front of him.

"Twice in only a few days," he said. "I'm flattered."

"By what?" Her voice was leaves drifting in wind.

"Your presence."

"I'm always here." She lifted her hands as if to indicate all of some undefined space. "Everywhere."

"My son thinks you are becoming part of the web."

Her face softened, a trace of her former vibrancy revealing itself. Then it faded again. "It all points to you," she said.

He tried to absorb her mood. Although he had shared the Triad with her for decades, he knew her only as a presence, a swirl of sublime mental intricacies he never fully fathomed. "What points to me?"

"I still haven't the right initial conditions."

"What are initial conditions?"

"The starting point for the evolution of a mathematical solution." She made a circle in the air with her finger. "The calculations go around and around, never converging." She pointed at him. "Around you."

He gave her a wry smile. "As flattered as I am to play a role in your equations, Dehya, I'm afraid I have no idea what you are talking about."

"It's about Soz. And you."

Eldrinson had been meditating to ensure he remained calm when faced with questions about Soz. Now he brought up images in his mind to invoke that tranquillity: Roca's voice, Eldrin's songs, Vyrl's farm, Aniece's laughter. Then he asked, "What about Soz and me?"

"It all comes back to you," she said. "The equations won't converge. The initial conditions are wrong. I put Soz back in the model and it improved, but it still doesn't converge. You're a singularity."

"I don't know what you mean," he said, which was honest.

She leaned forward. "Eldri, listen. This isn't a game. In the future extrapolations I'm calculating, I cease to exist. I don't die. I just *stop*."

He blinked. "How can you cease to exist?"

"I have no idea." She pushed her hair away from her eyes. "I can't find what happens after the divergence."

"I don't understand. What do you mean, 'divergence'?"

"The future."

"It splits into different paths?"

"Mathematical divergence. It blows up."

"Your equations predict the future explodes?" He rubbed his chin. "I should hope not."

"I mean their solution becomes infinite."

"How can the future be infinite?"

"Not the future. The equations that predict what happens. They don't behave in a logical way." She spread her hands. "My model is wrong."

He didn't know what to make of the conversation. Although he had wondered if Dehya would suspect he had an involvement in Soz's disappearance, he hadn't expected this. "Equations are only abstractions. They aren't real."

"They tell me that people we both love are in danger. Eldrin: my consort, your son. Taquinil: my son, your grandson."

He tensed. "In danger how?"

"I don't know." Frustration shaded her voice. "The calculations are off. I'm missing something. Something important. Something about you."

"But why do you think Eldrin and Taquinil are in danger?"

"I get hints of it in the model. Just hints, almost buried in noise." She paused. "I've asked Taquinil to come home."

He understood the impulse to draw one's children near when they were in danger. "Does his presence change your equations?"

"I can't tell yet. There's too much noise in the results."

What disquieted Eldrinson most was her fear. He had seen her in many moods, but this understated dread was something new.

"Why do you think I hide anything?" he asked.

She answered with a non sequitur. "Did you know that the Allied flotilla that will be taking you to Earth has arrived?"

The abrupt subject change puzzled him. "At the Orbiter?"

"Yes. They're rendezvousing with the ISC forces that will be your escort." She tilted her head. "You must go to Earth. Soz is right. You're safer there."

"Roca and Ami will go. I'm needed here."

"You should go too."

"I can't. You know that."

"Please, Eldri. Do it."

He touched her arm, sensing more to this. "What else did you see in these equations?"

She swallowed. "If you stay here, you also cease to exist."

He smiled uneasily, unsure what to make of this. "I certainly have no desire to stop existing."

"It would be a loss."

Dryly he said, "I'm glad you think so. There have been more than a few times I've wondered."

Her smile sparkled, reminding him of less somber times. "Ah, well, think how boring our lives would be if we didn't have each other to argue with about whether the inheritance of power should go through male or female lines."

He glowered at her. "I seem to be losing that argument lately, what with all these Imperators and Pharaohs and Empresses everywhere. I'm outnumbered."

Her voice gentled. "Then let us both survive to argue it another day."

In truth, he saw the logic in splitting up the Triad. The danger of all three Keys being in the same place was too great, and Earth was a sensible place to go, neutral ground, an unlikely target if the war escalated. His emotions, however, refused to acknowledge his logic.

"I can't leave you to support the Web alone," he said.

"Soz is here."

"The Triad link isn't stable."

"Even so. You have to go. You're too valuable to risk."

"So are you. You go to Earth."

"Eldri, hear me." She looked genuinely frightened. "Kurj didn't stay on Skyhammer. He died. I don't want you to end."

He shifted his weight. "You truly believe my life will end if I stay here?"

"Cease to exist."

"What does that mean?"

"I don't know. Maybe you will start to exist again later."

He couldn't help but smile. "Dehya, do you think perhaps you spend too much time with these equations of yours?"

"Eldri, please."

His voice gentled. "When does Taquinil arrive?"

"In a few days."

"And my son Eldrin will be here with you?"

"Yes."

He knew if he tried to stay, he would also have to fight the Inner Assembly over it. For all that his tornado of a daughter disconcerted them, they agreed with her in this matter. Strange how life went, when the children began to protect the parents.

"Eldri?" Dehya asked.

He exhaled. "Very well. I will go to Earth."

Her relief suffused the chamber. "Good."

"Do your equations say whether or not my leaving helps Eldrin and Taquinil?"

"I don't know. It's buried in the noise."

He made an exasperated sound. "You keep saying this. The 'noise.' How can equations make noise?"

"It's like static, but in the numbers. So much static I can't find the solution."

The comm in the chair chimed. Eldrinson frowned at the interruption. "Yes?"

His bodyguard answered. "Lord Valdoria, we just had a message from First Councilor Tikal. The Allied flotilla has arrived. They're rendezvousing with the ISC forces that will accompany you to Earth."

He raised his eyebrows at Dehya. He doubted she had "calculated" the flotilla's arrival before Tikal let anyone know it was here. More likely, her spy monitors had told her. He spoke into the comm. "Have you notified my wife and daughter-in-law?"

"Yes, sir. They went to meet the Allied commander."

"Very well." Eldrinson closed the link and grimaced at

Dehya. "Knowing Tikal, he will try to bustle us off right away."

She smiled. "Probably."

"I haven't even packed."

"He'll send people to do it for you." Softly she said, "You have to tell me before you go. What am I missing? What happened with Soz?"

"Did you ever think," he said, "that knowing answers may cause more damage than not knowing them?"

"What answers?"

"I have none for you. I'm sorry."

She stood up, her gaze intent as she leaned her hands on the arms of his chair. "And if those answers you don't have could save the lives of people we love? Eldrin and Taquinil?"

The comm chimed again. Eldrinson resisted the urge to growl *not now* and instead flicked it on. "What is it?"

His bodyguard answered. "First Councilor Tikal requests you meet him and the Allied commanders in the Strategy Room."

Eldrinson scowled. He had experienced enough of Tikal's "requests" to knew the councilor would continue haranguing him until he did what Tikal wanted. "I will be out in a moment."

"Very well, sir."

As he closed the link, Dehya said, "We can never know the answers for certain. But if making better guesses protects the people we love, isn't it worth it?"

He thought of Eldrin, his firstborn, the son most like him; of Taquinil, the vulnerable genius, the grandson he loved. Standing up, he said, "Put Jaibriol Qox into your equations."

"I already have."

Softly he said, "Not in the right way."

She watched him, her eyes green behind the sunset. "What is the right way?"

"Gently."

"Gently?"

"Yes. Gently." He took her hands. "Take care, my sister."

She squeezed his hands. "And you, my brother."

23

It was three in the morning when Seth Rockworth walked into the living room of his house. He found Jai standing in front of the glass doors that opened onto the patio, looking out at the Appalachian Mountains.

"Couldn't you sleep?" Seth asked.

Jai turned to him. At sixteen, Jaibriol Qox Skolia stood six-foot-two and was still growing. His shoulders had filled out, and he had the strapping vigor of a youth who thrived outdoors. The horizontal ribbing on his sweater made his chest look even broader. His jeans were old-fashioned denim, which had been popular for centuries. Gold highlights streaked his black hair, looking for all the world as if he had done it on purpose, after a style popular among young people now. Although his red eyes were hidden behind lenses that turned them brown, anyone familiar with Eubian aristocracy would recognize his features as Highton. But who would think to look for such in an American schoolboy?

"I still have trouble with the length of the day," Jai said. "I don't know if I'll ever get used to it being so short."

"Are you worried about tomorrow?" Seth asked.

Jai shrugged. "The tests said we're ready."

"More than ready."

The three older children had taken exams for the private schools where Seth had arranged to send them. They all placed beyond their age level in academic subjects and tended to shyness in social situations. Jai was entering school as a senior, thirteen-year-old Lisi as a freshman, and seven-year-old Vitar as a first grader. Del-Kelric would stay home with Seth and a nursemaid, an older woman who soothed the toddler when he cried for his parents. Seth knew the older children cried as well, but in private, with no one to see.

He had told the authorities they were his wards, Skolians who lost their parents in the war. He hadn't known what to call them. He certainly couldn't use Qox Skolia. He finally gave them his own name, which they accepted as if he had done them an honor, becoming Jay, Lisa, Peter, and Kelly Rockworth.

Jai walked into the darkened living room and picked up the remote for a holoscreen on the wall. He clicked it on and a news broadcast appeared, one he had apparently recorded earlier. He turned off the sound, so the newscaster spoke in silence. Her image faded and a scene of the Assembly Hall on Parthonia filled the screen.

Seth saw why Jai had recorded the broadcast. In one corner of the image, at a bench assigned to the Ruby Dynasty, the Skolian Imperator sat listening to the Assembly proceedings, the lights on the bench where she "sat" indicating she was present as a holographic simulacrum.

"It must be hard to see them on the news," Seth said.

Jai turned off the broadcast. "Do you think it's true, what the Allied leaders say? That the Ruby Dynasty overstates their case against the Hightons?"

Seth spoke carefully. "There was a time when I would have said no. People change, though. Trader pirates no longer prey on our ships. Their leaders appear to have a genuine interest in allying with us." In truth, he doubted the Hightons would ever change. But what could he say to this boy whose father ruled from the Carnelian Throne?

Seth had no doubt Jai's father wasn't Highton. No Aristo could have raised the four miracles Seth had cared for these past months. Gentle, intelligent, loving, well-adjusted, with a deep compassion for humanity and an innocence that belied the cruelty of the universe that had born them, they astonished him. He had agreed to take them, and hide their secret, out of honor to the dynasty whose judgment in matters of family he trusted, even if he found them otherwise impossible to live with. He honored his oath now out of love for the children.

Vitar and Lisi ran to Soz. She knelt in the grass, reaching out her arms. Her children collided with her and they all fell into a laughing heap. Jaibriol and Jai came out of the forest at a more sedate pace, grinning, bathed in sunlight . . .

Soz opened her eyes into the dark. "What?" she mumbled. A tear ran down her face.

I have a page from Admiral Jon Casestar, her node repeated.

She wiped the tears off her cheek. **How long have I been sleeping?**

Three hours.

Three hours? She had intended to take only two. **Tell Jon I'll be in the War Room in ten minutes.**

Soz limped to the bathroom. What she wouldn't give now for a eighty-one-hour night where she could sleep as long as she needed. She stared at her reflection in the mirror. Her body had recovered from her last pregnancy, become too thin even. She brushed the stretch marks on her abdomen. They were all she had now of her children. Even if she had wanted to remove the marks, which she didn't, she couldn't have done it. She never let doctors examine her and she kept her shadowmaker active all the time. If anyone found out she had children, they would ask what happened to them. And who fathered them.

She took no one into her confidence. She declined all friendship. She attended social functions only as duty demanded. But she did look up the files on the Jag squadron she had commanded seventeen years ago. Taas, the youngest member, had continued flying and was now a Secondary. Helda had earned many promotions, leaving active duty to become an administrator.

And Rex.

Her best officer and her best friend, he had been injured

in unexpected combat with ESComm just hours after he had revealed that he wanted to retire from ISC and marry her. After the battle, in pain both physical and emotional, he withdrew his proposal. They never had the chance to find out if time could have healed the wounds of war and grief that so scarred them.

Although Rex never regained full use of his natural legs, advances in surgery and synthetic enhancements made it possible for him to live a normal life. He became a diplomat for the Office of Planetary Development and eventually married a prime minister on the world Foreshires Hold.

Soz exhaled. That part of her life was gone. She knew the Assembly thought she was too single-minded in her pursuit of ESComm. That she stalked through the Orbiter always shrouded in a shadowmaker added to their disquiet. It didn't matter. Better they thought she was driven by an obsession to bring down Jaibriol Qox than they knew the truth.

She finished dressing and went to the War Room. As she took her place in the Command Chair, Jon Casestar swung up on a crane. Starlight bathed them. Fake starlight. The holodome over their heads produced it, rather than a genuine window to the stars. Given that the War Room was near the Orbiter's equator, the outer hull actually formed the floor of the amphitheater rather than the dome.

"We're ready," Casestar said.

Soz nodded. "Good. Let's do it."

Casestar swung in his crane to a monitoring station on the periphery of the dome. Submerging into the web, Soz extended her mind through the Orbiter web and then outward to the stars. She was traveling in deep space with eight Jag fighters. Only seven pilots joined her in the link; the eighth Jag was a drone piloted by its EI brain.

Ready. That came from seven minds at once.

Proceed, Soz thought. The word rumbled with the Rhon power of her mind.

The eighth Jag twisted out of reality and disappeared.

At first Soz noticed no difference. She was linked to the EI of the vanished ship, and it continued to send stats on its condition within the giant Klein bottle in complex space where it now existed.

Then a curious effect manifested; the data were *dripping* into her mind.

I am loooosing coheeeesion, the Jag's EI thought.

According to the chronometer on her mindscape, the Jag had been in its bottle for only three minutes. **Continue test,** she thought.

Coooooontinuuuuuuuuuuuu . . .

Soz waited. **JG-8, respond.**

We still have it on monitor, Jon Casestar thought. *It just isn't transmitting.*

Soz frowned. If an EI computer couldn't maintain contact, how would a human? Fifteen years ago she and Jaibriol had kept their mental cohesion for eight minutes in complex space on a ship with a far less sophisticated EI than a Jag fighter. Their speed had been complex, though, rather than their mass or charge.

Perhaps the EI brain is the problem, someone thought.

Identify, Soz thought.

Alis Rasmuss, Glenmarrow University.

Ah. Good. Soz had requested Rasmuss for the project. A mathematician at the Advanced Theory Institute at Glenmarrow, she was the undisputed genius in Klein containment theory.

What about the EI brain? Soz asked.

It's sophisticated enough to know it's in trouble, Rasmuss thought, *but may be too primitive to deal with it. An EI doesn't have the flexibility of the human mind. When reality dissolves, you may need that flexibility.*

Soz directed a thought to the Jag squad leader: **Primary Ko, drop the JG-8 back into normal space.**

Done, Ko thought.

The eighth Jag twisted into view. It looked normal, moving in formation with the seven other Jags at 0.05 light speed.

Data poured into the Soz's internal systems, the new array of nodes she had in her spine. She studied the JG-8 on her mindscape, viewing schematics of its interior systems.

In terms of equipment, it looks fine, a new voice thought.

Identify, Soz thought.

Jase Furlon, ma'am.

Soz's **P** node identified him as an engineer with the Radiance Project, traveling on *Anvil,* the dreadnought following the Jags in space. **Where is the data on its stint in Klein space?** she asked. **All I have is gibberish.**

We also, Furlon thought.

The data is in there, Casestar thought. *We need to unravel it from the noise.*

Imperator Skolia? That came from Stellart Heald, one of the Jag pilots.

Go ahead, Soz thought.

I'd like to go in, he thought. *Try the bottle.*

You're volunteering to go into Klein space? Soz asked.

Yes, ma'am.

Hold on. Soz directed a thought to Casestar: **Any progress deciphering the JG-8 data?**

Some, Casestar answered. *Rasmuss, respond.*

It's fluid flow! Rasmuss thought. *The data is hidden in noise that obeys Bernoulli's equation for an ideal fluid with steady flow in a pipe at varying heights. The flow "speed" is the change of noise with time. Fluid "density" is the magnitude of the noise. The "height" of the pipe is the data we want, specified according to its storage in computer memory. The "gravitational constant" is the position in complex space, so it isn't actually constant but varies according to the imaginary part of charge and mass. The only deviations from Bernoulli follow known corrections for fluid turbulence, friction, and compressibility. We can extract the data by pulling out the "pipe height" from the flow equations.*

Soz blinked. **That's amazing.**

The sense of a grin came from Rasmuss. *Truly.*

Did the JG-8 suffer any ill effects? Soz asked.

Jase Furlon replied. *None we've detected.*

Heald, do you pick up all that? Soz asked.

Affirmative, the Jag pilot answered.

That we've found no problems so far doesn't mean they don't exist, she cautioned.

Understood, Heald answered.

All right, Soz thought. **Give it a try. Good luck.**

Aye, ma'am. Activating Klein bottle.

His Jag twisted out of space.

Heald? Soz thought. **Can you still read me?**

Clear as cousins. After a pause, he thought, *Hold on that. My mindscape appears to be melting.*

Soz focused, trying to access the three-way link among his brain, his Jag's EI, and psiberspace. As she made contact, his mindscape *pooled* in hers, melting into a blur.

Rasmuss entered the link. *Heald, our calculations give you about fifteen minutes until your grid dissolves.*

Understooooood, he thought.

If at any time you think you're losing touch with our web, Soz thought, **twist back into normal space.**

Ayyyyyyyye, maaaaaaaa'am. His thoughts flowed like viscous oil.

Heald, we have an idea, Rasmuss thought. *We're extracting the data you're sending by using the Bernoulli equation. If you apply that extraction process to the data in your ship's EI, it might compensate for the melting effect you're experiencing.*

Tryyyyyyyyyyyyyy . . . His thought trickled away.

Heald? Soz thought.

No answer.

She sent a thought to the dreadnought: **Have we lost him?**

We still have him on monitor. That came from Jase Furlon. *Same as we did the JG-8 in Klein space.*

Soz submerged into the *Anvil* web and studied the data.

Heald's Jag was present and accounted for, though just what "present" meant in Klein space wasn't well-defined.

Heald here. The thought burst into the link, crisp and clear. *The extraction process appears to work.*

Soz grinned. **Welcome back.**

The sense of a grin came to her from the pilot, who had been in the Klein bottle now for sixteen minutes. His mindscape had stopped melting and was re-forming itself.

Good work, everyone, Soz thought. **Heald, drop back into normal space.**

Heald's Jag reappeared—

The JG-8 drone detonated in a burst of high-energy gamma rays and expanding antimatter plasma.

Heald, report! Soz thought. The piloted Jags and dreadnought had all gone into quasis during the explosion, but she wasn't sure if Heald had made it in time.

I'm still here, he thought.

What the hell happened? Soz thought into the general link.

We're not sure, Casestar answered. *Furlon?*

I can't figure it, Jase Furlon thought. *No, wait. The Klein fields for the antimatter fuel bottles in the JG-8 had some kind of instability. When Heald dropped into normal space, fluctuations in his Klein fields triggered the JG-8 instability and collapsed its fuel bottles.*

You better get Heald out of his Jag. That came from Professor Rasmuss. *It looks like his bottles have the same instability.*

Will the approach of another craft endanger him? Soz asked.

Yes, Rasmuss thought. *The closer the ships, the greater the effect. The fluctuations that triggered the JG-8 were large, from the collapse of the bottle holding Heald's ship. But if a Jag gets closer to him, even minor field fluctuations could trigger an explosion.*

Heald, abandon ship, Soz thought. **Ko, pick him up. All ships maintain present course and speed. Don't fire thrusters.**

Got it. The response came simultaneously from Heald and Ko.

The air lock of Heald's Jag dilated and he floated out, wearing an environment skin with its hood inflated. As he moved away from his Jag, Primary Ko began maneuvers to rendezvous with a "man overboard" at 0.05 light speed. A probe glided out from Ko's Jag, tethered by a spider-thin line of reinforced fullerene tubes, and homed in on Heald. As soon as he caught it, Ko reeled him in. The air lock of her Jag dilated—

And Heald's ship exploded.

Ko, report! Soz thought. **Did you get him?** The ships had gone into quasis, but Soz had no need of protection on the Orbiter. Even seeing the explosion, though, she couldn't tell if the field of Ko's ship had caught Heald in time.

He's here, Ko thought. She sounded subdued.

Soz eased her mind into Ko's Jag. Its EI also felt subdued. She was startled to find that with the Triad enhancing her already Rhon-powered mind, she could even submerge into the picoweb formed by repair nanobots in the ship's hull. She saw Heald floating in the cabin, his head down. Ko had peeled herself out of the cockpit and was moving toward him.

Gently Soz thought, **Heald?**

He lifted his head. *I'm all right, Imperator Skolia.* Grief saturated his thoughts.

Soz's mindscape registered the relief of personnel on the dreadnought and Orbiter as they picked up Heald's thought. But Casestar remained silent, as did the Jagernauts and a few others who realized the magnitude of the loss Heald had suffered. His ship had been part of his mind.

Ko took Heald into her arms and they floated, holding each other, while the Jag's EI controlled the ship. Soz and the other pilots offered regrets and praise for the lost ship.

Eventually Soz withdrew and checked the rest of the team. Professor Rasmuss and Jase Furlon were studying the explosions, trying to understand the problem. Apparently twisting an object that contained its own Klein fields in or out of a larger Klein bottle created instabilities.

Eventually Soz withdrew from the link and became aware of the War Room again. Jon Casestar swung up to her in his crane.

"Well, we did it." He looked fatigued, but a wary sense of jubilance touched his thoughts. "We actually put ships in a Klein bottle."

Soz blew out a gust of air. "Hiding in Klein space does us no good if we blow up when we come out of it."

The signal made no sense.

Domino Squadron consisted of sixteen ISC Wasps headed for the ISC army base in Edge Sector. They had just dropped into sublight space to run the standard checks when Lieutenant Jen Bollings picked up a telop signal. Still plugged into her telop station, she said, "Captain Kaller, I just got a signal over the web on an unsecured channel."

Kaller glanced back from his pilot's seat. "What source?"

"Unknown," Bollings said. "It was clumsy. Like a child trying to hack the web."

Kaller frowned. "Did the other ships pick it up?"

"I'll check." Bollings submerged into her link with the other Wasps. *Anyone pick up a hacker? Awkward, like a kid?*

Fourteen telops answered: ***No.*** The fifteenth had picked up a whisper he couldn't identify. But even the faintest murmur could be a warning. As soon as Bollings informed Kaller, he said, "Prepare to invert—"

The blare of a siren cut him off. All around them, eight ESComm ships dropped into real space, Solo starfighters, the Trader equivalent of Jags, appearing all at once in perfect formation, their hulls glinting silver and black.

Bollings identified them immediately: Hawkracer Squadron. That name was her last thought before an

ESComm missile hit the abdomen of her Wasp and exploded its antimatter bomb.

Jon Casestar paced Soz's office on the Orbiter. "The Hawkracers dropped out of inversion simultaneously."

Soz was sitting at the long table that had been Kurj's desk, a clear slab embedded with web components. She mourned the loss of Domino Squad. "Maybe the traders hadn't been superluminal long enough to lose cohesion."

"It was too precise." He stopped in front of her. "They came out at Domino's exact location, obliterated them, and then inverted out of there, all within seconds."

Soz swore. "It sounds like a web extraction."

"Yes." Casestar resumed pacing, his face creased with worry. "They may be using psibertech now, but we still have the advantage. I doubt ESComm will go into full-scale psibertech development, given their attitude toward their providers. If they do try, they face severe limitations. They have almost no trained telops and no access to a psiberweb. Even with the tech they steal from us, they can't link more than a few nodes. They don't have power for more."

Soz nodded. Without a web, ESComm could access psiberspace only by hacking Skolian nodes, which they had been doing, or trying to do, for decades. She looked over the report of the Domino massacre. "Their telops are clumsy." But that hadn't helped her people.

"We can set up a system to detect them," Casestar said.

"For now. They're bound to get better at it." She scowled. "*Any* psibertech ESComm uses cuts our edge. And we don't have much edge."

He halted again. "I'll check with Professor Rasmuss. Maybe they've solved the problem with the Radiance Project."

"Our web-extraction program also needs work." She leaned forward, her fingers laced together. "We need a way to locate other extractors in inversion."

Casestar grinned. "Train extractors to extract extractors?"

Soz felt her face relax into a smile. "It would seem so."

After Casestar left, Soz sat back in her chair. **A, attend,** she thought. With more than one node now, she had to distinguish among them. The first still had no name, so she simply called it **A** and labeled the new ones accordingly, by letters.

Attending, **A** thought.

Do I have any mail in the urgent queue?

One message, from First Councilor Tikal: It reads: "Imperator Skolia, please meet me in the Mentation Chamber."

Any idea what he wants?

Based on records of his behavior patterns, I assume he is in a perturbed state due to actions by one or more members of your family.

Soz smiled. **That sounds like his normal state of mind.**

He apparently retires to the Mentation Room when the perturbation rises past what he considers an acceptable level.

Ah well. I should go see what he wants.

Accompanied by her bodyguards, Soz headed for the Mentation Room. As she walked "uphill," her weight lessened. The room was near the north pole, 180 degrees around the Orbiter from the Solitude Room. The two chambers were similar, except Mentation had no command chair, only a small table.

Soz left her Jagernauts outside the chamber with Tikal's bodyguards. She found him inside, sitting at the table, staring at its surface.

"My greetings," she said.

He looked up. "My greetings, Imperator Skolia."

She sat across from him. "I got your message. Is anything wrong?"

"Your nephew arrived."

"You mean Taquinil?"

"Yes. Taquinil." Tikal rubbed his eyes. "He disappeared as soon as he got here. I tried to reach him at the Pharaoh's residence, but no one answers."

"That's why you wanted to see me?" What could be so dire about Dehya and Eldrin's son arriving on the Orbiter?

"You aren't concerned?" Tikal asked.

"Should I be?"

He grimaced. "It's bad enough having one invisible genius loose in the web. At least the Assembly Key is sane."

Soz tensed, a snap of anger ready in her voice. Then she paused. She felt Tikal's concern. He was genuinely worried. She made herself speak in a quieter voice than she had first intended. "Taquinil is sane."

"Is he?"

"He's been stable for decades."

"It was my understanding he assaulted his psychiatrist at Harvard."

"You mean while he was a student?" When Tikal nodded, Soz thought, **Node C, get Taquinil's college file. Give me a summary of anything about an assault.**

He attacked Doctor Maria Sanchez after she determined he was suffering from multiple personality disorder, C thought.

What did he do? Soz asked.

Trapped her in a building, struck her, and threatened to kill her.

That doesn't sound like Taquinil.

One of his personality fragments exhibited violent tendencies. However, Sanchez managed to draw out his core personality. He let her sedate him and call in help.

That's incredible. Soz knew Taquinil only as a gentle scholar, with a humble nature that belied his staggering intellect. She could no more imagine him committing violence than she could see herself as an Aristo. **Does that personality still exist?**

No.

Tikal was watching her. "Do you have a record of it?"

She nodded. "Yes. I do. Barcala, you don't need to worry. That was over thirty years ago. Taquinil has been fine since then. He's a charming man. You'll like him when you get to know him."

"How?" he growled. "He's just like his mother. Invisible. No one has seen him since he arrived."

"Do you want me to check on him?" She had a mind to do that anyway, to growl at her aunt, if Dehya really hadn't welcomed her son home.

"I'd appreciate it, Imperator Skolia."

"Soz."

"Soz?"

"That's my name."

He blinked. Then he smiled. "Ah. Well. Good. Soz."

After she left Mentation, she rode the magrail to Valley, where she was staying in the stone mansion Kurj had used as his second residence. His first residence, the desert house, had remained untouched since his death. Soz couldn't face it yet, that memorial to the brother she had admired, feared, criticized, and loved.

She walked to Dehya's home among the trees. The pager at the door played a ripple of music that brought to mind a whisper of insect wings, the burble of water, a bird's trill. Soz liked it.

The door slid open and a man gazed out at her. He stood about five-foot-ten, with a slight build and glossy black hair. His most notable features were his eyes, which shimmered gold and were fringed by long black lashes.

"Soz!" Taquinil smiled at her. "Come in."

"My greetings." She stalked into the house. "Where is Dehya?"

"In the web."

She scowled. "What, your mother calls you home, then ignores you?"

Taquinil laughed. "Ah, Soz, you're as ornery as ever." He pulled her into a hug. "Gods, it's good to see you."

She hugged him back, her annoyance softened by his good spirits. "I'm glad to see you too."

Stepping back to look at her, he said, "I thought you would be working in the Lock."

"Tikal told me you were here."

"Tikal? I haven't even seen him yet."

"He was concerned you hadn't been properly welcomed."

"Mother and Father met me in the docking bay. We had lunch here together."

"Well. Good." Soz stopped being annoyed at Dehya. "Tikal is a bit . . ." She stopped, feeling awkward. "I think he'd just like to know what you're doing."

His smile faded. "Why? To see if I foam at the mouth?"

"I didn't say that." Gently she added, "Barcala means well."

Taquinil sighed, a fey sound Soz recognized. Regardless of what anyone else thought, she liked her nephew. Given his background, a B.S. summa cum laude in economics from Harvard on Earth, a doctorate from the Economics Institute at Royal College on Metropoli, and tenure as a professor at Imperial University on Parthonia, he could have been an arrogant pain. Instead he was humble. She knew he considered himself flawed because of the personality disorder created by his Rhon mutation, but as far as she was concerned his ability to succeed despite so many obstacles made his prodigious accomplishments that much more impressive.

As they talked, she felt his distraction. He spent most of his time in the web, far more at ease in its universe than with people, whose minds he had such trouble blocking. He was the extreme end of a spectrum, a telepath so sensitive it was impossible for him to survive without medication and solitude.

Unlike Tikal, Soz had no concerns in regards to Taquinil's sanity. She was far more worried about what he and Dehya might come up with when the two of them combined their phenomenal intellects.

24

Empress Viquara sipped from her goblet of wine. The only light in her bedroom came from a lamp by her armchair, just enough to read the Hawkracer reports she held. The guards in her female contingent of Razers were stationed around the walls, along with four women in Calope Muze's secret police. In a room so large, they almost disappeared into the deepening shadows of night. Viquara often forgot they were there.

On the bed, Judge Calope sat dozing against the headboard, her long legs stretched out, her body covered in a gray tunic that extended to her thighs. Shimmering white hair curled in disarray around her face. Viquara wondered if the judge had aged past the stage where biotech would keep her hair black or if she simply didn't care that it had turned white. Given that the centenarian otherwise kept herself bodysculpted to look at least a half-century younger than her true age, Viquara suspected Calope had no choice about her hair.

Cayson lay on his side next to the judge, his eyes closed and his arms stretched over his head. The bedcovers were bunched up around his calves after his exertions with the elderly Calope. Viquara didn't think he was asleep, though. She saw too much tension in his beautiful body.

She set down the reports and her wine and went to lie on the bed, fully dressed, on the other side of Cayson. He turned onto his back to look at her, his arms still stretched over his head. They had to stay that way, after all, given that Calope had locked his wrist cuffs into a ring in the headboard.

Viquara pushed up onto her elbow and kissed him, tickling his lips open with her tongue. He responded well. But when she pulled back, he jerked his head, trying to move a curl of hair that had fallen into his face. She watched him struggle with it, oddly aroused by his attempts. Then she rolled over and took a bowl of fruit off the nightstand. When she turned back, Cayson was staring at the fruit.

She spoke in a low voice, so she didn't wake Calope. "When did you last eat?"

"This morning," he said. "Before the Razers brought me here."

No wonder. She had been called away and had forgotten she sent an escort for him. He must have been lying in bed all day with nothing to eat.

"Here." She held a cluster of fat berries over his mouth. He grabbed one with his teeth and ate it in seconds. But when he went for another, she pulled away the cluster. "Not so fast. You'll make yourself sick."

Calope opened her eyes and smiled lazily. "Let him eat, Viquara." She brushed the curl out of Cayson's eyes, her hand lingering on his forehead.

Viquara gave him a berry. To Calope she said, "What do you think of the Hawkracer reports?"

The judge stretched her arms. "The experiment was more successful than I expected. But I still think it's inhumane, putting providers in combat." She bent over and kissed Cayson. "Better to stay in bed, hmmmm?"

Cayson stared up at her. "Yes, Your Honor."

Viquara smiled. Then she slid off the bed and stood next to it. "I will see you two later."

The judge gave a satisfied stretch of her arms. "Your hospitality is unequaled, Viquara."

She wondered if Calope would feel so pleased if she knew how proficient the beautiful Cayson had proved at spy work. Viquara knew a great deal now, including the fact that Calope considered her cousin Corbal Xir better suited to the Carnelian Throne than Jaibriol.

Viquara paced through the palace, brooding, her bodyguards accompanying her like shadows. She climbed up shimmering white stairs to the emperor's suite. Keeping Jaibriol imprisoned had proved easier than she expected. The Aristos found his seclusion logical. For years his father had hidden him against ISC. And indeed, only months after his first public appearance, ISC captured him. For fifteen years he had evaded a death chase, until finally he returned to Glory in triumph. It surprised no one that he reigned as a recluse, surrounded by security.

Viquara left her guards outside the emperor's suite. Inside, she found Kryx Quaelen in the office connected to the rooms where they kept Jaibriol. Her new husband was reading a copy of the Hawkracer reports. It disturbed her to see him sitting behind the desk where once Ur Qox had sat.

She paused in the doorway. "What do you think?"

He looked up. "Six of the eight telops went into shock."

"That wasn't in the report for the War Cabinet."

"I deleted it." Quaelen set down the holograph. "The two Skolian telops were all right, but the six providers we trained almost went catatonic. Apparently they can't handle experiencing death in combat."

Viquara frowned. "Putting telops on warships does no good if they can't function after even the simplest engagement."

"The stability of the Skolian telops gives us something to work with," Quaelen pointed out. "It suggests their minds can be protected."

Like my son, Viquara thought. "Have you spoken to Jaibriol yet?"

"Not yet." He stood up. "Shall we?"

She walked into the room, still stiff in Quaelen's presence. He came around the desk and stopped in front of her, studying her face. Then he touched her nose. "It goes up too much."

Viquara pulled her head away, watching him with a cool gaze. She had spent a great deal of thought on the specifications she gave the bodysculptors for fine-tuning her face. One reason Ur had never appointed Admiral Kaliga to a Ministry position, despite the old warrior's venerable bloodline, was because Kaliga refused to have his ugly face molded into heroic proportions. Appropriate decorum included a favorable appearance.

"I find myself pleased with the work," she said.

"Perhaps you should find your husband pleased." Quaelen turned away and left the office. With a frown, Viquara followed.

They found Jaibriol reading in the library. When they came in, he looked up and tensed, like a beautiful trapped animal.

Quaelen and Viquara took up chairs opposite the emperor, facing him like a bulwark. With his chair almost flush against the bookshelf behind him, he had nowhere to go.

Viquara read the title of his book. "*The Ascendance of Eube.* A good choice."

He spoke in a cool voice. "That depends on how you define 'good.' I'll grant this much: as a treatise on how to subjugate populations using indoctrination, drugs, genetic manipulation, the granting or denial of affection, sexual abuse, and erratic positive reinforcement, it has no equal."

Quaelen considered him. "According to the palace records, you received a prodigious education, Your Highness."

Jaibriol closed the book. "Kryx, make your point. I've no interest in verbal dances."

The minister regarded him with shadowed eyes. "One wonders, though, if perhaps certain aspects of your admirable education were neglected. Such as the means of civilized discourse."

Jaibriol got up and went to the bookcase. As he slid his book into its slot, Quaelen asked, "Have you ever thought, Jaibriol, that it is to your advantage to be more cooperative?"

The emperor just stared at his books, ancient texts, written in calligraphy. "What do you want?"

Viquara spoke softly. "Sauscony Valdoria."

He turned to them. "Why come to me?"

"It occurs to me," Quaelen said, "that you have a remarkable talent for evasion."

"It occurs to me," Jaibriol said, "that you have a remarkable talent for sounding articulate without saying a single flaming thing."

Quaelen stiffened and Viquara saw his arm tense, as it did when he meant to strike a slave. "Fifteen years' worth of evasion," he said.

Jaibriol looked from him to Viquara. "A world is a large place. She and I weren't even on the same continents at first."

"At first." Quaelen watched him. "I imagine you were at the end, though, hmmm? She must have been close, to have found your communications equipment so soon."

"Apparently," Jaibriol said.

Viquara was certain he knew more than he admitted. After decades among Hightons, she had become an expert at reading the nuances of body language, and Jaibriol had never learned to disguise his. She touched the pager on her bracelet.

Jaibriol tensed. "What are you doing?"

"It would be unfortunate to miss your medication," she said.

"I'm not sick."

A rustle came from the doorway. Two medics stood there, humanoid robots, one platinum and the other gold, their polished surfaces agleam in the light.

Her son swallowed. "I don't need anything."

"Have you ever heard Kri's work?" Viquara asked.

He was still watching the robots. "Who?"

"Carzalan Kri," she said. "I find his epic *Beneath the Lowering Night* haunting."

Jaibriol turned to stare at her. "It made me ill."

"It is beautifully written," Quaelen said.

"A poem about the torment and death of a people who resisted enslavement?" Jaibriol said. "The beauty of the language doesn't make the subject matter any less horrific."

"More so, if anything," Viquara said. "It is a chilling work." She paused. "A lesson, one might say."

Jaibriol glanced at the medics, then back at her. "I don't have anything to tell you."

She touched her bracelet and the robots entered the library, moving with smooth mechanical steps. They had human shape but only horizontal slits for eyes and no mouth or nose.

Jaibriol backed up as the robots walked forward. They trapped him in a corner where two shelves met. Flattening himself against the books, he gave Viquara a look she recognized. Cayson watched her that way sometimes, as if making a mute appeal for her to change her nature, to become weak and empathic like a provider.

When the gold medic reached for Jaibriol, he tried to lunge between the robots. They caught him easily and pinned him against the shelves. A gleaming metal needle snicked out from the fingertip of the platinum medic. Viquara supposed she could have had an air syringe installed instead. Metal seemed more aesthetic to their design, though.

Jaibriol stared at the needle, then at Viquara. "Mother," he said.

She spoke gently. "Don't be afraid. The medicine will make it easier for you to cooperate with us."

"No!" He jerked as the robot inserted the needle. Viquara clamped down her mental defenses, blocking out his psion's mind to ensure she had no inappropriate responses to his pain.

So they waited, Jaibriol staring at them while the medics held him against the wall. Gradually he sagged in their grip, as the drug took effect. The robots helped him to his armchair and took up posts on either side after he was seated.

"How do you feel?" Viquara asked him.

"Tired," he said.

"What is your name?" Quaelen asked.

"Jaibriol Qox the Second."

"Where are you?"

"In the emperor's palace on Glory."

"How old are you?" Viquara asked.

"Thirty-eight."

"How many children do you have?" Quaelen asked.

No answer.

"What was the name of your mistress on Prism?" Viquara asked, using his name for the planet.

"I had no mistress," Jaibriol said.

"You didn't live with anyone?" Quaelen asked.

He just looked at them.

"What are the names of your children?" Viquara asked.

His mouth worked as if he were trying to form words. But nothing came out.

Viquara motioned at the medics. A needle snicked out from a gold finger and the robot injected Jaibriol. Again Viquara strove to shut out the transcendent flare of his pain.

Quaelen leaned forward, his lips parted. "How many children do you have?"

"None." Jaibriol's voice sounded strained.

"How long was Sauscony Valdoria your mistress?" Viquara asked.

His shoulders relaxed. "She was never my mistress. What an absurd idea."

The confident response gave Viquara pause. Were they worried over nothing? She glanced at Quaelen and he gave an almost imperceptible shrug. Then he turned to Jaibriol. "Who is the mother of your child?"

Jaibriol's mouth worked, but no sound came out.

Quaelen glanced at the platinum medic. "If we give the emperor more serum will it damage him?"

The robot extruded a thin rod from its finger, clicked it into Jaibriol's wrist cuff, then extracted it. "It could cause a loss of consciousness or convulsions."

"It's too risky," Viquara said.

Quaelen frowned. "And what of the risk in his silence?"

Viquara considered her son. Was he actually resisting the truth serum or did he really have nothing to tell them? "Sauscony Valdoria was an Imperial Messenger once, wasn't she?"

"I've no idea," Jaibriol said.

Quaelen spoke. "How much training did she give you in techniques to resist interrogation?"

"I don't know what you're talking about," Jaibriol said.

Viquara tried another tack. "Tell me about your father."

"What do you want to know?" Jaibriol asked.

"What was his name?"

"Ur Qox."

"How did you feel about him?"

His voice became strained again. "I loved him."

Viquara wondered at his reaction. Could a slave truly be capable of familial affection? "Why?"

Bitterness edged his voice. "I don't know." After a moment he added, "I suppose he loved me, in his own way."

"Could you pick that up from his mind?"

"Yes."

Viquara shifted in her chair, aware of Quaelen. Although they both knew the Jaibriol was a psion, it disconcerted her to hear the emperor verify it. Still, it provided a means to test how well the serum was working.

"What was your father's Kyle rating?" she asked.

Jaibriol's forehead furrowed. "What?"

"The emperor's Kyle rating. What was it?"

"Zero," Jaibriol said.

"Are you sure?"

"How could he be a psion?" Jaibriol asked. "You have to get the genes from both parents. Hightons don't have them."

Quaelen considered him. "And both Ur Qox's parents were Hightons?"

A bead of sweat rolled down Jaibriol's temple. "No."

Gods of all heaven, Viquara thought. She looked at Quaelen and he stared back at her, his face mirroring her reaction. With one word, Jaibriol had just shattered a century of deception. That she and Quaelen already shared the unspoken secret did nothing to lessen the shock of hearing it.

Quaelen turned back to Jaibriol. "Which of his parents wasn't Highton?"

"His mother."

"I see." Quaelen waited, then suddenly said, "How many children do you have?"

"None," he whispered.

Viquara spoke gently. "Jaibriol, dear, you can tell us the truth. We won't hurt you."

"I don't believe you," he said.

"How long were you an ISC prisoner?" Quaelen asked.

"Eleven days," Jaibriol said.

"Where did they keep you?"

"An installation in the desert. I don't know its name."

"How much did you see of it?"

"My cell. The interrogation rooms. Several corridors."

"Kryx, wait," Viquara said. When he glanced at her, she said, "Jaibriol's mind is conditioned and he has a cyberlock in his brain. It's similar to the conditioning Althor Valdoria has to prevent him from breaking under interrogation."

Quaelen nodded. "A logical precaution."

"It's more than that," Viquara said. "He shouldn't have been able to reveal Ur to us."

Quaelen raised his eyebrows. Focusing on Jaibriol again, he asked, "How did you alter your conditioning so you could reveal your father?"

"I didn't."

"Then who did?" Viquara asked.

"No one."

"It was Sauscony Valdoria, wasn't it?" Quaelen asked.

"I told you she wasn't my mistress."

"Where did that boy on Prism come from?"

"He was the son of a hostage I took during my escape."

"What was her name?"

"Lyra Merzon."

"Maximilian," Quaelen said.

The emperor's computer answered. "Attending."

"Identify 'Lyra Merzon.' Search Skolian databases."

After a pause, Maximilian said, "I have fifty-two matches."

"Do any correspond to a woman who disappeared at the same time as Jaibriol Qox escaped from ISC?"

"Yes," Maximilian said. "Lyra Merzon was an ISC medic. On the night Jaibriol Qox escaped, she was at the palace. She is listed as killed with Qox and Valdoria."

"Neither of whom seem to be dead," Viquara murmured.

"Perhaps we're asking our questions the wrong way." Quaelen leaned his elbow on the arm of his chair and rubbed his chin, regarding Jaibriol. "Why can you tell me devastating information about your father when it should be locked in your brain?"

"Because you already know it," Jaibriol said.

Viquara tensed. "Why do you think he knows it?"

"He told me," Jaibriol said. "Seventeen years ago."

Quaelen spoke smoothly. "Apparently you misunderstood, Your Highness. At no time did I ever make such a comment, nor would I ever have insulted your esteemed father's name in such a manner."

Viquara looked from Quaelen to Jaibriol. "Why did you think he told you?" she asked her son.

"As a threat." A muscle twitched in Jaibriol's cheek. "To keep me from telling anyone about his methods of tutelage."

Viquara's anger simmered like coals. Glancing at Quaelen, she said, "And what would these methods be?"

He regarded her steadily. "Whatever I felt necessary."

She turned back to Jaibriol. "Did Minister Quaelen ever use force against you?"

"Yes."

"What kind of force?"

"Enough, Wife." Quaelen motioned to the medics. "Knock him out."

"No," Viquara said.

She discovered then just how well Quaelen had infiltrated her security. The gold medic ignored her command and jabbed its needle into Jaibriol's arm. As the emperor gasped, Quaelen leaned forward, intent on his prisoner.

Viquara's anger surged. She stood up and spoke in an icy voice. "I think we should leave His Highness to rest."

Quaelen glanced at her, his face inscrutable. "If you wish."

As they left the library, she looked back. Jaibriol had sagged in his chair, unconscious now, guarded by the medics, his lowered lashes dark on his skin, like bruises.

She didn't speak until they were in Quaelen's office. Then she turned on him. "How *dare* you misuse the Highton Heir."

"Misuse?" He spoke in a mild voice. "I am surprised you let the histrionics of a provider cloud your judgment. It is unlike you."

Viquara took a breath to steady herself. Her husband might have the ultimate blackmail with what he knew about her son, but Quaelen also had a great deal to lose now. He was so close to the Carnelian Throne, he was almost emperor himself.

"I am surprised," she said, "that you would risk the position you worked with such diligence to attain."

He leaned against the doorjamb and crossed his arms. "Risk is relative, my lovely wife."

"Have you ever noticed," she commented, "that the loss of power to one person often results in losses to their associates?"

He watched her with shadowed eyes. "Perhaps."

"On the other hand, I've heard it said support inspires reciprocal support."

"So have I heard."

Viquara waited, hoping she hadn't pushed him too far.

Finally Quaelen said, "It pleases me that we have such compatible ideas."

Although relief trickled over her, she didn't let herself relax. Not yet. "Particularly in regards to the well-being of my son."

"Your son?"

"The emperor."

"I would of course always wish for our esteemed emperor's well-being."

Viquara's tension eased. "It pleases me to hear that."

Quaelen nodded. "Then we are in accord."

After an appropriate pause, she said, "What did you think of our conversation with him?"

"Half-truths?" Quaelen shook his head. "Lies?"

"I doubt he could lie under that strong a dosage. Certainly not with the ease he denied Sauscony Valdoria was his mistress."

"Perhaps. But she was a Jagernaut and ISC has its ways." He came over to her. "Vitrex tells me Prince Althor's mind is erasing itself."

"At least they're finally getting information out of him."

"He won't be much use to us with no mind."

Viquara shrugged. "Izar just plans to breed him with Cirrus when they're done interrogating him." She intended to take Althor as her provider then, also, but she was willing to work out an arrangement with Vitrex. "Althor and Cirrus are top-quality. They will produce top-of-the-line providers."

"You and Izar think too small," Quaelen said.

She raised her eyebrows. "And what would you do with him?"

"We need more Keys for the psiberweb."

"If you mean breeding Althor and Cirrus to make Rhon psions, it won't work." Viquara thought of the girl's son Kai. Never would the empress send Kai to Cirrus now, after the girl had dared to try hiding her knowledge about Jaibriol. Cirrus would suffer the price of that betrayal for the rest of her life. Viquara granted Kai his life in honor of Ur's memory, but the boy would never leave the isolated area where he lived now with the old slave woman Azzi. "Cirrus isn't Rhon. She can't make web Keys, not even with Althor."

Quaelen moved his hand in dismissal. "I have no interest in Cirrus. Althor is our path to the Ruby Dynasty." He tilted his head. "Did you know Eldrin Valdoria writes folk ballads? Or that the Ruby Pharaoh is the smallest member of the Imperial family? A pretty little waif."

"Entertaining, Kryx love, but hardly useful."

"Everything has uses." He paused. "According to Althor, our bard and his waif queen live together on the Orbiter."

That caught Viquara's interest. "Indeed."

He began to pace the office. "Through Althor, we can get more of his family. We need them. Althor can create a psiberweb and Jaibriol can maintain it, but they are scarce resources." His voice became crisp. "Two possible scenarios exist in regards to Jaibriol. Either he got children on this Lyra Merzon and Sauscony Valdoria is a fanatic who pursued him for fifteen years, or he got children on Valdoria and she seeks vengeance for their deaths. Either way, she is dangerous." He paced back to Viquara. "Previous ESComm extrapolations gave a good probability of eventual Eube victory, but now it is less certain. Waiting centuries to wear down ISC is too risky. We need a Lock, we need more Keys, and we need to break the Ruby Dynasty. Now."

Dryly Viquara said, "While we are at it, perhaps we could create a new universe or two."

His smile exuded a feral arrogance. "Think big, my love. I've discussed it with General Taratus and Admiral Kaliga. The more trained telops we install on our ships, the more we lessen the technological edge ISC holds over us."

She stared at him. "You're talking about Onyx Platform."

"You've a quick mind."

"I've seen Vitrex's reports on the interrogation. The Third Lock is at Onyx."

"So Intelligence says."

"It also says Onyx is prohibitively well defended."

Quaelen came over to her. "Well defended and sufficiently defended are not the same. Right now ESComm has the largest inventory of ships, equipment, and personnel in its history, whereas ISC is weakened by upheavals in the Ruby Dynasty. If ever there was a time for such a move, it is now."

Viquara wondered if she had misjudged her consort. Whether or not his plans would withstand scrutiny remained to be seen. But she knew Quaelen. He grounded his ideas in well-researched reality. If this bore out its promise, ESComm might bring the Imperialate under control within her lifetime. The Allieds would follow easily after that. It could be prudent to cultivate a more amenable relationship with this man who might soon rule all humanity from the shadows behind the Carnelian Throne.

She softened her posture, her hips settling just *so* to accent her figure. "This could be a best time for many things."

His gaze lingered on her body. "Indeed."

"Indeed," Viquara murmured.

25

All four of Soz's top officers attended the Joint Task Force meeting. General Stone and Primary Tapperhaven projected their simulacrums from HQ. Admiral Tahota projected from Onyx Platform and General Majda from Raylicon. Four people were actually present in the Strategy Room: Soz, Jon Casestar, Soz's brother Eldrin, and Barcala Tikal, all seated at the table. They kept this preliminary conference small, to lay the JTF groundwork before bringing in their staffs.

"A fleet the size we're talking about would be detectable to the most incompetent web extractor alive," Stone said. "You can't hide hundreds of thousands of ships."

"They don't need to travel together," Soz replied. "If we use telops linked through the web, the fleet could assemble anytime, from smaller groups."

Tahota spoke. "To avoid detection, the groups would have to be small, a few dozen ships or less. Coordinating the assembly of an entire fleet from such units, during superluminal travel, may be beyond even our best EI brains. We're talking trillions of coupled spacetime-psiberspace transforms per second."

General Majda leaned forward. "I understand the Pharaoh's son is on the Orbiter."

"That's right," Soz said.

"Perhaps he and the Pharaoh would consider bending their mental capacity to this problem."

Tikal sat up straighter. "Excellent idea." He sounded relieved. "It will keep them occupied. Out of trouble."

Irritation flashed across Brant Tapperhaven's face. "I wasn't aware they were in trouble."

"I think it's a good idea," Eldrin interposed.

Dryly Casestar said, "We have to find them first."

Soz glanced at her brother. "Can you talk to them?"

Eldrin nodded. "At the house."

Soz picked up a holograph on the table and cycled through its displays. "Even if Dehya and Taquinil can develop algorithms to coordinate assembly of the fleet, we still have the problem of the defenses in Platinum Sector and at Glory."

"My people have looked at it from every angle," Tahota said. "I don't see any way to bring in a fleet that size without triggering every alarm within five light-years of Glory. No matter how we assemble the fleet, Platinum Sector will still have more than enough warning to mobilize."

"Given the extent and strength of the Glory defenses," Stone said, "and its proximity to Platinum Sector, then unless I've missed something, we have no chance of success."

"Unless," Soz said, "our incoming fleet appears small enough to avoid detection until it's too late for ESComm to mobilize."

"I see no way to disguise so large a force," Majda stated.

Casestar glanced at Soz. When she nodded, he said, "The Radiance Project."

Tapperhaven snorted. "That business with the Klein bottles? It didn't work."

"A problem with instabilities in containment fields, wasn't it?" Tahota said.

"The instabilities come from interference between the larger Klein field and the fields it contains," Casestar said. "If we can shield the smaller bottle, that might take care of it."

"Might?" Stone asked.

"So far no shields have worked," Casestar admitted. "As soon as matter twists into Klein space, it loses cohesion. Melts, so to speak."

"Then don't use real matter," Tapperhaven said.

"You know another type?" Tikal asked. When Tapperhaven shot him an irritated look, the First Councilor raised his eyebrows.

"What would you propose, Primary Tapperhaven?" Soz asked.

"Something with quasis," he said. "Or tachyons."

"Quasis doesn't extend into Klein space," Casestar said. "It just protects the real space equipment that creates the bottle."

"Can you apply it to the bottle's contents?" Tahota asked.

Casestar shook his head. "That puts the fuel itself into quasis. Then the ship can't use it. Same for weapons. Annihilators do no good if we can't fire them."

"Tachyonic matter can exist in an imaginary state," Tapperhaven pointed out.

"Professor Rasmuss has been considering superluminal particles," Casestar said. "She might be able to do something with it. But that would mean we couldn't put the ships into Klein bottles until we were in superluminal space and we would have to bring them out before we dropped into normal space. It would add more complications and reduce our element of surprise."

Soz.

Soz nearly jumped out of her chair. Without equipment to enhance the fields produced by their brains, even strong psions rarely spoke mind to mind. Kyle activity depended on physical processes in the brain, dominated by Coulomb interactions, with higher order effects such as spin and momentum. In theory the interactions extended to infinity; in practice they became so small so fast that most telepaths could only pick up thoughts within a few meters and only from another psion, someone who could project strong enough signals.

She knew Dehya wasn't close to the Strategy Room. Yet her aunt's thought came as clear as a chime of crystal. Even odder, Soz could see the barest trace of a mesh around her now, as if Dehya had brought a ghost of psiberspace into the room.

Yes. That was from Eldrin. **I see it too. Strange.**

Soz regarded her brother uneasily. He knew Dehya better than anyone. If even he found this disquieting, she had no idea what to make of it.

Dehya? she asked.

The sense of a smile came from her aunt. *You all endow me with far more mystery than I possess, I'm afraid. I'm in the web. It makes it easier to link to you. That's all.*

Where are you? Soz asked.

In the Solitude Room. I had an idea for the Radiance Project.

"Imperator Skolia?" Tahota asked. "Are you all right?"

"She's in a Kyle link," Tapperhaven said. As a Jagernaut, he would recognize the signs.

Distracted by their voices, Soz held up her hand, urging them to silence. **Do you have a solution?** she asked Dehya.

Unfortunately, no. However, a thought does occur to me.

Go ahead, Soz thought.

If you have a problem with interference, perhaps you should look at phases instead of shielding.

You mean phases of matter? Soz asked. **Solid, liquid, that sort of thing?**

No. Light waves, actually. Waves out of phase undergo destructive interference. They cancel. Waves in phase interfere constructively. They add. Perhaps instead of shielding, you need to consider phases.

Does Klein space have phase? Soz asked.

I don't know, Dehya admitted. *I'm not that familiar with Rasmuss's work. But imaginary quantities often involve oscillation.* Her thought receded, fading into the mesh. *It may be worth a look.*

Then she was gone.

Soz blinked and shook her head, trying to clear it.

"Imperator Skolia?" Tapperhaven asked.

"That was Assembly Key Selei," Soz said. She had discovered different people thought of Dehya by different titles. Majda, General of the Pharaoh's Army, referred to her as the Pharaoh. Tapperhaven, whose own mind was inextricably linked to the web, thought of her as the Assembly Key. "She suggested we look at phases of Klein fields." Soz glanced at Casestar. "She compared it to the interference of light. Can your people do anything with that?"

He looked intrigued. "Possibly. I'll talk to Rasmuss."

"If we solve this problem of the bottles, it may give the project a chance," General Stone said.

General Majda shook her head. "The magnitude of the project is prohibitive. The logistics alone boggle the mind."

As the debate continued, Soz listened. They were right, of course. *If* they solved the Klein instabilities, they still had a thousand and one other problems that had to be solved before the invasion had a chance.

Vitrex glowered at his wife Sharla. "Last time all they did was lie on the cot. I can't breed them if they won't mate." He motioned at Cirrus, who was sitting on an examination table in Sharla's office, dressed in a silk robe. Cirrus tried to imagine she was someplace else. Anywhere else.

"You're the doctor," Vitrex said to Sharla. "You must have a way to, ah, increase his enthusiasm."

Sharla smiled. "Izar, love, just look at her. All you have to do is put her in his cell. Nature will do the rest."

"I did. It didn't."

"Let me check her profile." Sharla slid a needle out of her palmtop, inserted it into Cirrus's wrist cuff, twirled it around, and returned it to the palmtop. Studying the display, she said, "This is nice work."

"What is?" Vitrex asked.

Sharla flipped the screen open on her palm. The holo above it showed a blue, a red, and a gold line floating in the air. She pointed to the lowest line, the blue one, horizontal to her palm. "This is normal pheromone production for someone resting." She indicated the red line, also horizontal and higher than the blue. "This is Cirrus's normal level. Her nanomeds produce it."

Vitrex shrugged. "I know she smells good."

"It's more than smell. Even I feel the effect and normally I never react to women." She pointed to the gold line, higher then the red, with hills, valleys, and spikes. "This happens when she's handled. The spikes are off the scale." She flicked off the display. "On top of which, as a psion she produces pheromones targeted to other psions. Given that Althor is Rhon, he'll have an even more intense response to her. And she to him."

"So why didn't they *do* anything last time?"

She shrugged. "I don't know. Maybe she didn't want to."

"Then it's her enthusiasm you have to increase." Vitrex scowled. "It isn't easy, believe me."

"Have you tried Leratin?"

He waved his hand. "Leratin. Halcasic acid. Kerradonna. Nanogels. Either she gets sick or else she has these bizarre moods. One time she just kept crying."

You would cry too if you had to make love to you, Cirrus thought.

"You probably used the wrong dosages." Sharla plugged an air syringe into her palmtop to get its recommended prescription, then gave Cirrus a shot. She took a vial out of her lab coat pocket and pressed it into Cirrus's hand. Gently she said, "Give this to Althor. He may enjoy putting it on you and you may enjoy his doing it."

Cirrus considered the vial, blue glass with a gold stopper. She shook it and oil sloshed within.

Vitrex took the vial. "If he thinks he needs nanogels to make her want him, he'll lose interest." He gave it back to his wife. "You apply it."

Sharla smiled, and Cirrus caught her thought: *Ah, Izar, you want to watch me play with your favorite toy, hmmm?* She took off Cirrus's robe, speaking in a gentler voice. "This won't hurt. Just lie down."

Cirrus lay on her back and stared at the ceiling, imagining Vitrex and Sharla as repair bots up there, their exalted selves reduced to squeedy little mechanical bugs in casecrete. Sharla rubbed the nanogels over Cirrus's body, and

Vitrex watched, leaning against an adjacent table with his arms crossed, his gaze devouring them both. After Sharla finished, she helped Cirrus off the table.

"How do you feel?" Vitrex asked Cirrus.

Strange, she thought. She wanted to touch someone. Putting on her robe, she deliberately gave him a blank look. "Fine."

Vitrex scowled at his wife. "You see? Nothing."

Sharla was working on her palmtop. "According to this, she's having a huge response."

"Really?" Vitrex touched Cirrus under the chin. "Would you like to play later, pretty cloud?"

No, Cirrus thought.

Sharla gave Cirrus her robe. "If you do, Izar, she could end up with yours instead of Valdoria's. I've got her primed."

"I'll be careful," Vitrex said. "Give her a suppressant. I don't want your work wasted on Althor Valdoria."

After Sharla gave her another shot, Cirrus put on her robe and Vitrex took her out of the lab. His bodyguards were waiting outside, including Xirson, a Razer gifted to Vitrex from the palace. Xirson smiled at Cirrus, catching her by surprise. Razers were usually more like the other guard, Kryxson, hard-edged and cold, daggers in snow. They never smiled.

As they walked down the hall, two ministry aides intercepted them, along with more Razers. Vitrex went with them, leaving her in the care of several guards, who took her through secured halls until they reached a cell. Inside, Althor was lying on the cot. He sat up when they entered, and the guards removed his chains. Then the Razers left, locking Cirrus in with Althor.

"So you're back," Althor said.

She bit her lip. Did he hate her for revealing Jaibriol Qox?

He laid his palm on the cot. "Come sit with me."

Relieved by his mild tone, she went over and settled on the cot. Although he was still drugged, he seemed more coherent now. "Are you feeling better?" Cirrus asked.

"About what?" he asked.

"Last time you were unhappy."

He pushed his hand through his hair. "I don't remember."

I tried not to tell, she thought. *About Jaibriol Qox.*

His face gentled. **I know. I picked that up from the empress.** He took her hand. **I'm sorry if they hurt you because of it.**

She tried not to think of the son she would never again see. *I'm all right.* At least being with Althor distracted her. She rubbed the gold skin of his arm, below the short sleeves of his gray prison shirt.

He folded his hand around hers. "What did they do to you?"

"Do to me?"

"It's more than just Rhon pheromones. I can feel it."

She flushed. "I'm sorry."

"Why? They're the ones who should apologize to you." He let go of her hand and stroked her hair, from the top of her head to her shoulder. "They should be on their knees begging your forgiveness."

Cirrus slid her arms around his waist, feeling his muscles under his clothes. She rubbed her cheek on his shoulder, then turned her face up to his. Watching her, he moistened his lips and bent his head. As they kissed, he took off her robe.

Cirrus moved her lips to his ear. "You're wonderful."

"Hardly."

"I love you."

Althor sighed. "Ai, beautiful girl, you don't love me." He rubbed his hand up her spine. "They made you this way. Right now, you would love a slug under a rock."

She smiled. "You are no slug."

"I'm a shell without a memory."

"You're beautiful." She tugged at his shirt, to unfasten it. So he helped her, undressing while she explored him. Then they lay on the cot, their limbs tangling together.

What Althor did with her was no different than what Hightons did when they weren't transcending. Except she liked Althor. He had a gentleness she had never before encountered. But she was trying to reach something, she wasn't sure what, and she couldn't get there.

Finally he climaxed and then went still on top of her, his weight sinking in to her body as his breathing calmed. Even knowing he would soon want to sleep, she kept pressing against him. He brushed his lips over hers, then slid to her side and caressed her between the legs, trying to help. It wasn't enough. She almost cried out with the frustration.

"They gave you Damzarine, didn't they?" he said.

"What?" Opening her eyes, she saw him through a haze of desire and tears.

"A suppressant."

"Yes." She tried to calm her breathing. "What is it? Why would they give it to me?"

He swore softly. "To be cruel. Damzarine blocks the neural receptors in your brain that process the sensations of orgasm. You can become aroused but you can't climax."

She folded her fingers around his, not understanding, just wanting to hold his hand.

He felt her face with his other palm. "You have a fever."

"Hot," she agreed.

"Did they give you kerradonna?"

"I think so. What is it?"

"A poison."

Poison? "Have I done something wrong?"

"Gods, no." He kissed her, running his tongue over her swollen lips. "You're an angel."

"Why would they poison me?"

"In low dosages, kerradonna is an aphrodisiac."

"A what?"

"It makes you want to love me."

"I do."

He laid his head next to hers. "Why is it so important to them that we make love?"

"I'm your reward. For cooperating. Last time I wasn't enthusiastic enough. So they made me better."

"You were fine last time." His face gentled and he fitted her to him, bringing his lips to hers.

The next time they went slower. Through his mind she felt him trying to help her finish. But she couldn't. Finally he groaned and let go, this release even more intense than the first. When she realized he was done, she was so worked up from the drugs that she cried, as much from anger at Vitrex as from frustration. Althor held her, murmuring comfort, until she calmed down. His embrace relaxed then and she felt him submerge into sleep.

Too restless to sleep, she lay watching him, almost content in the shelter of his kindness.

Soz floated in psiberspace, within a shimmering mesh. As she slowly came awake, she realized she couldn't be in the web. She wasn't even plugged into the chair here in the Solitude Room.

Starlight bathed the chamber. Her neck ached from sleeping on it at an odd angle. She pushed her hands through her hair, trying to wake up. Too many days with too little sleep had left her groggy. She could almost feel the meds in her body trying to compensate, synthesizing molecules to provide energy.

"Soz?" The voice came from behind her.

With a jerk, Soz looked around. Dehya was standing in the shadows.

Her aunt walked to the chair. "I'm sorry I woke you."

"How did you get in here?" Soz rubbed her eyes. "I didn't hear the door open."

"You were asleep."

"Only dozing. I would have heard."

Dehya leaned against the console in front of her. "Taquinil and I finished our work on the fleet assembly problem."

Soz tried to focus on her. For some reason, her aunt's body seemed blurred. "You found a solution?"

"Many of them, some cumbersome, others less so. We gave Tahota the least clumsy ones." Dehya shrugged. "To implement any of them will require many telops, working together, solving as many simultaneous coupled equations as there are ships in the fleet. But it should work. In theory."

"In theory."

Dehya spread her hands. "That's what I am. A theorist. The engineering I must leave to others."

"Professor Rasmuss says you were right about Klein space phases. If we can find a way to keep the larger field in phase with the smaller, it will probably solve the problem."

"I hope so."

Soz rubbed the kink in her neck. "We're going to do it. We're going in to Eube. I'm not sure when. But we're going."

Her aunt continued to watch her, and Soz had an eerie sense that Dehya was dissolving. When the Pharaoh spoke, her words seemed to drift in from a distance. "Don't wait too long."

"Why?"

Dehya exhaled. It was a curious sound, like a wind blowing in trees as a storm approached. "The solutions converged. But I can't read much from them."

Soz poked her ear, trying to fix whatever problem in her audio enhancements made Dehya sound so odd. "The solutions?"

"My predictions."

"What do you predict?"

"Upheavals. But it's buried in noise. The noise of many possible futures." Dehya tilted her head and her eyes caught the starlight. "Right now the future is malleable. But I can say this: Go to Eube now. Don't wait."

"We aren't ready yet."

"It's something about Glory. There may be somewhere else you have to go? You have to make a choice. You have to lose something." She turned her head as if looking at visions Soz couldn't see. "You have to choose."

"War is always a matter of choices," Soz said.

"I asked Eldrin to go to Earth."

Soz had given up trying to follow her aunt's mental leaps. Dehya's mind formed connections so fast, in such detail, that her comments only touched the surface of her thoughts. Soz had discovered that if she just went with it, she could usually fill in her gaps of understanding later. In any case, she could guess what her brother had said. "He's not going to leave you here."

Dehya scowled. "He told me I should go to safety, not him."

"That sounds like Eldrin."

"He is as stubborn as a hammerheaded skybolt."

"He's a man who loves his wife and son. Did you really think he would leave without you?"

"You don't see." Dehya leaned forward, her words collecting in drifts of sound. "He could be hurt. Killed. Worse."

"How?"

"I don't *know.*" Frustration creased her face. "I get glimpses and glimpses, a million futures fluttering, fanning, filling my mind. He's there; he isn't. You're there; you aren't. I exist; I cease to exist."

Soz squinted at her. "I think you spend too much time in the web."

"Go to Glory now. Don't wait."

"We need more preparations."

"You won't have this chance again." Dehya became translucent, her body fading into the ghost web that spanned the Solitude Room. The chamber dissolved, leaving only the web to fill space, a shimmering mesh floating in space.

Go now, Dehya whispered. *Don't wait.*

Soz's eyes snapped opened and she sat up with a start. She was in the Solitude Room, her neck aching from sleeping in the wrong position. She looked around the chamber. No ghost web, no ghost sea, no ghost Dehya.

The comm on her chair arm buzzed. Rubbing her neck, she touched the glowing button. "Skolia here."

"Imperator Skolia, this is Admiral Tahota. We have results from the Pharaoh and her son for the fleet assembly problem. Do you want to meet to go over them? They gave me several possible options."

Soz stared at the comm, remembering her dream. Coincidence? "Yes," she said. "We'll meet in—" She checked her chronometer psicon. "Fourteen minutes, at oh five hundred this morning. Notify the cabinet."

"Will do, ma'am."

"Very good. Switching out."

After Soz closed the link, she stared at the stars. **Dehya?** Her aunt's thought whispered across her mind. *Go now.*

26

Onyx Platform glittered, twenty-three habitats, ranging from small wheels with a few thousand inhabitants to double-barreled giants that housed millions. It resembled a cluster of gem-studded flowers that on approach transformed into a mammoth city of space stations alive with sparkling lights. "Smooth" surfaces resolved into cranes, antennae, docking ports, control towers, all dwarfing the ships that came to call. And many came: Wasps, Cobras, Asps, Scythes, Leos, Scorpions, Jack-knives, Starslammers, Thunderbolts; Jag starfighters, Needle Spacewings, Ram camouflage tanks; tugs, bolts, masts, rafts, booms, blades, fists. Firestorm battle cruisers loomed among their smaller brethren, metropolises themselves, yet only specks next to the habitats.

The Third Lock was a small wheel a quarter-kilometer across, with a tower at its hub that extended perpendicular to the wheel. From far away it looked like a spire of glistening lace above a gilded disk. The Lock rotated in space, protected by the most massive military complex ever built by humanity.

In year 372 of the Imperial Calendar, a sentinel one light-year from Onyx sent warning: a Eubian force had been detected on approach.

A large force.

Two million vessels.

* * *

Soz strode toward the Orbiter docking bay, the gold helmet of her armor under her arm, her Jagernaut bodyguards ahead and behind her. With his long legs, Tikal had no trouble keeping up. Nor did the pace interfere with his anger.

"Get this straight," he said. "ISC is under civilian control. I don't give a flaming damn how many people say otherwise. You answer to me, Imperator Skolia. And I forbid it."

Soz came to a halt and Tikal stopped next to her, as did the Jagernauts. "How do you plan on keeping me here?" she asked.

Tikal glanced at the Jagernauts. "Take Imperator Skolia to her home in Valley. She is to remain there until the Fourth Squadron of the Pharaoh's Army leaves the Orbiter."

"I'm afraid I can't do that, sir," the first Jagernaut said.

"Negative, sir," the second said.

"Do you understand the word 'court-martial'?" Tikal gave them a chance to consider the question. Then he said, "Perhaps I didn't make myself clear. You are to hold the Imperator in her home until the Fourth Squadron has left this base."

Soz watched the Jagernauts. She knew the magnitude of what she was asking from them; if Tikal pressed charges, their military careers had just ended. The question of who truly ruled Skolia had long plagued the relations of her family with the Assembly, and through them, with the rest of the Imperialate.

"I'm sorry, sir," the first said.

"I can't obey your order, sir," the second said.

Tikal gave them hard looks. Then he turned to Soz. "You won't leave this base without my permission."

"Barcala, I need to do this."

"Why? You can monitor almost everything from the War Room."

Soz shook her head. "I can only access web nodes. That hardly includes 'everything.' And what if something happens to the web links?"

"We can't risk you." He made a frustrated noise. "How do I get through that cast-iron skull of yours?"

She grinned and knocked her head with her fist. "Can't do it."

He didn't crack a smile. "Do you see Empress Viquara going into space? The days when warrior queens rode at the front of the army ended five thousand years ago."

"What 'front of the army'? I'll be inside the Asteroid weapons platform, far behind the Radiance Fleet. And my officers are even more fanatic about my safety than you are."

"You're safer here."

"You have two Triad members here. That's not safe. We need to split up."

"Then go to Parthonia."

"I'm needed on Asteroid."

"Ur Qox believed he was safe. You see the result."

"He made a mistake. He underestimated Kurj."

"And you're going to die taking out Qox's son?"

If only you knew, Soz thought. "I'm asking you to trust my judgment."

"Skolia can't afford to risk a member of the Triad."

"Skolia can't afford to risk failure of this operation."

"You think your presence could make that difference?"

"Yes."

He rubbed his head, pushing his fingers against his temples. With a wince, he dropped his arms. "I served in the Imperial Fleet forty years ago. But I've no military mind. When the cards are played, I'm a politician. My advisers tell me you're a military genius. They say if you believe we should send the Radiance Fleet to Glory now instead of waiting, they support you. What does that leave me with? Do I trust my judgment or yours? Mine screams to keep you here."

She spoke in a quiet voice. "I know what I'm doing."

"You've been Imperator less than two years. Why are you so sure?"

She spread her hands. "What can I tell you, some cliché

about how it's in my blood? When I was six years old I started organizing the other children into infantry. When I was ten I spent all my free time reading military strategy texts meant for adults. When I was fourteen I took Althor's Jumbler apart while he was home on leave and put it back together keyed to my mind instead of his. I entered DMA a year early and took three years to finish a four-year program. I was the youngest person in ISC history to receive the rank of Jagernaut Secondary. Do you want me to continue? Don't ask me why I'm sure. I just am."

For a long moment he stood watching her. Finally he blew out a gust of air. "I'm going to regret this."

"You won't." She set off again, headed for the docking bay.

"Soz," Tikal said.

She stopped to look back. He was standing in the corridor, his lanky form silhouetted against the gleaming walls.

"Good luck," he said.

She smiled. "Thanks." Then she took off, striding to meet the Pharaoh's Army.

Starjack Tahota's voice snapped in the air of her office. "How many sentries have picked up the incoming fleet?"

"We've reports from thirty-seven now," Colonel Raines said. "They all say the same. The incoming fleet consists of about two million ships. They're forming a sphere around Onyx Platform five light-years in diameter."

Tahota swore to the empty air. Physically she was the only person in her office on *New Metropoli,* the largest space habitat at Onyx. But consoles and holobooths filled the room, alive with images and sound. Some displays showed Onyx, others the Trader fleet assembling out of superluminal space, yet others her staff meeting with simulacrums of herself. They all sent her reports via IR signals. Her spinal nodes analyzed the data and either responded or else queued the analysis for download into her mind. A file labeled *urgent* she read immediately; otherwise she went through the queue in order.

Unlike with Jagernauts, no regulations required that

Tahota have a biomech web. As a naval officer trained at Jacob's Military Institute on the world Foreshires Hold, she had an impeccable and conservative background, one as bound by the traditions of Ruby Empire warfare as by modern cybernetics. But like most high-ranked ISC officers, she chose to have extensive biomech added to her body. It was the only way to handle the flood of information needed to do her job. Now she paced her office, her mind swapping among her nodes, her thoughts, her queue of files, and her staff.

She stopped in front of a holo that showed the sphere of ESComm ships. "How fast are they dropping into normal space?"

"Too fast," Colonel Raines said, his voice coming out of the air. "It's only taken thirty minutes to reassemble what we estimate is over 10 percent of their fleet."

Tahota whistled. With two million ships, the fleet should have acquired a huge spread in space and time. To reassemble this fast, they had to be using telops. Without a psiberweb, they could maintain only crude links, but it would be better than nothing.

"Do you have a reply from Rail Sector yet?" Tahota asked.

"They're giving us two thousand ships," Raines said. "ETA is two hours."

"That's it. Two thousand?"

"That's it."

Tahota clenched her fist. She knew where the bulk of the Rail Sector forces had gone, along with ISC forces from all over the Imperialate. Hidden in inversion, they were stealing toward Glory like a cloud of stealth raiders, assembling into a camouflaged fleet of 800 thousand ships.

The Traders, however, were making no attempt to hide their attack on Onyx. No way existed, within ESComm's technological capabilities, to disguise such a massive fleet.

"Colonel Raines," Tahota said. "Verify our numbers here at Onyx. I'm reading 283 thousand ships."

"With the reinforcements from the Reef Periphery, we're up to 286 thousand."

"How many more do we have coming in?"

After a pause, he said, "We'll probably make it to 300 thousand before the Traders arrive."

Tahota didn't need her huge staff to state the obvious. The normal complement of ships at Onyx numbered 600 thousand. Had the usual reinforcements been available, they could have kicked that up to over 900 thousand. Given the superior ISC technology and communications, they would have had a chance against the monster assembling out there in space. But a child could read the odds now. They had less chance than an ice crystal in hell.

Except that hidden out in space was an ISC fleet that could swell their ranks to over a million, a fleet armed with technology the Traders had no clue existed.

Tahota went to a console set apart from the others. She clicked her wrist gauntlet into it and a voice rumbled, "Security verified. Dedicated line open."

"Put me through to Imperator Skolia." And then Tahota said, "Code One."

"Absolutely not!" General Stone hit the table with his fist. "If we split the Radiance Fleet, we lose everything."

Like most everyone in the Strategy Room, his "presence" was a simulacrum. His fist made no sound, but his anger needed no physical manifestation to give it reality. People packed the room: General Stone, General Majda, Primary Tapperhaven, Admiral Tahota; the generals and admirals who served as Operations, Plans, Communications, Logistics, Intelligence, and Security; deputy officers, lower ranked generals and colonels; telops from Onyx, HQ, Raylicon, and the Radiance Fleet; and the Inner Assembly. As a simulacrum herself, Soz "stood" in a corner, behind the crowd. Across the room, the flesh-and-blood Tikal also stood in silence, also listening.

General Majda thundered at Stone. "If we leave Onyx out there with only 300 thousand ships, it will be a massacre."

Logistics spoke. "Onyx has almost no civilians."

Tahota's face took on an inward quality as she accessed

her biomech web. "The current population is 2.2 billion. About 4.9 percent are civilians." Her attention focused out again. "That's 108 million, including 1086 children under sixteen."

Domestic Affairs stared at her. "What the hell are you doing with children on weapons platforms?"

Someone muttered, "You try putting two billion people in one place without producing children."

At almost the same moment, Stone said, "Can you get them out?"

Tahota shook her head. "We asked ESComm to let us evacuate the children. They refused. They've blasted every one of our decoy attempts."

"Send ships out in inversion," Brant Tapperhaven said. "ESComm can't extract every single one of them."

"They've been doing a damn good job of it," Tahota told him. "They've got telops on those ships. A lot of them."

Someone swore. Someone else said, "How long have they been assembling the sphere?"

"It's 2.3 hours now," Tahota said. "We estimate they will be ready to collapse it onto Onyx in another 2.8 hours."

Operations spoke. "Even with telops, they can't collapse a sphere five light-years across with complete accuracy. They have to invert, get their fleet through two and a half light-years to Onyx, and re-form. The fleet will spread in both space and time."

An officer on Tahota's staff spoke. "Whether or not they can maintain enough cohesion to keep us trapped depends on how much they know about our peripheral defenses." He paused. "Althor Valdoria was the primary officer involved in setting up those defenses."

Silence greeted his statement.

Finally Brant Tapperhaven said, "Commander Valdoria's mind is protected. ESComm won't have found him an easy source."

Soz knew her brother's strength. If anyone could resist interrogation, it was Althor. But *two years* of it? Even the strongest human alive, with the best biomech defenses in existence, couldn't hold out.

She spoke quietly, hating what she had to say, hating what it implied about her brother's last two years. "We have to assume the security of the Onyx periphery has been compromised."

Although Tahota nodded, Soz recognized her strain and saw it reflected in faces all around the table. Her brother was well regarded by all branches of ISC. No one wanted to think of how he had spent the last two years.

A naval captain spoke. "This sphere they're assembling is a show. It's meant to demoralize."

"It's working," someone muttered.

General Majda spoke. "If we don't divert the Radiance Fleet to Onyx, we lose the Third Lock. ESComm already has a potential Key. And they're trying to use telops now. Give them the Lock and they will build a web. Better we give up the invasion of Glory than risk losing everything."

Dayamar Stone leaned forward. "Take that conservative approach, General, and we lose our chance to break Eube. ESComm has its critical nodes dispersed in the Platinum Sector around Glory. If they've pulled this many ships off their defenses, we've an even better chance of getting the Radiance Fleet in there. They don't even know we're *coming*. We'll never get this chance again."

"Onyx Platform is our most critical node," Communications said. "Losing it will cripple ISC."

"If we break ESComm," Judiciary added, "we can repatriate any prisoners they take at Onyx."

"There may be no prisoners to repatriate," Tahota said.

Admiral Casestar spoke. "Have they contacted you with conditions of surrender?"

Tahota nodded. "They want the Lock, the space habitats, myself, my top officers, and all the ships at Onyx."

Someone swore, someone else said, "That's an outrage," and Stone said, "Starjack, you can't surrender. You know what they'll do to you."

"If we divert the Radiance Fleet to Onyx," Tapperhaven

said, "we save the Lock and lose Althor Valdoria. ESComm then has a Key and no Lock. If we go in to Glory, we have a chance to save Valdoria, but we lose the Lock."

"We can blow up the Lock," Tahota said.

"We don't have the tech to rebuild it," Logistics said.

"Lose the Lock and we lose the Triad," Operations said.

"We have two more Locks," Tapperhaven said. "Even with only one, the Triad could exist."

"Exist how?" Majda demanded. "Hanging by their fingernails?"

Soz spoke, and the room became silent. "Don't blow up the Lock unless you have no other choice." She regarded Tahota. "We can survive with two Locks, but it would be difficult. If ESComm has no Key, then destroying the Lock to keep it out of their hands becomes less imperative. If the only choice is to give ESComm both Lock and Key, then blow it up."

Tahota nodded. "Understood."

"What we need," Operations said, "is an alternate strategy."

"Split the Radiance Fleet," Plans said.

"No!" Stone boomed. "Split it and we lose everything."

"You don't know that for certain," Majda said. "It offers a chance to salvage both operations."

Tahota spoke. "We've run extrapolations. Unless you send most of the fleet to Onyx, it won't be enough."

A man spoke out of the air, a voice with a fey quality. "We're also running extrapolations. With so many ESComm ships pulled off Platinum Sector, we predict a probability of success for the Radiance Fleet of 63 to 81 percent if it remains at full strength. But even small reductions in the size make those numbers plummet. Cut the fleet in half and both the Onyx and the Glory efforts have a less than 5 percent chance of success."

"Who the hell is that?" someone said.

Taquinil? Soz thought. **Identify yourself.**

"I'm Taquinil Selei," he said. "Assembly Key Selei and I are working on the calculations."

"If the Pharaoh and Lord Taquinil are correct," Stone said, "then splitting the fleet gives us a lose-lose situation."

Security turned to Tahota. "What do the surrender terms specify for Onyx personnel?"

Her voice hardened. "They would be 'appropriated' by ESComm and 'assigned work contracts.' "

Dayamar Stone scowled. "Sold into slavery, in other words."

"That's the least of it," Tahota said. "Only 'units' considered 'suitable for salvage' would be retained."

"What the hell does that mean?" Majda asked.

Intelligence spoke. "ESComm will execute most of the Onyx personnel. They take slaves only from certain categories, people who are easy to control, have high Kyle ratings, are worth interrogating, or are sexually desirable. What they don't want is a big influx of ISC personnel into their slave pool."

"We're talking a massacre here," Communications said.

Tahota leaned forward. "There is no way in any ten hells of the Vanished Seas that I would turn my people over to that fate. We've kept communications on this wide open on the Onyx intranet. It's unanimous from every sector. No surrender."

"Far better to do as much damage as you can," Operations said. "The Traders have concentrated a huge portion of their resources into this effort. You could cripple ESComm."

"If we turn our attacks into suicide runs," Tahota said, "we can maybe take out three ESComm vessels for every ISC ship destroyed. That's almost a million. Half their force."

Soz didn't want her forces turning themselves into a fleet of suicide pilots. "There has to be another way."

"Divert the Radiance Fleet to Onyx," Majda said.

"Then we win the battle and lose the war," Tapperhaven said. "We won't have this chance at Glory again. Damn it, this is our chance to end the *war*."

"At what cost?" Life demanded. "*Two billion* people? Will you sacrifice them to torture and death? Because believe me, that's what will happen. When have Hightons honored the Rules of War? I sat in the negotiations for the Halstaad Accord. I've seen how the Highton mind works. They don't consider us human, and the Allieds can rot in hell if they refuse to see that. Have you read *The Ascendance of Eube*? It's all the more horrifying because it's so brutally effective. Let ESComm have Onyx and we will never see any of those people again, the Halstaad Code be damned."

Majda hit the table with her fist. "Then *divert Radiance.*"

"Do it," Tapperhaven boomed, "and you condemn us to a war that will kill far more than two billion!"

An almost inaudible chime came from the palmtop Soz held. She opened her hand to see Barcala Tikal's face on the screen in her palm. Three words scrolled below it: Code One conference?

Soz understood. He offered advice. No orders this time. The dance of power played between the Assembly and Ruby Dynasty had almost no rules; where the authority of one left off and the other began remained a constant source of conflict. But in this the boundaries were clear. Code One. Invasion. In such a situation, military decisions belonged to the Imperator, the commander in charge of all the ISC forces. The Assembly couldn't tie her hands.

Nor could she give the decision to anyone else.

She responded via one of her spinal nodes, which uploaded the message to a secured picoweb in the walls of the Strategy Room, using IR. The picoweb sent it to the section of the wall closest to Tikal and signaled his palmtop, which then downloaded it. They used the picoweb rather than transmitting across the room because the signals were harder to intercept this way.

What do you think? she asked, via her computer.

Divert to Onyx, he answered.

And Glory?

Fight that battle another day.

This may be our only chance.

After a pause, he wrote: I know.

They watched each other while their advisers argued. Then Tikal added, I don't envy you this decision.

Soz sat alone in the dark. All around her, in bays, halls, and chambers, on deck after deck after deck, the crew of the battle cruiser *Roca's Pride* carried out their duties. She had never left the ship; during the entire conference, she had been sitting in this chair by the console table.

Now she sat alone in the dark.

You have to choose, Dehya had said. Soz remembered well the answer she had given her aunt. *War is always a matter of choices.* So facile. So smooth. So stupid. She hadn't had a clue what Dehya meant.

Two billion people.

Onyx or Glory.

Lose two billion and end the war; rescue two billion and lose how many more over the centuries? Lose the Lock and rescue the Key; lose the Key and rescue the Lock. Break Glory and lose Onyx; rescue Onyx and spare Glory.

And it was worse than any of them knew. ESComm didn't have one Key, it had two. Rescuing Althor wasn't enough; they had to get Jaibriol out as well.

In 1.8 hours ESComm would converge on Onyx. If she intended to divert the Radiance Fleet, they had to start recoordination as soon as possible.

A chime sounded in the dark. She touched the comm on the arm of her chair. "Skolia here."

"Imperator Skolia, this is Admiral Barzun on the bridge. We have a transmission from Admiral Casestar on the Orbiter."

"Can you handle it?"

"He's relaying you a Prime transmission from Earth."

Soz tensed. What could have provoked a call on her hot line to the Allied president? "Put it on."

"For security, we're routing the signal through the Orbiter, using a scramble code," Burzan said. "It will cause a delay of three seconds. President Cohen is almost certain to realize you aren't on the Orbiter."

"I understand."

On the table in front of her, a screen rose. As she brought up the lights, the screen cleared to show a handsome man with curly hair graying at the temples. Although Soz didn't know Cohen as well as the previous Allied president, she had always found him straightforward and likable.

After three seconds he said, "My greetings, Imperator Skolia."

"My greetings, Mr. President."

Another pause. Then he said, "We seem to have a problem with the link. We're getting a three-second delay here."

"We're aware of the problem," Soz said.

This time his delay was longer than three seconds. When it became clear no more information was forthcoming, he said, "Your father wishes to speak with you."

Her *father?* What was going on? "Very well. Put him on."

Cohen moved out of view and Eldrinson appeared. "Sauscony."

"What's wrong?" she asked.

He didn't waste words. "The Triad link is dissolving."

Soz stared at the screen. Five words. That was it. Five words. With them, he had just described an interstellar crisis of a scope so large it had no precedent. For an instant her mind hung in a limbo where those five words had no meaning.

Then reality crashed in. "No," she said. *No.*

"I've no doubt of it," he said.

Soz absorbed the implications. If the Triad link dissolved, psiberspace would implode. The web would collapse. No communications. No way to assemble the Radiance Fleet. No way to keep sane the crews on 750 thousand ships in Klein space.

"How do you know it's dissolving?" she asked.

"I feel it," Eldrinson said. "I see it. Like a ghost web."

"Dehya," Soz said.

He nodded. "You and she are too alike. The link can't support both your minds. She's been holding it together somehow, but something has to give."

"How long do we have?"

"A day? Probably less." Frustration showed on his face. "The overlap doesn't affect me. If I could link to a Lock, I could hold the Triad together, at least long enough to arrange a solution."

"No!" Soz leaned forward. *"Stay on Earth."* Losing the web would shatter Skolia, but webs could be remade. If they lost their Keys, they lost the web for good. And she lost her father.

After three seconds, he said, "Very well." That he gave no argument, despite the danger, told Soz he understood the import of that three-second delay even if he didn't know the cause.

"Is there anything you can do from Earth?" she asked. "Even just a few more hours could make a difference."

"I will try," he said.

"Can you put Harry Cohen on again?"

"Here he is." Eldrinson moved aside and Cohen reappeared.

"Mr. President," Soz said. "I need to invoke the full protection clauses in the Iceland Treaty. I'm asking for Allied forces to defend Lyshriol. Most of my family live in the Dalvador region of the North continent, except for my brother Denric, who is on the planet Sandstorm. You'll need to pull out Denric and get him to Lyshriol. My father can give you details."

Cohen nodded. "We'll protect your family, Imperator Skolia."

"Can you put my father back on?"

"Here he is."

When Eldrinson reappeared, Soz said, "I have a question for you. It may seem odd, but the answer is important."

"Go ahead," he said.

She spoke carefully. "When Eldrin was sixteen years old, he rode into battle with you for the first time. The army was gone for two months. Do you remember?"

"Yes. Your brother showed great courage."

"When he left, all he took was a sword."

"That's right."

"We had laser carbines and EM pulse rifles. He didn't even consider them."

"It was a matter of honor for him. He felt that to use such weapons against men armed with swords was wrong."

"He killed three men," Soz said. "In two months."

In a quiet voice her father said, "He had to fight one with his bare hands. I also saw him refuse to kill when he didn't have to." He paused. "Your brother may have had trouble in his youth, adjusting to life on the Orbiter. But he has always been a man of honor."

Soz nodded. It was true of all her brothers. "Two years later, when Althor was sixteen, he rode into battle with you."

This time the pause was far longer than three seconds. Then he said, "Yes."

"With a laser carbine."

"Yes."

Softly Sauscony said, "He stood on a hill above the Plains of Tyroll and slaughtered 316 men in five minutes."

His voice came from light-years away. "And ended a war that might otherwise have dragged on for decades, killing many more."

"Which way do you think was right?"

He had a look she recognized, one she had seen before, the day they held the funeral services for her brother Kelric. The look of a father who knew the anguish of outliving his children.

"I can't answer that," he said. "All I know is this: Eldrin and Althor each made the best decision they could."

"What would you have done?"

"I don't know." Pain touched his voice. "I can't begin to know what you are facing right now, Soshoni. All I can say is that I have always, no matter what our differences, had confidence in your judgment and sense of honor."

She swallowed. "And if there is no way of honor?"

"You make the best decision you know how."

Softly she said, "Gods' blessing to you, Hoshpa."

His voice caught. "And to you."

"Good-bye."

"Good-bye, Daughter."

Then they broke the link.

She had run out of time. Whatever she decided, they had to move now, before the web failed.

"Charon, attend," she said. "Set up a dedicated link to Admiral Tahota at Onyx Platform. Security codes in 3-11-S."

"Codes verified," the computer said. "Link established."

The screen on the table in front of her rippled, and then Soz was facing Tahota. The admiral was seated at a console, the blur of holos visible behind her. With her six-foot-six frame and strong features, she looked like the reincarnation of a Ruby warrior queen from five thousand years in Raylicon's past.

"Imperator Skolia," she said.

Soz felt as if she were in a suddenly muffled room. Her words came out in quiet, still tones. "I'm sorry, Starjack."

It was a moment before the admiral answered. Then she said, "I understand." She took a breath. "I will keep you posted as the situation evolves."

"That may not be possible," Soz said. "We're losing the web. It shouldn't affect you within the Onyx complex, given the proximity of your habitats, but we won't be able to communicate across interstellar distance."

Tahota stared at her. "Gods, what's going on?"

"I'm not sure." Soz spoke quietly. "Whatever happens, I've faith in your abilities and your decisions."

Tahota nodded, acknowledging her words. "My thanks."

Soz paused. "Kurj told me something once."

"Yes?"

"That you were his closest friend."

The admiral exhaled. "I am honored."

"Gods' blessings, Starjack."

"And to you."

Then they closed the link.

Soz pushed a hand through her hair. "Charon, get me Admiral Barzun."

"On channel three." The screen rippled again, clearing to reveal a man with iron gray hair, a beak of a nose, and a square jaw.

"Imperator Skolia," Barzun said.

"We have to assemble the Radiance Fleet now," Soz said. "The psiberweb is collapsing. We have a day, perhaps less."

Barzun swore. "Why is it collapsing?"

"The Triad link isn't stable."

"Gods almighty." The admiral stared at her for a full count of five before he asked, "Are we going to Eube or Onyx?"

Quietly Soz said, "To Eube."

27

Admiral Starjack Tahota and Colonel Claymore Raines strode side by side along the gravel path in *New Metropoli*. The ground curved up ahead of them, barely discernible as deviation from the horizontal. Trampled gardens stretched on either side and starlight flooded through dichromesh windows overhead. All around them, personnel jogged by, duffels slung over their shoulders.

"I'm getting confirmation from the other habitants," Raines told her. He held his hand to his ear as data came over the comm on his headset. "They've almost finished loading evacuees."

"Good," Tahota said.

Ahead of them, people were converging on one of the great elevator columns that would ferry them out to the docking areas at the hub of the space station. She and Raines made their way through the crowd to a lieutenant directing traffic.

"How many more loads do you have scheduled?" Tahota asked.

"This is the last group, ma'am," the lieutenant said.

Tahota nodded. "Well done."

As she and Raines took off again, Tahota pushed back the tendrils of hair that had escaped the braids on her head. Her people had implemented a contingency plan for evacuation, using computer databases to dictate what units took what personnel and equipment where, coordinating every last action, from the flow of people down to thousands of minute details that a less prepared force might have missed. But for all that, she still knew this was a desperation move.

Instead of gearing the 300 thousand ships at Onyx for battle or suicide runs, she filled them with Onyx personnel. When ESComm moved in, the evac fleet would move out. The stations were almost empty now, a sparkling cluster of deserted islands in the sea of space.

To "collapse" their sphere, the Trader ships would have to invert into superluminal space, converge on Onyx, drop back into normal space, and re-form the sphere close enough in to attack. Any ISC ships trying to flee would be extracted by ESComm telops. But Tahota suspected most of those telops were untrained providers struggling to monitor a huge volume of space. Their job would be even trickier during the collapse, particularly with the Onyx periphery defenses harassing the ESComm fleet. Whether or not that would distract the telops enough to let any ISC ships slip through undetected depended on how well prepared ESComm was to counter the Onyx periphery defenses.

Tahota had no idea what was happening out on the periphery. Onyx had lost psiberweb contact with its outlying bases. The fragile thread of hope for a successful evacuation depended on the answer to one question: how well had Althor Valdoria kept the secrets of Onyx?

Messages flooded Tahota's mind, almost all from volunteers reporting for duty. Not everyone had boarded the evac ships; a few hundred thousand were staying behind to help the last strike Onyx would ever make against ESComm. Even knowing the price they would pay, still they volunteered.

The observation bay where Tahota and Raines were headed was in the hull of this cylinder in the gigantic double-barreled habitat that made up *New Metropoli.* They entered the bay by a trapdoor in the "ground" under their feet and climbed down a ladder to a platform. With the apparent gravity directed out from the axis of the cylinder, the observation bay lay "below" them, a dome of dichromesh glass bubbled out from the hull. Platforms were scattered throughout it, linked by catwalks and ladders. Standing above the transparent bubble, looking out into space, Tahota felt as if she were poised over a great abyss.

As *New Metropoli* rotated, other habitats came into view, including the Third Lock. The stations were dangerously close to one another, given their immense sizes. On Tahota's order, her people were drawing them together into as small a volume as possible.

Reports poured into her nodes. In only two hours, almost two billion people had boarded the evac ships, a tribute to the efficiency of a force linked by a web that permeated their lives, even their minds, though most weren't psions. Tahota rated only two on the Kyle scale, having more empathic ability than 99 in every 100 humans, but not enough to qualify as psion. Even so, the extensive biomech in her body allowed her to develop a symbiosis with the electro-optic webs almost analogous to telepathy. But she could never enter psiberspace, a fact she had always regretted.

Hundreds of people already filled the bay, gathered on platforms and catwalks, and many more were streaming in from other trapdoors. Monitors around the bay showed similar scenes throughout Onyx.

"There's so many," Tahota said to Raines as they climbed to the main platform, about halfway down the bubble, near its curving wall.

"It's the same on every station." He sent her a copy of a file she also had waiting in her queue. All together, 400 thousand people had stayed behind.

"Gods," Tahota murmured. "ISC better have enough medals for them all."

A buzz came from the comm in her wrist gauntlet. Raising her arm, she said, "Tahota here."

"Admiral, this is Colonel Oppendayer, on the battle cruiser *Pharaoh's Shield.* We've packed in the last stragglers. The evac ships are ready to go."

"Good work," Tahota said. "Launch on my order."

She called up a continually updating file from one of her spinal nodes. Her biomech web accessed her optic nerve and a display appeared in front of her, a translucent image in the air. When she winked her right eye, the image moved to the right, toward the glass wall of the bubble, leaving her view of the bay unobstructed. The image showed the ESComm sphere enclosing Onyx, two million ships spread over a shell with an area almost eighty light-years square, roughly sixty billion kilometers on average separating vessels. Without a psiberweb, the sphere was far too big for real-time communication among its constituent ships. It could take well over fifty hours for a light signal just to go from a craft to its nearest neighbor.

However, ESComm telops were monitoring the sphere and had so far caught every decoy ship Onyx sent out, extracting them from both real and superluminal space. Soon ESComm would collapse the sphere, bringing it in to only a few million kilometers from Onyx, just far enough out for the ships to dump their velocity on approach to the stations. Tahota already knew they could pull off the maneuver on a much smaller scale; they had used it with vicious success on ISC outposts. But seeing it from a force of two million daunted even her experienced eye.

Raines was listening to his ear comm. "Admiral, we have hookups now to every station and ship. You're all set."

"Good work." Tahota drew in a breath, knowing this was the time she should produce a stirring oration that would inspire the billions waiting to hear her voice. Given her limited oratorical abilities, she would have to make do with a few simple words instead.

She spoke, and her voice carried throughout Onyx. "In a few moments, you will all make history." It wasn't the most original opening line, but it would do. "We expect ESComm to collapse their sphere within five minutes. That's when we'll launch the evacs. Gods know, I wish I could promise you will all make it. I can't do that. But I know of no force better trained to make this work, no force with greater courage or skill."

A rumble of approval rippled through her listeners. When it quieted, she said, "We know ESComm has state-of-the-art quasis tech for dealing with large accelerations, so we expect it will only take them ten minutes to converge on Onyx, maybe even less." To collapse the sphere that fast meant the ships had to travel at about a hundred thousand times light speed. The speed itself was easily attained, but the accelerations were daunting. "What that means," she said, "is that the evac ships will have less than ten minutes to get out."

Tahota took a breath. "Those of you who volunteered to stay behind should have been assigned fuel bottles by now. With 400 thousand of you, we've covered almost every bottle on every station. We all know ESComm can stop our self-destructs now, but try to engage them anyway. They will expect it."

She glanced at her display. The habitats had moved farther inward, leaving the Lock on the edge of the cluster. "ESComm wants these stations intact. As soon as they're within range, they'll go after our electro-optic webs, to control our systems so we can't blow anything up. After you try to engage the self-destructs, simply surround each of your assigned bottles with a second Klein field." Whether it would actually be "simple" remained to be seen. It wasn't a procedure they had ever had reason to test on this scale, given that putting one fuel bottle inside another achieved nothing except making the fuel inaccessible. However, the apparent stupidity of such an action meant ESComm had no reason to have countermeasures for it either.

"You must wait until the last evac ship has inverted out of here before you make the new bottles," she continued. "*Under no circumstances* should you start before the evac ships invert." Looking out at her people, she raised her voice until it resonated throughout the bay. "I am honored by the service of every last one of you. Your courage will be remembered throughout history, when parents tell their children how the heroes of Onyx broke the back of the Eubian Empire."

They gave a subdued cheer then, from all over Onyx. Tahota swallowed, moved by the bravery of all these men and women who volunteered to follow her despite the enormity of the threat they faced. She saw no sign of regret from anyone.

Colonel Oppendayer spoke over her ear comm. "Admiral, the Trader ships are accelerating in preparation for inversion."

"Ready on my order for evac launch," she said.

On her display, the ESComm sphere began to shrink and fade as its ships accelerated inward and then vanished into inversion. Data reeled off in her mind; hundreds of Trader ships inverted, thousands, hundreds of thousands.

"Three ESComm battle cruisers inverted," Oppendayer said.

Tahota studied the sphere. Only forty-six ESComm vessels remained yet to invert, the largest cruisers, monsters the size of cities.

"Admiral!" Oppendayer said. "We've got ESComm Stingers dropping into normal space out at only seventeen million kilometers."

Damn. They had come in faster than she expected. "Launch the evac!" The last ESComm weapons platforms had yet to invert, but she dared wait no longer.

The evac force surged out from Onyx like spherical light waves diverging from a point source. The bigger the area of space they scattered across, the harder they would be to catch.

Raines cupped his hand to his ear. "Admiral, we've got about 10 percent of the ESComm fleet now, at about fifteen million kilometers out from Onyx in a spherical distribution."

Oppendayer spoke in her ear comm. "The forward wave

of our evac force is inverting. Jag starfighters, Wasps—there go the Asps. Cobras—we've got a destroyer into inversion."

At her side, Raines swore. "And we've got ESComm Stingers on approach to Onyx. The first wave of their weapons fire will hit the evac in forty-six seconds."

"Oppendayer, get our ships out of here," Tahota said.

"We're 60 percent inverted," Oppendayer said. "Seventy-two. Eighty. Eighty-eight."

Her display showed which of her ships hadn't yet made it: the battle cruisers, still lumbering up to inversion speed. "Come on," she muttered. *"Go!"*

Raines said, "About 30 percent of ESComm fleet now on approach to Onyx."

Three ISC cruisers remained. As Tahota watched, two inverted. Only the largest, *Pharaoh's Shield,* remained.

"Oppendayer, get out of here," Tahota said.

"*Shield* hasn't enough speed," he said.

"Do it anyway."

"ESComm Annihilator fire incident on *Shield,*" Raines said.

No answer came from Oppendayer as the cruiser went into quasis. On Tahota's display, beams of energy highlighted in red hit *Pharaoh's Shield.* One deck of the cruiser imploded, only a fraction of the mighty ship's girth, but a warning of its overtaxed quasis.

"*Shield,* invert, damn it!" Tahota said. *"Now!"*

With a ripple of spacetime, the giant cruiser *melted* out of space, flowing around a singularity in reality. The ship was large enough that the effect wasn't instantaneous; it poured out of the real universe.

Then it was gone.

As a cheer went up from the bay, Raines spoke to Tahota in a low voice. "Evac fleet launched, Admiral."

Tahota let out a breath. She raised her voice and directed her next words to the 400 thousand volunteers still at Onyx. "Make your Klein bottles."

All around her, in the bay and on the monitors, she saw

soldiers directing their attention to palmtops, gauntlets, and control bands as they went to work.

At her side, Raines said, "We've got 90 percent of the ESComm fleet converging on Onyx."

Tahota nodded, intent on the data flowing into her spinal nodes. The overlap between the emergence of the ESComm vessels and the departure of the evac ships had been too big. But the evacuation was out of her hands now. All she could do was pray.

Then Raines said, "The ESComm battle cruiser *Flagstone* is hailing *New Metropoli.* Admiral Kaliga on comm."

Tahota stared at him. "Xirad Kaliga? The admiral who commands ESComm?"

"Not that Kaliga," Raines said. "A cousin, apparently."

"Put him on," Tahota said.

A four-meter screen lowered from the ceiling until it hung about five meters in front of Tahota. An image formed on it, a tall officer in a black uniform and knee boots, with carnelian ribbing on his sleeves. His gaunt face had a cold Highton ascetism.

Tahota nodded. "Admiral Kaliga."

"So," he said. "The infamous Starjack Tahota."

Tahota hardly thought she rated "infamous." She was more known for her organizational skills. Given that those skills were all focused on waging war against ESComm, though, she supposed that could qualify her for infamy from their point of view.

"We accept your terms of surrender," Tahota said.

"You haven't much choice," Kaliga told her. "It's remarkable, in fact. A base that had 300 thousand ships to defend it now has none."

"Remarkable," Tahota agreed.

"Did you really expect that game to work?" he asked. "Tuck your tails and run? We caught the pups, you know."

She felt a sinking sensation. "I don't know what you mean."

"No? Can you see the screen behind me?" He motioned to someone outside her field of view, and Tahota's screen suddenly filled with the image of an ISC frigate tethered to an ESComm destroyer. She recognized the frigate. It was one of her evac ships.

Damn. "Yes. I see it."

"Watch," Kaliga said.

Tahota watched. The two ships continued to drift in space.

An ISC officer spoke in her ear comm. "Admiral Tahota, this is Major Byr. I may be able to eavesdrop on the comm chatter among the ESComm ships. It's scrambled, but I think I can break their code."

She didn't want to speak into her comm with Kaliga watching, so she sent a thought to one of her nodes. *Can you link me to Byr?*

Yes, it answered. I can transmit to the picoweb in the hull of *New Metropoli,* which can then link to his console.

Major Byr, can you read me? Tahota thought.

"Loud and clear," he said.

Get that spy line on their chatter.

Out in space, the captured ISC frigate drifted next to the ESComm destroyer that tethered it. Still nothing—

The explosion made no sound. The frigate simply disappeared in a burst of debris and radiation. The ESComm ship remained unaffected, having gone into quasis.

Tahota clenched her teeth. Next to her, Raines muttered, "So much for Halstaad."

Kaliga appeared on the screen again. "You were foolish, Admiral, trying to deceive us."

"You had no cause to destroy that ship," Tahota said. "You've also just violated the Halstaad Code of War."

Dryly Kaliga said, "You can lodge a complaint with ESComm."

Major Byr spoke in her ear. "Admiral, according to my sensors, they only have a handful of ISC ships out there."

Good work, she thought. Byr's information implied three possibilities: ESComm had destroyed the evac ships, taken them elsewhere—or missed them altogether. She prayed it was the last.

Admiral Kaliga put his hand on his ear and tilted his head. For a moment Tahota feared he was listening to her chatter with Byr. Then he said, "Double Klein bottles, Admiral Tahota? What were you thinking?"

"I've no idea what you're talking about," she said.

"I'm sure you do." He listened on his comm again, then laughed. "Good gods. Hiding Klein bottles inside bigger Klein bottles." He dropped his hand. "How bizarre."

"I see." Tahota let a note of strain enter her voice. It wasn't hard, given the situation.

"We've taken your fuel bottles out of the silly Klein fields you put them in," he said.

"Admiral Tahota!" Byr said. "They're moving the Lock."

On her display in the observation bay Tahota could see the Lock surrounded by the specks of ESComm ships. The Lock's huge thrusters were firing, propelling it away from Onyx.

"Admiral, I'm disappointed," Kaliga said.

"Disappointed?" Tahota asked.

"We've downloaded the Onyx web into ours," he said. "Your codes were far too easy to break."

Is he bluffing? Tahota asked Byr.

"Sorry," Byr said. "It's true. They have everything."

"That gambit with the bottles was foolish," Kaliga said.

"What gambit?" Tahota asked.

"We have your 'secured' orders. Hiding antimatter in double Klein bottles was hardly likely to fool our sensors or stop us from freezing the self-destructs."

Tahota blew out a gust of air. "So."

"Yes. So. Your ploy failed." Kaliga put his hand to his ear. "We dock at *New Metropoli* in four minutes. Prepare for boarding."

Boarding. *Boarding.* Tahota contemplated the implications of becoming an ESComm prisoner and sweat beaded on her forehead.

"Admiral Tahota," Byr said in her ear comm. "I've got that spy line on their comm."

Pipe it through, Tahota thought.

A woman's voice came over her comm, speaking Eubic. "Over seven billion Klein bottles. Gods only know what they thought they could do with them."

"Double-check the bottles," a man said. "Look for anything—trick triggers, hidden web links, anything unusual."

"We deactivated their links to the Onyx web," the woman said. "We found self-destruct triggers, but our quasis generators countered them."

Tahota lost the rest of the chatter as Kaliga spoke to her. "Admiral, we have the Lock secured." Triumph glinted in his eyes. "Here is something for you to ponder while you await my guards, my dear Starjack. Eube has a Lock and Key now. Think on it."

Tahota didn't want to think on it. Nor did she like being called *My dear Starjack* by a Highton Aristo.

Kaliga's image disappeared, leaving the screen blank. The chatter from the spy line was still going. "We've run double and triple checks," the woman was saying. "The bottles look normal."

The next voice on the line surprised Tahota. It was Kaliga. "Warn the troops boarding the stations to be careful anyway."

Out in space, the Lock was shrinking to a point as it accelerated toward inversion, attended by its ESComm captors. The other habitats huddled around *New Metropoli.* A flash of light came from a station on the outer edge of the cluster.

Tahota stiffened. No! *Not now.*

Kaliga spoke on the spy link. "What the hell was that?"

"One of the Klein bottles had an instability in its field," someone said.

"Is it part of a self-destruct sequence?" Kaliga asked.

"Apparently not," another voice said. "Faulty equipment. The Klein field had a flaw."

"I don't like it," Kaliga said. "Put me through to Arez."

After a pause, a voice said, "Colonel Arez here."

"Are you ready to invert the Lock?" Kaliga asked.

"Speed-wise, yes," Arez said. "But I'm concerned about our proximity to Onyx. Inverting a platform this size will cause spacetime ripples all over this area. It could damage the other habitats."

"That doesn't matter," Kaliga said. "As long as we get the Lock. Invert now."

"Yes, sir. Engaging."

Tahota directed a message to Major Byr: *Can you show me the Lock on long-range sensors?*

"I'm not sure," Byr said. "I'm losing my link here. ESComm has most of—wait, here we go. Incoming."

Got it, Tahota thought. A detailed view of the Lock came up on her display. As she watched, the space station melted out of reality. It was astonishingly beautiful, like watching sparkles liquefy and run through space in rivers of radiance. Then the light faded into blackness and the Lock was gone.

"We've got it!" a voice exulted.

So, Tahota thought. She felt as if she had just finished a marathon race. She looked at the chronometer psicon in her mind.

In the third second of the sixth hour of the eighth day in the tenth month of year 372 ASC on the Imperial Calendar, the Traders inverted the Third Lock, capturing a prize that had eluded their grasp for almost four centuries.

In the fourth second, the backlash from the inverting Lock hit Onyx Station—and set off instabilities in the out-of-phase fields of 7.32 billion Klein bottles.

Tahota raised her hand to salute the volunteers watching her from throughout Onyx. "Gods' blessings to you all," she said.

In the fifth second, 7.32 billion Klein fields on every space station collapsed—and dumped 700 billion kilograms of antimatter plasma into real space.

In one majestic sweep, every habitat at Onyx detonated. Plasma exploded, spewing out radiation, gamma rays, and brutal showers of high-energy reactions. Gargantuan chunks of debris hurtled in every direction. On the scale of a universe that knew supernovas, quasars, and black holes, the result was a splutter of energy.

In human terms, it had no precedent.

Expressed in terms of matter to energy conversion, the combined explosions produced a million trillion trillion joules of energy, greater than the output of a hot yellow star, more powerful than 100 trillion nuclear bombs. The waves of destruction swamped *New Metropoli* in a great, raging maelstrom of fury.

So Onyx died—and in doing so, it also obliterated two million ESComm ships.

28

Eldrin sat bolt upright in the dark. He jumped out of bed and pulled on his robe as he strode out of the bedroom. He heard Taquinil's door snap open, then heard his son run into the darkened living room. They left the house together, racing through the soft night of Valley. They had both felt the cry for help.

The trip on the magrail seemed to take forever. By the time they reached the Orbiter's hull, Eldrin was so tense he couldn't stop clenching his fists. They ran through the hull corridors, their bare feet slapping the ground. Neither he nor Taquinil had taken time to put on shoes. Taquinil was wearing his black pants and black sweater, having fallen asleep at his web console, and Eldrin wore only sleep trousers under his robe.

No one was posted outside the Solitude Room. They ran inside—and found Dehya screaming in silence.

A fragile figure in a blue sleep shift, she clutched the arms of the control chair, her body rigid. With horror, Eldrin realized he could see *through* her. He also saw a translucent web spread through space all around them, as if she had pulled psiberspace out of itself and overlaid it on the universe they inhabited.

She kept screaming, but he heard no sound. He was at her side in two steps. As he closed his fingers around her hand and felt its solidity, relief poured over him. But when he tensed to pull her out of the chair, Taquinil grabbed his arm.

"We don't know what will happen if we yank her out of it," his son said. "It could rip apart her mind."

Dismayed, Eldrin let go of his wife. She stared through him, from some other place, with no sign of recognition. Tears streamed down her cheeks.

"Can you help her?" he asked Taquinil.

"I think so." But Taquinil's fear saturated the air. He touched a panel on the arm of the chair, another, and another. One by one the glittering lights on both the chair and the console faded into darkness.

As Taquinil worked, Dehya became more solid. She focused on Eldrin, and he was sure she saw him now. When he touched her cheek, he felt her tears.

"Dehya?" he asked. "Are you here?"

She tried to speak, but her voice drifted like leaves blown by a far wind, over a remote plain, too distant to hear.

Taquinil came to stand in front of her, moving his lips so she could read them. "Mother? Can you understand me?"

Her lips moved. *Yes.*

"Can Father unfasten you from the chair?"

She formed more words. *Yes. Hurry.* Her body rippled as if it were the surface of a lake disturbed by a falling rock.

Eldrin turned to his son. "Are you sure I should do this?" What if he erred and caused his wife to dissolve into some other universe?

"I can't do it," Taquinil said. "My mind is too much like hers. In psiberspace we're too close together."

The prospect of losing them both shouldered its unwelcome way into Eldrin's thoughts. "You mean you could fall into wherever she is?"

Taquinil nodded. "Just standing this close to her, I feel my mind trying to dissociate."

Taking a deep breath, Eldrin leaned over Dehya and reached behind her neck. The psiphon prong felt smooth in his fingers as he tugged it out of her socket. He unplugged the prongs in her wrists next, then put his hand behind her waist and pulled out the one in her spine. Going down on one knee, he removed the plugs in her ankles. When he disconnected the last one, ripples swept over her body as if she were *resetting.*

Dehya fell forward, out of the chair. Eldrin caught her and sat back on the floor with a jolt, wedged between the chair and console. She felt *real,* the softness of her hair, the tickle of her breath on his skin. He cradled her in his arms and she hung onto him, her head against his chest. Dressed in only a flimsy sleep shift, with her childlike face, she seemed painfully vulnerable to him, ready to break at the least touch.

Taquinil knelt next to them. "Mother?"

Her thought came like the gurgling of a distant muddy brook. *Dryniiiiiii . . . heeeeeelp . . .*

Eldrin held her closer. **Tell me how.**

Dissooooooolving . . .

He surrounded her mind with his, trying to hold her close in the web as well as in his arms. **Come back.**

Aiiii . . . cold, she thought. *I'm so cold.*

Eldrin peeled off his robe and wrapped it around her, then enfolded her in his arms again. **Dehya, come back!**

Ah. She heaved in a ragged breath, holding him tight around the waist.

Dehya?

"They've gone," she whispered, her voice like dust in the wind. "The warriors of light."

A relief almost unbearable in its intensity poured over him. "The warriors of light?"

"Onyx," she said.

"You were there?"

"They have the Third Lock."

"Who?"

"ESComm."

Taquinil stiffened. "Mother, are you sure?"

"Yes. We must warn Soz." She was starting to shake as a

reaction set in from whatever had happened. "ESComm put someone into the Lock and tried to link to the Orbiter. I stopped them."

Eldrin suddenly felt cold. "If they add a fourth person to the Triad, the power surge will kill all four of you."

"Only if they use a Key. They didn't. Just a telop." Dehya shuddered. "It killed him instantly."

Eldrin blanched. It was an ugly way to die. "Dehya, you can't go back in the web."

"They have the Orbiter's location," she whispered. "We have to warn Tikal. We have to hide the Orbiter."

Eldrin hung onto her, rocking back and forth, looking at Taquinil over her head, knowing they all shared the same thought. The Locks were inextricably connected through the web. If ESComm had a fix on the Orbiter through the Third Lock, nothing could hide them.

Soz sat in a control chair above the bridge on *Roca's Pride.* Her guards wanted her on Asteroid, the hollowed-out planetoid that served as a stand-off base for the invasion. But she was needed more here, where she could hold together their corner of the web. She felt as if she were running on an edge, keeping her equilibrium only through speed, that if she paused, she would fall into the raging seas on either side.

The cruiser rumbled in her mind. Entering Platinum Sector One.

Soz exhaled. This was it. Accelerating their timetable to outrun the web collapse had fragmented some of the Radiance Fleet, but they kept most of it intact. Whatever happened now, they had no way to turn back.

Major Coalson's voice burst over the comm. "We've been detected. A squadron of Solos—all right, here it is. A fleet of ESComm ships is dropping into real space. About 500 thousand ships, stats in file D5m."

"Got it," Soz said.

ESComm signal on channel 6, Admiral Barzun thought.

Ready, Soz thought.

A Highton voice came over the comm in her ear. "*Roca's Pride,* this is Colonel Jaibriol Izarson aboard the *Rapier.*"

Soz's entire body went rigid. *Jaibriol.* Even though she knew the name was common among Traders, the sound of it still sent her adrenaline roaring.

"You have violated Eubian territory," Izarson said. "This sector is under ESComm protection and interdicted to ISC ships. Surrender and prepare for boarding."

Soz knew how her fleet looked, a paltry force of 50 thousand ISC ships trying to sneak through Platinum Sector. "Colonel Izarson, this is *Roca's Pride.* We don't acknowledge your interdiction."

"Surrender now and you will be escorted to one of our bases," Izarson said. "If you refuse, we will have no choice but to respond with force."

"You are holding a member of the Ruby Dynasty in violation of the Halstaad Code of War," Soz said. In truth, nothing in the Code actually forbade ESComm from taking Althor prisoner. Torturing him violated it with a vengeance, but she had no proof they were doing it. "Release him to us and we'll leave."

Imperator Skolia. That came from Garr, her ISC psiberweb wizard. *Our links to the ships in Klein space are slipping.*

Slipping? Soz thought. **Be more precise.**

It's because of the collapsing web. We can't keep our Klein space links stable.

Izarson spoke over her comm. "*Roca's Pride,* be reasonable. You're outnumbered ten to one. Surrender and we won't fire. You have one minute."

"Where is the rest of your force?" Soz asked. "I thought Platinum Sector had over a million ships."

"Admiral Barzun, you have fifty-five seconds," Izarson said.

Barzun sent Soz a dry thought. *Their intelligence leaves much to be desired, if they think you are me.*

Despite his amusement, Soz felt his tension. Izarson had made the logical assumption. ESComm had no reason to think the Imperator would be on the flagship of an invasion fleet. To Garr, she thought, **How long before we lose the links?**

Garr thought, *I can give you 1.03 minutes on the Klein bottles. Any longer and our links to the ships may become too diffuse to recover.*

"I've picked up another ESComm force," Major Coalson said. "Coming out of Platinum Sector Five."

"Got it," Soz said. It didn't surprise her that ESComm had to reach all the way to Sector Five for reinforcements, given how many ships had gone to Onyx. **Any report from Onyx Platform?** She asked Garr.

Nothing, he thought. *But those web links are all down.*

Prepare to open the Klein bottles, Soz thought. She submerged into a VR simulation and arrowed through space with the Radiance Fleet, a cord of ships spread out over billions of kilometers and traveling at half the speed of light. The ESComm ships showed as distant specks in a cylindrical formation around Radiance.

"Barzun, you have forty-five seconds," Izarson said. "Do you really intend to engage a battle you can't win?"

Even though she knew her telop communications went at almost light speed, it still surprised Soz that only ten seconds had passed. **Barzun, can you distract him?** she asked. To Garr she thought, **Open the Klein bottles.**

Barzun spoke on an intership channel. "Colonel Izarson, this is Rear Admiral Chad Barzun. We demand the release of Althor Valdoria."

"You have forty seconds," Izarson said. Then he added, "If you're Barzun, who was I talking to before?"

Klein bottles collapsed, Garr thought.

Space rippled.

The effect spread along the Radiance Fleet. As the ripples intensified, Soz tensed. They had no way to be sure what would happen now. There had only been time for preliminary tests. On a small scale, matching phases in Klein space solved the instability problem. On this large a scale, who knew? When the hidden ships entered real space, the Radiance Fleet might well vanquish itself with no help at all from ESComm, disappearing in a cascade of destruction caused by massive Klein field collapse.

The ripples swept through space, first swamping the Radiance ships and then extending to encompass even the ESComm ships. A chronometer in the lower corner of Soz's mindscape showed the countdown to Izarson's deadline. Thirty seconds.

Garr, how are the Klein fields holding up? she thought.

We've instabilities in about 8%. His thought came in the blur of fast-mode, all symbols and numbers.

Soz directed her thought into the general Radiance web. **Those of you with instabilities, abandon craft.**

The damaged craft fell back, accompanied by recovery ships that would pick crews up out of space. Only about 10 percent of the ships in the fleet carried humans, the rest being crewed by EIs. The recovery partner of one ship was itself damaged but switched smoothly to its backup.

The distortion in space continued to increase, making it difficult to see any ships, let alone the reinforcements. Twenty seconds remained to Izarson's deadline.

Then, with a silent majesty, in perfect synchronization, 750 thousand ISC ships twisted into real space.

Someone, on some channel, said, "Gods almighty."

Soz spoke into the comm. "Colonel Izarson, I suggest you surrender."

All Izarson said was, "Your time is up." But he sounded strained now, his earlier confidence gone.

ESComm collapsed its cylinder formation around the Radiance Fleet, forming a pipe a ten billion kilometers long but only 100 thousand kilometers in diameter, with the Radiance ships in a long "cord" down its center. Traveling at half the speed of light, the ships covered 150 thousand kilometers a second. The ESComm force numbered 600 thousand ships to Radiance's 800 thousand, a total of 1.4 million ships.

Annihilator beams and Impactor smart missiles crisscrossed the pipe. The formation favored ESComm in that it made the ISC ships easier targets, but it worked against them when the beams passed through the widely spaced ISC ships and penetrated the far side of the pipe. Unlike smart missiles, which could evade and pursue their targets, beams had no such intelligence. They annihilated whatever they hit.

To catch anything in such a diffuse formation, however, was no simple task. Now in the "thick" of battle, the ISC cord of ships contained on average one craft every 12.5 thousand kilometers. Annihilator shots hit their targets only if the gunner correctly calculated the intersection of the target's trajectory with the antimatter beam. With the split-second timing and huge distances involved, even minute course changes by the target made the beams miss.

Taus flooded the pipeline, brutal missiles with starship drives that let them invert into superluminal space. The ISC Jags and ESComm Solos, the most maneuverable craft in the fleets, were the only crewed ships that deliberately engaged the taus, inverting if necessary to chase the superluminal missiles. Jags normally achieved far better precision in such maneuvers than their Solo counterparts, using psiberweb links to guide them in superluminal space. But now the Jags were doing almost no better than the Solos, as the psiberweb unraveled.

A tau surged out of superluminal space almost on top of *Roca's Pride* and detonated against the quasis shield.

Quasis jump, *Roca's Pride* thought.

Barzun thought, *Blackstars, stay on* Roca's Pride.

Aye, General. That came from the commander of the Blackstars, a legendary Jag squadron so renowned for its combat successes that it had become notorious even among ISC forces.

Soz frowned and sent Barzun a message on their private channel. **Why aren't the Blackstars guarding Asteroid?**

We need them on Roca's Pride.

Her scowl deepened. **You're compromising the safety of Asteroid to protect mine. Put them back on Asteroid.**

A sense of refusal came from Barzun. *Imperator Skolia, contrary to Councilor Tikal, I agree with your decision to accompany the fleet. In fact, your value to this operation exceeds that of Asteroid. That's all the more reason for precautions. The Blackstars stay on* Roca's Pride.

She blinked. **How did you know Barcala tried to stop me?**

He told me. Dryly Barzun added, *He also informed me that if you returned in any condition other than your "normal ornery self," he would "flay my flaming carcass."*

Soz smiled. **That sounds like Barcala.**

At web speeds, their exchange took less than a second. The battle between the Radiance and Platinum fleets went on at relativistic speeds, a form of combat ISC forced on ESComm because it favored the faster communications capability of ISC. Drone missiles pursued targets and evaded each other, while clouds of smart dust fogged space, moving with the ships. Directed by picochips embedded in the grains, the dust mucked up signals and corroded surfaces. When a grain disintegrated, the miniature warhead it carried ignited.

At 50 percent light speed, the ships, missiles, and dust all contracted relative to slower objects. For two ships moving at the same speed, the contraction offered no benefit to one craft over the other, because they both experienced it by the same amount. But it favored the quicksilver Jags, which could outpace most any other class of ship. Nor was it only speed that gave the Jags an edge; they also had the ability to alter their shape and so exaggerate the contraction effect, better using it to decrease the target they presented to slower ships. The advantages were small when all the ships were moving at relativistic speed, but for such closely matched forces it made a difference.

Time dilation could jump ships up to a full two seconds into the future for every ten seconds of travel. The consequent complications in communications normally favored ISC, because the psiberweb made them less dependent on signal transmission times. But as the web weakened, that advantage decreased. With growing disquiet, Soz realized she could *see* the web filling the void like a ghost, rippling, unraveling, and tearing.

The battle was also hurtling through an interstellar cloud of gas and dust natural to this region of space. Although they encountered far less dust than gas, the natural grains wreaked havoc with their smart-dust. A particle of smart-dust raced past Soz at 50 percent light speed, smashed into a mundane grain of the interstellar muck, and exploded, wasting its warhead on an innocent fleck of matter.

The gas in the cloud was diffuse, only about ten molecules per cubic centimeter. Compared to a planetary atmosphere, which might have ten million trillion particles per cc, it was nothing. Nor was the gas itself dangerous. Most of it was simply atomic hydrogen. But for ships covering over five billion centimeters per second, it became a scouring fog of corrosion. Here ESComm fared better than ISC, having designed ships and weapons adapted to dealing with the foggy weather in their home territory.

An ISC frigate loomed ahead—and vanished in a flash of radiation as an ESComm Stinger hit it with an antimatter bomb. Then the Stinger exploded, caught by an ISC tau that dropped into normal space almost "on top" the Stinger. Another ISC tau flashed by Soz, chased by an ESComm drone. The tau inverted out of real space—and reappeared behind the drone, having come around at superluminal speed. It impacted the ESComm ship and both exploded in a shower of energy.

Data flowed into Soz's nodes. ESComm had lost 200 thousand ships, a third of their force, leaving them with 400 thousand. ISC had also lost 200 thousand, but that was only a fourth of their fleet. Most of the destroyed craft were drones piloted by EI brains. But the losses in human life wrenched Soz, as many thousands gave their lives in the gargantuan engagement.

A glittering fog of dust spread around her. The reason for its scintillation fast became clear: an ESComm Starslammer shot straight "through" her, its huge bulk dwarfing her virtual body, the lights on its hull sparkling. Two ISC Asps were chasing it and she arrowed after them. The ESComm smart-dust came with them, harassing the Asps, igniting in tiny explosions against their hulls, forcing them into quasis again and again. The continual quasis jumps made it difficult for the Asps to increase their speed, and the ESComm Starslammer pulled farther ahead.

A Jag suddenly dropped out of inversion right in front of the Starslammer, matching its trajectory with a precision coordinated through the psiberweb—and the Jag blasted the Starslammer out of existence with its relativistic exhaust. Then the Jag hurtled on, leaving Soz alone in space.

Soz read her displays—and exhaled a long breath of virtual air. ISC still claimed 450 thousand ships and ESComm had dropped to 90 thousand. As she watched, the ESComm number decreased to 85 while ISC stayed constant.

Imperator Skolia, Admiral Barzun thought. *Colonel Izarson on channel 6.*

Got it, Soz thought, withdrawing her awareness back into the control chair above the bridge.

Izarson spoke in a quiet voice. "*Roca's Pride,* this is the ESComm *Rapier.* We surrender our forces to you."

"Surrender accepted," Soz said.

Then she saw the red light on a panel in front of her chair. Izarson was using his captive telops to blast a message through a hacked node in the disintegrating ISC psiberweb. The job was so sloppily done that every ISC ship picked it up, but by then it didn't matter.

Izarson's warning cut straight through to Glory: *Code One. 450 thousand ISC ships incoming from Platinum Sector.* And then he added: *Their web is failing.*

29

Dehya sat on the couch in Tikal's living room, still in her sleep shift, her arms wrapped around her torso, her body shaking. People surrounded her, officers and telops, many in sleep clothes themselves, having been summoned out of bed. Tikal was kneeling in front of her, his eyes level with hers, while General Majda had taken a seat on one side of her and Admiral Casestar on the other.

"Are you sure?" Tikal was saying.

"Yes." Dehya's voice had an eerie distant quality. "ESComm has located the Orbiter."

"Can you give us any more details on their force?" Majda asked. "How many? What weapons?"

"Ahhh . . ." Dehya's body rippled like the surface of a lake. "I'm trying to reach them."

Watching his wife literally fade in and out of reality, Eldrin struggled to stay calm. "Don't push her so hard. If she goes any deeper into the web, she'll never get out."

Tikal glanced at him, compassion showing on his gruff features. "I'm sorry, Lord Eldrin. But we have no choice."

Knowing Tikal was right made it no easier. Eldrin pressed the knuckles of his fists together in front of his body, willing Dehya to keep her tenuous link with reality. He was in a Rhon meld with her now, giving her his stability, but he feared it wasn't enough. How could she be in the web without a link? What if he lost her altogether, as her mind, perhaps even her body, dissolved into a place where space and time had no meaning?

He felt their son Taquinil in the next room, linked into the web via a console. Like Dehya, his work consisted of subtle intricacies, all nuances and finesse. Dehya spun the web, Taquinil held it together, and Eldrin supported them like a deep sea.

"ESComm is using their Lock to reach ours." Dehya shivered in her flimsy shift, her gaze focused on a point between Tikal's head and the leg of the hulking Jagernaut standing next to him. Seeing her surrounded that way made Eldrin grit his teeth. He *felt* them penning her, like a sense of compression.

"You're crushing her," he said. "You have to ease up."

"Dryniniiii." Dehya's voice echoed. "I have to do this."

"If you lose yourself in the net," he said, "you won't be able to do anything."

General Majda looked from Eldrin to Dehya. "Pharaoh Dyhianna, are you still able to pull out?"

"Yes . . ." Dehya took a breath. "They're in! ESComm just linked into Orbiter web."

Casestar stiffened and an officer behind the couch swore. General Majda spoke into the comm on her wrist gauntlet. "Colonel Gaithers, we have reason to believe the incoming ESComm force has broken into our web."

"We're on it," Gaithers said. "We're already countering them. We'll keep you posted."

"They only have a few ships," Dehya said. "Onyx broke them."

"You made contact with Onyx?" Majda asked. "We haven't heard anything out of there for hours."

"Onyx is . . . gone," Dehya said.

"Gone?" Tikal asked. "How?"

"Broken. Onyx. ESComm."

"You mean ESComm is broken?" Casestar asked.

"Almost no ships," Dehya said.

Casestar glanced at Majda. "Do we have news from Radiance?"

She shook her head. "Our web links with them have been down almost as long as the Onyx links."

Suddenly Dehya said, "Two ESComm Starslammers are

incoming to the Orbiter. And a few Solos. That's it. No, there's a Stinger too." She pulled her arms around her torso for warmth. "Desperate."

"Desperate?" Tikal asked.

"The ESComm force that went into Onyx is gone." She took a breath and sat up straighter. Eldrin could feel her pulling her mind back into her body. "They've nowhere near enough forces to secure the Orbiter," she said in a stronger voice. "They're sending a special operations team, meant to get in and out fast. They're after something specific."

"You," Tikal said.

Dehya swallowed. "Me. Taquinil. Eldrin. They know the web is collapsing. They want as many Keys as they can get and they want to kill the rest, to make it easier for them to rebuild the web, after this is over, and harder for us."

Tikal turned to General Majda. "What about the rest of the Ruby Dynasty?"

"We heard from the Allieds before we lost our links with them," Majda said. "They pulled Denric Valdoria off Sandstorm and took him back to Lyshriol, to stay with the rest of the family. The Allied forces have tripled the Lyshriol defenses. Web Key Eldrinson and Councilor Roca are on Earth, which is even better defended."

Casestar spoke into his gauntlet comm. "Security, send the Abaj Jagernauts here."

"On their way," Security answered.

"General Majda." Gaithers's voice crackled from her comm. "We've a problem. The ESComm lines into our web are locking up our operations."

"Can you get a reciprocal fix?" Majda asked "Follow their lines back into their web?"

"We're trying," Gaithers said. "So far they've evaded us."

"ESComm is hacking our web with provider-telops." Dehya's fist clenched in her lap. "Their providers can't do it. They're *dying*. But they're just equipment to the Traders. ESComm is using them up almost as fast as they install them." She shivered. "They don't care what it takes. They don't want to lose this chance at the Orbiter. If the psiberweb fails, that's it."

Tikal watched her face. "Will it hurt the Triad if the web collapses?"

"I don't know." She looked almost translucent, her delicate beauty hollowed by exhaustion. "Never happened before."

Tikal stared at her, then at Majda. "It's never gone down?"

"Not all at once," Majda said.

"Parts have crashed," Admiral Casestar said. "Sections of the EO network or small regions of the psiberweb. But it's always been localized. We've never had a full-scale shutdown."

"It might not all go this time either," Dehya said. "We've lost the long-distance nodes, but psiberspace itself is intact."

A chime sounded and Eldrin heard a door open. Boots thudded in the entrance foyer of the house. Then eight Abaj Jagernauts strode into the living room. They towered, seven feet tall or more, their height inherited from their ancestors, the Abaj Tacalique that six thousand years ago swore to defend the Ruby Dynasty and still honored that pledge. They wore black Jagernaut uniforms and black boots, massive leather-and-metal gauntlets all the way to their elbows, and huge black Jumbler guns glinting heavy on their hips.

Casestar assigned four of the Abaj to Eldrin and Dehya, adding them to the four Jagernauts already on their bodyguard, and sent the other four into the next room. They reemerged with a wearied Taquinil in rumpled clothes, his hair in disarray from pushing his hand through it, his expression disconcerted as the Abaj towered around him, two heads taller than he and more than twice his weight.

Majda spoke into her comm. "Gaithers, do you have any more on the incoming ESComm ships?"

"Our web is still locked up," Gaithers said. "The whole flaming thing. But we've followed their lines back to their web and have locks on their computers now. We can't shoot at them, but they can't shoot at us either."

"They'll try infiltrating the docking bay system," Casestar said. "So they can board."

"They're already in the docking web," Taquinil said.

"All over it," Dehya said. "Even the auxiliary bays."

Majda spoke into her comm. "Gaithers, don't let them dock! I don't care how you do it. Ram their ships with your own if you have to. But keep them off the Orbiter."

"We're trying to regain control with manual overrides," he said. "But the systems won't respond. We could end up ramming the Orbiter."

Casestar swore. "We have a city full of civilians here, with no defenses against ESComm commandos."

"It's the Ruby Dynasty they want," Tikal said. "Not City."

Dehya looked at him. "They want you also, Barcala."

Casestar spoke into his comm. "Security?"

"We're monitoring you all," Security said. "Almost every defense system within the Orbiter is focused on the house. Right now it's the best protected place in the station."

"It's not enough," Dehya said.

Casestar turned to her. "Why?"

"ESComm is worming holes in the security web."

Casestar spoke into his comm. "Security, do you have a breach? Assembly Key Selei says ESComm sent in worms."

"Affirmative," Security said. "We're killing them as fast as we find them. We've dropped several nodes altogether because of the infestation."

Gaithers spoke on Majda's comm. "General, we estimate the ESComm ships will arrive in about two minutes."

"You've got to block them," Majda said. "If your navigation systems are frozen, theirs must be too."

"We're trying. The damn web is fluctuating all over creation. We can't—*that's it.*"

"Gaithers?" Majda asked.

"Our estimate was off. They're here. Two Starslammers, four Solos—*hell,* that Stinger is—"

In the sudden silence, another voice said, "General, this is Colonel Marland. The Traders hurled a Stinger right into Gaithers's ship. Both craft were destroyed."

Majda clenched her fist and a surge of anger mixed with grief rolled out from her mind. "What about the other ships?"

"Our Jags have engaged the ESComm Solos," Marland said. "We're holding off one Starslammer, but the other is docking."

Eldrin stepped forward, aware of his towering guards moving with him. "We can't stay here."

Tikal stood up next to him. "You heard Security. This is the best defended place on the Orbiter right now."

Eldrin felt Dehya's mind straining to follow ESComm's invasion into the Orbiter web. "It's not enough."

Security spoke from Casestar's comm. "Lord Eldrin, we're giving it everything we have. Hell, we'll attack them with our bare hands if we have to. I swear to you, we won't let ESComm take your family."

"And you have our abiding gratitude." Eldrin watched Dehya, feeling what she felt, the silent relentless invasion. "But it's not enough. If we stay on the Orbiter, ESComm will capture us."

"You can't get off the Orbiter now," Majda said.

"We can," Dehya answered.

"Take us to the First Lock," Eldrin said.

"No," Casestar said. "The War Room is harder to secure."

"You have to take us there," Dehya told him.

"The Lock is our only chance," Eldrin said.

"Why?" Casestar asked. "You're more vulnerable there."

"I can do it from there," Dehya said.

"Do what?" Majda asked.

"Dissolve," Dehya said. "Into the web."

Majda frowned. "What?"

"Transform," Taquinil said. He glanced at his father. "But

I don't know—" Strain showed on his face. "Father, you aren't as interwoven with it as we are."

"What are you talking about?" Casestar asked.

"My wife and son are—" Eldrin struggled for words to describe what he understood only on an intuitive level. "They are here, but not fully. They've extended into psiberspace." He knelt in front of Dehya and took her hands. "That's what you've been doing, isn't it? Becoming part of the web."

"Our bodies are wavefunctions," she said. "Psiberspace is just another Hilbert space. It should be possible to transform our wavefunctions from spacetime into psiberspace." She cupped his face in her palms, holding him as if he were a treasure. "Taquinil's mind is like mine. But yours is different. That has made it harder to find the right transform. I don't know if it will work yet for you. I just don't *know.*"

Casestar spoke. "You're talking about turning your bodies into thought, aren't you? Becoming part of the psiberweb."

"Yes," Eldrin said.

Majda gave Dehya an incredulous look. "Even if you could do such a thing, how would you get out again?"

"Reverse transform," Dehya said.

"How?" Casestar said.

"I'm not sure," Dehya admitted. "But I would rather risk being lost in the web than becoming a Trader captive."

Eldrin glanced at Taquinil and his son nodded. Standing up, Eldrin held his hands out to Dehya. When she took them, he drew her to her feet. "We have to go now," he told General Majda. "While we still have time."

The general spoke into her comm. "Marland, what's the situation?"

"We're holding off the Solos and one Starslammer," he said. "The other slammer docked." A murmur of voices came from the background. Then Marland said, "ESComm waroids have boarded the Orbiter. Four—no, make that five commando units."

"We have to go *now,*" Eldrin said. "Or it will be too late."

Majda made up her mind. "Do it."

Casestar jumped to his feet. Surrounded by bodyguards, he, Eldrin, Dehya, and Taquinil ran from the house. The lighter gravity made their motions surreal, their steps taking them long and far. The magcar the Abaj had taken to the house waited on its platform, its door opening for them. Six of the Abaj jumped inside first. As Dehya reached the car, an Abaj grabbed her around the waist and heaved the Pharaoh inside as if she weighed nothing. Eldrin pushed Taquinil after her and jumped in himself, followed by Admiral Casestar and the other six Jagernauts.

As the car sped across the mountains, Casestar used his gauntlet comm to monitor the commandos and ISC teams. The unraveling communications made it difficult to track the invaders, but it sounded as if the teams had split up.

The car jarred to a stop on a platform at the hull. It took only seconds to run to the War Room. As they raced into the amphitheater, a sound came from the catwalks in the stardome above them. Eldrin looked up to see four waroids, ESComm warriors in full body armor, walking fortresses eight feet tall, ESComm's answer to Jagernauts, better protected but slower in speed than their Skolian counterparts. Their mirrored surfaces splintered light.

"RUN!" Casestar shouted.

Eldrin, Dehya, and Taquinil raced for the amphitheater dais. Some of their bodyguards ran with them while others fired at the waroids. The Jumbler shots made a shimmer of orange sparks in the air, as their abiton beams annihilated subelectronic bitons. With a rest mass of 1.9 eV and a charge of 5.95×10^{-25} C, abitons only needed an accelerator with a 50 cm radius and 0.0001 Telsa magnet. The air was too diffuse to attentuate the beams any significant amount, but where they hit the waroids the mirrored armor evaporated in explosions of orange light.

Eldrin had no time to see if the beams took out the warriors as well as their armor. He and Dehya sprinted across the dais, with Taquinil behind them. One of the Jagernauts running next to Eldrin made an odd sound, like a puff of released air. His body hurtled to the side and flew several meters before it slammed into a console.

"Gods, no," Dehya whispered. Another Jagernaut went down, shot from behind. Looking back as he ran, Eldrin saw more waroids pouring into the War Room, through the same entrance he and the others had used moments before.

Taquinil stumbled, going down on one knee. An Abaj warrior grabbed him around the waist and swung him to his feet, carrying him for several steps until the Ruby prince regained his balance. As soon as Taquinil started to run on his own, the Abaj whirled around and fired at their pursuers.

A crane swung down from the stardome straight at Dehya. Even before it stopped above her, a waroid was vaulting out of the cup at its end. With horrifying clarity, Eldrin saw the armored mammoth land behind her, the force of its impact vibrating through the dais. Still running, Dehya looked back, her unbound hair flying around her body. With one long step it caught her, its arm closing around her waist. She cried out as it swung her into the air. She looked like a small child in its massive grip, or a rag doll it could smash in one blow.

Before the waroid had a chance to take more than one step with its captive, two shots blasted into it. A Jagernaut on its right side fired a Jumbler beam that pulverized the waroid's helmet in an orange flash, eating through the metal and beyond. On the left, a second Jagernaut fired an EM pulse rifle, hurtling razer sharp projectiles into the waroid's armor. The projectiles couldn't penetrate it, but the impact threw the giant to the side and it toppled, falling with Dehya still in its grip.

Eldrin was already running toward them, but he knew he couldn't reach Dehya before the waroid crushed her beneath its massive bulk. Then the Jagernaut with the pulse rifle fired again, and the force of the shot changed the waroid's trajectory enough so it fell on its side, missing Dehya.

One of the Abaj reached Dehya and yanked the waroid's arm away from her body. She was already struggling; as soon as she was free, she scrambled to her feet and started running.

Eldrin skidded to a halt and reversed course, then took off again for the Lock corridor. He stopped at its entrance long enough to make sure Taquinil and Dehya made it past him, into the corridor. In that instant, an Abaj ran up behind him. Eldrin was a large man, over six feet tall, with a strong physique, but the Abaj picked him up as if he weighed nothing and almost threw him into the corridor. Eldrin caught his balance and sprinted forward, a few steps behind his son and wife, racing down the long, long hall into the Orbiter's heart, to the First Lock, the birthplace of the Skolian web.

Translucent columns packed with clockwork machinery flashed by, lights spiraling inside pillars. Eldrin heard the clang of boots behind them, their Jagernauts running, fewer than before. The end of the hall came nearer, no longer a point of perspective, but an octagonal arch with lights racing around it.

They ran into the Lock.

The power of the web filled the chamber with a great hum. Octagonal in shape, the room was only a few paces across. A singularity pierced its center, a pillar of light that rose through an octagonal opening in the floor, rupturing the fabric of reality. It came out of a sparkling fog and disappeared over their heads back into a hazed glitter.

The pillar was a Kyle singularity, a needle piercing the fabric of spacetime. The technology to create it had been lost, gone with the Ruby Empire. The three Kyle singularities—the Locks—were all that remained of the eerie Kyle sciences created by the Ruby Empire.

Time became torpid within the chamber. Eldrin saw Dehya and Taquinil moving in slow motion as they ran to the pillar. Reality thickened, like a heavy gel. Turning in slow motion, he saw his Abaj bodyguard look back at the Lock corridor. Only a few steps behind the Abaj, four ESComm waroids were entering the chamber. With excruciating slowness, the Abaj and a waroid fired at each other. The waroid stumbled back a step—and the Abaj slowly collapsed, shot in the chest.

Dryyyyyninini, Dehya's voice echoed. He turned to see her coming toward him. *We can't get a fix on you . . .*

Leave, he thought.

She reached her arms to him. *Not without you . . .*

Eldrin felt a massive arm close around his waist and knew they had run out of time. With a huge push, he shoved Dehya toward the pillar. In slow motion, her face flushed with desperation, she toppled against Taquinil—and together Eldrin's wife and son fell into the singularity.

Their bodies *flowed* around the pillar. Eldrin saw their faces smear across the singularity and fade into translucence. It took a bare fraction of a second, but he felt as if he stood forever watching the two people he loved more even than his own life dissolve into unreality.

The waroid who had grabbed him around the waist was lifting him now. Eldrin's feet left the ground and the chamber moved past his vision. Then he was facing the entrance, falling at it in slow motion as the waroid pushed him forward.

The instant Eldrin fell through the archway time sped up and he sprawled across the floor with a jarring impact. Before he could catch his breath, two waroids hauled him to his feet. Seeing the lifeless bodies of Jagernauts sprawled on the corridor floor made his mind reel. Jon Casestar wasn't here, but Eldrin felt a void in his mind where he had once known the admiral. It was too much to absorb so fast, that a lifelong friend and his sworn bodyguards could suddenly be gone.

Before Eldrin could regain his feet, the waroids took off, one on either side of him, each with a gauntleted hand gripped around his upper arm. His toes scraped the floor as they dragged him, until he got his feet beneath him and could run with them. He struggled to breathe. The flashing lights added to the confusion as the waroids propelled him down the corridor at a speed almost impossible for him to match.

They ran out to the same magcar he had taken to the War Room and dragged him inside it. As the car sped across the mountains, the waroids reported to their superiors in rapid-fire Eubic that went by too fast for Eldrin to decipher. All he picked up was that units had broken into Tikal's house but hadn't bothered to search for the First Councilor when it became clear their primary targets were no longer there.

Everything seemed to speed up as his mind struggled to readjust to the wild swings in reality he had experienced in the past few moments. The time it took for the car to cross the Orbiter compressed into what felt like seconds. Eldrin knew he had gone into Kyle shock, thrust to the brink of psiberspace and then yanked back again, but he had no idea how to deal with it.

When the car reached the opposite side of the orbiter, the waroids pulled him out and took off with him, once again running through corridors in the hull, headed for the docking bays. They passed more bodies, both ISC and ESComm. Eldrin wanted to shout his protest against what he saw, his dismay and his anger, that so much violence had been committed, all for three people who wanted no more than to be left alone, to solve equations and write songs.

A docking bay blurred around him. He could no longer keep up with the waroids, so they dragged him, uncaring as his feet snagged on cables, ridges, and bodies. They threw him through the open hatchway of a Starslammer and he rolled across the deck. As the growl of engines rumbled in the ship, the surface under his body vibrated.

Eldrin tried to absorb the tumult, tried to slow down his sense of time, but it had gone out of control. He could neither see nor hear, barely even feel the deck. The Starslammer left the bay, and his nausea told him they were dropping in and out of quasis, jumping so fast that no one had yet had a chance to secure him in a berth. He lay sprawled on the deck, flattened by acceleration, while his mind imploded.

Gradually his mental tumult eased. Quieted. Slowed. He became aware of his breathing. His vision cleared and he saw that he no longer lay on the deck. He had drifted into the air, weightless.

A man wearing the black uniform of an ESComm major floated toward him across the bridge. Other officers sat in control chairs, facing away from him, monitoring their banks of consoles. At first Eldrin thought a view port stretched the length of the bridge, showing the stars in gem colors. Then he realized it was a holoscreen, giving its radiant version of the inverted universe outside.

Eldrin had little idea how to manage in free fall, but it made no difference. The major moved with practiced ease, using grips in the hull. He took hold of Eldrin's arm and drew him to a chair at the back of the bridge. Like all Hightons, the man was tall, with glittering hair and red eyes. Watching his face, Eldrin felt as if he were falling into a soulless cavity, dragged down into the grasping mind of the Aristo.

The major strapped Eldrin into the chair, locking his wrists to its arms and his ankles to a bar along its lower edge. Eldrin spoke in his limited Highton, his halting words heavy with his Skolian accent. "You ESComm, yes? Highton major?"

"Yes." He answered slowly so Eldrin could understand him. "You're on the *Prevailer*."

"You take me to Glory?" Eldrin asked.

"Possibly." With brooding fascination, the major watched as Eldrin jerked his head, trying to move a lock of hair floating in his eyes. He traced his finger along Eldrin's jaw. Then he shook his head, as if trying to clear his mind, and spoke into the comm on his gauntlet. "We're secure here."

"How many of them did you get?" a voice asked.

"One," the Highton said. "The consort. The Pharaoh and her heir committed suicide."

Suicide? Until that moment, Eldrin hadn't realized how it must have appeared, with Taquinil and Dehya dissolving out of real space. He prayed the appearance didn't become reality. He had felt the effect of their entry into the already besieged web.

Psiberspace had imploded.

30

At first no one knew. The implosion initially seemed a localized phenomenon. At ISC headquarters, they thought it was a glitch in new software being installed in the security web. Operators at Imperial University on Parthonia assumed the school's aging nodes had gone off-line again. At consoles all across Skolia, users lifted their heads, tapped their psiphon prongs, checked their equipment.

Then the web began to unravel.

On every planet, habitat, and ship throughout the Skolian Imperialate, the psiberlinks that bound civilization together simply disappeared. Users tried to reach other nodes, searching for a web that no longer existed. Mail that required psiberspace connections bounced back to its sender. Complaints trickled in to systems operators. As sysop after sysop tried, without success, to access psiberspace, the effect intensified and the trickle became a river, then a deluge.

No official count existed of the electro-optical links to the psiberweb. EO systems were localized, unable to span more than a world or two, limited by light speed. The main EO networks were well-known, but smaller webs changed too rapidly to keep track of in a systematic manner. The sum total of all single-user links underwent a continuous flux, billions of changes per second.

When psiberspace imploded, those links lost their moorings. Trillions of EO connections snapped free. Outside the psiberweb, the only way messages could travel from a web in one star system to a web in another, in a reasonable amount of time, was via starship. So at first no one realized that on every planet and space habitat within the Imperialate, only moments after the psiberweb ceased to exist, the EO webs also collapsed.

No full map existed of links among the Skolian, Allied, and Trader webs. Large Imperial centers kept records of their psiberlinks to non-Imperial systems, but those only skimmed the surface of a deep, deep sea. Trillions of humans lived among three civilizations that teemed with computers. Picowebs threaded buildings, ships, habitats, every form of construction created by humanity, including the human body.

The web knew no political or spatial boundaries. It existed in and of itself, an organism that had been growing for centuries. When the Imperial web imploded, it pulled down the Eubian and Allied nodes connected to it. That precipitated the failure of any EO nodes linked to those that had collapsed. The breakdown spread throughout Eube and the Allied Worlds like a roaring tidal wave, as the combined webs of three interstellar empires ceased to exist in a great, monumental, star-spanning crash.

The Radiance Fleet made no sound in space, but to Soz, clenched in the grip of the web collapse, the ships seemed to scream into the Glory star system. She sat rigid in her command chair, her muscles pulled so taut that cords stood out in her neck. As psiberspace imploded, she held onto the Radiance Fleet's corner of the web, relying on the sheer power of her Lock-enhanced mind to hold off the implosion in this small corner of reality.

Radiance dropped into real space, proceeded by tau missiles at 95 percent of light speed, fast enough that their impacts would have the energy equivalent of many megaton bombs. Glory outmanned and outgunned Radiance, but the web collapse had crippled ESComm. The Radiance Fleet tore a swath through Glory's planetary defenses, vaporizing drones, satellites, and weapons platforms. They hurtled past the planet, headed straight for the sun. With exact synchronization, the Radiance ships inverted and continued to accelerate, looping around Glory's star. They arrowed back toward the planet and dropped into real space again, coming out of the sun in a silent scream of relativistic power.

In the Radiance Fleet's second pass, ESComm vaporized 80 percent of the remaining ISC drones. The crewed ships fared better, more adept at evading the lethal energies with their telops still in the web. Nor were losses confined to Radiance; ISC destroyed most of what remained in Glory's orbital defenses.

As the remains of the Radiance Fleet came back for a third pass, Soz sent a shout into the fragment of psiberspace she had been holding together. **Get out of the web! NOW.**

Her people had one instant to act. Then, with a great wrenching surge of power, the last piece of psiberspace imploded, thundering in on Soz's mind with the crashing force of a tidal wave.

Soz groaned, slumping back in her chair, suddenly aware of her surroundings again. Medics were crowded around her, floating in free fall, plastering her with diagnostic tapes and poking things in her arms.

"What are you doing?" she growled.

One doctor, a plump woman with graying hair, exhaled in obvious relief. "We thought we were going to lose you."

Soz sat up straight, then grimaced as her muscles protested. She didn't know how long she had been sitting rigid in her chair, but every part of her ached.

"Imperator Skolia!" Barzun's voice came over her ear comm. "Glory has called in reinforcements from all over Eube. If we're going in to the planet, we have to do it now. If we aren't out of here by the time reinforcements arrive, we're dead."

She rubbed her face, trying to focus. "What's our status?"

"Eighty thousand ships," Barzun said. "We're cleaning up Glory's orbiting defenses and firing on planetary nodes. We just got the Silicate Rift Military Complex on the Tarja Cape of Kuraysia. We're avoiding civilian areas, except for the palace, which is packed with ESComm nodes. We're trying to carve them out without destroying the rest of the palace."

"Good," Soz said. "Only military sites." Billions of civilians lived on Glory, only a tiny fraction of them Aristos, and killing civilians violated both the Halstaad Code and Soz's conscience.

She slapped her face, but it didn't make her any more alert. The strain on her resources had gone beyond what her nanomeds could handle. She couldn't remember when she had last slept. Focusing on the plump doctor, she said, "Give me a stimulant."

"I don't think you should," the woman replied. "You're pushing the limits of your endurance as it is."

"Advice noted," Soz said. "Now give me something."

The doctor opened her mouth to protest. Soz glowered, and the woman raised her hands, conceding defeat. Then she dialed a prescription into her syringe and injected Soz.

A new clarity came over Soz's thoughts. She spoke into her comm. "Barzun, are the d-teams ready?"

"They're assembling in the drop-down bay," he said.

"I'll see them off." Soz extricated herself from the chair, and the doctors moved back to give her room. She floated free, over the platform that anchored the catwalks stretching through the stardome to her command station. Below, the bridge personnel worked at consoles.

Soz pulled herself to a catwalk. As her boots touched it, one of her spinal nodes sent a command to her ankle sockets, which conveyed the command to the nanobots in the soles of her boots, ordering them to extend their molecular hooks so her boots adhered to the catwalk.

The walk swayed as she made her way to a hatch in the back wall of the bridge. The rotating body of the cruiser was separate from the bridge and extended out from it in a double-walled cylinder half a kilometer in diameter and several kilometers in length. She entered the cylinder at the center of its end cap, on its rotation axis, where no pseudo gravity would disorient a person transferring from the bridge to cylinder.

Soz floated into a circular chamber with chutes leading out in all directions, like spokes. When she entered one, weak gravity pulled her "down" toward the rim. As she progressed outward, gravity increased until she was slowly falling down the chute. She grasped the rung of a ladder on the wall and climbed the last ten meters.

At the bottom, the gravity was about one-tenth human standard. She opened a hatch and entered the main body of the cylinder, which ran parallel to the rotation axis. She ran along the metal hall in loping strides, sailing. When she rose into the air, Coriolis forces pushed her to the side, and she compensated with practiced nudges against the bulkheads.

Instead of heading to the drop-down bay, she went to her office. People crammed it. Jagernauts. Twenty of them. They stood holding their drop-down gear, at attention as she entered, gauntleted men and woman in black uniforms. They raised their arms to salute her, fists clenched, wrists crossed.

"At ease," Soz said. She had selected this group with excruciating care. Two were Blackstars. Four were Abaj. All were at least Secondary in rank and several were Primaries. None had families. No ties to a home or life. But their personality profiles showed they desired such ties, that indeed they sought them. As Jagernauts, they were all psions. She chose only those with the highest ratings, telepaths, seven or more on the scale. They came from across the Imperialate, men and women of many cultures, races, and backgrounds. A wide genetic pool.

"I want to make sure you all understand what being on this team means," she said. "Regardless of what happens on the mission, you won't be coming back. Ever. I can't tell you more at this time, other than to say you will be serving Imperial Skolia. It will be a good life, one your profiles suggest suits you well. But you won't be going home." Quietly she added, "I've no intent to take anyone from a life you value. If you wish to join another drop-down team, there will be no loss of honor. But you must let me know now."

They all stood watching her. No one spoke. They had already made their decisions.

"All right," Soz said. "Let's go."

They moved through the cruiser in formation. Elevators took them "up" spokes to the nonrotating hub that stretched along the cylinder's center like a giant pipe. The hub ended in launching pods at the aft end of the cruiser, where instead of having a second end cap, the cylinder was open to space. The huge thrusters mounted around its rim could provide an immense push, adding a component of gravity to the cruiser that pointed along the rotation axis instead of perpendicular to it.

At the hub, they entered a cavernous bay crowded with drop-down teams, all Jagernauts. Unlike special operations forces of the past, they brought only light packs for gear. Most of what they needed, they already carried within their bodies. It left them better able to carry more weapons, including laser carbines, EM projectile rifles, and missile launchers.

As Soz floated to a weapons rack, she spoke into her comm. "Barzun, the teams are ready to go."

"We're all set here," Barzun said.

"Good." At the weapons rack, Soz took a Jumbler she had already set to her brain patterns.

"Imperator Skolia," Barzun said. "My sensors indicate you are arming yourself with weapons meant for the d-teams."

She strapped on the Jumbler. "You're a hell of a good commander, Chad."

His voice exploded over her comm. "Are you out of your flaming mind? You will NOT go with them!"

Surrounded by her team, she floated to the launching chute and boarded a drop-down shuttle. Even without the psiberweb, her biomech still worked and EO signals still flooded *Roca's Pride.* Being a Triad member had its advantages: she was thoroughly integrated into what remained of the Radiance web. So she monitored Barzun's attempts to evade the blocks she had set up. His people tried everything from emergency shutdowns to short-circuiting the docking bay doors. They tried to deactivate the shuttle nodes and engines. When the launch sequence initiated anyway,

Barzun started swearing, language she had never before heard from the conservative admiral.

Then the shuttle launched and dropped away from the cruiser, headed for the planet.

Althor lay on his back in the sweltering heat. When the door of his cell opened, he sat up, combing his fingers through his hair. But it wasn't the girl with sky eyes and sun hair. He hadn't seen her since the day she had cried in his arms and sworn she loved him. Today eight guards entered, accompanied by a tall man with Highton features.

The Highton regarded Althor. "Do you recognize me?"

Althor tried to remember. "You're one of the palace ministers."

"Which one?"

Althor shook his head.

"Do you know your own name?" the Highton asked.

"Althor."

"That's all? Althor?"

He hesitated. "Prince Althor Izam-Na Valdoria kya Skolia, Fifth Heir to the throne of the Ruby Dynasty, once removed from the line of Pharaoh, born of the Rhon."

"That's it?"

Althor knew there was more, but he couldn't remember. So he said nothing.

The minister considered him. "You're going to have a son, you know."

Althor froze. "What?"

"Cirrus is pregnant."

"Who is Cirrus?"

The man smiled. "The little trill was all over you the last time she was here. Couldn't control herself."

"You mean that beautiful girl?" Althor couldn't believe it. "She's going to have a son? My son?"

"Quite so."

His pleasure was fast replaced by a hollow sensation. "Why? She wouldn't be pregnant unless you wanted her that way."

"She's prime stock, you know. I paid ten million for her."

Althor tensed. "What are you going to do with my son?"

The minister beamed. "With you as the father and Cirrus as the mother, he will be top-quality. Better than top. I may even get more than ten million—ah!"

The Highton stumbled back as Althor lunged at him. Althor's chains brought him up short before he even reached his feet, and he fell back on the cot. Rage hazed his mind. *Provider.* They were going to make his son a provider. His vision went red and he saw only the chains that kept him from killing the Aristo who would enslave his son. Althor fought with a single-minded violence until finally he dragged a ring out of the wall, the one that secured the chain attached to his left ankle.

A needle hit his chest. He ignored it, struggling with his other chains. Then languor spread through his body, draining his strength until he fell onto the cot and sagged against the wall. As his mind went dull, he saw the guards staring at him. The Highton tried to look calm, but nothing could hide the pallor of his face.

"Gods," one of the guards muttered.

Althor watched them, his rage blunted by whatever drug they had given him. Gradually he absorbed what had happened. He had gone berserk. It had never happened before, even in battle. Apparently the past two years of interrogation had affected more than his memories. His higher functions had suffered as well, the shadings of intellect that separated civilized behavior from barbarism. He didn't care. He had to protect his son.

A woman spoke. "I thought you deactivated his hydraulics."

Althor turned to look. A woman stood in the doorway of his cell, a beauty even by Highton standards. He knew he should recognize her, but no memory came, only a sense of disquiet. And pain. He didn't want to remember how he knew her.

"We did deactivate them," the minister answered. He

glanced uneasily at Althor. "It seems he has more reserves than we realized."

"Reprogram him, Vitrex," the woman said. "Now that you're done with him, you can get rid of that speed and strength."

Althor had known they would eventually redesign his biomech so they could use it to control him. If they were done with his interrogation, they no longer needed to worry about erasing data and could proceed with a full reconfiguration of his internal systems. It would take extensive operations, including brain surgery. Even more than the operations, though, he dreaded what he would lose. Having lived his entire adult life with enhancements, he would feel crippled without them.

He finally associated a name with the woman's face. "Empress Viquara."

"My greetings, Althor." Her expression gentled. "Would you like a nicer home than this cell?"

"Yes," he said, which was the truth.

"I'm going to bring you to the palace."

He could guess why. His son wasn't the only one they intended to make a provider. The drugs blunted his revulsion, but the idea still sickened him.

The other Highton, apparently Minister Vitrex, said, "I don't think it's wise to move him yet, not until we're sure he can't go berserk again."

"How long do you need?" she asked.

"We should be able to deliver him this evening."

She nodded. "Very well. Proceed."

"Yes, Your Highness." Vitrex bowed, his fist placed to indicate optimism.

The empress departed with her Razers, leaving four guards with Vitrex. Two had air-syringe rifles, what they must have used to drug Althor. The other two had EM pulse rifles, which would have killed him instantly.

"Are you hungry?" Vitrex asked him.

"No." It struck Althor as a strange question until he saw

one of the guards working on a palmtop. That jogged his memory. They were checking his physiological responses while Vitrex talked to him, to see how he reacted to the drugs.

"Tell me something," Vitrex said. "How did it feel to live without an owner? Did the lack of structure frighten you?"

"No," Althor replied. "Does it frighten you?"

"Why would it frighten me?"

"No more reason exists for me to need an 'owner' than you."

"Do you really believe that?"

"Yes."

"Amazing."

"How about you tell me something?" Althor said.

"You may ask."

An edge came into Althor's voice. "How is it that you people have convinced yourselves the rest of us are less than human? Do you think your wanting it to be true makes it that way?"

"Astonishing," Vitrex said. "Even with half your mind gone, you still sound articulate."

"My mind isn't half-gone."

"No? Perhaps we need to question you more."

Althor tensed. "On the other hand, I can't even remember your name."

"Pity."

He wasn't sure what Vitrex considered a "pity," that his prisoner couldn't remember his name or that he had no excuse to interrogate him anymore.

"Minister Vitrex," one of the guards said. "He's responding normally."

"Very well," Vitrex said. "Bring him."

The guards removed Althor's chains and locked his wrists behind his back. They helped him stand up, but when they let go, his legs gave way and he sat back down on the cot.

Vitrex scowled. "Get him up, Kryxson."

One of the guards unhooked an E-spring from his belt, a

metal truncheon he activated by a switch in its handle. When he motioned at two other guards, they took Althor's arms and stood him up. He tried to stay on his feet, but as soon as they let go, his legs folded and he sat down with a thud on the cot.

Althor looked up at Vitrex. "I can't do it."

Vitrex appraised him with a speculative glance, then gave a slight nod to Kryxson. The guard touched his truncheon to Althor's neck, and a spark jumped from it to his skin. Althor jerked away, clenching his teeth against the shock. He tried to get up again, but his body wouldn't cooperate.

As Kryxson raised the E-spring again, Althor said, "For gods' sake. I'm *trying*."

The other guard was working on his palmtop again. "Minister Vitrex, he could be telling the truth. We may have given him too much of the muscle relaxant."

"I don't like it." Vitrex nodded to Kryxson. "Make sure he's not faking it."

Althor ducked as Kryxson swung the truncheon, but his locked wrists and the drugs in his body slowed him down, and the E-spring caught him square across the back. He gasped, from both the blow and the electric shock. Again he tried to rise and again he fell back on the cot.

Vitrex considered Althor, then glanced at the guard with the palmtop. "Can you counter the relaxant in his body without affecting the sedatives or neural dampers?"

Neural dampers? No wonder he felt groggy. Too much damper and he would walk around in a mental vacuum. It wouldn't mute his empathic projection, though, which was all that mattered to the Aristos.

"I can start with a small dose," the guard said.

"Proceed," Vitrex said.

The guard injected Althor, and as the drug took effect his strength returned. This time when they helped him stand, he felt well enough to stay up. He sat down anyway, pretending to collapse.

Vitrex scowled. "Now what?"

The guard worked on his palmtop. "I'm checking, sir."

Basalt, Althor thought. **Synthesize a chemical to resemble what they're looking for, but that doesn't relax my muscles.** Although he had lost contact with Basalt long ago, the fact that his enhanced strength kicked in when he went berserk suggested the node still functioned, at least in part.

"The antidote isn't working," the guard said. "He has more relaxant in his system now than before."

More? **Basalt!** Althor thought. **Don't overdo it.**

"How can he have more?" Vitrex asked.

The guard hesitated. "I may have given him the wrong drug. The menu choices are right together."

"Did you record what you did?"

"Not for one shot."

Vitrex made an exasperated noise. "Next time record it."

Althor felt the Razer's uncertainty. He wondered if the Hightons realized that in training their taskmakers not to think for themselves, they conditioned them to make errors. Even this Razer, who was part Aristo, hesitated when he should have questioned.

"Try another dose," Vitrex said. "But keep it small."

The Razer administered a shot. After waiting for it to take effect, the guards stood Althor up again. And again Althor let himself fall back on the cot.

The guard checked his palmtop. "The levels are decreasing, sir. Not enough, but we're getting there."

"I don't trust this." Vitrex motioned to Kryxson. "Encourage him to get up."

So Kryxson went to work again. Althor tried to evade the blows, but the Razer worked him over with an expertise that suggested a long practice in beating people with pipes. Althor gritted his teeth—and when they put him on his feet he let himself collapse again.

So it continued, Kryxson alternating "encouragement" with the other guards' standing Althor up. He soon regretted his deception. He kept at it only because he feared even more what would happen if they realized he had feigned the whole thing. Kneeling on the floor where he had fallen the last time, he closed his eyes, trying to dissociate his mind from the blows.

Finally Vitrex said, "Enough, Kryxson."

Relief swept over Althor as Kryxson stopped. He felt the Razer's reluctance to quit. What surprised him wasn't that Kryxson was transcending, but that Vitrex resisted it. A memory toggled: Vitrex had also suppressed his transcendence during Althor's interrogations. It hadn't always worked, but that he tried at all astounded Althor. It had never occurred to him that Hightons might be capable of, even see honor in, quelling their impulses to sadism. That they could deny their nature and yet still chose to indulge it made their cruelty that much worse.

Althor focused on Vitrex, trying to fathom him. He hadn't thought Hightons capable of love, yet Vitrex's thoughts revealed a great depth of affection for Cirrus. It stunned Althor. Having loved Cirrus himself, even if that reaction was medicated into him, he felt driven to protect her. That Vitrex's love translated into images of brutality sickened him.

"I don't think he's faking it," the guard said.

"All right." Vitrex sounded impatient. "Try another dose."

So they gave Althor another shot. This time when they stood him up, he stayed up. He wasn't sure what he had achieved with his ploy, but his strength felt normal.

"Good." Vitrex looked relieved. "Take him to Chemical."

Althor tensed. "Chemical?"

"Showers." Vitrex grimaced. "You need a bath, Ruby prince, and clothes that will please the empress." A smirk played around his mouth. "And other things."

Althor regarded him warily. "What other things?"

Vitrex waved his hand to dismiss the question. Then he paused, and Althor felt his urge to boast. "My wife is very good with such things, you know. Pheromones. Drugs. Inducements, you might say." He gave Althor a malicious stare. "You ought to see what she does for me with Cirrus. Imagine it, the mother of your child on her knees begging me to love her."

The lie of that exuded from Vitrex's mind. Althor gritted his teeth. "Go rot in hell."

When the guards slammed Althor against the wall, his reflexes kicked in and he tried to stop them. Had he succeeded, it would have revealed the deception of his supposed reduced physical capacity. But with four guards pinning him and his hands locked behind his back, even he couldn't do much.

"I should let Kryxson work you over for that," Vitrex commented. "But I feel benevolent today. Besides, that look on your face when I told you about Cirrus was enough." He seemed more amused than anything else. "You know, Althor, when Sharla is done with you, your enthusiasm for the empress will outdo what you feel for Cirrus."

Althor stared at him, wondering how the Highton's neck would feel in his hands. Crack. No more Vitrex.

The minister turned to Kryxson. "Have Sharla contact me when she's done with him. I will be with the Sphinx delegation."

Kryxson bowed. "Yes, sir."

Vitrex strode through the doorway, and four Razers waiting outside fell into formation around him. After the group had swept away, gone from sight, Althor's guards took him out of the cell. They led him along glossy white halls that twisted, turned, and backtracked until he lost all sense of placement. He hoped Basalt could still make maps.

They brought him to a large room tiled on every surface with glassy black squares bordered by white lines that glowed. The guards left him standing there, wearing nothing but his cuffs and collar, his hands still locked. With grating scrapes, nozzles extruded from the walls and drains punctured the floor like inverted kisses. Sudden jets of waters blasted out the nozzles, pummeling him from all sides. He felt like a statue being sandblasted, but it was a relief to be clean.

Finally the water stopped and the nozzles retracted, turtles pulling their heads into their shells. The guards returned with a large towel and clothes and helped him dress. The black leather pants resembled his Jagernaut uniform, except these were skintight, designed to accent his muscular build. When he saw the velvet shirt, he realized the guards would have to unlock his wrists to put it on him.

The neural damper they had given him blunted his analytic capacity. It took no great analysis, however, to see that trying to escape was stupid. Even if he managed it, he would be caught within minutes. But he also knew he would rather walk through hell than be a Highton's pleasure slave.

Basalt, he thought. **I could use some help here.**

No response.

Kryxson took a magnetic key out of his pocket and stepped behind Althor. He lifted Althor's wrists, manipulating his slave cuffs. A tingling ran through Althor's arms as they fell free.

Combat mode toggled on, Basalt thought.

Althor didn't stop to ask how Basalt could respond, after so long a silence. With enhanced speed and strength, he kicked up his leg and rammed his bare foot into the chest of the guard in front of him, at the same time throwing his body sideways into a guard with a pulse rifle. With a crack of breaking ribs, the first man flew over backward. The guard with the rifle fired as he stumbled back a step, and the shots went wild over Althor's head. To Althor the Razers looked as if they were moving in slow motion. He ripped the pulse rifle out of the guard's hands and whirled in a circle, firing the weapon.

Serrated projectiles riddled the Razers. Even protected by the neural damper, Althor reeled with the shock of their dying and almost blacked out. He stared at their bodies crumpled around him on the tiled floor, stunned by the depth of his remorse. They had helped subject him to over two years of brutal interrogations, yet still the killing tore at him.

Althor rubbed his eyes, trying to clear his mind. He limped to the doorway and leaned his forehead against the doorjamb, trying to think. He felt no minds in the vicinity. Where was everyone? He concentrated on Cirrus and caught a distant sense of her. Fear. The intensity of her emotion reached him even across whatever kilometers separated them.

He had no idea where he was, other than in an unnamed ESComm base. All he could remember picking up from Vitrex's mind was that the minister had a mansion in the vicinity, convenient but not too close.

Basalt, he thought. **Show me a map to the Vitrex mansion.**

No response.

He tried a different tack. **If you have an idea how I can find Cirrus, take over my hydraulics and start me walking.**

Nothing.

He started off down the hall. Then, suddenly, his legs moved of their own volition. He turned around and went in the other direction.

31

Cirrus sat at the white lace-draped vanity in her white chair within her white bedroom and fidgeted with her glass of water. Although her pregnancy didn't show yet, she always felt thirsty now. But her joy at having a child had turned into a depression saturated with grief. Vitrex intended to take the baby away from her. She would never see her second son.

She missed Kai, her firstborn, so much it ached like a physical pain. Did he still laugh, climb trees, sing off-key? Was his hair still black? He had been born with yellow hair and blue eyes, like her, but the emperor had altered them to make him look Aristo.

"Ai." Cirrus wiped the tears on her cheeks.

As she stood up, the door opened and four Razers entered, including Xirson. One guard carried a large gold towel and another had a gold box inset with emeralds and sapphires. She flushed, wondering why Vitrex sent people to bathe her when she had already done it herself. She suspected he used it as a reward for his favored Razers.

Xirson came over to her, his normally impassive face relaxing into a smile. "My greetings, Cirrus."

She reddened. "My greetings, Xiri."

He stopped in front of her and picked up an end of the sash that kept her thigh-length robe belted around her waist. When he tugged on the sash, it came undone and her robe fell open. He nudged the garment off her shoulder and it rippled to the ground, where it pooled around her feet in waves of gold Hesterian silk.

"Ai, Cirrus," he murmured.

She kept her eyes averted, unable to look at him.

Xirson took her hand and drew her across the room to an arch in the wall there, a keyhole-shaped doorway bordered by gold mosaic flowers. The bathing room beyond was an octagonal chamber, every one of its surfaces tiled with green and gold fish. An octagonal dais filled most of the small room, with an octagonal pool sunken into it. The life-sized jade statue of a girl stood on the dais, in one corner. Emerald-tinted water arched up from a huge spiral shell that she held and fell sparkling into the pool, like liquid gems.

As Cirrus slid into the pool, Xirson sat on its edge with one booted leg in the water and the other stretched out on the dais. He bathed her gently, lathering her hair and body with scented creams. Then he held her in his lap, sitting with both boots in the water now, murmuring endearments, oblivious that she was dripping all over him.

But Xirson wasn't Althor, the father of her child. No one was like Althor. He reached her at a fundamental level no one else had ever found. It made no difference, though. She would never have any relationship, let alone a husband. Providers were forbidden it.

One of the guards cleared his throat. Xirson sighed, then helped her out of the pool. After she dried off, they returned to the bedroom. For one panicked second, as he led her to the bed, she feared he would go too far with her and anger Vitrex. But he only opened up the jeweled box that another guard had left there.

The vials in the box held a gold powder that glinted with sapphire and diamond grains. The Razers covered her body with it, using soft brushes. She tried rubbing it off, but it stayed, with no creases or flaws, only the excess swirling to the carpet. It was apparently set to her DNA, because it clung only to her skin, not theirs. As the Razers applied it, they ribbed one another about this dangerous assignment they had pulled, powdering a naked woman. It surprised Cirrus as much as it embarrassed her. Except for Xirson, she had never seen any of them smile. She hadn't thought they knew how.

The box also held clothes. The thong for her hips consisted of gold wires, with a gold plate for the triangle between her thighs. The halter was no more than sapphire-inlaid strips of gold that framed her breasts. She didn't see the point. It covered nothing. Xirson put sapphire rings in her nipples, with a gold chain hanging from one to the other. The gauzy mesh didn't show when they put it over her hair, only the jeweled specks on it, glittering like blue and white stars. Xirson activated the nanobots in her hair and they contracted, making the strands curl into huge waves to her hips. Like a cloud.

She would rather have worn a sack. Xirson watched her with an intensity that disconcerted her. Still, she liked him far better than Kryxson, the other top-ranked taskmaker at the estate. Both Razers were educated, rich themselves, loyal to Vitrex, and half Highton. But Cirrus had long ago sensed what no Aristo realized. Despite his Highton genes, Xirson had no trace of the cruelty that drove Aristos to seek providers.

They took her through the mansion to a room with ivory rugs patterned with birds and translucent screens painted with the same design. Vitrex and several other Hightons sat in loungers around a low table, deep in discussion, their holographs and palmtops spread everywhere.

Vitrex glanced at her. "Pour for my guests, pretty cloud."

Cirrus knelt next to him and took a carafe on the table. As she filled the goblet of the Highton to her left, Vitrex and his guests went back to arguing, something about merchant guilds. Vitrex was considering an investment but didn't like the terms they offered.

When she knelt by the next delegate, he placed his hand over his goblet. Startled, she looked up. It was Corbal Xir, the elderly Highton with white hair. She remembered him from the palace auction, the unexpectedly gentle Aristo who had simply wanted affection from her, no transcendence. He smiled now with an enamored look much like the one Xirson had given her. When she blushed, his face gentled and he moved his hand to let her pour.

The next Highton was big. Huge, really, with folds of fat under his chin. Usually Aristos went to the bodysculptors when they gained weight. Cirrus could tell this one irritated Vitrex; like most Aristos, the minister considered ugliness a sign of weak character. Cirrus thought otherwise, though she never dared mention it. She had always liked the homely Xirson far more than Kryxson, though Kryxson molded his face to Highton perfection.

After she poured for the big Highton, he grabbed her wrist. His stale breath wafted in her face. "I should like a polly-berry," he said.

Cirrus glanced at Vitrex. He had told her to pour for his guests, not to feed them. But he was talking with Corbal Xir and would grow angry if she interrupted. Flustered, she took a berry out of a bowl on the table and raised it to the Highton's mouth.

He shook his head, his chins waggling. "From your lips."

She flushed. But Vitrex was still talking. So she held the berry in her lips and tilted up her face, as she had been taught in the Silicate pavilion. Bending his head, the Highton closed his mouth around the berry, sliding one arm around her waist while he fondled her breast with his other hand. As he pulled the fruit into his mouth, he kissed her, his tongue tasting of polly-berry. She struggled not to gag.

A throat suddenly cleared. The Highton released Cirrus and she looked across the table to see Vitrex scowling. Mortified, she grabbed the carafe and poured for the last delegate, then went to kneel by the minister.

As the meeting continued, Vitrex's annoyance increased. Although her presence made the Sphinx delegation more amenable, especially Corbal Xir, they were too savvy to let the presence of a pretty provider cloud their judgment. So in the end, no one got what they wanted.

When everyone was standing up, preparing to leave, Corbal Xir smiled at Xirson. The Razer bowed to him, obviously pleased to see the elderly Highton. His father? Vitrex was angry at everyone, but he hid it until the delegation left. Then he snapped several commands to Xirson and stalked out of the room. Cirrus was relieved to see him go.

Xirson drew her to her feet, but he wouldn't meet her gaze. She tried to pick up what was wrong, but he hid his emotions. The Razers took her back into the mansion, this time to Vitrex's suite. In the bedroom, where almost no sunlight diffused through the heavy curtains, the guards laid her on the shadowed bed, on her back. When they stretched out her limbs and fastened her wrists and ankles to the bed's corner posts, she struggled not to panic.

"I'm sorry," Xirson whispered. "Cirrus—I—I'm sorry."

Her voice shook. "Why, Xiri?"

Another guard cleared his throat and Cirrus felt his anger. They feared Xirson would cause them all trouble by paying too much attention to her. Xirson swore, then went to his post by the wall.

A moment later, Vitrex stalked into the room, bringing his anger with him. He lay down next to her and began touching her body. "They negotiate like old iron ingots," he muttered.

"You know better than they," she said, even though it wasn't true.

"I want to show you something." Propping himself up on his elbow, he unhooked his palmtop from his belt and flipped it open so the screen lay flat on his palm. When he brushed his thumb through one of the tiny holicons glowing above the border of the screen, a larger holo appeared, an unclothed ten-centimeter-tall Cirrus standing on his palmtop. The image faded into a silver network of lines in the shape of her body.

"Those are your nerves," he said.

"Inside me?"

He nodded. "Do you know how your wrist cuffs work?"

"I don't think so."

Vitrex highlighted a group of lines that ended in the wrists of the image. "Your cuffs extend neural threads into your body. Each thread is specific for a certain nerve. When the cuff sends a pulse through the thread, it stimulates whatever nerve the thread touches."

Cirrus stared at him. She understood now, all too well. She had screamed her throat raw from the effect of those threads.

His voice gentled. "Don't worry, love. I won't activate the cuffs."

She almost closed her eyes with relief. "You are most kind." He wasn't kind, he was a monster, but she could hardly tell him that.

"This gold powder is pretty." He rubbed her arm. "It has nanobots in it, you know. Molecules that hook into your skin. That's why it doesn't come off." He watched her face. "The bots also extend neural threads into your body. I can activate them from my palmtop."

As his meaning sank in, panic swept over Cirrus. The powder covered her entire body. "Minister Vitrex, no. Please."

He spoke in a deceptive voice that would have sounded loving had she not recognized its undercurrent of hungry anticipation. "Have you ever heard the Tale of the Fire Prince?" When she shook her head, he said, "The prince descends to the depths of the world. His journey demands more than he thinks he can endure, but in the end he is rewarded for his labors. He ascends to an exaltation he could never have achieved without the trials of his suffering."

"Please," she whispered. "I don't want to be exalted."

"Ah, Cirrus. I'm disappointed in you." He indicated the holicon of a neuron on his palmtop. "This extends the threads into your skin." He flicked his finger through it. "Can you feel that?"

"No." Her voice caught. "Not yet."

He poised his finger over a dragon holicon. In a husky murmur, he said, "This one will stimulate the threads."

A siren suddenly cut through the air, from somewhere far away. Scowling, Vitrex sat up. "What the hell is that?"

Xirson was reading a display on a screen embedded in his wrist gauntlet. "It's Bunker Base, sir."

"Nexus, attend," Vitrex said. "Why the sirens?"

His computer answered, "It's a general raid warning."

Dropping his palmtop on the bed, Vitrex got up and strode to a console by the wall. "Lieutenant Azez, what is going on?"

A voice snapped into the air. "ISC has invaded Platinum—"

Vitrex waited. "Lieutenant?"

"The palace web is down," Nexus said. "Please try later."

Vitrex activated his wrist comm. "Azez? Are you there?"

"Yes, sir. We've lost the house web."

Vitrex headed for the door, motioning the Razers to accompany him while he spoke into his wrist comm. "Azez, get me a line to Bunker and get me details on the ISC invasion."

"Aye, sir." Azez sounded relieved to have orders.

Then Vitrex left the room, leaving Cirrus alone in the gathering shadows.

At first Althor thought the sirens meant his escape had been discovered. Pressing flat against the corridor wall, he reached out with his Kyle senses and touched the minds in a group of soldiers jogging down a nearby hall. None had thoughts about his escape. Instead he caught an impression of an ISC invasion in Platinum Sector. Then their minds faded, as they moved away from him.

He took off at a jog, letting Basalt choose his path. At times it had him hide in recessed doorways or empty rooms, when he wouldn't have thought to do so. He knew he used to understand how it made such decisions, that he used to make far more complex ones every day, as second in command of ISC. That he operated now only on reflexes and biomech left him with a sense of loss too great to quantify.

He used his mind to detect other minds and so avoid running into people, but his efficiency wasn't 100 percent. Once he came face-to-face with an ESComm pilot as the man stepped out of a lift. Before Althor had a chance to think, his combat libraries accessed his hydraulics and his enhanced reflexes kicked in. He grabbed the pilot's uniform and yanked the soldier off balance, then bent over and rolled him across his back. Althor slammed him down on the floor, on his back, smashing his skull and breaking his neck and spine.

The pilot's death convulsion wrenched through Althor's mind and Althor almost threw up. Somehow he hid the body in a storeroom. He started to run again, then ducked into a rest chamber and barely made it to the sink in time. When his convulsive heaving finished, he cleaned his face, wondering if he had always reacted this way to death. He couldn't remember.

As he was leaving the chamber, a soldier came in. Althor snapped his spine. The man's unvoiced scream reverberated in his mind and Althor staggered, reeling from the mental backlash. He realized then that the neural damper had protected him when he shot the Razers, muffling his ability to pick up brain waves. As the damper wore off, his brain became more sensitized.

The soldier's only weapon was a dagger as long as Althor's lower arm, almost a short sword. It hardly ranked as state-of-the-art arms, but he belted it around his waist anyway. He hid the body and took off again, his long legs covering ground.

He heard no alarms. He was supposed to be on his way to the palace, so no one had reason to look for him here. Normally someone would have discovered the bodies by now or detected him running through the base. But none of the consoles he found worked. The web for the entire base was down. In many places the lights were out and he had to use his IR vision. When the sterile halls didn't produce enough heat to register in the IR, he relied on his acoustics, bouncing ultrasonics off the walls.

As he jogged, he planned. If ISC had a force in Platinum Sector, Glory had to be their target. How could they pull off such an invasion? It seemed suicide to Althor. But if they made it to Glory, they would look for him. Locating a person on a planet was straightforward with a good satellite system, but he had no way to predict what would be available if and when ISC arrived. He needed to increase his chances of recovery, but he couldn't think how to do it. He clenched his fist, frustrated by his inability to plan. He knew he used to excel at this, yet now he felt as if he were swinging in the dark.

A thought came to him. Jaibriol Qox. Soz would send people in to get him. Now he had a plan. Go to the palace. Find Qox. First, though, he had to find Cirrus. And his son.

For some reason, Basalt sent him underground. He began to doubt the node's coherence when it directed him to a room crowded with dusty equipment. He slammed his fist against the wall in frustration, then swore, knowing his violence was another sign of his brain damage, like his earlier berserker rage.

When his legs moved again, he almost told Basalt to leave off. But he let it go, to see what happened. He went to a window on the opposite wall, a pane of glass rather than the glassteel used in most of the complex. It smashed easily under the blow from his fist. He felt nothing when blood ran down his arm from the cuts in his hand; his biomech web produced chemicals that muted his ability to register pain. The anesthetic worked far better for cuts than it had during his interrogations, where it had been like trying to stop a flood with a spoon.

The window was just under the ceiling, but outside it was at ground level. He climbed out into the moon dazzled night of the Jaizire Mountains, beneath the radiance of eight icy-pastel moons. A breeze ruffled his hair as he stood up at his full height, the pulse rifle gripped in one fist and his dagger-sword strapped to his waist.

Althor moved around the building, keeping to the shadows. On his left, a bank of lights came on, flickered, and went off. He evaded human sentries by using his empathic senses. That Bunker Base had mainly people monitoring the area now, with almost no artificial systems, gave another indication of the extensive collapse their web had experienced. But if the organized competence he sensed from the sentries was an indication of Bunker as a whole, it wouldn't be long before someone detected his escape, even with the web down.

The building he had just left was one of several embedded in the mountain, big structures gleaming like gunmetal, with cylindrical towers and convoluted pipes. He came around the front and saw mountains sloping away from the installation. On an unlit airfield about fifty meters to his right, two fliers stood in the dark.

He jogged out onto the field. **Basalt, can you guide a flier to Minister Vitrex's estate?**

No answer.

Althor rubbed his chin. A flier did no good if he had no idea where to go. His legs kept moving, though, to the second craft. Inside, it had seats for a pilot and copilot and two passengers. At first he didn't recall how to operate a flier, but when he sat in the pilot's seat the knowledge started to come back. There wasn't room to taxi, so he lifted straight up. That the thrusters made no sound caught him by surprise. Although some ISC fliers had that stealth capability, he hadn't thought ESComm could do it. This flier suggested their technology was more advanced than ISC knew. Either that, or he had forgotten the information.

The comm crackled. "Arrow-Jay-Gee-Three, this is Bunker Base Tower. You aren't cleared for takeoff."

Before Althor could put together a response, a voice said, "I filed a flight plan, Bunker. You tower boys approved it."

Althor blinked. According to the comm in front of him, the flier's computer had just spoken. Holding the craft at a hover above the airfield, he scanned the controls. A flickering button indicated the computer was receiving IR signals from *within* the flier. But how? He was the only possible source. His biomech sockets could handle IR, but they were plugged into his slave cuffs and collar, which controlled them, except for the socket in his lower spine, which Vitrex's people had deactivated.

"We've no record of your flight plan," Bunker said.

The computer answered, sounding for all the world like a frazzled pilot. "I was supposed to take this load of DNA samples to the Vitrex estate."

"Arrow-Jay-Gee-Three, land immediately," Bunker said. "Under no circum—wait. Stand by." After a pause, the traffic controller said, "Sorry. Your authorization is in the system. It's a flaming mess down here. You better get going. You're half an hour behind schedule."

"On my way," the flier said. "Switching out."

With his hand on the stick, Althor watched the comm go dark. The stick moved on its own and the flier veered to the east.

After they had flown for several moments, he said, "That was amazing."

His arm moved again, this time to click his wrist cuff into a panel in the arm of the chair. A "voice" he hadn't heard in over a year thought, Althor?

He swallowed, hit by a sudden intensity of emotion. If

he hadn't known better, he would have thought he was going to shed some tears. **I thought you were broken, Basalt.**

I can't "break," his node answered.

You know what I mean.

I am damaged, it admitted. Right now I'm using the flier's computer to talk to you. I'm also downloading codes from it to help rebuild our interface.

Good. Having Basalt back relieved Althor more than he knew how to say. He had missed the EI. This reunion made him feel as if he were becoming whole again. **How did you get that fake shipment manifest into the Bunker web?**

I didn't. This flier is scheduled and programmed to make that run.

How do you know?

I contacted it, using IR signals.

That answer bothered him, though he couldn't place why. **Where is the real pilot?**

You killed him a few minutes ago.

Oh. Althor shifted in his seat. Had death always bothered him this much? He couldn't ask. He didn't want to know if he had been a calloused killer. **Was that you talking to the tower?**

Yes. I sent a signal through the picoweb in your cuffs to the flier's computer.

Now he caught what had bothered him earlier. **Why can you control my slave restraints now, when you couldn't before?**

I don't really have control now, either, Basalt thought. But the web collapse cut off all IR signals in this area, so I can act in their absence. Even the IR leashes are down. I'm trying to gain control of the picowebs in your cuffs and collar before it all comes back up.

IR leashes?

If an Aristo wants a slave "leashed," he or she registers you with the Bureau of Recovery, which assigns you a signature. If you leave the area flooded by the IR signals specific to your signature, your collar notifies your owner and immobilizes you.

Althor didn't like the sound of it. **Immobilizes how?**

Drugs. Electric shock. Neural threads.

"Gods," he muttered. **Ingenious bastards.**

We do have a problem, Basalt thought. Your leash is set for Bunker and the Qox palaces. If you are outside those regions when the leashes come back, you will be in a lot of trouble.

Can you do anything?

I'm trying to deactivate the leash, but so far it hasn't worked.

Can you fool its trigger instead?

In what sense?

Make it think it's receiving the right signal when it isn't.

Basalt paused. I may be able to do that.

The comm crackled. "Arrow, you are entering Vitrex airspace. Land immediately or we will shoot."

"*Shoot?*" Basalt gave a remarkable impression of a startled pilot. "Hey, I'm just delivering lab supplies to Doctor Azer."

"We're downloading your ID." After a pause, the voice spoke in a friendlier tone. "Arrow-Jay-Gee-Three, go ahead. We're having a hell of a time with our web here."

"Sure." Basalt sounded relieved. "It's wild out there, with the webs crashing."

The traffic controller grunted his agreement. "I can't get any messages out."

"Glad I'm not the only one," Basalt said.

"Eventually they'll get the webs up," the controller said.

"It's taking too damn long," Basalt grumbled. "My wife will steam me in a sewer."

Althor stared at the comm. What the hell was Basalt doing, making small talk with a Eubian air traffic controller?

The controller chuckled. "If she's anywhere on this continent she has the same problem."

"She's not," Basalt said. "She's on duty in Kuraysia, in Rakajan Sector."

"I can probably link you through to her."

Basalt perked up. "Hey. Thanks."

After a pause, the controller said, "Skolia be damned, all the Kuraysia connections are gone too."

Skolia be damned? Althor scowled. **What kind of oath is that?**

"It's a mess," Basalt told the controller.

"People can survive without the web," the controller said.

"I suppose." Basalt sounded skeptical. "Seems primitive to me. I can't believe an entire planetary web could go this way."

"We don't know that the whole planet is down."

"If both Kuraysia and this continent are, there isn't much else left." Basalt paused. "Anyone know why the flaming thing collapsed?"

"I haven't heard." The operator's voice became clipped. "Arrow-Jay-Gee-Three, I've another craft coming in and we don't have any monitors on traffic control right now. Out."

"Out." Basalt cut the connection.

Gods, Althor thought. **How could the web of an entire planet collapse?**

I don't know. But it helps us. And right now we need a great deal of help.

Elaborate.

You can't land this flier at the Vitrex airfield. It's obvious you aren't the true pilot.

Why?

You don't match his ID. You also have gold skin, the slave restraints of a war prisoner, and no clothes except sexually suggestive black leather pants. You look like a cross between a Jagernaut and a sex toy.

Althor blinked at the description. **Any uniforms on board?**

No. But it doesn't matter. The cuffs and collar will still give you away.

He considered. **With no web, the air controllers have to depend on more primitive systems. Radar. Even visual sightings. If I come in low enough, maybe I can evade detection.**

It's possible. Basalt paused. I calculate a 14 to 85 percent probability of success.

Dryly Althor thought, **That's precise.**

Too many variables exist to narrow the range.

Does the flier's computer have—what do you call it? A navigation macro?

Do you mean an automatic pilot?

No. It's a— Althor searched for words to describe what had once been second nature to him. **A way to make the flier skim just above the terrain. We feed the computer a map of the area and it picks the best route. As pilot, I can compensate for unexpected changes in terrain.**

A stealth function matching this description is available. I've uploaded your specifications to it.

The ship's computer spoke. "What is your destination?"

"The estate of Izar Vitrex," Althor said. "I need a site close to the house and big enough hide this craft."

The screen projected a holo of a mansion in front of Althor. A forest bordered it on the east, climbing into the mountains. Meadows stretched on the other three sides, rising to mountains in the north and west and sloping down toward the flatlands in the south.

"It looks like the forest is our best bet," Althor said.

Basalt sent a thought to the flier's computer. Magnify region and highlight possible hide sites.

The forest expanded to fill the holomap. Two hide sites glowed in red on it. One, about a kilometer from the mansion, was a sunken crevice with rock walls. The second was only twenty meters from the mansion, a clearing with no real protection from monitors.

I recommend the crevice, Basalt said.

A kilometer is too far, Althor thought.

With your speed, you can cover it in less than two minutes.

Althor's fist clenched on his knee. He no longer even knew his own capabilities. **Isn't that assuming level ground? And no load?**

Yes. Load wouldn't be much problem, given your strength. But your weight does slow you down, particularly in these areas where the terrain is so uneven.

I don't know Cirrus's condition. He concentrated on the sense of her in his mind. **All I can tell is that she's scared.**

If she's frightened, she's probably conscious.

That doesn't mean she can run.

If you choose the closer site, you risk detection.

Be realistic, Althor thought. **What chance do I have of getting in, getting Cirrus, and getting out without detection?**

Not high, Basalt admitted.

We go with the closer site.

I've input the data. The map disappeared, replaced by a map of the ground below the craft. A ghost schematic overlaid it, giving a real-time view of the terrain. The two maps were almost identical, differing mainly in the size of plants.

Althor watched the ground pass underneath them. **Basalt.**

Yes?

I may have to make more kills at the mansion.

This is an accurate statement.

An outcropping jumped into view on the real-time map that wasn't on the older map. Althor pulled on the stick and the flier angled up to clear the rocks.

After a moment, he thought, **Have I always been troubled by death?**

Yes.

Althor wasn't sure why it relieved him to know he didn't like to kill. But it did.

He altered course, going farther south as they passed the mansion. Although it added several minutes to their flight, time they couldn't really afford, it also allowed them to go lower, using the mountain itself to shield the flier.

They settled into the clearing in a silent whirl of leaves. The exhaust billowed, but nothing burned, rumbled, shrieked, or otherwise drew attention. When he opened the hatch, he saw the lights of the mansion glowing through the trees.

Basalt? he thought.

I'm receiving you.

Relief flowed over him. Basalt must have made good use of the codes it had pirated from the flier; his interface with the node remained operational even without the flier's computer. **Are you getting anything from the house? Web signals?**

Some IR. Most of the mansion's web is off-line.

IR? Althor tensed. **What about the leashes?**

None so far. I've set your collar to "see" the correct leash no matter where you are, but we won't know if it works until the leashes come back on-line.

Althor left the flier and headed through the woods, moving like a silent shadow. He didn't recall learning how to walk without making twigs or leaves crackle, but his body knew what his conscious mind forgot. He paused at the edge of the forest, then sprinted to the house, a graceful structure made from wood, a far more extravagant building material than the usual synthetics.

Extending his awareness, he picked up many minds. Most were slaves, but a few had that sense of *cavity* he associated with Aristos, an emptiness that made his skin crawl.

Then he found Cirrus. This close, the intensity of her fear wrenched at him. What had Vitrex done to so terrorize her? Althor slipped through shadows, picking his way around bushes. When the intensity of her emotions increased, he kept moving in that direction; when it decreased, he went the other way.

He ended up under a balcony. The wall offered neither an entrance nor any toeholds to climb on. He started toward the nearby corner of the house, then froze when he heard voices. Raising the pulse rifle at his side, he extended his awareness.

"... DNA shipment from Bunker," a man around the corner said. "The flier dropped off scan, but we don't know if it crashed."

"I don't like it," another man said. "I want extra guards on Minister Vitrex and the Sphinx delegation, and more people searching the grounds."

Althor almost snorted. **I'm not after Hightons.**

That you want his provider works to our advantage, Basalt thought. His police are unlikely to think of guarding a slave.

Althor tried to keep his senses extended, but his mind was tiring. His brain damage made it harder to use his Kyle senses, and the Aristo-like minds of the Razers were sandpaper against his. He turned and headed back the way he had come, searching for a less dangerous entrance.

Then he paused.

With enhanced speed, Althor whirled around to see a Razer standing at the corner of the house, raising a gun. Althor fired and the projectiles from his gun hit the Razer with such force, the man flew back several meters before dropping to the lawn. Althor was already running. Gritting his teeth against the mental backlash from the first Razer's death, he came around the corner of the house and fired again, focused on the second Razer standing there. His shot threw the guard against the crystal doors behind the patio, and they shattered, shards flying everywhere like an explosion of broken ice.

The shock of the man's death hammered at Althor as he ran through the broken doors, into the house. His enhanced ears registered sounds and his hydraulics threw him to the side just as the door across the room burst open. He hit the ground and rolled, shooting the Razers as they ran into the room. They had already fired, the projectiles from their guns hissing through the air where he had been an instant earlier. He finished his roll and was back on his feet, coming at the door from an angle now.

Four bodies lay on the floor. Althor ran past them and out into a broad corridor. At the end it widened into a foyer where a staircase swept up to the second story. He took the stairs three at a time. At the top, he found three antique-style doors. The first opened into a library and the second into a sitting room. Although starlight poured through the glass doors of the balcony, he didn't see Cirrus. Search the room or check the third door? He didn't have time to do both.

Althor ran to the third door. It opened into a foyer that he crossed in two steps. The next door refused to budge, so he threw his weight into it again and again, until finally it crashed open.

Cirrus's terror hit him like a tidal wave. The bedroom was dark, but his IR vision showed her bound spread-eagled to a bed. As he ran to her, her voice came out in a ragged sob. *"Who's there?"*

"It's Althor." He stopped at the bed, gulping in air, and freed her as fast as he could, at the same time blending his mind with hers. Fear swamped her thoughts. She had been lying here for hours with her limbs stretched tight, long enough that she probably couldn't walk right away.

As Althor helped her stand up, Basalt thought, Take the palmtop. Carefully. Don't activate any icon on it.

Holding Cirrus around the waist, he grabbed the palmtop and hooked it to his belt. Then he lifted Cirrus, sliding one arm under her knees and the other behind her back. When she put her arms around his neck, he felt better, competent after all, despite his brain damage.

As he strode to the windows, his augmented hearing caught a quiet footfall. Moving with blurred speed, he let Cirrus's feet drop to the floor, holding her at the waist as he simultaneously spun around, fired at the door, and lunged to the side. His IR vision picked out four Razers. He caught three in his sweep, but then his pulse rifle quit, out of ammunition. His lunge just barely managed to evade the blast from the Razer's rifle. Althor hurtled his rifle at him with enhanced force as projectiles from the Razer's rifle stabbed the wall behind him. The narrow snout of Althor's gun rammed into the guard's head, and his death scream reverberated in Althor's mind.

With a groan, Althor lurched backward. He knew ways existed to protect himself from empathic backlash during combat, but he remembered none of them. Fighting his nausea, he hefted Cirrus into his arms and stumbled to the window.

A needle-gun hissed behind him. His shocked systems didn't respond fast enough and the needle buried itself in his back. A relaxant immediately spread to his muscles. As his grip on Cirrus slipped, she slid into a crumpled heap on the floor. Swaying, Althor sank to his knees next to her.

Engaging hydraulics, Basalt thought. Play dead.

Althor forced himself to hold still. He wanted to recoil from what he felt in the doorway, that mental *cavity* that sought to consume him, to pull his mind into its depths and suck him dry. Vitrex strode across the room with the surety of IR-enhanced sight. The minister fired again, pumping more drugs into Althor, to make sure he was immobilized. Basalt sent commands to the meds in Althor's blood and they made him appear unconscious, slumped forward, his head hanging down.

After waiting yet another moment, to make doubly sure Althor was incapacitated, Vitrex knelt next to him. "Gods," he muttered. "How did you get out of Bunker?"

Althor's hand shot up and clamped around Vitrex's neck. For one instant Vitrex froze. Had Althor been in top condition, that hesitation would have finished the minister. But Althor's hydraulics didn't kick in fast enough. Vitrex clawed at his hand, and Althor's grip slipped as Basalt and the relaxant vied for control in his body. With a choked sound, the minister yanked his head free.

In Althor's IR vision, Vitrex glowed red, like a fire demon. Althor's sense of time slowed. The minister's hand went to the pulse gun at his hip and Althor reached for his dagger. In slow motion, Vitrex grasped his gun while Althor's hand closed around the hilt of his weapon. As

Althor drew the short sword, Vitrex drew the gun. Althor gritted his teeth, struggling to speed his hydraulic-driven motion. He had farther to go than Vitrex, having to thrust forward with the dagger where Vitrex needed only to fire. If he couldn't go faster, he would be dead before his blade found its target.

Despite their enhanced speed, every motion seemed to take ages. Vitrex raised the gun and Althor brought his dagger level with his chest. When Vitrex aimed, Althor could almost feel the projectiles tear through his body. He thrust forward with the dagger, watching its tip cross the chasm that separated him from the Highton.

As Vitrex's thumb descended on the firing stud, Althor's blade touched the minister's chest. Falling forward with the momentum of his thrust, Althor plunged his dagger into Vitrex's heart. His body plowed into the minister, knocking them to the side while Vitrex fired. With an eerie flare of IR light, projectiles exploded out from the gun and a honed edge sliced Althor's arm.

The shock of pain snapped Althor's time sense to normal. He sprawled across Vitrex, his knife embedded to the hilt in the Highton's chest. Vitrex died, not in trauma or horror—but with an abiding confusion, unable to believe a slave had ended his life.

Althor lurched to his feet. According to Basalt, the fight had taken only seconds and less than two minutes had passed since he had landed the flier. With the smooth motions of hydraulic-driven responses, he gathered Cirrus up into his arms.

Her voice shook. "Who is that?"

"Althor." He went to the curtains and pushed them aside. The window had no latch, so he smashed it with his fist, running his cuff around the jagged edges to grind them smooth. Wind rushed into the room and threw Cirrus's hair around their bodies.

The click of a cocked projectile rifle sounded behind them.

"Turn around," a voice said in Highton.

Althor froze. Then he turned slowly. A few meters away, a man held a rifle trained on Althor. He had the face of a Highton and uniform of a Razer, yet despite his obvious Aristo heritage, his mind had no sense of a cavity. He looked Highton, but he had a normal human mind.

He spoke with a gentleness that stunned Althor, until he realized it wasn't directed at him. "Cirrus?" the man asked. "Is this really what you want?"

"Ai, Xirson," Cirrus murmured. "Let me go. Please. I would rather die than keep providing for Hightons."

Xirson swallowed. Then he jerked his gun at Althor and spoke in a hard voice. "You have sixty seconds. Then I 'discover' what happened here."

Althor nodded. He turned to the window and spoke to Cirrus in a low voice, praying the love-struck Razer didn't hear. "I have to drop you out the window. I'm sorry. The bushes below will break your fall." Then he hefted her over the sill.

She made almost no sound, only a choked gasp, before her body hit the bushes. He hauled himself up on the sill and jumped after her. He landed in spiky foliage that tore the unprotected skin of his upper body. Cirrus wasn't moving, so he picked her up and ran for the forest. Shouts came from the house and someone gave an order to fire. His back itched as he anticipated death by laser fire, pulse projectile, who knew what. Instead another voice cursed, damning the failed web.

Then he was among the trees, then at the flier. As he climbed inside, Basalt thought, You can't take Cirrus.

What? Why not? Althor fastened her into the copilot's seat, then slid into the pilot's seat.

The IR leashes are up and she's tied to this estate. Right now every single grain of dust on her body has threads extended into her skin. Take her out of range and it will set off a massive neural shock throughout her entire body that I can't stop.

Flaming bloody hell. Protect her! Althor started the engine. **Do for her what you're doing for me.**

I'm trying. But I have less connection to her systems.

If we don't leave now, they'll catch us.

Give me twenty seconds.

We don't HAVE twenty seconds. Althor's mind raced. Any moment the flier would explode—

Done! Basalt thought. GO.

As the flier leapt into the air, two laser beams crossed below it. Leaves on the ground ignited and trees around the clearing caught fire. When Althor kicked the thrust even higher, acceleration slammed him into his seat. The instant they cleared the woods, he dropped the flier low to the ground and programmed a new destination into the autopilot. Within seconds they were skimming through the mountains, dark and hidden, a stealth hawk running in silence.

Finally he turned to Cirrus. For the first time this night he got a good look at her. She gleamed, her skin a gold sheen dusted with tiny gems, her thigh-length hair spread everywhere in a luminous sparkling cloud, her spectacular body glittering with jewels and little else. He swallowed, absorbing the golden vision. *Beautiful* hardly began to describe her. How in any ten hells of the Vanished Seas could Vitrex have wanted to *hurt* her?

Your pulse and blood pressure are too high, Basalt thought.

Never mind. How is Cirrus?

I deactivated the neural threads.

Cirrus stirred. She opened her eyes and looked at him. No recognition showed either on her face or in her mind. No reaction. Nothing.

Basalt! What's wrong with her!

Calm down, Basalt thought.

I am calm. Answer the damn question.

She's stunned. It is a logical reaction given she has just been hauled around by people she can't see, shot at, and tossed out a window. I suggest you comfort her.

Oh. Yes. Of course. Althor flushed. It had been decades since he had felt this self-conscious around a lover.

"Cirrus?" he asked. "Are you all right?"

Her emotions stirred, fear bubbling to the surface. "He cut your arm."

Startled, Althor looked down. The projectile from Vitrex's rifle had sliced his biceps. He couldn't even feel the wound. Yet. He had taken worse, though. "I can patch it up with the flier's med supplies. It'll be fine."

"He was there."

"He?"

"Minister Vitrex. I heard him." She sounded calm, but terror simmered in her thoughts. "The dragon."

When Althor picked up from her mind what she meant by *dragon,* he nearly gagged. Every time he thought he had the measure of the Hightons, they astonished him anew with their capacity for brutality.

"Vitrex can't hurt you now," he said. "He's dead."

"Are you sure?"

"Yes. Positive."

Grim satisfaction flickered on her face. Then she hesitated. "Who do I belong to now? You?"

That caught him off guard. "Cirrus, listen. No one owns you. *You* own you." She smelled so good it was fuzzing up his brain. All he could think was how much he wanted to hold her. "But I, uh, I would like—will you stay with me? If you want."

"Stay with you?"

"Yes." He knew they had little chance of escape, but faced with this spectacular woman, the mother of his child, he didn't want to admit it. "We can take care of our son together."

Her smile dawned like a sun. "I would like that."

"Good."

"But where are we going?"

"To the palace." He took a breath. "To find the emperor."

32

The image of Admiral Barzun on the holoscreen was the only light in the shuttle. Soz was aware of the d-team around and behind her, silent in their berths.

"That you came on Asteroid—this made sense to me," Barzun said. "Your presence on *Roca's Pride* carried more risk, but it still made sense. You have unique capabilities. Without you there, holding the net when it collapsed, I doubt we would have made it this far. But a drop-down?" He shook his head. "To risk the Imperator in such a manner is neither acceptable nor necessary."

She spoke in a low voice. "Chad, why do you think the web collapsed?"

"ESComm got the Lock and tried to use it."

"They couldn't crash the web with that."

"Then what did?"

"It's me," Soz said. "We talk as if the web is a mesh in a sea, but in some ways it's more like a room. The Triad holds up the walls, and the Assembly Key and I are trying to stand in the same place. We can't do it." She shook her head. "I don't know what drove the final collapse, but if we bring it up again, it's going to kill either Dehya or myself."

He watched her uneasily. "It was my understanding that no way exists to extract a Key from the Triad."

"When the web is up, no. It has too many links into our brains. Ripping them out would kill us."

"We can find a solution," he said. "It isn't enough reason for you to risk your life this way."

"I have other reasons."

"What?"

"I can't say."

Barzun leaned forward. "Then I will say for you. You think you have the best chance of locating your brother. You consider it worth risking your death, particularly since you think you're going to die anyway. It's either that or cause the Pharaoh's death, right? You don't want to repeat Kurj Skolia's history. But you want revenge for his death. You want Jaibriol Qox dead. Well, I have news for you. Those aren't good enough reasons." He made a frustrated noise, as if he were trying to reach her and kept hitting a wall. "We can solve this thing with the Triad."

Although she couldn't deny his summation had validity, the truth was far more complex. But she would let all Skolia believe as he believed, that she went to rescue one brother and avenge the other. It fit with the legends of the Ruby Dynasty, tales of atavistic warrior queens who marauded across the stars. It made no difference that she led a modern, egalitarian military rather than an ancient army of female warriors who owned their men and subjugated worlds. Reality would have little effect on the legends that grew around her final acts as Imperator. Those who knew her better, like Naaj Majda and Dayamar Stone, would question that "truth," comparing it to the pragmatic officer of their experience. But their questions would go unanswered.

"Chad." She watched him from the dark. "Don't fight me."

"I have to. Skolia needs you alive."

She snorted. "Skolia doesn't need more warriors. We need diplomats. People to stand up and say, 'Let's make peace.' "

"We tried that. Didn't work."

"I have to go now." Softly she said, "Give my regards to my family. Tell them I thought of them."

"Soz, come back."

"I can't. Out." Then she closed the link.

She felt the d-team around her, felt their questions. But no one spoke. They knew better than to ask questions. As long as the risk of capture existed, she had no intention of going into more detail than what they needed to complete this mission.

They landed at night, a few kilometers from the palace. Sections of the ethereal residence were in flames, from surgical strikes by the ships in orbit or the Jags that had come down to harry the ground forces. ISC wasn't trying to destroy the palace, only cripple its defenses. The palace was returning fire, but without web control neither side was having much success fighting off the other.

After landing on a hill behind a bank of tall bushes, they disembarked and moved into the woods at their right. Each Jagernaut called up a tactical map produced by *Roca's Pride.* Had the web still been up, the map would have been continually updating. But even without that, it was still only a few minutes old.

Soz's biomech web superimposed the map over the terrain like a ghost. Her IR vision showed the area in fiery hues, letting her match landmarks with psicons on the map. A compass psicon in one corner of her mindscape verified their direction, and she also carried a compass in her gauntlet, should the mindscape fail.

The woods sloped down to the palace, with rocky ground in front of them and a drop-off to the river on their right. Soz stepped into a hole, grimacing as her ankle twisted. She extricated herself and kept going, stepping over roots. Vines brushed her face and caught on her rifle. She had no doubt the woods looked charming, but they were a pain to walk through.

The d-team moved as a unit. This close together, with their Kyle abilities augmented by neural implants, they formed a psiberlink, twenty-one nodes in all.

Wait, Soz thought.

The team stopped. A security line cut through the woods ahead, highlighted in red on her map. From orbit it had been hard to determine details, but here they could get more. **Caser, I need your help.**

On my way.

Her mindscape showed a man-shaped icon walking through the woods. As it reached the icon marking her position, the real Caser came up next to her. An expert in both intelligence and security, he was an ace at outfoxing defensive systems.

The line is about 500 centimeters north, Soz thought.

I'm getting a fix on it. Caser probed the line with various signals, using routines he had programmed into himself, drawing on years of experience and his natural aptitude. Then he laid a red line over the map's curve, one closer to their position. *It's a sensor and spike biter. The sensor would be sending data to palace security if the web was up. This type usually monitors a cylindrical area about ten centimeters in diameter around the line and also in a vertical plane that extends out of the ground.* He highlighted the geometry on the map.

What about the spike biters? Soz asked.

Primitive but lethal. He grimaced. *If you cross the line and you aren't broadcasting the correct IR codes, spikes shoot up. You die by impalement.*

Can you figure out the IR codes?

This is a well-secured system. It could take an hour.

Too long. Soz considered the curve. **How accurate do you think your fix is? Enough to risk a jump?**

I'd say yes. About 60 to 80 percent accuracy.

Soz directed her thought to the listening d-team. **The spikes have to come through a meter of ground. That gives us time to jump if we use hydraulics. Make your leap long, but don't give up speed for distance. Have your nodes calculate a trajectory and apply it to your hydraulics.** She paused. **Ready?**

Yes. The response came from twenty minds.

All right. Go.

They started running from several hundred meters back and leapt with hydraulic-enhanced grace when they reached the line. Spikes shot out of the ground, shearing up plumes of soil. One missed a Jagernaut by less than two centimeters.

Backing up, Soz released control to her hydraulics. She took off and ran forward, then jumped the line, her legs stretching out in an airborne split. A spike ripped through her sweater. Then she was on the other side, landing with bent legs to cushion the impact. Despite Caser's mental barriers, she "heard" him swear at himself for not making a more accurate estimate of the line's position.

She sent him a mental grin. **Keeps us alert.**

Caser gave her a dry smile. *Aye, that it does.*

Within minutes they came on another line. This one had already been triggered, the soil around it churned and torn, with spikes everywhere. And bodies. Both ESComm and ISC soldiers had been caught in the carnage. Soz swallowed, wishing they had time to bury their dead. Even after so many decades, she had never grown inured to the killing.

Increase kylatine production, she thought. **Level four.**

Done, her node thought. With kylatine damping their psionic reception, Jagernauts had a better chance of surviving combat. Turning empaths and telepaths into weapons had been condemned by many among the Allieds and Imperialate, even by critics within ISC. It was no coincidence Jagernauts had the highest suicide rate among all ISC personnel. But despite the price she paid in combat for her Kyle-enhanced abilities, Soz would never have given them up. They had saved her life too many times, and more than that, they kept her human in the dehumanizing force of war.

They reached the edge of the forest, which came closer here to the palace than anywhere else. According to the map, 162 meters separated them from the closest section of the palace, visible now, a patio bordered by fluted columns and topped by a dome.

She sent a thought through the link. **Remember: I want Qox alive. Understood?**

Twenty responses came back. ***Yes.***

All right. Go.

They ran to the palace and gathered under the dome. Soz was picking up other minds now, flickers all around them. Several resolved into people running in their direction. Her team melted into the shadows just before six ESComm soldiers jogged across the patio and disappeared into the night.

Soz sent a private message to her node. **Halt kylatine production.**

Recommend you continue, her node thought.

I need full probe ability.

Halted.

As the kylatine decreased, her awareness spread into the palace, searching. She found other psions, probably providers, but no trace of Jaibriol or Althor.

Imperator Skolia, I'm picking up a pulse cannon. That came from Jinn Opdaughter, a weapons expert as well as a parachuter with the Blackstars. She highlighted the cannon's position on the map. *If we split up, my people can take it out.*

Go, Soz thought.

Jinn and her subunit of nine Jagernauts crossed the patio like shadows.

Still monitoring the area, Soz detected an ESComm unit moving in from the south. **Evade,** she thought.

Her ten Jagernauts melted off the patio, headed for a preset destination. They easily found the crystal doors that opened onto a dining hall within the palace. Inside, diamond chandeliers and lacquered vases gleamed in the dark.

Caser? Soz asked. **What's in there?**

Lasers, he answered. *Keyed to brain waves. If ours deviate from the right signature, we're fried.*

Can we use decoys to map the lasers?

Won't work, Caser thought. *They track on their target.*

Brain waves vary, Soz thought. **The detectors can't be too specific, or they would kill people they're meant to protect.**

True, Caser thought. *But they're specific enough to know we don't belong.*

Imperator Skolia? That came from Cy Merzon, one of the younger Jagernauts. *May I make a suggestion?*

Go ahead, Soz thought.

Have our nanomeds damp our mental processes while our nodes broadcast signals. It might mask our brains, make us look like machines. Cy paused. *I volunteer to try it.*

Soz considered the idea. **All right. Go. Good luck.**

Cy stood still while the dampers did their work. Her face blanked and she walked into the palace with the hydraulic-driven grace of a machine. As she crossed the dining room, the rest of the d-team waited, tense and silent. When she reached the far side of the room, a silent cheer went through the psiberlink.

Caser, is she safe over there? Soz asked.

As far as I can tell, yes, he answered.

Good. Everyone go. Soz set up the commands for her node to take her across the room after damping her neural processes . . .

She came to on the other side of the dining room, right in front of Cy. The Jagernaut grinned and saluted her. Soz smiled, then turned to watch the rest of the team. Most were over now. Caser stepped into the safe area, and then only Secondary Matolinique was crossing the dining room.

Soz didn't know if Matolinique's node miscalculated or if the room's defense node finally registered what was going on. Whatever the reason, lasers suddenly crisscrossed the room, intersecting at Matolinique's body.

The Jagernaut died instantly. Not only was Soz connected to Matolinique through the d-team psiberlink, but she also had her Kyle senses at full expansion. She almost screamed with the backlash. Several of her team stumbled back and another moaned, not an audible sound, but in the psiberlink.

Soz swallowed, knowing time to mourn would have to come later. She hated that they had to leave the body.

From the dining room they entered a white diamond corridor, with ceiling lamps made from carnelian, ruby, and onyx. They jogged down the sparkling hall, surrounded by its deceptive beauty as they penetrated the palace.

Eight waroids ran with Jaibriol and Viquara through the tunnels below the palace, headed for the underground magrail that would take them to safety. Viquara glanced at her son. No emotion showed on his face and he refused to look at her.

At least he had stopped fighting his two guards, armored waroids who so far outmassed and outmaneuvered him that his resistance had been absurd. They ran on either side of him now, each gripping one of his upper arms, forcing him to run between them. Neither had hesitated when the dowager empress and Quaelen ordered them to escort Jaibriol to safety. That Jaibriol had resisted with uncharacteristic violence made no difference; he was their emperor and it was their duty to protect him—even if he didn't want it.

Viquara wondered if Quaelen had reached a magrail yet. They had split up to decrease the chance that all three of them would be killed or captured. If all went well, they would meet at Safeguard, a buried ESComm base high in the mountains.

They were a mere hundred meters from the rail station when the explosion hit. Viquara wasn't sure if a bomb or beam drilled into the ground, but the result was the same. The blast threw them back and part of the tunnel imploded, showering the area with debris. Had the corridor not been designed to withstand such attacks, all of it would have collapsed and buried them.

As it was, the debris claimed four waroids, leaving only Jaibriol's guards and two more. Even as Viquara scrambled to her feet, another explosion vibrated the walls. The mobile waroids tried to contact the buried soldiers, but a fast check by their linked communication systems showed the others hadn't survived.

When yet another blast shook the area, they took off, running back the way they had come. Viquara silently cursed the web breakdown that had delayed warning of the ISC approach. But would it have mattered? The advantage of an intact web might well have gone to ISC rather than Glory.

The waroid on her right grabbed her arm and swung her into a cross tunnel. She recognized it: this way led to another rail station, an alternate escape route. They came around a corner—and skidded to a stop. The tunnel ahead had collapsed, debris still falling from the ceiling.

They whirled around and retraced their steps. Jaibriol kept the grueling pace, forced to it by the waroids, but Viquara was beginning to lag. The waroid on her left suddenly put his arm around her waist and lifted her against his side, carrying her with her feet half a meter off the ground. Disconcerted, she put her arms around his "neck" and hung on. She saw lights flashing on his face screen and knew he was trying to contact palace operations.

An explosion came from behind, throwing them forward. As Viquara hit the floor, she felt weight press down on her. But the waroid held himself up enough to keep from crushing her, as debris thundered down all around them.

The thunder lessened and then stopped. Viquara struggled out from under the metal giant. He had locked his armor to make his arms remain straight, creating a protective shelter that stayed up despite the chunks of debris piled on him. But the explosion had claimed its price. A panel on his wrist gauntlet flashed: *Inactive.* Dead.

She set her hand on his armored shoulder. "Thank you." Had he not sheltered her, she too would be dead.

Jaibriol was pulling himself out from under an arch formed by his two bodyguards. She didn't see the fourth guard, but a gauntleted hand extended out from under a mass of rubble. The *inactive* symbol glowed dully on the armor of all three waroids. Even armored fortresses couldn't survive tons of casecrete.

Jaibriol stared at the guards with a stunned mixture of gratitude and hatred. Then he climbed to his feet and limped along the hall. Viquara took a laser carbine from a fallen guard and followed him.

They stumbled through the clogged tunnel, clambering over mounds of debris. When she caught up with Jaibriol, she said, "We must get you to safety."

"Why?" He pushed his hand through his hair, loosing a shower of casecrete dust. "What is it you want from me?"

"To live, my son."

Bitterly he said, "All my life you made me beg for your love with your silences and distance. Now you want me safe and well. Why? Because without me you lose the throne?"

His undisguised emotion and blunt words unsettled her. No innuendo for Jaibriol; he broke every rule. What did she feel? He was a slave. Yet he was also the emperor. Most and least, Highton and slave, son and not-son.

"I don't know," she admitted. "It is wrong for me to treat you like a Highton, as if you were human."

He stared at her, disbelief and anger warring with grief on his face. "Do you know how it feels to hear your own mother say that? But I forget. You aren't my mother, not in the true Highton sense." Pain edged his voice. "None of that matters, though, does it? You are the only mother I have now."

Viquara felt as if she were breaking inside. "You weaken me."

"The worst of it is that I do love you." He spoke as if the words were broken glass, each scarring him as it came out. "Gods know why. Now that I know what a true family is, you would think I would no longer care. But the feelings you have as a child—they never leave."

True family. *True family.* Like a dragon, Viquara's anger raised its head. "She's come for you, hasn't she?"

"Who?"

"Imperator Skolia."

"She's come to avenge her brother."

"No, she hasn't." The anger breathed into her heart, burning with its pain. "She's come for you. The father of her children."

"She's not my mistress. I told you that under every truth serum you and Quaelen pumped into me."

She gave a bitter laugh. "I never saw even when it stared me right in the face. We asked the wrong question. You *married* her. You married that contaminated provider. The Skolian Imperator is also Empress of Eube."

In a dull voice Jaibriol said, "Tell me you hate me, Mother. Tell me the truth. Then I can stop caring."

"I can't."

"Can't what? Tell me the truth?"

She swallowed. "Can't tell you I hate you. Gods forgive me, but I can't." Her universe was disintegrating. Imperator as Empress. The abomination was beyond her capacity to endure.

They finally found an intact staircase. As they climbed it, Viquara heard sounds of battle and tightened her hand around the laser. But all she could feel was the abiding horror of knowing that her position, her throne, her son, her power—all had been taken by an Imperator Empress.

The stairs exited at ground level, in the ruins of a garden that looked like a giant animal had torn it to pieces. The lamps were shattered, but fires lit the area, as well as spotlights from aircraft overhead, Jags and Solos trying to engage each other without destroying the palace. An explosion shattered a nearby statue, spraying chunks into the air, and the roar of battle surrounded them.

Viquara pointed to a nearby wing, the one that housed the emperor's private suite. She had no doubt it was more than coincidence that it remained in such good condition. They ran to a stairwell in it and climbed until they came out on a balcony. To their right, night-shrouded hills rolled away to the woods; to their left, wings of the palace smoldered or roared in flame, interspersed with blasted gardens. In front of them, a quadrangle separated them from another wing.

Jaibriol froze, staring across the quad. A bomblet hit a nearby roof and sprayed out shattered tiles, showering them with dust and debris.

"This is madness." Viquara drew him back, against the wall, under an overhang. They couldn't go down the stairs now; she had caught sight of ISC soldiers below. "I hope Kryx made it to Safeguard."

"I doubt it." Jaibriol continued to stare at the wing across from them. "The ISC strikes are too thorough."

"Why are you looking at over there?"

"I thought it might be safer."

She slapped the wall behind them. "This is the safest.

The wing with your suite." Clenching her fist, she added, "Apparently your *wife* gave orders to take you alive."

He motioned at the other wing. "She's in there."

"The Imperator would never come down on-planet."

"She's here." Jaibriol increased his Kyle concentration, focusing it outward. Perfect, lush empathic wealth emanated from him, stronger and purer than anything Viquara had ever felt. She reeled from it, too stunned to react as he walked forward.

Explosions rumbled and a pillar in the quad toppled in a great crash, roiling dust and debris into the air. Jaibriol went to the edge of the balcony and stood there, gripping the rail, his hair flying in the dusty wind, his face caught in the spotlight of a flier, then cast in shadow again.

Recovering herself, Viquara went over to him. She had to shout to be heard above the explosions and aircraft. "You have to come back! You're a target out here."

He was still staring across the quad. When a dark-haired woman ran out of a doorway there on the ground level, Jaibriol shouted, "Up here!"

The woman looked up, her face obscured by swirling dust. Then she took off, running in a zigzag course around the perimeter of the quad. Jaibriol climbed up on the rail, preparing to jump to the ground one story below. Viquara had no doubt then as to the identity of the woman coming toward them.

The roof behind Viquara exploded, spraying her and Jaibriol with debris. In the quad, the running woman shouted. Viquara didn't need to hear the words to know she had ordered someone to stop shooting. Commandos were crossing the quad, darting for the cover of fallen pillars and piles of debris, Jagernauts invading her palace. Viquara ignored them, her focus narrowing to the thief who had stolen everything that mattered in her universe, including her Highton detachment. She backed away from Jaibriol, out of his reach.

Then the Empress of Eube raised her laser carbine and sighted on the Imperator of Skolia.

"Not my son," she whispered.

"NO!" Jaibriol jumped back onto the balcony and lunged at her. Viquara danced out of his reach, then turned back to the quad, trying to find Sauscony Valdoria again.

But it wasn't the Imperator she saw. On a balcony level with theirs, in the wing of the palace across the quad, a tall man was raising an EM pulse rifle, a Highton whose form and face she knew well.

Kryx Quaelen.

At first Viquara thought he was aiming at her. Then she understood; as would any Highton, Quaelen would kill his emperor rather than let him suffer the ultimate humiliation of ISC capture. At least that would be Qualen's excuse. She knew his true reason: he feared exposure. If Jaibriol escaped to his Imperator wife, he could make public devastating truths that would wreak a far greater havoc than the whirling chaos around them.

Viquara saw Quaelen sight on Jaibriol. She knew Jaibriol's death would end her anguish. No more agonizing over her slave son. No more Imperator Empress. No proof of it existed beyond Jaibriol. In one shot, Quaelen would put the universe right again.

In one shot, Quaelen would kill her son.

Raising her carbine, Viquara stepped into the line of sight between Jaibriol and the Trade Minister. She and Quaelen fired in the same instant.

Even as she felt the projectiles stab deep into her body, she saw the laser flash envelope Kryx. Dying, he reached his hand out to her, as if he could bridge the chasm that separated them, though whether to embrace or strike her, she would never know.

Viquara was falling. Someone caught her and eased her to the ground. She saw Jaibriol's face above her, saw the tears on his cheeks. Behind him in the sky, the waning crescent of the Diamond Moon shone through the whirling dust of battle. A fading portion of her mind knew it was impossible, that a moon in that phase could never be overhead late at night. Next to it shone another impossibility, the waxing gibbous disk of the Unnamed Moon shedding unadorned light down from the heavens.

Softly she whispered, "It seems . . . I do love you, my son."

Then blackness enveloped her and her universe became forever, eternally silent.

33

A bomb exploded only meters from Althor's flier as he skimmed above the lawns around the palace. At least, they had once been lawns, many acres of lush green waves. Now blast holes pockmarked the terrain. He had taken the flier so low to the ground, it was almost sliding instead of flying. He didn't dare turn on the lights for fear of drawing attention, but it made the flying even more difficult.

He had tried raising the ISC forces on the planet and even the ships in orbit. The comm barely had the range to reach even the palace, but by now he was willing to try anything. Cirrus sat rigid in her seat, dressed in a thigh-length sweater she had found in the flier's locker.

An explosion came too close to the flier, and the shock wave tossed it forward like a giant throwing a toy. Its nose rammed the ground and plowed a furrow for a good twenty meters before it jolted to a stop. Cirrus hunched up in her seat, covering her head with her arms.

"It's all right," Althor said. When she looked up, he added, "It's another kilometer to the palace. We can make it in less than two minutes." Then he realized Cirrus could never keep up if he went that fast. "Run the best you can. I'll stay with you."

She nodded, silent, concentrating all her attention on

what had to be, for her, events extraordinary to the point of disbelief. They clambered out of the wrecked flier and took off across the lawns. Spotlights swung over them, came back, held, and then went on. Althor suspected it was because of the slave restraints and civilian clothes they wore. ISC would want only military personnel, not civilians.

But the chaos still endangered them. An ESComm infantry unit was jogging only a few hundred meters to their right. A bomblet exploded on their left, flinging them to the ground. Althor scrambled to his feet, reaching for Cirrus, but she was already up and running again. The palace rose before them, stark with fires, clouds of smoke roiling about its ragged spears. A Jag arrowed out of the night and exploded the palace roof below it in a burst of debris.

Cirrus ran with him until they reached the wreckage of a garden. Then she sprinted at right angles to their route.

"Cirrus, wait!" He went after her, straining to reach her mind. He picked up a wash of deep, deep fear and beneath that an even more intense emotion, a protective sense as deep and as wide as a sea.

Althor caught up with her and threw both his arms around her waist, jolting her to a stop. "We can't go that way!" He had to shout to be heard above the explosions and sirens. "We need to find the emperor's wing."

"NO!" With an unexpected ferocity she raked her gold-tipped fingernails along his arm. Stunned, Althor loosened his hold. She tore away from him and took off for a cluster of small houses, most of them in smoking ruins.

Althor went after her, devouring distance with his legs. She ran to the smoldering remains of a house, slammed open its door, and disappeared inside.

He found her kneeling in a scorched corner of the one-room dwelling, tears pouring down her face as she cradled a charred sweater in her arms. She rocked back and forth, crying, while outside explosions showered the area, some distant, others too close.

Althor knelt next to her. He spoke more softly now, able

to make himself heard with the walls shutting out the worst noise. "What is it?"

"My baby." She showed him the sweater. "This was his favorite." Tears rolled down her face. "My baby is dead."

Althor took the sweater. "You have a son?" The garment didn't look like it belonged to a baby. "Eleven? Twelve?"

"Ten." She drew in an ragged breath. "He needed me and I wasn't here. Now he's gone."

He folded her hands around the sweater. "This doesn't look like anyone was wearing it. Probably it was lying here when the house burned."

A desperate hope flickered on her face. "But where is he?"

"Who has been taking care of him?"

"Empress Viquara."

Althor knew the empress would never care for a slave. "What about a nursemaid?"

Her face brightened. "Azzi!"

Dropping the sweater, she jumped up and ran past him. Althor caught up with her outside, and they crossed a ravaged garden to a house with its roof caved in. Inside, a table had cracked in two when part of the roof hit it, and a bed in one corner creaked under piled debris, straining with the load, ready to collapse.

Cirrus froze. Althor felt her mind reach out, searching, untrained, but with the natural instinct of a Kyle parent for a Kyle child.

A choked sob from the corner, followed by a boy's voice speaking in Highton. *"Mama!"*

"Kai!" As Cirrus ran to the corner, the sound of scrabbling came from under the bed. A tousled head of yellow hair appeared, followed by the rest of a small boy with blue eyes. Cirrus pulled him to his feet and they clung together, the boy crying, "Mamamamama," while Cirrus said, "It's all right," over and over.

Althor went to them and spoke gently. "We have to go. If we stay we'll be recaptured." These had to be quarters of the emperor's favored providers. He doubted Jaibriol Qox kept slaves; these would have belonged to his father.

Cirrus and Kai looked up at him with an unsettling trust. How was he going to get them out of this mess without being recaptured, blown up, blasted by lasers, or otherwise killed?

"Did you used to live here?" he asked Cirrus. When she nodded, he said, "Do you know the way to the emperor's suite?"

"Yes." She wouldn't look at him. "I was there. Often."

Althor touched her arm, offering comfort, though he wondered if she would ever consider touch a form of comfort after the life she had lived. "Can you take us there?"

"I think so."

She led him to a path that wound through the remains of the slave quarters. Kai couldn't keep up with their long-legged gait as they ran, so Althor carried him on his back. The boy was an easy load, but Althor worried what would happen if he needed enhanced speed. Although he had cleaned and bandaged his arm, it was in bad shape, with damage to his hydraulics as well as his natural tissues. He couldn't carry both Kai and Cirrus.

Cirrus took him to a discreet entrance at the palace. An instant after they entered the foyer, lasers shot across the doorway. Althor felt he should have realized the danger, but if he had ever known ISC intelligence on the Qox palace, that information was gone now. That the laser fired after they passed could mean the system recognized Cirrus and Kai and didn't identify him as an intruder until too late. Then he realized it should recognize him, given that he was the empress's provider. Perhaps Cirrus had triggered the lasers, since she no longer lived here. Or else it had been a mistake caused by damage to the palace defenses.

Cirrus motioned to a stairway. "That goes to his suite."

Althor extended his empathic senses. He caught traces of psions, but nothing strong enough to be Qox . . .

Then he hit it: a brilliant glowing star among embers. It wasn't Jaibriol Qox; this nova he knew far better.

Soz.

For one horrific instant, when the laser cut the night with its harsh flash, Soz thought someone had shot Jaibriol on the balcony. Then she saw him crouched down, holding a woman in his arms.

Two of the Abaj Jagernauts ran into the stairwell to the balcony, but before Soz could follow, a unit of ESComm Razers jogged around a corner of the building. She dropped behind a fallen statue and fired, sniping Razers. They blanketed the area with rifle fire, the wrong tactic against ISC commandos, wasting ammunition while the hidden Jagernauts picked them off. But for every Razer they stopped, more came from behind, and more, enough to overcome even her crack d-team.

The two Abaj suddenly reappeared, striding out the doorway—with a prisoner. They held him by the arms the same way waroids held captives, forcing him to run with them. Soz had one instant to see his stunned, beloved face. Then she shouted a thought into the d-team psiberlink: **Retreat to the shuttle!**

They raced through the burning palace. The Razers pursued, well organized despite the depletion of their ranks, but unable to keep pace with the enhanced Jagernauts. ISC weapons fire continued to harry the palace, providing cover for the d-team.

As they ran, Soz both rejoiced and mourned. They had found Jaibrol but not Althor.

By the time they reached the lawns, they had left the Razers far behind. With luck and speed the d-team would reach the shuttle in time. They ran through the dark, up the hill to the ship, crossing the lawns in blurs, faster than any normal human could follow. One of the Abaj had lifted Jaibriol into his arms and was carrying him.

They sailed across a security line, legs stretched out long

and graceful. Spikes shot up like avenging specters, but they missed the flying Jagernauts. They continued their mad race, and the crest of the hill came into view, including the bushes that hid the shuttle. Relief touched Soz. They were almost there—

Soshoni?

Soz froze, and was almost knocked over by a Jagernaut who barely managed to avoid her. The call echoed in her mind. Soshoni. A name only Jaibriol and her family called her.

She swung around to the palace. **Althor!**

Where are you? he asked.

She sent him an image of their location and the tactical map, magnifying her signal through the d-team link. She felt his confusion: he no longer knew how to read the map.

She input a command into the link. **Get the emperor to the ship. If I'm not there when you're ready to go, leave anyway.** Then she ran back down the slope.

Althor sent her an image of the slope below. **We're following you. But we have Razers after us.**

I've got a fix. Make a 30° turn from your current direction. Soz kept going, letting her node choose her way, as it calculated the least-time intersection of her path with Althor's.

She saw figures on the hill below, a waroid pulling a woman. Then she realized it was Althor carrying a boy on his back, jogging in a zigzag path with the woman struggling to keep up. He apparently couldn't carry both companions, which meant he had to go at the woman's speed or leave her behind.

Soz ran out to them and Althor thrust the boy at her. As she put the child on her back, Althor hefted the startled woman into his arms. Soz had no chance to greet the brother she hadn't seen in seventeen years; she and Althor took off like pulse projectiles, covering ground in tendon-ripping strides that strained even their augmented systems. The boy clung to Soz, his hands clutched in her hair, while her internal biomech sent out every signal it could come up with to confuse their pursuers.

They were within a few hundred meters of the shuttle when Soz's map showed a flood of Razers pouring up the slope. She kept running, but a sinking sense came over her even before her node gave warning. She and Althor weren't close enough to the shuttle. It was a good target for the missile launchers the Razers carried. If it didn't leave now, it would be destroyed.

GO! she shouted into the team link. **Get Qox out of here. Contact my father about him!**

The shuttle engines rumbled into life, but its air lock stayed open, two Abaj silhouetted in its oval of light.

GO, damn it! Soz shouted. She and Althor were meters from the ship, but it was within range of the Razers' weapons and they surely saw it by now.

A missile shrieked above them—

Quasis jump, the shuttle thought.

For an instant Soz thought the world had stopped. Then she realized some insane member of her team had thrown the shuttle into quasis as the missile exploded, catching her and Althor in the field as well. It was madness. Quasis had never been meant for ground combat. Conditions changed too fast. With the momentum she and Althor had now, they would hurtle through the air like a rigid bodies while they were in quasis—and when they came out, the altered forces of their environment could tear them apart.

Soz stumbled, her entire body clenching in pain. Althor let go of the woman, shoving her to one side to keep from crushing her as he fell. Soz lost her hold on the boy and barely managed to swing him at the mother. "Run!" she shouted. "Get in the ship!"

Another missile screamed over them—

Quasis jump.

Soz fell forward, slamming into the ground as Althor struggled to his feet. Another missile—

Quasis jump.

Soz lurched to her feet and staggered to the open hatch. Hands reached out—

Quasis jump.

—and pulled her inside. The Abaj lost their grip on the heavier Althor—

Quasis jump.

—both Abaj grabbed him again—

Quasis jump.

—and heaved him inside. As they slammed the hatch, Soz sprawled across the deck—

Quasis jump.

—thrusters fired—

Quasis jump.

The ship nearly lost cohesion, trying to hold fixed the molecular wavefunction of its billowing exhaust. The billows became a rigid cloud, but the ship had to keep going up, caught in quasis. Then the quasis failed and the ship faltered in its takeoff. The thrust kicked back in and they leapt at the sky again, the ship's structure groaning under the strain of so many counterforces. Acceleration flattened Soz on the deck and she heard the boy gasp.

Escape velocity achieved, the pilot thought.

Still pressed to the deck, Soz thought, **Go to phase three.**

The ship's computer said, "Detonation primed," in the same instant that Jinn Opdaughter, their weapons expert, thought, *Explosives on decoy are set.*

Make it work, Soz thought. **This is our only chance.**

Preparing to enter Klein space, the shuttle pilot thought.

Releasing decoy, the computer warned.

Klein field activated, the pilot thought.

Nausea grabbed Soz as the ship twisted into Klein space—and in normal space a decoy "shuttle" exploded in a blast of energy, hurtling slagged debris through space. To the thousands of people monitoring their flight, it looked as if the shuttle had just blown up.

The Klein-enhanced rumble of the engines increased as

they gained speed. Soz couldn't focus *her thoughts, water pouring through a tube, rushing under pressure, quasis jump after quasis jump as the shuttle accelerated . . .*

Inversion twisted them into superluminal space in the same instant they twisted out of Klein space. Soz almost threw up, but she managed to hold it. Then they were free and hurtling through space.

Taking a deep breath, Soz reoriented herself as she floated up from the deck in free fall. The boy's grip on her head before had pulled down her hair, and now it swirled around her in sweeps of black, red, and gold. She heard the boy cry and the woman murmur to him in Highton. The woman had to be a provider; she emanated Kyle strength, but with no training on how to hide her fear. Then Althor's mind flowed around her, rumbling with power, reassuring and protective.

The d-team was eerily quiet, securing themselves and their gear in silence, with none of the relieved chatter that usually followed a successful mission. Soz knew why. None of them knew why they had faked their destruction or what she intended for the captured emperor. Everyone was waiting to see what came next.

Across the cabin, a medical bunk had unfolded and Althor was sitting on it, holding himself in place by a grip. Soz saw why the bunk had responded to his condition; blood was running down his arm from a torn bandage, bruises and welts covered his torso, and cuts scored his hand.

The woman floated next to him, her hand on his shoulder and her other arm around the boy. Soz didn't know what to make of her. She had the face of a girl, but her sweater-dress did nothing to hide her womanly build. Either her skin had been altered to match Althor's or else she wore gold makeup. Her diamond collar and cuffs threw out prismatic sparkles and her eyes were a blue too vivid to be natural.

Althor watched Soz from across the bustle of the cabin,

as the Jagernauts stowed their gear. **My greetings, Soshoni,** he thought.

She sent him a mental grin. **Here I thought I was rescuing you from a dire fate and instead I find you in the arms of a gorgeous woman.**

He smiled. **It's good to see you.** Then his gaze shifted and she followed it.

The Abaj had Jaibriol in a corner where two bulkheads met. They held him by the arms and kept themselves in place by hanging onto grips in the hull. So they floated with the emperor between them, waiting, like everyone else was waiting, to see what would happen when the two potentates came face-to-face. Only once before had such a meeting happened, and both rulers had died for it.

No one yet knew whether ISC or ESComm had won the war. At this moment, no one in the shuttle cared. Soz felt the question that burned in all their minds: when she and Jaibriol spoke, how would the centuries of conflict finally be given voice?

Soz floated to him, closer, and closer, until she was a meter away. She discovered she felt an overwhelming sense of disbelief. Only now did she realize just how much she had doubted she would live to see him again.

"Let him go," she said.

The Abaj hesitated and she felt their conviction that they had misunderstood. So she said it again. "Let him go."

She waited, watching them, until finally they released Jaibriol. As he grabbed a handhold and pulled himself closer to her, every Jagernaut in the shuttle reached for a weapon. She and Jaibriol ignored them, caught in a dance they had begun eighteen years ago on Delos, the planet of sanctuary.

They floated to each other, nudging against bulkheads to control their movement. When they met, she put her arms around his neck and he embraced her, pulling her to him. They kissed each other then, slowly rotating in the air until they bumped up against another bulkhead.

"Saints almighty," someone whispered.

After a long, long moment, Soz and Jaibriol separated. She cupped his cheek with one palm. "My greetings, Husband."

He watched her with the gentle expression she knew so well. For the first time in two years he spoke to her. "My greetings, Wife."

So they came together, their union having survived through the miracle of their love.

34

Seth Rockworth stood in the entrance hall of his house, watching the youth before him. At seventeen, tall and broad in the shoulders, with a natural grace and quiet reserve, Jai Qox Skolia had stopped being a boy and become a man.

Seth knew Jai considered himself nothing special. Although the boy did well in school, his problems adapting to life away from Prism had masked the full extent of his intellect. But Seth saw. Jai had inherited both the Selei analytic brilliance and the Qox political acumen. He mixed his mother's military genius with his father's abiding gentleness. He had the steel-edged strength of his Ruby and Qox heritages, tempered with the love he had known as a child. But he was more than the sum of Skolia and Qox. Rather than the failing remnant of an inbred bloodline, he was a genetic cornucopia, hale and hearty in mind and body.

Jaibriol the Third had no idea he was a miracle.

But Seth didn't know how to ease Jai's pain, or the pain of the other children, who had learned of their parents' deaths in the harshest way possible. They had all been in the living room a few days previous, Lisi and Jai playing chess, Vitar reading, del-Kelric building with blocks, and

Seth watching an old movie, half-asleep. A broadcast interrupted the movie, news that came with no warning. Jaibriol Qox and Sauscony Valdoria had died in the final battle of the Radiance War. That the children had to learn it from an impersonal news broadcast convinced Seth that if fates truly existed, they had no heart.

Now Jai stood by the hall mirror, holding a holograph.

"You don't have to do this," Seth said.

"I can't go unless you sign." Jai gave him the graph.

Seth scanned it, cycling through the forms in its memory. They were straightforward, permission forms for Jai to join the Dawn Corps, a humanitarian organization formed in the wake of war. No one knew the exact situation between Eube and Skolia yet, but rumors proliferated. Some said ESComm was broken; others said it was the Ruby Dynasty. This much was clear: the galaxywide collapse of the psiberweb had destroyed communications throughout settled space, ESComm was either decimated or destroyed, and the governments of both Skolia and Eube were in chaos. Eubian slaves were pouring into Skolian and Allied worlds asking for sanctuary. People everywhere were spilling across boundaries: soldiers, merchants, pirates, scouts, even Aristos, mixing on worlds where no one knew who claimed what.

Then came the survivors of Onyx.

It started as a trickle, a few ships running fast and hard. Then they came by the thousands, limping into ports across the stars. The flow turned into tens of thousands, then millions, then tens of millions.

Then billions.

Two billion people escaped the massacre of Onyx. When history turned its critical focus on the Radiance War, none doubted certain names would rise in honor: Starjack Tahota and those who had died with her so that billions could live. And Althor Valdoria.

The survivors of Onyx made it out because ESComm knew too little about the Onyx periphery defenses to stop the evacuation. Althor Valdoria never divulged to his captors his knowledge of the Onyx defenses, at a price to himself too grim for most even to imagine. And so two billion people survived.

In the aftermath of Radiance, the Allied Worlds of Earth moved into the chaos, treading with care, still too small to reach openly for what their mammoth neighbors had lost, but strong enough to take advantage of a situation that let them increase their power base. They also stepped in to help. The military needed volunteers to organize relief efforts, relocate refugees, and carry out the million and one other details of cleaning up after a war with no clear winner. So the Dawn Corps was born.

"But why now?" Seth asked. "Can't you give yourself more time?" Time to mourn.

Jai watched him with an unsettling intensity. "Have you read *The Ascendance of Eube*?"

Quietly Seth said, "Yes."

"It was written by my grandfather's grandfather."

"You aren't responsible for the sins of your fathers."

"I'm two parts of a whole, one Skolia, the other Qox." Jai spread his hands. "Do I believe the Skolians, that my father was a sadistic monster? The Eubians, that my mother was an obsessed dictator? The Allieds, who say both were flawed?" He watched Seth with a haunted gaze. "Or do I believe what I remember, that they were the most decent human beings I've ever known?"

"Believe your heart." Seth's voice gentled. "To raise children such as you four, they must have been remarkable."

"I have to know they died for something," Jai said.

Seth indicated the holograph. "How will this give you answers?"

"I need to go out there. See for myself."

"But to leave now—" Seth shook his head. "Your sister and brothers need you."

"No." The voice came from behind them. Seth turned to see Lisi in the archway to the living room. At fourteen, she already showed signs of her Ruby grandmother's striking presence. Vitar stood with her, eight now, with his mother's eyes and hair and his father's Highton features. Three-year-old del-Kelric hung onto Lisi, his gold hair and skin gleaming, his red eyes solemn.

"We've talked about it," Lisi said. "We want him to go." Her voice caught. "We have to know, Seth. It's all wrong. What people say about them. It's all wrong. Isn't it?"

Seth longed to take away their pain. "Of course it is."

"Will you do this for us?" Jai asked.

Seth turned to him. "Do you have a lightpen?"

Jai gave him one. And so Seth signed.

Corbal Xir walked through the empty Hall of Circles, one of the few undamaged sections of the palace. At its center, he mounted the steps to the dais. Then he sat on the Carnelian Throne.

He had never wanted to be emperor. That he had no interest in politics, that he far more preferred working out trade agreements to royal intrigue, that he felt too old now, at 132—none of that mattered to the DNA in his body.

A rustle came from the benches in the Circles. He looked to see a woman get up from one and walk toward him, a tall figure with glittering hair. White hair. Like his. She came up the dais and sat in a chair someone had left next to the throne.

"Have they brought him in yet?" she asked.

Corbal shook his head. "The last I heard, they were at the starport."

She looked around the Hall. "It's yours. I don't want it."

"No?" He regarded Calope Muze, High Judge of the Hightons, the only other Aristo besides himself with Qox blood. "The Carnelian Throne promises great power."

"Even more so, now."

That surprised him. "It would seem less so to me."

Calope turned to him. "The Ruby Pharaoh is dead. Her heir is dead. The Imperator is dead. The Allieds hold the Web Key and his wife on Earth and the rest of the Rhon on their own home world. They won't let them go, Corbal. They've made that clear. And why? To ensure power for Earth, yes, but even more because they fear the war will start again if they do." She clenched her fist on her knee. "The Ruby Dynasty is broken. After so many centuries, they're finally *broken.*"

He scowled at her. "We too are broken. ISC shattered ESComm and put a spike through its brain. And you want to rejoice."

"We won. We have a Lock and a Key."

"So why don't you want the Carnelian Throne?"

Calope shrugged. "I'm an old woman. I would rather spend time with my providers."

He considered her. "I had a request from one of Empress Viquara's providers. Her favorite, in fact. A boy named Cayson."

Calope smiled. "I remember him. Charming."

"He wants me to sell him to you. He says you are 'kind.' "

She chuckled. "With such a fellow, how could one be anything but kind?"

He watched her for a long time. Finally he said, "How long has your hair been white?"

"You are rather blunt today, dear Cousin."

He touched his own head. "I've the same silver mane. And I am even older than you. I am allowed blunt questions."

Calope smiled slightly. "Ah, so. Perhaps." She shrugged. "It's been white since I was about ninety."

"Ninety." He nodded. "I was closer to 110."

"A strange thing, genetics." She wound a lock of her hair around her index finger. "Change the hair color of a non-Aristo to look Aristo and it changes nothing of their nature. They still aren't Aristo. But you can't change the nature of a Highton without changing the hair."

A strange dance we do, Corbal thought, stepping so carefully around the truth lest we say too much and betray ourselves. "Genetics is always complicated."

"Indeed."

"Have you ever thought, Calope, how sobering it would be if it took a century for a Highton to learn human compassion? A frightening proposition."

"I can think of one more frightening."

"Yes?"

"To never learn it at all."

" 'Kind.' " He shook his head. "My providers also use this word to describe me. Are we kind? Why? They are still slaves. I like having slaves. I like having beautiful providers kneel to me, please me, satisfy me. That girl who died with Althor Valdoria—ah, you don't know. I would have given all my wealth to own her. I almost did. But Vitrex outbid me. I grieve for her death. Is this compassion? Or just the lust of an old man who wanted to own an incomparably beautiful girl regardless of how she felt about it?"

Calope snorted. "She would have been happier with you than Vitrex."

"I would never have hurt her."

Calope laid her hand on his arm. "Perhaps we should speak with more care, Cousin. Should words such as these slip to the wrong ears, it could do us great harm."

"Ah, so."

A chime came from the control band on his wrist. When he activated the comm, a man said, "We're at the palace, Lord Xir. Shall we bring him to you?"

"Yes," Corbal said. "The Hall of Circles."

A few minutes later the great doors swung open and a unit of Razers entered, accompanied by two ESComm officers, Hightons in black uniforms with red piping on their sleeves. Their prisoner walked barefoot, his glossy hair brushing his collar, his hands locked behind his back. Corbal couldn't see if he wore cuffs on his wrists, but a diamond collar glittered on his neck and diamond cuffs showed on his ankles. They had given him the restraints of a provider rather than a prisoner of war.

His exotic appearance pleased Corbal. The captive had violet eyes, large and dark, in a handsome face with the barest hint of freckles across the nose. His hair was the color of fine burgundy and his features classic in their lines, more refined than his brother's square-jawed visage. Nor was he as tall or a massive as his brother or even as Corbal himself. This captive prince was about six-foot-one, broad in the shoulders and narrow at the hips.

When they reached the dais, the Razers shoved the man on his knees in front of Corbal. He stared at the ground, his head bowed, his torn shirt slipping down his arm. Corbal scowled when he saw the bruises on the man's shoulder. His captors had obviously beaten him, a glaring violation of the Halstaad Code, which Corbal had worked so hard to set up. He would look into this, have the officers in charge removed if necessary.

Corbal spoke. "My greetings, Prince Eldrin."

Eldrin raised his head. He spoke Highton with a heavy accent, his voice hoarse. "My honor at your presence, Your Highness."

"I'm not actually 'Your Highness' yet," Corbal said. "These things take time."

Eldrin had no ISC background. That, combined with the chaos in the Ministry of Intelligence following Vitrex's death, had made it almost impossible for Vitrex's people to put together a good case for interrogating Eldrin as they had Althor. Corbal intended no stark cells for this sensuous captive. He would keep Eldrin for himself.

"You will come to Xir estate as my guest," Corbal said. "When the Lock arrives, you will build a psiberweb for ESComm."

Eldrin swallowed. "As your guest?"

Corbal wondered if in another hundred years, if he lived that long, he would find himself unable to own human beings. Perhaps. But not now. Right now he had no qualms at all. "Ah, well. Guest of a sort."

The hope in Eldrin's eyes faded. "I see."

Watching him, Corbal knew Eube had its triumph. They had their Lock and Key. Yet for all that, he felt a loss of something valuable. He had trouble defining it. A chance for peace slipping away because Hightons knew only one way? He saw no way for Eube and Skolia to succeed at the peace table if it took centuries for one to understand, at a basic level, what motivated the other.

* * *

Seth shifted del-Kelric on his lap and turned the page of the picture book he was reading the boy. Across the room an angry cry sounded, followed by a crash. Looking up, he saw Lisi holding a plate with a sandwich. Her glass lay in pieces on the floor, a pool of water spreading across the parquetry. She stared at it, then sank to her knees crying, trying to soak up the water with her hands.

"Ai, Lisi." Seth set del-Kelric on the couch and went to the girl. Kneeling next to her, unheeding of the water soaking into his trousers, he put his arms around her and rocked her back and forth, murmuring comfort. When a small hand touched his face, he turned to see del-Kelric. Vitar put down his book and came over as well, to hug them. They stayed that way, kneeling on the floor in the water, their arms around one another, fighting the darkness of their grief together.

Finally Lisi sat back and pushed her tear-soaked hair out of her eyes. Vitar tried to smile at her, his face just as wet. "Don't cry, Lisi," he said. She squeezed his hand.

"Pizza come," del-Kelric announced.

"Oh, Kelly." Lisi laughed, a shaky sound, but one that encouraged Seth. "What pizza?"

"We ordered it," Vitar said.

"Pizza man at door," del-Kelric stated. The doorbell rang.

As Seth stood up, del-Kelric ran across the room and into the hall. When Seth heard him activate the release on the door, he said, "Kelly, wait!" He didn't want the boy opening the door to a stranger.

As soon as del-Kelric squealed, Seth ran to the hall. Then he stopped. No wonder del-Kelric had cried out. His brother had come home. Standing in the entrance foyer of the house, Jai had picked up his little brother and was hugging him, obviously overwhelmed, so much that it startled Seth given the older boy's reserved personality. But then, the children had been separated for a while now, during a time when they all needed each other.

Still, something seemed off. Jai looked an inch or two

shorter than normal. Seth wasn't sure; perhaps he remembered the boy as taller than he actually was—

Then Jai lifted his head and Seth knew it wasn't the boy he faced. It was the father.

The emperor spoke in perfect English, with a Highton accent. "My greetings, Admiral Rockworth."

As Seth stared at him, speechless, a cry came from behind him. Vitar ran past, followed by Lisi. Both children threw themselves against their father, laughing and crying at the same time. It was like the dreams Seth had been having where their parents came back, but always he woke to know it was a false hope, one that hurt more each time he dreamed it. Except this was no dream.

A slender woman stepped out from behind Qox and gathered the children into her arms. Seth moved back then, to let the family reunite. The parents had somehow, incredibly, come home. He felt an immense, incredulous joy for the children, but sorrow too, that they were no longer his.

Finally Soz looked up at him, her face wet with tears. "You have our eternal gratitude."

Seth managed to find his voice. "But how? We thought—the shuttle—everyone saw it explode."

"Ah. Well." She gave him a rueful look. "That was a bit dramatic, yes? But we wanted to leave no doubt."

"A bit?" As an understatement, that had no equal he could think of right now.

"We've been trying to send a message," Soz said. "But it's been difficult with the webs down."

That didn't surprise Seth. "What will you do now?"

"Go back into exile," Jaibriol said. "We're going to build a community. A community of psions."

"It wasn't stable with just us and the children," Soz said. "But we've more now, people willing to build with us."

Seth tried to absorb it all. "Will you ever come back?"

"I don't know," Soz said. "Not soon. We've found closure. Completion for our lives. Peace."

Jaibriol looked around the hallway. "Where is Jai?"

"He flew into a star," del-Kelric explained from the safety of his father's arms.

Jaibriol smiled at the boy. "Into a star?"

"He means to the stars," Lisi said. "Jai joined the Dawn Corps."

Soz stiffened. "He's not here?"

"I'm sorry." Seth suddenly felt awkward. "I wouldn't have signed the papers. But I had no idea."

"Why the Dawn Corps?" Soz asked.

"It was his way of mourning," Seth said. "He wanted to understand why you died."

Jaibriol exhaled. "Yes. That sounds like Jai."

"You must tell him where we've gone," Soz said. "Tell him that he can come home."

"I will." Seth paused. "Can you stay awhile?"

Jaibriol shook his head. "If it becomes known we lived, it could start the war again. Gods only know what would happen if our marriage became public."

"We've heard rumors that ESComm captured the Third Lock," Seth said. It was the most recent news come in by star ship, as of yet unverified.

"But they have no Keys," Soz said. "Both Althor and Jaibriol are with us now."

"Is Althor all right?" Seth asked.

It was a moment before she answered. "He has some brain damage. Many of his memories are blurred or erased."

"I'm sorry," Seth said.

"He's still essentially the same person." Her face gentled. "My big brother."

"So the war really is over," Seth said. When Soz nodded, he asked, "Who do you think won?"

"If you mean," she said, "ISC or ESComm, I would say neither. Both took immense losses. At least most casualties were military." She paused. "I would say the peoples of Eube and Skolia won. Apparently Trader slaves are going free by the millions. What's happening with Skolia is more subtle, the easing of ISC control and the psiberweb, but in the long run, the effect may be just as dramatic."

"Eventually the web will come back up," Seth said.

"In a limited sense," she agreed. "But without a full Triad, it will be impossible to maintain on the same scale."

"Won't you still be in the Triad?"

She shook her head. "With the links frozen, I was able to get out. I suffered neural damage, but nothing drastic."

He stared at her. "You've already done it?"

"We went to Raylicon before we came here," Jaibriol said. "That's why it took so long."

"I used the Second Lock," Soz said. "It's in the ruins of a city that was the ancestral home of our hereditary bodyguards, the Abaj Tacalique."

Seth began to understand. The presence of the Second Lock on Raylicon was one reason it was so well defended a world. "What you're doing with all this—it's a way for Skolia and Eube to make peace, isn't it? Without ESComm to back up Eube and the psiberweb to back up Skolia, your peoples have to meet at the peace table."

"We can hope," Jaibriol said. "The chances are better now than ever in the past."

Seth regarded them uneasily, wondering if they knew Soz's parents were being held in Stockholm and her siblings confined to their home world of Lyshriol. The Allied authorities had turned their protective custody into imprisonment. As far as Seth knew, they had no intention of ever freeing the Imperial family.

"We certainly have every wish to see peace prevail among your peoples," Seth said.

Soz snorted. "And if it means keeping my family prisoners in their own homes, so be it, hmmm?"

"Ah. Well." He cleared his throat.

She started to speak, then stopped. Then she said, "I realize you can't give me secured information."

"I don't know any. I'm retired." It wasn't exactly true; he still did some work for the navy, training SEALs.

"I wondered if you had news of Dehya," Soz said.

The mention of his ex-wife's name caught Seth off guard. "She's on the Orbiter, isn't she?"

"Not anymore. She's—" Soz hesitated, as if unsure of the right word. "Gone, somehow. I can feel it. I'm afraid she, Taquinil, and Eldrin are dead."

Quietly Seth said, "I'm sorry." He didn't want to believe they had died. He put that knowledge away for when he had privacy to deal with the complicated forms of grief that came with it.

He understood why Sauscony and Jaibriol wanted to vanish, to set up their own community. Even after having lived several decades among the Imperial court, as the Pharaoh's consort, he still found it hard to believe one family could be so coveted by so many powers. Empires rose and fell in attempts to control the Ruby Dynasty. It was no wonder they wanted their own hidden community, where the rest of the universe would leave them alone.

"I hope you succeed with what you're trying to do," he said.

Jaibriol offered him his hand. "I don't know words enough to thank you for taking care of our children."

Seth shook his hand. "You honored me." He looked at the children and they smiled back, Lisi, Vitar, and del-Kelric, so beautiful to him. He would miss them until his last day alive.

Jai's first posting took him to the city of Porthaven on the Allied world known as Edgewhirl, near the border regions of Trader territory. The small, sparse planet had formerly supported an atmosphere rich in chlorine as well as oxygen. Biosculptors adapted it to human life, though chlorine still remained in the biosphere, dissolved as salts in the oceans. The sun Whirligig, also called Clement's Star to honor one of the great literary names of Earth's Golden Age, spun so fast it resembled a squashed orange, huge and golden in the green sky.

Porthaven had grown up around a bustling starport. Now

refugees poured into the starport from all over settled space, and races from a thousand different worlds jammed the city.

With his ability to speak Iotic, Highton, Eubic, Skolian Flag, and English, Jai worked as a translator, helping people fill out forms. So he heard their lives. The taskmakers wanted freedom, education, and the right to go where they pleased, when they pleased. He was surprised to learn some had considerable financial resources or lands on their home worlds, often all used to pay for their escape.

One morning a huge, taciturn man came to his office. He had brown hair and eyes, but in the light they glinted, suggesting a metallic sheen hidden by the genetic alterations available in tattoo parlors. His gold wrist guards looked ancient, with no picotech, only engravings in a language Jai didn't recognize, though it resembled ancient Iotic. The outline of armbands showed under his sleeves, five on one arm and six on the other. The pouch hanging from his belt clinked when he sat down, as if it contained coins or perhaps dice.

Incredibly, the man knew almost nothing of the war. He asked many questions but refused to answer any. When he learned that every living member of the Ruby Dynasty was a prisoner and that both the Allieds and Traders intended to keep it that way, he became even more wary. In the end he declined to fill out any forms and left the office without giving his name.

Jai met one provider. Spectacularly beautiful, soft-spoken and frightened, she could barely talk. The director of his unit called him in to translate for the girl, who spoke only Highton. When Jai entered the director's office, the girl was standing by the window. She turned to him and froze, panic flushing her face. Then she came over and knelt in front of Jai, her head bowed. Flustered, he looked around at the director and his staff, but no one seemed to know what to do.

Finally Jai got on his knees in front of her and spoke in Highton. "What are you doing down there?"

For a long moment she stared at him. Then she said, "You have brown eyes."

He understood then. She saw what no one from Earth noticed: he had the classic Highton facial structure and build. Without his contacts, his eyes were Highton red.

Jai gave her a reassuring smile and touched the patch on his Dawn Corps uniform. "I'm with the Allied Worlds."

Her relief flowed around them, unhindered, impossible to miss. She had never learned to hide or mute her emotions.

He took her back to his office and helped her fill out forms. And so he heard her story. Somehow he managed to stay calm. Somehow he managed to translate every last horrific detail without falling apart.

That evening he lay on his bed and stared at the ceiling, unable to sleep, unable to free his mind of the images she had left him. He felt sick for days.

Then a message came into the corps office from the Eubian world Garnet. A group of taskmakers there requested aid in "releasing a pavilion." It took a few back and forths before it became clear they wanted to relocate people who lived in the place they called a pavilion.

The corps rated the assignment at the highest risk level. Garnet was inside Trader territory. At the moment the Aristo presence there was nonexistent, the owners unwilling to stay without ESComm protection. With Garnet cut off so thoroughly from Eube, some taskmakers had decided to flee. But if ESComm returned while the Dawn team was on Garnet, the team members could lose their own freedom and become slaves themselves. So the corps took only volunteers for the mission. With his linguistic abilities, Jai was one of the first chosen.

They landed in Agate, a city on a southern continent, in the evening. A welcoming committee of taskmakers put them up at an inn. The taskmakers had a simple request, in addition to their immigration concerns. They wanted their slave restraints taken off. Usually it was a matter of jimmying maglocks or breaking silicate-metal alloys, but the more complex cuffs and collars carried picotech linked to implanted systems within the taskmaker's body and had to be removed with the utmost care.

Despite the obvious competence the taskmakers had at running their lives and society, they were tentative, unable to make even minor decisions. Toward their owners they expressed a disquieting mix of worship and fear. Most wrestled with guilt over their decision to seek sanctuary and several changed their minds.

Jai couldn't sleep that night. He lay staring at nothing while scenes of the cruelty his kind had wrought played over and over again in his mind.

A day on Garnet lasted twenty-three standard days, so the sleep period ended when night had barely begun. In the starry darkness, the Dawn team and their hosts boarded carts drawn by six-legged animals. Rocking and jolting along in the cart during the dark hours of a long night reminded Jai of Prism and his mood dimmed again.

A question haunted him: were his parents to give humanity no more than epic legends of the leaders who brought two empires to their knees? The myths growing around them had no reality he recognized. It was as if the truth had been thrown away by the cold immensity of a universe with no place for flimsy human love.

So were his thoughts as they rode to the Silicate pavilion. When the taskmakers said they didn't know what to do with the providers in the pavilion, the Dawn volunteers didn't understand. Everyone in the pavilion was an adult, yes? *Yes,* the taskmakers said. Couldn't they be retrained? *How?* the taskmakers asked.

Once at the pavilion, Jai understood. He saw the testing rooms, the bodysculpting labs, the examination tables. He walked through the isolation rooms, discipline rooms, memorization rooms, erotica rooms, silence rooms. He met the "adults" huddled in their sterile cubicles, slaves his own age, some even younger, staggeringly beautiful, terrified by the upheaval in their rigidly controlled lives, robbed of their humanity. He saw their glittering restraints, picotech so interwoven with their bodies that the team didn't dare remove the cuffs and collars.

Jai started his shift handing out food and blankets to slaves who watched him in silence. At first the Dawn team thought none of the providers could talk. It was Jai who discovered that they understood Highton. Once again he became the completer of forms. He almost broke down. None of the providers had a name. A few gave him a number that listed them in some inventory, but most didn't even know that. None knew their age. None could read or write. For the section requesting their reasons for seeking sanctuary, they simply stared at him. Finally he wrote their descriptions of their daily routines. It needed no other explanation.

At the end of his shift, Jai walked into the Garnet night. He went into the whispering woods outside the factory and knelt down, surrounded by the beautiful forest the Silicates had grown to adorn their pavilion. And then he was violently sick. He leaned over with his arms around his stomach and retched again and again, until he felt as if he were tearing out his insides.

Sometime later a hand touched his shoulder. Looking up, he saw Mik Fresnel and Carol Sanchez, two other corps volunteers. As Jai stood up, Mik handed him a handkerchief to clean himself. Jai wiped his mouth, unable to think of one word to say. This went beyond what he had expected even when he believed he knew the worst.

Carol spoke in a subdued voice. "We were wrong."

"Wrong?" Jai wiped the tears off his cheek. He hadn't realized he was crying.

"About the Traders," Mik said.

Carol shuddered. "How could anyone believe that without seeing it?"

"We must make sure it's recorded," Mik said. "Broadcast to the free worlds. Seen by everyone. So no one can ever forget or deny this existed."

Softly Jai said, "I will never forget."

After they finished on Garnet, they went to a new posting, a place like Porthaven. Again Jai filled out forms.

The news of Eldrin Valdoria's capture hit the settled worlds one by one. Without a central web, it had to be carried by star ship and so spread slowly. Dismay greeted it. The hope for peace, the dream that Eube and Skolia would finally be forced to the negotiating table, was false. Eube had their Lock and Key.

So also came the reports of Eube's atrocities, adding layer after layer of horror. The Allieds finally spoke in condemnation of what they had so long doubted existed. But even as free humanity struggled to regroup, to build defenses and offenses, so Eube rumbled with the beginnings of a power that could devastate the fragile accords being established all over settled space.

The golden thread of hope everyone had nourished, that glistening tendril called *peace,* was about to break.

Skolia was tired. Eube was tired. The Allieds were tired. No one wanted another war. Even the Hightons desired calm. But regardless of that desire, the Aristos knew only one mode of thought. With the uniformity of a glittering machine, an inflexibility that took centuries to change, and an innate arrogance that never died, the Hightons responded as they had always responded. They sought to conquer.

Late one night Jai went to a tattoo gene parlor in the Old District of town. When he told the tattoo artist what he wanted, the man said it was impossible, that it couldn't be done unless Jai carried at least some of the necessary DNA. Jai insisted until finally the artist checked Jai's gene map. Subdued and uneasy, the man acknowledged that what Jai wanted was possible after all. But he refused to do it. Finally Jai paid him a great deal of money, both for the process and for his silence.

Jai returned to his rooms with no visible difference except a shaved head. He bought a cap and wore it everywhere after that, never removing it.

35

The planet Delos was a member of the Allied Worlds. Earth had long ago declared it a neutral zone, sanctuary, a place where ISC and ESComm soldiers could walk together in harmony. *Harmony* was the Allieds' word, however. No Skolian and Traders had ever walked together on Delos, in harmony or otherwise.

Except two.

When the Dawn Corps landed on Delos, Jai went to the Arcade, a vibrant, booming boardwalk crowded with people. He tried to find the bar, Constantinides, where his parents had met, but no trace of it remained. So he walked on, a tall figure in jeans and sweater, his hands in the pockets of his leather jacket. He still wore his cap, though his hair had grown back, altered forever by a top-of-the-line tattoo artist.

On an overcast day, he left the inn where the Dawn Corps was staying and went out into a large plaza. Pulling up his collar against the drizzle, he crossed to the embassies on the other side. Inside a glittering white building, he arranged to send a message. He wrote it in a language almost no one alive spoke, and he included a lock of his hair.

Then he returned to his inn. To wait.

Soz sat with Jaibriol on the hill. Spatula grass rustled around them, blown by the breezes of Prism. Only a few people in ESComm had known the planet existed and they were all dead now.

"Do you think he'll come home?" Soz asked.

"I don't know." Jaibriol spoke in a contemplative voice.

"Jai is an adult now. He needs his independence. He was restless even before all this happened."

Soz felt a hotness in her eyes. She still remembered her firstborn as a baby in her arms. "Whatever he does, I hope he's happy."

Jaibriol swallowed. "Yes. I also." He watched the meadow below, where the Jagernauts and Althor had almost finished building a gazebo for the wedding. Vitar, Kai, and del-Kelric were running around the structure while Lisi watched them.

The pilot and first mate of *Tailors Needle,* the ship Soz had commandeered, were bringing over food for the celebration. All things considered, they were adapting well to their forced exile on Prism. Neither had a spouse nor children, so their situation hadn't broken apart any families.

"Do you think Althor will be happy here?" Jaibriol asked.

Soz considered her brother. "I think so. He's always liked this kind of life." Quietly she said, "He can't be what he was. And he knows it. If he returned to his former life, he would face constant reminders of it. Here he will be a leader."

Cirrus strolled into the meadow, dressed for her wedding in baggy pants rolled up at the cuffs and a huge sweater that belonged to the largest Jagernaut. She had scrubbed herself clean of the gold dust as if shedding a hated shell.

"I don't understand why she wanted to get married in those clothes," Soz said. "They're so drab."

"After the life she's been forced to live,' Jaibriol said, "it wouldn't surprise me if she never wanted to be looked at again." He started to say more, then stopped.

"What is it?" Soz asked.

"I wonder if it's fair to Cirrus for Althor to marry her. Or fair to him."

"Why do you say that? They like each other."

"Like, yes."

Soz tilted her head. "I think she wants exactly what he

has to offer—companionship, gentle affection, and a protector. It's the symbolism too. As a provider she was forbidden to marry." She paused. "As to my brother, he can go either way. He seems genuinely happy with her."

Down in the meadow, Althor was talking to Cirrus. Kai ran up to them, said something, and took off before they could answer, leaving Cirrus and Althor laughing.

"They will be parents to my brother," Jaibriol said. "I would like to be sure he is well taken care of."

"Althor is a wonderful father," Soz said. "And you've seen Cirrus with Kai. It's like magic."

Jaibriol curled his fingers around hers. "We should get down there. Everyone looks ready to start."

They stood up together, hand in hand, and walked to the future.

"I don't understand," Mik Fresnel said. "It sounds like you're asking me to be your bodyguard." He sat on his bed in the room he shared with Jay Rockworth in the inn on Delos and listened while Jay moved around in the bathroom, getting dressed after his shower.

"I just want you to come with me," Jai said. "I'd rather not go alone." He came out of the bathroom toweling his hair. Instead of his usual jeans and sweater, he had on black trousers and a black shirt, both with a cut as severe as it was expensive.

"Where did you get those clothes?" Mik asked.

"At a store. On the Arcade."

"They look like Aristo clothes."

Jay sat on his bed, across from Mik. He pulled away the towel—revealing hair that glittered in the light, like black diamonds.

Mik stared at him. "Have you flipped out? You look like a Highton."

Jai reached into his shirt pocket and took out a small case. With his eyes downcast, he removed a lens Mik had never known he wore, then repeated the procedure with his other eye. Then he looked up.

With red eyes.

Mik spoke uneasily. "What the hell are you doing?"

"I want you to remember something," Jay said. "No matter what happens, no matter what you hear, know that I will never forget what we've seen." He stood up. "Come with me, Mik. Stand as my friend."

Still puzzled, Mik rose to his feet. "You know I'll always stand by you."

Jai swallowed. "Thank you."

Together they went out into the drizzle that saturated the city of New Athens on Delos.

Corbal Xir stood at the window and watched the Delos rain. He still hadn't made his decision.

The formal Highton language the boy had used in his message had made it possible for the note to reach him despite the various spies who intercepted it. They probably smirked over the content, a lost son claiming Xir blood. Ah well, bastard children have a tendency to show up, or so their thoughts would go. Corbal wondered if anyone had taken a strand of the hair to analyze. It didn't matter. None of them had access to the right genetic files for verification.

Corbal had seen beyond the obvious message in that letter. With a sophisticated innuendo worthy of the most adept Highton, the boy told another story between the lines. So Corbal analyzed the hair himself.

The DNA match was exact.

Corbal was tired. He had lived a long time. He didn't want to rule Eube. Even with the potential for glory, vengeance, and sheer power, he didn't want the throne. Now a new voice had spoken. No doubt existed: that message had come from one of his relatives. But this was no illegitimate son of the Xir line.

Jaibriol II had left an heir.

It would invigorate Eube. With Jaibriol III on the throne, a vital young emperor just beginning his ascendance, victory was complete. Corbal had checked pictures of the boy. He was the image of his father, even taller and more classic of feature, with a robust quality most Highton bloodlines had lost. Eube needed him. The decimated empire crawling on its knees needed this miracle.

However, Corbal also knew the rest.

Corbal had given up what made him Highton. He made the choice when he could no longer justify taking his pleasure at the pain of others. He knew the changes in his DNA, knew them well. And so he recognized the anomalies in the boy's gene map. When he realized the magnitude of what he was uncovering, he tried ever more obscure tests, going far past what was needed for proper determination of the youth's heritage. He pulled out the records of past emperors and tore them apart. Many had been tampered with. It took him a long time to uncover the truth.

Eube Qox had been pure Highton.

Jaibriol I had been pure Highton.

Ur Qox had been half Highton.

Jaibriol II had been one-fourth.

Jaibriol III was one-eighth.

In Corbal's darker moments, he suspected the identity of the boy's mother. It didn't matter. A Highton mother could be created. What mattered now was his decision.

I can walk away from this, he thought, watching the rain. I can assume the throne and start over.

Or I can even the balance.

And there lay the crux of the matter. Jaibriol III hadn't come to claim the throne. Corbal sensed the boy had even less interest in it than he. In the oldest tradition of Eube, Jaibriol III had come to trade.

Corbal knew his limitations. He had told Calope the truth. He liked owning slaves. He liked his providers, even loved some of them. Eldrin Valdoria pleased him no end. That Eldrin loathed him made no difference; Corbal was the owner and Eldrin the owned.

Yet Corbal questioned his actions. It had taken him a century to learn compassion. He lived now with the guilt for what he had inflicted on his providers before he changed himself so he could never again transcend. What would he learn in another century? How long would it take to reach whatever enlightened state waited the final evolution of the Highton mind? Centuries? Millennia?

And what would the Hightons have done to humanity by then?

Perhaps his guilt was misplaced. Perhaps he and Calope, in their doddering old age, had lost their intellectual acumen. Maybe in making it impossible to transcend, he had made himself less than human and as a result confused weakness with compassion. He didn't know the answers.

No Highton had ever before asked such questions.

Jai was halfway across the plaza when a group came out of the Eubian embassy. Through the drizzle and distance, he couldn't see their faces. What did they come to say? Yes or no? He prayed the answer was no and hated himself for that hope.

He stopped in the center of the plaza with Mik. The Traders walked toward them, six men total. Four were large, bodyguards it looked like, probably Razers. Watching them, Jai wished he had brought more people. He had been naive, assuming that regardless of the answer, it would be given with honor. What if he was wrong?

He could make out the tallest man now. Corbal Xir. It wasn't until the Traders reached him, however, that he recognized the sixth man. He knew then that his life had changed forever.

Eldrin Valdoria stood with a numb expression, arms locked behind his back, a collar glittering around his neck. He watched Jai with no sign of recognition. Corbal spoke to him in a low voice, and Eldrin tilted his head as if unsure whether or not to believe whatever he heard.

Corbal turned to Jai. "I suggest we make a simultaneous exchange. You and Prince Eldrin walk forward at the same time."

"Very well." Jai turned and offered Mik his hand. "Thanks for coming."

Mik shook his hand. "I'm not sure what you're doing with this, but I'll remember what you said."

Jai nodded. Then he turned and saw his uncle watching him. Jai could feel his mind. Until this moment no one had given Eldrin an inkling of the offered trade. He hadn't even known he was on Delos.

"Are you ready?" Jai asked.

Eldrin took a breath. "Yes."

They walked forward, passing each other on the right. It took six steps, and then Jai was among the Traders. He turned and saw Eldrin join Mik. As his uncle looked back at him, the Razers closed around Jai. Then they and Corbal Xir started for the Eubian embassy, taking him with them, cutting him off from his former life forever.

Jai set his shoulders and faced his unwanted future. He knew he had a great deal to learn. Self-protection. Intrigue. Deception. He had no desire for the title he had just accepted, but he meant to be sure of one thing. He would be no puppet emperor.

It never struck him as a self-sacrifice that he gave up his life, his happiness, perhaps even his humanity, to make possible the dream of peace humanity craved. Knowing the legacy of the Hightons who had produced him, he felt as if he carried a guilt so deep it crushed him. At least with this trade, he could ensure one thing.

His parents hadn't died in vain.

With the psiberweb gone, Roca and Eldrinson had no way to attend the ISC funeral service, even as simulacrums. But they saw a recording later. ISC gave full military honors to Soz, with all the pomp and ritual due an Imperator. So too they honored Althor. Leaders from across the free worlds attended. Cannons thundered and music played.

Eldrinson and Roca held a private ceremony in Sweden. Accompanied by their daughter-in-law Ami, her two-year-old child Kurjson, the soldiers in the United Nations peacekeeping unit that guarded them, and Tiller Smith, the Allied Liaison to the Ruby Dynasty, they went to a wind-torn section of coast on the Gulf of Bothnia. On a cliff lush with trees, above an isolated beach with icy rolling waves, they spoke for their children, quiet words drifting on the wind. Tiller also gave a eulogy for Soz, who had been his patron when he was the only Allied citizen ever admitted to the Skolian institute that trained psions.

So the parents mourned their children. Eighteen years ago Kelric had died, their beloved youngest. Twice they had mourned Sauscony, the grief no less the second time than the first. They lost Althor, first to Eubian violence and then to death. They lost Kurj just as they had begun to find the complex man beneath the hardened exterior. They lost Dehya and Taquinil to a void neither understood and Eldrin to the hell of Trader slavery.

Most of all they mourned the death of hope, represented by their children who had envisioned a universe better than they knew and died for it. Had the deaths realized that dream, they could have endured the grief. But that was not to be.

After the ceremony, they returned to the countryside estate where they now lived. Feeling at a loss, Eldrinson wandered into the web room. A telop was there, plugged into a control chair. Eldrinson went over and watched lights flicker on the console in front of her.

He spoke in Skolian Flag, the only language they had in common. "It almost looks as if you're linked into the psiberweb."

She smiled. "I'm trying to re-form the link we had here."

Eldrinson nodded. It was a way to rebuild, link by link. With only one person in the Triad, and he forbidden the use of a Lock, rebuilding even a limited psiberweb would take years. But this was better than nothing. Perhaps he could help. It would give him something to do, to stop him from dwelling on the knowledge that he had outlived so many of his children.

The telop was watching him. "I'm off duty now," she said. "You're welcome to use it if you would like."

"I might sit for a while," he said.

She disengaged herself from the chair, then bowed to him and withdrew, leaving him privacy.

Eldrinson settled into the chair. ***Open Ψ gate,*** he thought.

Nothing happened.

He let his mind soak into the tenuous space the telop had created and tried again. **Open Ψ gate.**

No response.

Ah, well. It had been worth a try.

A voice came from across the room. "Eldri?"

He turned to see his wife, a golden sight that soothed him. "My greetings, beautiful lady."

Her face gentled at the nickname, but then her smile faded. "A starship landed in London with a recording of the funeral ceremonies from Glory. It's on the news now."

"All right." Eldrinson detached himself from the mesh. As he slid out of the chair, he glanced at the console screen in front of it, which showed a record of his commands:

Open Ψ gate.

Open Ψ gate.

He was about to turn away when he saw a third line. For an instant he froze. Then he touched the screen, wonder filling him.

"Eldri?" Roca came over. "What is it?"

"They're *here.*"

She smiled. "Who?"

He felt a curious sensation. Given what he had been feeling lately, it took a moment to identify. Joy. He pointed to the third line on the screen:

I exist.

"What did you mean?" Roca asked.

"I didn't input it."

"Who did?"

"Someone in psiberspace."

"There is no one in psiberspace."

"There are. Two people." His voice caught. "Once Dehya said to me, 'In the future I predict I cease to exist.' Then later she said perhaps she would exist again."

"You know how Dehya talked." Roca took his hands. "She rarely made sense."

"She always makes sense. You just have to figure her out." He tilted his head toward the screen. "It's her."

Roca sighed. "It would be strange indeed, wouldn't it, if Dehya and Taquinil were in there, lost forever?"

He grinned. "Ah, but Roca my love, when have you ever known your exasperating, charming, brilliant, and hammer-headed sister to stay lost when it came to solving a computer problem?"

She patted his hand. "It is a pleasant hope, yes?"

Eldrinson knew she didn't believe him. But he had no doubts. He knew Dehya. The joy washed over him, sweet after so much grief.

They went to the house amphitheater and joined Tiller Smith to watch the recording from Glory. Made originally in the Hall of Circles, the three-dimensional image replayed here on the holostage. The ceremony consisted of various Hightons giving speeches, the longest and most ornate for the emperor, then the Empress Mother Viquara, then her consort Kryx Quaelen. Corbal Xir surprised them and gave Sauscony a eulogy, a short one, but still a speech in honor of his late Skolian counterpart. The Aristos clicked their cymbals twice for Jaibriol, once each for Viquara and Quaelen, and not at all for Sauscony.

When the rituals were done, Corbal stood before the Carnelian Throne and looked out at the Aristos. But instead of stating his claim to the throne, he spoke as if he were beginning yet another speech.

"A new age has begun for Eube," he thundered.

"Oh, get on with it," Eldrinson grumbled. "Why do they always say that?"

"Many of you have heard rumors of negotiations between my office and the Allieds," Corbal said. After a well-timed pause, he added, "These rumors are true."

Cymbals whispered in the Hall. When they quieted, he said, "The Allieds had in their custody a man. A Highton man. A trade was arranged, this man for a prisoner in my possession." As cymbals whispered, Xir held up his hand. "Eube has triumphed! As we will always triumph."

"Do you have any idea what he's talking about?" Roca asked.

"Not a hint," Eldrinson said.

Tiller turned to them. "Apparently the pilot who brought this in was so worked up he started to transmit before he landed."

"Do you know why?" Eldrinson asked.

Tiller shook his head. "Not yet."

"And so it was agreed between the Allied Worlds and Eube," Corbal said. "Our Skolian captive for their Highton captive." He paused. "That Skolian was Eldrin Valdoria."

An angry discord of cymbals filled the hall. Roca put her hand over her mouth and Eldrinson stared at the stage. His son? *Free?*

"It's a lie." Roca's voice cracked. "They're taunting us. No Highton alive would be worth giving away their Key when they have a Lock."

"I can check on it," Tiller said. "The ship that brought this in should know." When Roca nodded, he bowed and strode out of the amphitheater.

Corbal waited. Finally the Aristos became silent, watching him with cold marble faces, waiting to see what he could possibly offer to atone for what he had given away.

He raised his arm to the great arched entrance of the Hall and said: "I present to you, His Honor, Jaibriol Qox the Third, Emperor of Eube."

For the first time in her life, Roca heard voices come from the Circles. As one, the heads turned to the entrance.

Jaibriol III strode into the Hall. Barely more than a child, he walked with confidence, the image of his father, yet taller, larger, stronger, more regal. Razers surrounded him, but in the force of his personality their presence faded.

He reached the dais and climbed its steps. Corbal bowed to him, then withdrew to the front row of the Circles. So the emperor stood alone, looking out at the assembled Aristos. And he began to speak.

His voice resonated, with surprising authority for someone his age. As he lauded a new era for Eube, Eldrinson watched—and saw what no one else would see, because it was too incredible. He knew the way Jaibriol tilted his head, knew that cheek structure, which looked Highton but had subtle differences, knew the power in that voice, having long ago heard it himself from another seventeen-year-old.

In Jaibriol III Eldrinson saw his own daughter.

The emperor praised his Highton mother, a woman secluded with her son, following what had become a tradition for the Qox line, to hide their heirs. Born almost nine months after his father disappeared, Jaibriol III had lived during all the years of his father's assumed death in secret, with his mother who had only recently passed away. Eldrinson recognized the woman Qox described, knew the nuances of behavior he lauded. She was no Highton.

The emperor's listeners reacted with an uprush of emotion. Three times during his speech they chimed their cymbals, caught by the charismatic performance.

Tiller returned and spoke to Roca and Eldrinson in a low voice. "It's true. Your son Eldrin is in the custody of the Allied embassy on Delos."

"Thank you," Roca whispered. She looked at Eldrinson and he took her hand, squeezing it. Safe. Eldrin was *safe.* The Ruby Dynasty might all be prisoners, but at least they were free from the Traders.

On the holostage, Jaibriol turned to the camera, obviously aware his words would go to a far larger audience than the Hall of Circles. In a quiet voice, he said, "We have suffered the ravages of our conflicts. Let us now seek to heal. To the people of the Skolian Imperialate and Allied Worlds of Earth, I say this: Meet with me at the peace table. Let us lay to rest the hatreds that have sundered our common humanity."

Jaibriol III extended his hand, reaching across the stars.

So the first planks of a bridge were laid, a tenuous arch that could span a river of hatred and let humanity cross above, out of its grasping reach. The bridge might take years, even decades, to complete.

But it had begun.

Family Tree: RUBY DYNASTY

Boldface names refer to members of the Rhon.
The Selei name denotes the direct line of the Ruby Pharaoh.
All children of Roca and Eldrinson take Valdoria as their third name.
All members of the Rhon within the Ruby Dynasty have the right to use Skolia as their last name.

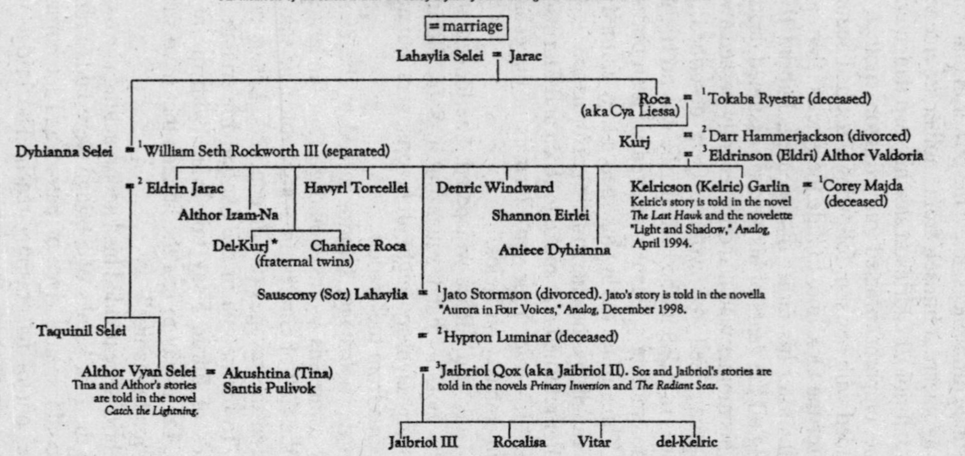

*The name Del-Kurj means "in honor of Kurj," and del-Kelric means "in honor of Kelric." The Del in Del-Kurj is capitalized because Kurj is a member of the Triad.

Family Tree: QOX DYNASTY

Boldface names refer to members of the Rhon.

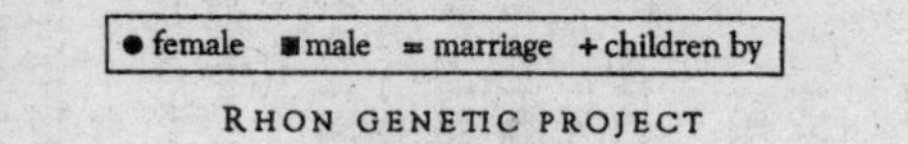

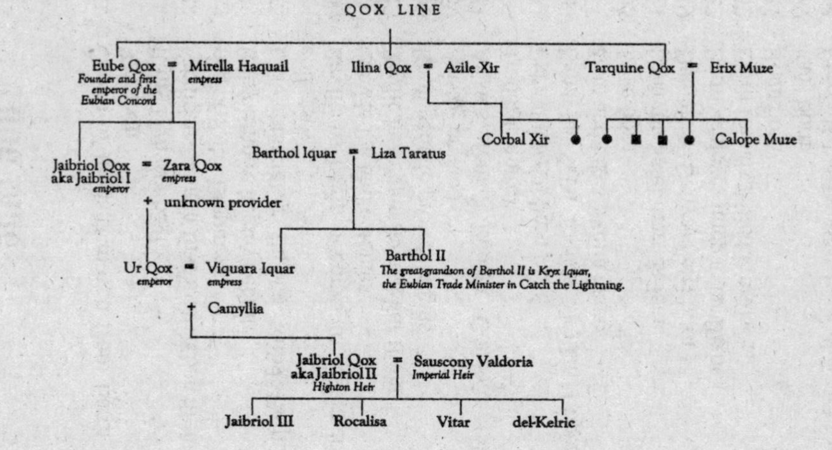

Time Line

circa 4000 B.C.	Group of humans moved from Earth to Raylicon
circa 3600 B.C.	Ruby Dynasty begins
circa 3100 B.C.	Raylicans launch first interstellar flights; rise of Ruby Empire
circa 2900 B.C.	Ruby Empire begins decline
circa 2800 B.C.	Last interstellar flights; Ruby Empire collapses . . .
circa A.D. 1300	Raylicans begin attempts to regain lost knowledge and colonies
1843	Raylicans regain interstellar flight
1866	Rhon genetic project begins
1869	Aristos created
1871	Aristos found Eubian Concord (aka Trader Empire)
1881	Lahaylia Selei born
1904	Lahaylia Selei founds Skolian Imperialate and takes Skolia name
2005	Jarac born
2111	Lahaylia Selei marries Jarac
2119	Dyhianna (Dehya) Selei born
2122	Earth achieves interstellar flight
2132	Earth founds Allied Worlds
2144	Roca born
2169	Kurj born
2204	Eldrin Valdoria born; Jarac dies and Kurj becomes Imperator; Lahaylia dies
2206	Althor Valdoria born
2209	Havyrl (Vyrl) Valdoria born
2210	Sasucony (Soz) Valdoria born

2219	Kelricson (Kelric) Valdoria born
2237	Jaibriol II born
2258	Kelric crashes on Coba *(The Last Hawk)*
early 2259	Soz meets Jaibriol *(Primary Inversion)*
late 2259	Soz and Jaibriol go into exile *(The Radiant Seas)*
2260	Jaibrial III born (aka Jaibriol Qox Skolia)
2263	Rocalisa Qox Skolia born
2268	Vitar Qox Skolia born
2273	del-Kelric Qox Skolia born
2274	Radiance War begins (also called Domino War)
2276	Traders capture Eldrin; Radiance War ends
2277	Kelric returns home (*Ascendant Sun*); Dehya coalesces (*Spherical Harmonic*)
2278	Kamoj Argali meets Vyrl (*The Quantum Rose*)
2279	Althor Vyan Selei born
2328	Althor Vyan Selei meets Tina Santis Pulivok *(Catch the Lightning)*

About the Author

Catherine Asaro grew up near Berkeley, California. She earned her Ph.D. in chemical physics and her M.A. in physics, both from Harvard, and a B.S. with highest honors in chemistry from UCLA. She runs Molecudyne Research and lives in Maryland with her husband and daughter. Among the places she has done research are the University of Toronto in Canada, the Max Planck Institut für Astrophysik in Germany, and the Harvard-Smithsonian Center for Astrophysics in Cambridge, Massachusetts. A former ballet and jazz dancer, she founded the Mainly Jazz Dance program at Harvard and now teaches at the Caryl Maxwell Classical Ballet, home to the Ellicott City Ballet Guild.

Catherine also wrote *Catch the Lightning,* which won the Sapphire Award in 1997, *Primary Inversion,* and the Nebula-nominated *The Last Hawk.* All three books are stand-alone novels set in the Ruby Dynasty universe (the Skolian Empire). *Primary Inversion* tells the story of how Soz and Jaibriol met. A tale of Soz from her younger days can be found in the novella "Aurora in Four Voices," which appeared in the December 1998 issue of *Analog,* won the AnLab and the Homer, and was nominated for both the Nebula and Hugo. The next three Ruby Dynasty books due out from Tor are *Ascendant Sun, Spherical Harmonic,* and *The Quantum Rose.*

Catherine can be reached by E-mail at asaro@sff.net and on the web at http://www.sff.net/people/asaro/.

Look for:

Moon's Shadow

by Catherine Asaro

Now available in hardcover
from Tor Books